REDEMPTION
Summer

PAYNE SCHANSKI

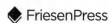 FriesenPress

Suite 300 - 990 Fort St
Victoria, BC, V8V 3K2
Canada

www.friesenpress.com

ISBN
978-1-5255-7311-8 (Hardcover)
978-1-5255-7312-5 (Paperback)
978-1-5255-7313-2 (eBook)

1. YOUNG ADULT FICTION, COMING OF AGE

Distributed to the trade by The Ingram Book Company

CHAPTER ONE

New Start

The first day of summer vacation after my freshman year of high school began with one of those rare perfect mornings. One where I woke up right at 7:30 with no alarm and didn't feel the slightest bit drowsy. One where all three of my favorite cereals were fully stocked to choose from out of the breakfast cupboard over the kitchen stove. One where I looked in the mirror after showering and thought I genuinely looked good.

My slightly crooked smile looked straighter than usual. My deep brown eyes penetrated the glass and looked excited and full of life for once, instead of vaguely sad. My typically unruly hair didn't even need any touch-ups before I was ready to leave the house; I would usually push it around for at least a few minutes unsatisfied, before eventually just screwing it up even more and saying forget it. Speaking of screwups, I had some of those from a year ago that I was ready to fully put behind me. What better way to start things off than a perfect morning on the first day of summer?

Maybe you've already heard about me from the local newspaper. Remember that "series of home invasions" up in Northern Michigan? Remember the "troubled youth" who got everybody all riled up and outraged, and maybe even a little bit scared? Yeah, that was me. Please don't pre-judge me, though—I've already had enough people dismissing me as just another teen delinquent (or something like that).

I know my past says otherwise, and there's some evidence that's not in my favor, but I'm really not that type of person. For one thing, I get straight A's in school. That's not because I feel like I'm all that smart, but mostly because my mom won't settle for anything less. Even so, how many "delinquents" do you know who make the all-A honor roll every semester? If you still don't believe me, consider this: I've never gotten in a fight, I don't drink alcohol or do drugs, I've never stolen anything, and I'm not even very good at swearing.

I mostly try to do the right thing, but the little angel and the little devil inside my head sometimes get into some heated arguments. Actually, it's not even an angel and devil in there; that would be too simple. It often seems like the guys inside my head guiding me are two little dudes wearing skullcaps and skateboarding around up there, and they are just as confused about how to make it in the world as I am. So they chase each other around in circles and try to punch each other in the balls when the other isn't looking, and a lot of the time they really aren't any help to me at all. So all this stuff gets built up inside, and I guess I need to release it sometimes. Maybe that means I'm a "troubled youth," or maybe it just means I'm trying to grow up.

Anyway, the past year of my life was pretty crappy. I was grounded for the entire school year, my "best friends" stopped talking to me, and I wasn't allowed to play basketball: the one thing that the little guys in my head are in full agreement on. That part probably hurt the most. I don't know anyone who has a three-point stroke that's as sweet as mine, and I couldn't even put it to use for nine months. That's messed up. Well, *I* messed up is more accurate.

Oh, and I also broke into another house towards the end of winter. I know what you're thinking, but I swear this one was a little different. Nobody lived there, and it was totally abandoned. I was trying to find out whether the old house is haunted or not; you probably won't believe me about this part either, but I'm pretty sure it is. I'm also pretty sure that whatever spirits are in there helped me out a lot that night too, so I'm going to leave it in peace and never go back.

Anyway, it was already sunny and over seventy degrees outside by 7:30, and I didn't want to waste a moment during my first morning of freedom. After breakfast, I made sure to take care of all my chores right away while my mom was at work, washing dishes, vacuuming, and even doing a massive load of laundry. It was the middle of June, yet I found shirts buried at the bottom of my hamper that were still covered in remnants of March. While I waited for the clothes to dry, I grabbed a notebook from my nightstand and carefully wrote out a list of everything I wanted to accomplish before the end of summer. The plan was to get started on them right after lunch.

THIRTY-SECOND TIME-OUT

PRESEASON RANKINGS

My Top 5 priorities for the summer before sophomore year:

1. **Stay out of trouble.** No more sneaking around in other people's houses. I really mean it this time. I'm done with the drama, done with the risks, and done with going looking for ghosts. I'm serious, too. If you're expecting this be another one of those books, I recommend you stop reading now.

2. **Set myself up to make varsity.** I missed a full year of basketball, but I'm almost two inches taller than when I last checked during winter. I'm still fairly short compared to the other sophomores, but at least it's some progress. I'm not worried about that part. I have a deadly three-point shot and such a quick release that bigger guys can't block it anyway. I can't wait to get back on the court.

3. **Enjoy my new freedom.** I have a lot of lost time to make up for. Freshman year sucked. I'm not saying it wasn't my fault to begin with, but it still sucked.

4. **Reconcile with Blaise.** Blaise asked me when we were

going to be cool with each other again. I told him it would take some time, but eventually we'd get back to being friends. Who knows if it will be exactly like the old days, but I think enough time has passed by now to get a fresh start in our friendship.

5. **Get a girlfriend?** Somewhere between the end of winter and the start of summer was when I really started to discover girls. The only issue is that they haven't seemed to discover *me* yet. Maybe I'll be able to change that.

*Notice that **"Find a summer job"** doesn't crack the Top 5. Well, not in *my* rankings, anyway.

CHAPTER TWO

The Hitch in the Plan

J**B**!"

My mom calling out to me from downstairs a little after 10:30 interrupted the second half of that perfect morning. She was back from work early. I was in the middle of folding laundry in my room, taking breaks in between to roll up my socks and practice three-pointers into the recently emptied clothes hamper. Neither the radio nor the fan could drown out Mom's shout from below, so with a slump of my shoulders, I cracked the door open and timidly walked downstairs to see what this could possibly be about. Past experience told me that I was being summoned because I was either (a) in trouble again, or (b) about to be given some sort of undesirable task.

When I got down to the living room, my mom's body language surprised me. No balled-up fists rested on her hips, no demanding stance, no accusing glare. Instead, she looked defeated—and almost nervous—to face me.

"JB, I need to tell you about something that's going on at the factory."

"The factory? What about it?"

— 6 —

For as long as I can remember, my mom has worked at the plastics factory about thirty minutes away, right outside of the Silverledge city limits. Her job was to pour huge barrels of plastic beads of different colors through a hot machine that melted it all down. The beads from her machine then get stretched, pressed out, and rolled into plastic bags.

One time when I was in middle school, I got a few bad grades on a report card. As punishment, my mom took me to work with her on a snow day to prove a point. By lunch-time, my ears were pulsating from the constant rumbles of the heavy machinery, and my stomach was so queasy that I didn't even want to eat; the stench of the factory is overpowering, like a constant thick glue weighing down the atmosphere. That whole time, I could feel my mom smirking at me from behind her safety goggles. She never went out and said it, but I knew exactly what she was telling me by taking me there:

"You're not doing this for a living. You're going to get good grades, you're going to go to college, and after that, you're going to do something other than waking up at 6:30 every weekday and driving out here to dump plastic beads into a loud machine for the rest of the afternoon."

The message sunk in. I hadn't gotten anything less than an A-minus in any class since. I also hadn't given much thought to that plastic factory, other than to remind myself that I never wanted to go back. Why would my mom bring that place up now?

"My hours at work have been cut, by a lot." She said it as quickly as possible, like diving straight into the lake to get the shock over with immediately. "I've heard rumors about it, but it became official today."

"What?! How come?"

She told me something I didn't fully understand—something about stricter emissions and clean air laws. For some reason, this all meant that the company had to update the way the factory operated. Apparently, the business needed to make a big shift that was very expensive, or else they'd get in a lot of trouble with the law. Mom shrugged and said it was probably a good thing overall. In the short term though, her hours were being cut back significantly, and she needed to figure out a way to make up the difference.

"Hopefully by the new year, everything will be sorted out and back to normal," she said. "In the meantime, I need help."

I wasn't going to be the one to say it, but I was starting to understand exactly where this conversation was headed. It was a direction that could severely change my entire vision for the summer. Mom shifted her feet uncomfortably before dropping the real bomb.

"I'm going to look for something else part-time, but you're old enough to work now too. I need you to find a summer job, sometime in the next week."

"But I can't do that!"

I sat my mom down on the couch and calmly explained that me getting a job wasn't going to be an option. After all, I would be far too busy with staying out of trouble, earning my spot on the basketball team, enjoying my freedom, repairing my friendship with Blaise, and getting a girlfriend. Unfortunately, that wouldn't leave any room to even entertain the thought of finding employment for the summer. Instead, her best option would be to just find a new job herself—one that pays a lot more money. Mom nodded and said that she fully understood, and then apologized for wasting my time.

Hold on—I seem to be getting a few of the details from the conversation wrong. Let's try that again.

What really happened was that my mom was the one who sat *me* down on the couch. It was like getting laser eye surgery: Mom's laser eyes cut into me and carefully removed any conflicting ideas that I might be having. And then she hit me with such a powerful "*Son. . .*" that all my preseason rankings melted into the couch cushions, somewhere between the loose change and stale pieces of cereal.

She asked me if I wanted to continue eating three full meals a day. Then she asked if I still wanted to have electricity in the house. And if I wanted to have a new pair of basketball shoes when the next season started up again. With the way my body sank into the couch, it must have looked like someone had let all the air out of it.

"Yes, Mom."

"Then this is what we have to do."

"Well, what about Rodney? He's the oldest—he should come back and get a job too!"

My older brother was a sore subject around the house for the time being. Right after his final exams, he'd decided that he was going to stay at college and rent a house with his buddies for the summer.

"We've been over this. Your brother has chosen to . . . assert his independence this summer."

"Well, it sounds more like he's being a complete—"

Mom's voice displayed a calmness that was undermined by the way I saw her hands shaking.

"That's the choice he made. He's twenty years old, and I

have to accept his choices if he decides not to live here."

That jerk and his full-ride academic scholarship to Notre Dame, I thought bitterly. *Staying in Indiana all summer without the slightest thought for the rest of us.*

"But I was supposed to be . . . because you see, the funny thing is . . . well, what if we just . . ."

I just sat there with my arms crossed, glaring at the floor while trying to conjure a magical response—one that could flip the situation back around. I couldn't get more than a half sentence out at a time. Even the skateboarders in my head cut me off each time I was about to say something that I knew didn't make sense. Mom wasn't doing this to be mean, and she wasn't doing it to ruin my summer; it was just the reality of things. I needed to put my other plans on hold and bring in some extra income. There was no way out.

"Fine—I'll go and look for a summer job."

"Starting as soon as possible," added Mom.

The worst part about the whole thing is what came next. I had a nearly impossible time trying to get something that I didn't even want in the first place.

CHAPTER THREE

Job Search

The first major heat wave of the season seemed to be passing through Northern Michigan much earlier than usual; it was only mid-June, after all. By the time I changed clothes, found the bike pump in the garage, and mentally prepared myself, the temperature outside was over ninety degrees. I decided that my Asics running shoes were the most mature-looking of my three pairs of sneakers, so I opted for them instead of the old black Reeboks that I preferred. Already sweating a dark ring into the collar of my nicest shirt, I rode towards downtown, where for the rest of the afternoon I would look for a job.

I paused at the top of the bluff before cruising down the steep hill to the town center, overlooking a messy collage that included colorful and tightly packed houses, old-fashioned church spires, and a thick border of trees that were now reaching their darkest shade of green. I made a mental map of all the shops, galleries, cafés, marinas, golf courses, and resorts that would soon be gushing with summer folks, requiring the help of younger locals to handle the busy season.

At the middle of the collage were just a few orderly rows for glossy storefronts and a concrete diet of uninspired rectangles and cylinders that made up city hall, the public library, the banks, and the post office. The farthest edge of the landscape was dominated by Lake Bellview and accented by the red-and-white striped lighthouse of the South Point Peninsula on the right-hand side. Pushing off the ground with my left foot, I didn't need to pedal again until getting to the bottom of the hill.

The first store I went into was something called "Number One Rebaires." It was a building that appeared right as I rounded the curve at the end of the slope, with a green awning that provided shade for a little bit as I stopped and leaned my bike against the outside wall. I was only inside for about thirty seconds total. I weakly asked the guy at the front desk if they needed any extra help, was shot down instantly, and walked right back out.

I had no idea what their business was, and still don't. To be honest, I misread the sign the first time and thought it was a repair shop. Not that it would have mattered; I can't repair anything to save my life. They made the right choice by sending me away.

I went back into the searing heat until making my next stop at a fancy restaurant called Rivera, another two blocks down the road and closer to the heart of town. It was darkly lit and had air conditioning, and there was a round-faced girl standing by herself at the hostess stand, maybe in her early twenties. She wore an apron over her dress shirt and was arranging menus, looking glad for something else to do when I came in and asked about a job. She smiled broadly at me, like she knew it was going to be my first job and thought it was cute, in a little kid sort of way. This annoyed me for a second, but I got over it immediately when she said they had a spot available for a dishwasher, as long I could work evenings.

My spirits soared as she went back to get an application from the day manager. I reasoned that if I worked evenings, that would still give me the best part of the day to take care of everything else that I wanted to accomplish. That wouldn't be so bad. Maybe the whole job thing wasn't as big of a deal as I first made it out to be.

It was still only a little bit past one o'clock, so as long as I sealed the deal here, that would still leave me with plenty of the day to myself. As soon as I wrapped this application thing up, I could swing by the public beach for a little while, and then ride around a little more and look for a pickup basketball game after that. Maybe today wouldn't be as perfect as it had started out, but it could end up being a great day all the same.

When the hostess came back with her manager, I wiped a streak of sweat from my forehead and stood up as straight as possible, trying to appear as mature and responsible as I could. I noticed him do a double take as soon as he caught a glimpse of me, like he recognized me from somewhere. I waved and nodded at him, but now he appeared doubtful.

"What did you say your name was again?" he asked.

Once I told him, he couldn't prevent his face from moving into a frown as he turned and whispered something to the hostess. The only part that I caught was something that sounded a lot like, "That was the kid . . ."

Upon hearing whatever the rest of the whispering was, her mouth dropped open, scandalized. The two of them walked back within hearing range, with the hostess now tucking the blank job application close against her ribs, as if she was protecting it from me. The manager stiffly cleared his throat and spoke again.

"I think we're going to . . . head in a different direction, for this position. Thank you for your interest."

"You're welcome."

I didn't get the hint at first and kept standing there like a coatrack. The manager repeated himself, a little more forcefully this time, and motioned towards the door. The hostess girl avoided any more eye contact and gave a fragile apology as she went back to arranging menus.

I slowly walked back out of the restaurant, partially to hang out in the air conditioning for few seconds longer, but mostly because the manager's reaction had stunned me.

It didn't take a genius to figure out what his problem was. Rumors travel fast in a town like Bellview—even faster if they're partially true, and faster still if the partially true parts end up in the local news for two weeks straight. My biggest mistake was literally the only thing he knew about me, but I realized that was enough. Momentarily blinded from stepping back out into the midday sun, I felt around the edge of the building for my bike.

The beach was put on hold as I continued my route through all the main tourist spots around town. Already, I noticed a rise in the number of luxury cars slowly maneuvering through the main streets, carelessly parking in handicapped spots and forgetting who had the right-of-way at stop signs. Summer was definitely on its way to Bellview.

The docks sat empty for a little while longer, but by 4th

of July weekend, I knew that sailboats and yachts with names like *Windjammer III*, *Sweetnorthern Saint*, and *Margaritaville* would pepper the harbor; sometimes I'd catch myself looking out to the bay and trying to estimate just how expensive the largest ones were, and who their owners could possibly be. I wondered what it was like to be one of their kids, the princes and princesses of the Peninsula who used my hometown as a playground every summer, with no money worries except that there might not be enough time to spend it all.

I spent the rest of the afternoon stopping into more places and practically begging for even the lowest jobs available. I saw that same look the day manager at Rivera had given me a few more times, and others told me their summer roles had already been filled weeks ago. The best I could do was fill out applications and be told, "We'll get in touch with you if something opens up." As the number of outright rejections piled up, so did my level of anxiety.

After debating with myself whether it would do any good, I made a phone call to my brother Rodney before going to bed. We hadn't talked in nearly a month, and by the slight tone of irritation in his voice, he wasn't all that excited to be hearing from me—especially since the first part of the conversation was spent trying to convince him to come back home. When it was clear that Rodney was unmoved by my appeals, I switched to asking for help finding leads for jobs.

"Whatever you do, just don't go on Craigslist. I'm learning that it's, uh . . . not all that reliable," was his response.

He vaguely mentioned his own negative employment experiences throughout the spring. It sounded like he'd been responding to listings online for work, only to find out that most of them weren't what they had seemed to be at all. He basically admitted that he was having a hard time paying his share of the rent at the house with his friends; scholarship money doesn't cover summer if you're not taking classes. When I pointed out that this was an even better reason to just come home, he dismissed the idea and changed the subject.

"Nah, boy, it's all good here . . . by the way, I went and saw Dad last week."

That wasn't what I had expected to hear. It had been long enough where I hadn't given much thought to what our dad was up to, even though deep down I probably really wanted to see him.

"That's cool," I said.

By the time I got to be Rodney's age, I might be more curious about what our dad was up to. For the moment, though, my guess is that the skateboarder guys shut him out of my mind completely as a favor to me.

"Yeah. Yeah, it's just an hour and a half drive from here. He says he's doing a lot better lately."

I knew that "a lot better" could mean many different things. Rodney should have known that too.

"Do you believe him?"

"Ehh—yes and no. You know it's hard to tell." He went quiet for a few seconds, searching for more to say. I stared down at my Asics, now fighting between the urge to hear more and hoping to just get off the phone. Rodney abruptly chose the second option for me. "Anyway, I have to get going now. H is having some of the boys over for beer pong. Good luck with the job search."

"Later, Rodney. Thanks."

Saying thanks was more of a reflex than anything else. He really hadn't helped at all.

The combination of concerns weighing on my mind turned falling asleep that night into another grim failure; the muggy heat that lingered long after the sun went down didn't improve the situation, either. A year ago, I might have used this insomnia as an opportunity to sneak out and go exploring. Instead, I blasted the fan in my room and lay alone in my head, stuck in neutral as the first day of summer silently dissolved into the next.

CHAPTER FOUR

Help Wanted

For an entire week straight, it was the same story repeating itself, like the *Seinfeld* reruns airing every time I needed a distraction and flipped on the TV. I woke up each morning with the same feeling of dread and finally dragged myself out of bed and got on with it. Half the day was spent biking around town from place to place, and my efforts turned into absolutely nothing. Each night when I got home, my mom would nag me to see if I found anything, and of course I dropped my head and told her no, and the small stack of unpaid bills on the kitchen counter seemed a little bit taller than the day before.

My older brother had recently warned me about trying to find a job on Craigslist, so I should have known better—I really should have, but desperate times call for desperate measures, I guess. Since seven restaurants, two ice cream shops, four clothing stores, the boathouse, three golf courses, a day care center, a car wash, and the fine people at the "Number One Rebaires" wanted nothing to do with me, my options were running low. It was the same thing over and over. Most places said there weren't any open positions, and for the few that did, the manager at each one seemed to know who I was and what I had done a year ago. The town apparently hadn't forgiven me yet. I kept looking, though—what else was I supposed to do? I needed a job for the summer, and I was getting frantic.

So I parked myself at the computer one morning. According to Rodney, the online classified ads section on Craigslist is loaded with scammers, predators, and weirdos. Once in a while there's a good opportunity sprinkled in somewhere—if you dig deep enough. "Just to keep up appearances at the site," he'd said. The fact that I ended up on that site that particular morning showed just how limited my options really were. Like I said, I was getting frantic.

I had to scroll back all the way into the April job listings before I found anything that really jumped out at me. I noticed that something about Craigslist headlines seemed to make people forget about all the punctuation, spelling, and capitalizing rules that every middle school kid is forced to learn about, but there it was:

> help wanted outdoor work. suMmer 2005.
> 180 $. dollars per wek.

I clicked on the link and read through the full description. Whoever posted it had edited this part much better, since the errors were gone.

> Hi, my name is Sara. I am looking for a
> reliable worker to help me this summer. I
> pay 180 dollars per week for a few hours of
> outdoor work, plus occasional help with
> cooking. Must be a nature lover.

A part of me was skeptical, but I guess it looked legitimate enough. Anyway, for just a few hours, it was a lot more money than I could make washing dishes at one of the restaurants.

Sara had left an email address and phone number at the bottom of the page. 180 bucks a week? Just for a few hours of outdoor work? This had to be too good to be true—right? I did not consider myself to be a nature lover by any stretch, but this Sara lady didn't need to know that. I could rake a few leaves, weed the garden, mow the lawn a little bit, chop wood, whatever. At home, these would all be chores that I dreaded, but for that type of cash—yeah, I could manage. I didn't know how to cook either, but I could figure that part out later. Thinking that this had better not be just another Craigslist scam, I decided to give Sara a call.

"Excited" isn't exactly the correct word to describe myself as I waited impatiently for the other line to pick up. Are you ever really all that "excited" for what you suspect is a scam, or at the very least, a chance to do manual labor in the hot sun? No, I wasn't excited, but my heart was racing, and I was doing tiny circles around the kitchen as the ring tone kept going.

I really hadn't spent much time on the phone over the past year. When I was grounded, no one was ever calling, seeing how I was, inviting me out, or wanting to chat—none of that stuff. Even before I got into trouble, I didn't talk on the phone much either, if I'm being honest, other than prank phone calls. At this time a year ago, if I was on the phone at all, it likely would have been in Blaise's basement, quickly passing it off and letting Darko (our old friend, seemingly one from a different life, who found a different crew to hang out with when high school started) try another accent out on the latest of our prank targets. For me, though, I could never keep my cool over the phone when the pressure was on. That was something I hadn't outgrown yet, even if the prank calls were ancient history.

"HALLO?"

Her voice was harsh and old-sounding. Raspy, like she'd been smoking for decades, with a little bit of a drawl. It caught me off guard.

"HALLO?"

"Hi, my name is JB."

"HUH?"

I raised my voice level a little bit and tried to speak more clearly. "I said, I am JB."

"No, it didn't. Not that I remember."

Something was clearly being lost between the two phones here.

"It didn't what?"

"Who is this?"

"My name is JB. JAYYY-BEEEE."

"Geezus, I hurrja the first time."

Well no, you didn't, I thought.

"State your business then."

Her voice bothered me, and the rocky start to the conversation made a part of me want to hang up the phone and forget about this. My words started to stumble badly on the way out as I became flustered.

"Yeah hi, hello? I'm JB. I uh—saw your internet . . . Do you need to find any more work for me to do?"

I was blowing this job interview, and I knew it. I couldn't even figure out what I'd just said.

"WHAAT?"

I firmly believe that her voice permanently scratched the speaker of my mom's landline phone. But never mind that—I needed to redeem myself. I gave it another try.

"Hi, I saw your ad-advertisement, on Craigslist? It says that you are hiring somebody? For some outdoor work?"

I was doing that annoying thing where you say everything as if it's a question. Even so, this time around, she actually understood what I was saying, so I guess it was better.

She barked back in response, *"Yup, yer a smart one. That's why I put it on the web."*

"Right. Makes sense. And do you really pay 180 dollars per week?"

"Yup. Hunnerd-etty bucks. Good honest work too. Need a strong pair a' hands."

I gave a small fist pump from my end of the phone. That toxic voice was suddenly music to my ears! I quickly responded.

"I want the job. I've got hands too. Strong ones," I added. "Really, really good hands."

"Well then . . . you'll do a good job, if that's the case."

"Is it okay if I stop by sometime in the next few days, to learn more about the job? I could even start working this week, if that's okay."

"Doesn' bother me. Come by tomorra' if you really want."

She was clearly a woman of few words. Then again, if I had voice as abrasive as hers, I'd probably keep quiet most of the time too. I did most of the talking from that point forward, working out the important details of my new job training session. She gave the address to her house, and I agreed to come over at 2:00 pm the following afternoon. After ending the call, I realized that Sara hadn't mentioned any of the actual work that I would be doing at this job. She also never said anything about the "must be a nature lover" part on her advertisement. It must not have been that important after all.

When 1:45 rolled around the next day, I laced up my old black Reeboks (no socks, of course—this was summer) and walked out to the garage. I was nervous about meeting this Sara lady and checking out the new job opportunity. The last thing I wanted to do was show up late. According to MapQuest, her house was less than two miles into the country, away from downtown, maybe a ten-minute bike ride is all.

Since there were only three turns to make, I found her house without much difficulty. She had a really tacky mailbox. It was painted bright green and had all these fake lily pads attached to the wooden post. The driveway was a winding dirt path that looped around a small pond before leading to a small and rustic-looking cottage next to the woods.

I approached the front door, took a deep breath, and thumped on the door. There was no answer. I waited for a few moments before knocking again, this time putting some extra force behind each hit. It was enough to make my knuckles a little sore. Pressing my ear to the door, I eventually heard Sara's distinctive rasp from inside.

"Geezus, hold on to yer crackers, I'll be with you in a sec!"

Fighting off the sudden urge to call the whole thing off and make a run for it, I reminded myself that I really needed this job. It's just one summer—I could put up with this for a few months, no sweat. As long as I was making some real greenbacks, I could put up with this lady, especially if it was only a few hours a week like she said. So I stayed put. A few seconds later, I heard at least four deadbolts and a chain slide out of place to unlock the house. The door swung open. Sara didn't look the way I thought a typical boss at a job would look.

She was wearing purple sweatpants—actually, not really purple, more like fuchsia. They had the elastic at the ankles, showing her thick gray socks and sandals. She wore an extra-long T-shirt with a picture of SpongeBob SquarePants on it. The caption on it said, "*You like Krabby Patties.*" I figured the dress code at this job wasn't very strict.

If I had to guess, I'd say Sara was about forty-five, maybe forty-seven years old. Flecks of gray showed in her shoulder-length black hair, and her sun-spotted face was etched into a mean perma-frown. She was currently brushing her teeth. I was the first to speak.

"Hi, Sara, nice to meet you. I'm JB." She stepped onto the porch, spitting her toothpaste out into a pot of flowers. Her perma-frown deepened as she stared accusingly at me.

"Thass not a name," she rasped. *"It's just letters."*

I had no response to that. I'm used to strangers messing up my name; even though I think it's pretty simple, people that I'm meeting for the first time always figure out a way to get the initials mixed up. No one had ever come right out and told me that my name wasn't really a name, though. I decided it was my turn to speak again.

"So, this is the place, huh?"

I knew it was a stupid thing to say, but after too many seconds of awkward silence (what is it about silence that makes it so awkward, anyway?) that's what I came up with.

"Of course it's the place. Kick yer shoes off and come have a look around!"

I did as she instructed and walked inside. Despite how irritated she seemed, her cottage actually seemed like a friendly enough place. Fully furnished, reasonably clean, no crazy paintings on the walls. Then again, even if the place was a mess, my job would be mostly outside anyway, so whatever. Scanning my gaze toward the kitchen, I tried to make a little more small talk.

"It smells pretty good in there—what're you making?" It actually smelled a little gross. Maybe that's why she wanted help with cooking.

"*Supper,*" she croaked.

"Oh, okay. Cool."

I prefer to call it "dinner" like everyone else under the age of seventy, but this wasn't the time.

"So, what types of jobs will I be doing around here?"

Sara motioned for me to follow her down the narrow hallway. I heard a faint bumping noise while we were walking past a broom closet across from the kitchen. A noticeable shiver of weirdness quickly shot down my spine.

"What do you keep in there?" I asked, trying to keep my voice sounding casual.

"*Pets,*" she replied.

Oh, I thought sarcastically. *That explains it.*

"Ohh, right. So is that what you meant when you said you wanted a nature lover to work for you? Do I need to help take care of the pets or something?"

"*Yeah . . . or something.*"

Sara's perma-frown twitched up to a neutral position as she moved over toward the closet, opening it a crack. To my disbelief, I watched as three frogs leapt out of the small opening! I started to fidget and back up from the closet. Amphibians make me pretty squeamish; in the same way that some people stay away from spiders or snakes, that's how I feel about amphibians—as in, get me the hell away from them. Reminding myself over and over again in my head how much money I could make by doing this job, I tried to convince myself that I could still make this work. But I was starting to sweat a little bit all the same.

"Sooo . . . what do you need help with?" I inquired. "You just need me to like, feed these guys once a day?"

Sara wasn't impressed.

"Not entirely, dear. You need to feed 'em, sure, but mostly gotta help keep the numbers up."

She turned away from me again and walked back into the kitchen. By the breezy tone of her voice, what she'd just said obviously made perfect sense to her. For me, this was going to require further explanation though.

"The uh, numbers? What numbers are you talking about??"

I dodged another frog (one with a vertical jump that I would kill for), and then followed her to the kitchen.

"Sara, how many frogs are you keeping in there?"

Very matter-of-factly, she grunted back, *"Twenty-five. Always gotta be twenty-five."*

"TWENTY-FIVE??"

I should have walked out right then and there. How in the world was I supposed to work for a grouchy middle-aged woman who wore SpongeBob shirts and had twenty-five frogs living in her broom closet? But I stayed put. Maybe it was the sheer shock of this sudden development that was keeping my feet planted in the floor like a pair of oak trees.

My senses gave out on me for about twenty seconds, leaving me in a state of mini-paralysis.

Sara must have been talking this entire time, because when my senses came back to me, I could hear her finishing up a previous thought.

"—*and when that happens, you'd head right out to the pond near the driveway and fetch up a few more of the rascals. Gotta be real patient and quick. Strong pair a' hands. I'm not as quick as I used to be, bad back . . . yep, always gotta be twenty-five.*"

She then casually turned back to the black frying pan steaming on the front of the stovetop. Completely oblivious to my shock and revulsion, she might as well have been asking me to empty the dishwasher once a week. Then again, maybe she was keeping something else in the dishwasher. I pushed the thought from my mind.

I could hardly bear to be in the same zip code with all these frogs, let alone scampering off to the creek every other day like Tom-freaking-Sawyer and trying to catch the slimy green bastards! I was opening my mouth to passionately protest when a random piece of trivia from an old science class flashed through my mind. This was the loophole I needed; I was saved!

"And that's the entire job?"

"*Well yeah, dear,*" she rasped. "*But it ain't easy, mark my words! That, plus a little of the cooking.*"

She pointed the frying pan at me, as if to emphasize the warning. I grinned for the first time all afternoon.

"You know," I began, putting that trivia to good use, "frogs actually have a relatively long life span. Most of them will live between about four and seven years, right? So odds are I'll never even have to, you know, 'keep the numbers up.' Right?"

This time, it was Sara who grinned.

"*Well, not exactly, TJ...*"

I had no idea what she meant at first—let alone her forgetting my name—but as I began speaking, my brain slowly put the pieces together while in mid-sentence.

"Sorry, I guess I don't really get what you could—wait, WHAT ARE YOU COOKING IN—? ERRHH!!!"

I was once told to never ask a question if you don't really want to know the answer. Sara had slowly tilted the frying pan downward, revealing four full frogs, sizzling and bubbling, neatly arranged in rows of two. One of them was still twitching. I instinctively started backing away from her, but my knees were now shaking so badly it caused me to stumble back and bump open the door to the closet. This set off a scene of utter bedlam within the house.

The series of events right after I knocked the door open: a mass of slimy amphibians jumping around in the hallway like hyperactive green popcorn, a flame erupting on the stovetop, and Sara chasing me through the house, screeching, "*YER LETTIN' ALL MY FROGS OUT*!! *THIS IS COMING OUT OF YOUR PAYCHECK!*"

The smoke alarm came to life after that, beeping out all of the swear words that were uncontrollably spilling from my mouth. I sprinted out of the house, puked in the front yard, and then biked away so fast that my quads almost gave out. It wasn't until I was back in the driveway at home that I felt sharp pains on the bottom of my bare feet. I realized that I had left my shoes back at Sara's froggy cottage. With no job, I didn't know how I'd get the money for a new pair of black

Reeboks—but I didn't plan on ever, ever, ever going back for them.

I was back to square one for finding someplace to work.

CHAPTER FIVE

Job Interview

It was still way too hot and muggy for me to fall asleep that night, but maybe that was a good thing; I'd probably have nothing but frog nightmares even if I did sleep. The fan in the window did nothing except hum and swirl away one set of warm, humid air and exchange it for another set that was somehow warmer and even more humid. Lying shirtless in a pair of yellow basketball shorts, my mind was exhausted while my muscles clenched and tightened and further prevented me from getting comfortable.

The skateboarder guys in my head must have crashed into each other, and somehow I was the one who ended up with a headache. I rolled over time and again, with both my exhaustion and anxiousness building as the restless hours of the night ticked down—or maybe it was the restless hours of the morning ticking up, I don't know. At some point, though, the somber and cavernous hooting of the night owls gave way to the insufferable chirps of the morning songbirds. Like flying messengers, they tweeted at each other, exchanging rumors and gossip from tree to tree and across Northern Michigan.

I hadn't slept more than a few hours by the next morning, and it was still way too hot to function, but I had an idea—one that would require asking a favor from an older friend. Well, technically, Jennie Rawlings wasn't old . . . sixteen or seventeen. She was only two grades ahead of me. Technically, she wasn't a friend either. I had only really even talked to her once before, and that had been back in the winter. Still, the thought lodged in my mind that Jennie was the one person at this point who would be able to help me out.

I knew that she was a waitress at Jimmy's Family Restaurant downtown. Jimmy's was only open during the summer, and plenty of high school kids got jobs washing dishes, bussing and waiting tables, scooping ice cream, or working the cash register there. I figured they would have already gotten all set with their new staff for the season in advance—probably weeks before school let out. Even if they were hiring, I had good reason for avoiding that specific restaurant up until now: Jimmy.

I knew my idea was a long shot. Through Jennie, though, maybe there was a way in.

"Come on, Jennie, help me out with this one. Please?"

It was getting late in the afternoon, and I was standing in the waiting area of a place that I was already certain wouldn't want to hire me; I had purposely skipped the door to Jimmy's Family Restaurant on all my other depressing job-hunting trips downtown. Now, with Jennie dividing her attention between me and writing out a chalkboard display for that night's dinner special, it seemed like my only chance. She finished chalking out "Mac n' Cheese Night, $9.99" in bubble letters and turned back to face me.

"Even if I wanted to, it would be no use. Jimmy hates you."

She was probably right. Jimmy knew about me even before I became infamous in town. My ex-friend Garrett had worked here a year ago, as a cashier. When Blaise, Darko, and I had too much time on our hands, we used to come in for lunch or an orangeade from time to time so we could keep him company. And maybe we were a little too loud at times and joked around a little too much. So yeah, Jimmy had had his eye on me, even before I was an outcast.

"Well, maybe you could talk to him. Put in a good word— you know?"

Jennie frowned as she thought my suggestion over. Something about her was different from back in the winter, and not just because her hair was pulled back off her shoulders and her skin was starting to get a tan. She had a tattoo now also—something written on the inside of her slender left wrist—but that wasn't it.

"What should I say?" she asked. "That you tried to put the moves on me in the basement of a haunted house?"

"I DID NOT!!" I said that way too loud. Some of the customers even looked over from their tables in the dining room.

"Yeah, well, you thought about it." Being much edgier than most girls that I found cute, Jennie really wasn't my type. Then again, it had felt like we'd shared some sort of connection when we'd talked on those haunted steps at Five Mile Creek.

"How do you—I did NOT!" After I said it, Jennie's frown broke, and she started giggling.

"Calm down, man, I'm just messing with you!"

Oh.

Now I was embarrassed for a new reason. I rubbed the spot

between my eyebrows with my thumb as my glance lowered towards the aging wooden floor of the restaurant.

"Just messing . . . yeah, I know . . . come on, it's ridiculous anyway . . . putting the moves. . ." I mumbled.

"You really want me to talk to Jimmy, though? He *does* hate you, you know. I wasn't joking about that part."

"Look, I really need a job this summer. Nowhere else will hire me. It's like they still think I'm some sort of criminal."

"Right. And what would make them think that?" She clicked her tongue. "Oh, there's the small fact that you robbed some rich guy's house or something, and the whole town found out."

"I never stole anything. And all that stuff is in the past. Look, I'm really reliable. I'll show up on time every day, I'll wash dishes, I'll mop the floor, whatever needs—" I couldn't finish, because Jennie was laughing at me again.

"Re-lax, dude, I'm not your parole officer. Look, I'll talk to Jimmy and see if he has anything available. Here, come sit at a table in my section. Get something to eat while you wait."

"Wait, you're going to talk to him *now*?"

"Yeah. Well, when I get a coupla' minutes. Come on."

She grinned and shook her head after seeing the relief on my face before gliding back towards the dining room. I followed behind and settled in an empty booth. I wanted to kiss her. Not in *that* way—just because I had a lot of gratitude for her helping me out. I swear.

It was a little after 4:00, and there weren't very many customers in the dining room. It seemed like Jennie was the one taking care of most of them. The difference I'd noticed comparing the Jennie from here to the one I'd seen in the halls at school—or even that night at the haunted house—was even more visible. She wasn't aloof, or bored, or scowling, or deep in thought. Judging by way she slid through the aisles in such a breezy demeanor and confidently greeted customers, and how she'd nonchalantly messed with me a few seconds ago, she almost seemed . . . happy.

Now if she could only convince Jimmy to give me a chance.

Since the whole point of being there was to earn money and not spend it, I didn't order any food; sipping ice water with a little wedge of lemon as I waited would have to do. As I watched an elderly couple limp up to the register to ask for a takeout box and pay for their club sandwiches, my eyes eventually gravitated up to the person working at the cashier's booth. I didn't remember ever seeing her before, but her whole demeanor drew me in. Immediately, I knew she must not go to my school, for two reasons: (a) there's no way I'd forget seeing a girl who looked like that, and (b) to my knowledge, girls who looked like that don't go to Bellview High to begin with.

She sat at the stool with her long legs crossed, her frizzy jet-black hair partially tamed by a white headband. Her navy polo shirt with "Jimmy's" embroidered on the upper left of the chest area shouldn't have been attractive at all, but something about the small knot that she tied at the bottom to hang just above the pocket of her shorts even made that work shirt intriguing on her. It occurred to me that if by some miracle I got a job here, I'd have the chance to get to know that girl a lot better.

Before any further daydreams could start to materialize, Jennie had returned from the back of the restaurant—not with the old and short-tempered Jimmy, but with a fit woman whose only hint at aging came from a few wrinkles on her face and a head of flowing gray hair. She smiled and gave me a friendly welcome, introducing herself as Gloria, the co-manager of the restaurant.

Seeing my confusion register, Jennie pointed to the woman and mouthed the words "Jimmy's wife," then left us and walked back to the entrance to get a new group of customers seated.

"Thanks for stopping in, Mister JB. Jennifer says you're looking for a job?"

I nodded yes, feeling grateful that Gloria hadn't given me a Rivera-type of look yet. Maybe she didn't recognize me, or maybe she just was the kind of person who believed in fresh starts.

"Well, let's go check in with the head honcho and see if there's anything we can do."

Gloria led me away from my booth in the dining room and around a long countertop, which split a corner and opened up for an aisle to bring us into the kitchen—a part of the restaurant that I'd never been before. My stomach tightened a little bit as I saw Jimmy back there, emphatically stirring a large metal vat of macaroni. His apron strings were tucked into his pants pockets, and a yellowing towel was draped over his shoulder. A single bullet of sweat reflected from his forehead. He scrunched his mouth to the side in concentration, which sent the gray moustache off at a forty-five-degree angle.

"Mister J.," Gloria announced cheerfully. "This is Mister JB. He's here for a job interview."

Jimmy nodded, but barely looked up from his mac n' cheese stirring motion. Maintaining the proper tempo of RPMs with that wooden spoon must have been a bigger priority for him than a handshake or making eye contact. He continued stirring as if there was already nothing left to discuss. Gloria shrugged and encouraged him with a gentle nudge.

"I can have Cal take that over, hun," she said. "You should take a break and get to know JB a little."

Jimmy wiped his forehead with that nasty yellow towel and turned to face us, clearly disappointed that now he had no excuse to avoid getting to know me a little. My nerves caused my voice to go slightly higher than what I meant, but I spoke first and tried to sound respectable.

"Thanks for meeting with me, sir. Are you busy?"

"It's summertime, I'm the busiest man in Northern Michigan. Let's make this quick."

"Yes, sir."

"I don't need all that 'sir' crap, either. It's just 'Jimmy' around here."

"Yes, Mister Jimmy."

He shaped his lip into a snarl. Apparently, being called "Mister Jimmy" was about as appealing to him as adding a cup of roach poison to his macaroni and cheese—either that or he was just trying to intimidate me. If I crumbled into dust right then and there, he wouldn't have to be the one to tell me to get lost.

"So, what are you here for? Got a few prank phone calls to make?"

Jimmy gave me a hard stare. He used to give my friends and I that same hard stare every time we would come into the restaurant to eat. It seemed like it had been much longer than a year ago since my friends and I had prank called Garrett while he was working here at the cashier's booth. We used to think it was hilarious. Jimmy did not, then or now.

In Jimmy's eyes, he must have seen us a nuisance and a threat to his machine-like seriousness. I never thought I'd have to face him, or to ask humbly for him to forgive and forget. Reminding myself of the end goal, and the stressed look on my mom's face every time a new overdue notice was added to her stack of bills, I steeled myself, set my feet, and stared right back at Jimmy.

"I need a job, sir—" I stopped myself. "Not sir—let me do that again. I need a job, Jimmy. I really need a job to help with a situation at home, and I can work hard if you give me a chance. I'm really sorry if I annoyed you in the past. I know I've made a lot of mistakes, but I'm trying to move on and be better. Please help me with this."

Jimmy moved to the sink and started rinsing off his towel. He twisted it tightly around to wring out the extra water before facing me once again. I honestly thought he was about to use the wet towel to smack me across the face. Without softening his expression, he gave his quick and final word on the subject.

"You're lucky I owe Jennifer a favor." Jimmy nudged his head to the back of the kitchen and pointed towards a thin screen door. "Be here at 9:30 tomorrow. Employees use the back entrance. You'll start off as a busboy."

My new boss grabbed his large wooden spoon and went back to stirring, and I wordlessly skipped out of that kitchen before Jimmy could change his mind. Now commanded by a wild excitement I hadn't felt since school had let out, I rushed out of the restaurant, sneaking a final glance at the cash register girl and calling out a heavy "thank you!" to Jennie across the dining room.

THIRTY-SECOND TIME-OUT

TRAINING DAY RANKINGS

My Top 5 things I learned on my first week of work:

1. **Jimmy wears Velcro shoes.** I don't know why that small detail stuck out so much to me. Out of at least two hundred different things that I was supposed to remember about the job, the grouchy boss's plain black kitchen shoes without laces were somehow what I remembered the most.

2. **The employee discount is only 25 percent off.** This one I learned about around lunchtime on my first day, when I was craving a cheeseburger and some of the fries that I'd smelled the moment I'd walked in that morning. I'd heard about places where workers got free food, but Jimmy's was not one of those places. For 25 percent off, I decided to just wait for lunch until getting back home.

3. **Don't ever get Dumpster Duty.** When somebody really gets on Jimmy's bad side, this is what he does instead of firing them: he assigns them Dumpster Duty. After finally finding out what it was, I thought I'd rather just get fired.

4. **It's okay to break up to three dishes.** After that, it starts to come out of your paycheck. At least, that's what one of the cooks told me after a sundae glass shattered while I tried to stack it back in its place behind the Fountain. I'm hoping I don't have to find out whether that's true.

5. **They take mopping the floor very seriously around here.** I'll explain that one a little bit later.

CHAPTER SIX

Training Day

I woke up an hour earlier than I needed to, wanting to give myself plenty of time to bike downtown; walking in late on the very first day wasn't the type of start that I wanted. I arrived with plenty of time to spare and locked my bike to an empty metal bench near a wooden fence. Like Jimmy had directed, I made sure to go in through the screen door at the back of the restaurant. Peeking through that door for the first time, my nose was met with the pleasant, greasy smell of French fries.

I'll admit that I was nervous going in there, half-expecting Jimmy to take one look at me and tell me to forget it as soon as I stepped inside. It was Gloria who happened to see me first though, and she greeted me with a warm smile and began showing me around.

Gloria explained that since it was my training day, I was going to be shadowing some of the other workers, following them around and getting a feel for how all the different parts of the restaurant worked. Every couple hours or so, she explained, I'd be paired with somebody different, and that she'd be giving me a full tour and covering some of the important things first.

"Before that, we need to get you into the system, though. And then get your uniform."

I followed Gloria into the main area of the restaurant, which was filled with rows of ice cream freezers and neatly arranged glasses and dessert dishes, along with a computer screen sitting near the edge of a crowded countertop, with notebooks, pens, and seating diagrams spread across it. Leaning back against a freezer was a bored-looking college kid with a pair of skinny arms folded across his chest.

Upon first glance, he looked like a guy who knew he'd be on to bigger and better things at a time in the near future. Until that time came, pouring sodas and scooping ice cream was an interesting enough way for him to spend the waiting period. He nodded at me and introduced himself, while Gloria went to the basement to find an extra shirt for me.

"They call me Staples," he said, extending his long right arm for a handshake. He had thin, slanted blue eyes and a pale skin tone that led me to believe he was more of an indoor cat than a guy who spent much time at the beach in his off-hours.

"Nice to meet you, my name's JB."

"Hmm . . . J . . . B . . ." He spent an extra breath or two letting my name sink in before shrugging and nodding to himself. "You know, I don't hate that. What's it stand for?"

"Try to guess."

Staples instantly dismissed my friendly challenge.

"Nah, I don't care enough to do that. Instead, I'm just going to assume that it's . . . let's go with 'Jelly Bean' then."

"Huh?"

"Yeah, Jelly Bean it is. Have a good first day, and let me know if you need anything. Try not to screw up too badly, though."

Gloria called me downstairs to get my work uniform: a royal blue T-shirt with the restaurant name in cursive on the front and a slogan on the back that said, "Summer starts *here*." Gloria said that khakis, either pants or shorts, were the other half of the dress code. Since I was a busboy and would be mostly clearing off tables, I had to wear an apron at all times too.

The aprons hung on a rusty metal hook down in the basement, and all of them were navy blue: the same color as the varsity team's away uniforms. Seeing them, I felt a surge of restlessness at the reminder that I still hadn't been on a basketball court since the start of summer; instead of "EAGLES" across the front in red block letters, my apron uniform for the moment said "Jimmy's Family Restaurant" in gold script. The aprons were faded, and most of them carried the permanent stains from years (maybe even decades) of spills from sugary drinks, hot fudge sundaes, and cooking grease.

Gloria showed me the staff bathroom at the very back of the basement and gave me a few minutes to get changed. When I met her back upstairs, she told me I could get three more T-shirts to take with me when I left at the end of the day. Jimmy made his first appearance at that point, popping across the way to remind me that the cost of the shirts would be coming out of my first paycheck.

I didn't realize how many little things there would be to remember. During my training day, Gloria must have shown me about two hundred different things, and I decided I would be lucky to remember even a tiny fraction of everything. How to sign in and out on the DigiServ computer system, what to do if a customer spills something, how to wrap silverware, when to start clearing off a customer's table, who to talk to if the cleaning solution is running low, why the dish racks need to be arranged a certain way before being sent back to the washer: the list ran on and on. By 10:30 a.m., my head was already spinning faster than the giant electric mixer that was stirring salad dressing in a back corner of the kitchen.

When she was ready to pass me off to somebody else, Gloria took me over to the grill area. Foggy clouds of steam were rising off the griddle, and a tall and stringy-looking guy wearing all black was cracking eggs onto it. After one sloppy attempt, he held his fingers close to the hot metal surface and tried to retrieve pieces of eggshell without getting burned. Gloria tried not to roll her eyes as she got the cook's attention.

"Mister Cal, I have a mission for you: can you handle our new trainee for the next forty-five minutes or so?" Gloria said it like a question, but the certainty in her voice indicated that it was more of a friendly demand than a question.

"Hey, how come nobody told me that there was a new guy?" The cook turned around smiling, but it was the sort of smile that suggested he felt slighted to not be alerted about this sort of thing sooner. He nodded towards me. "So, I have a new protégé behind the grill, do I?"

"Not exactly." Gloria frowned: something that I could already tell was unusual for her. "He's going to be a busboy, but our *friend* Arthur is running late."

"*Again?*" Cal looked both horrified and amused that

Arthur was running late again while Gloria checked her watch. "Need me to kick his ass, Gloria?"

"Not yet." Gloria laughed at the helpful threat.

"It's gotta be Dumpster Duty then," he urged while the co-manager patiently chuckled. "Come on, you know you want to."

"I'll decide on that later," she said, patting Cal on the shoulder. "What I do need, however, is for Mister JB to shadow you until our friend makes an appearance."

"Yeah, I can show him the ropes," Cal agreed importantly, cracking two more eggs before addressing me. "Just make sure you're not too distracting—I'm the only cook this morning."

Gloria seemed glad to have me (and maybe Cal) off her hands, leaving the two of us back at the grill. For someone worried about being distracted while he tried to cook, Cal sure got talkative in a hurry. Maybe this doesn't entirely make sense, but with his long and thin build, slightly angled posture, and his semi-bowl-cut hair that stuck up a little higher at the very crown of his scalp, I got an image of a carrot in mind when I looked at Cal.

"So, having fun yet?" he asked.

Not an *actual* carrot—nobody looks like that. I mean, like, if his class ever did a play about the food groups back in elementary school or whatever, Cal definitely would have played the part of the carrot. And for some reason, he wanted to know whether or not I was having fun watching him cook.

"Uh . . . yeah, I guess. I'm JB." I reached out for a handshake, but stopped when he held up his own, which now had egg slime starting to drip from his rubber glove.

I expected him also to wonder what my initials stand for,

but he was far more interested in talking about himself. In my first forty-five minutes with Cal, I don't think I learned anything about working at the restaurant. Without asking him a single question, though, I somehow got a pretty good chunk of his full life story. While watching him cook up a few more rounds of eggs and bacon, I found out that "Cal" is short for Calgary, his parents are Canadian, he broke up with his girlfriend a while ago but it's for the best, he was planning a "sick" party for his twenty-first birthday in a few weeks, he wanted to be head chef at a big restaurant, and he thought college is for suckers (and he didn't have good enough grades to get into any colleges, either).

In between lecturing his Cal 101 introductory course, Cal also found time to handle the slowly increasing load of orders coming through the small printer sitting on a corner of the metal countertop. All of the food orders from customers were entered by the waitresses and sent back to the kitchen through the touchscreen on the DigiServ computers. The printer made an annoying whirring sound with every new ticket that came through, and Cal grabbed and clipped the slips of paper to a metal wheel that rotated like a merry-go-round. As meals were started, finished, and placed on the window ledge for the waitresses to deliver, these little sheets helped make sure that the proper things were being cooked, that any special instructions were being followed (Cal seemed personally offended that someone wanted yellow mustard instead of Dijon on their ham sandwich), and that all the food made it back to the correct table.

Sometime between when I started with Cal and when Arthur finally arrived, the dining area completely transformed.

In the morning, it had been a sleepy series of neatly arranged tables and chairs—basically an oversized dollhouse, with no more than a booth or two occupied at any given time. Behind the scenes at the grill, I did hear the jukebox turn on for the first time, and the shift must have happened shortly after. I noticed the metal order wheel spinning at a faster rate, Cal began churning out burgers and sandwiches rather than eggs and hash browns, and different faces (including Jennie's) started to appear at the order window as new waitresses arrived for their shifts and entered the rotation.

By noon, the main section of Jimmy's was packed wall-to-wall with customers and staff. The frizzy-haired girl with the knot at the edge of her polo shirt was on duty now too, as an energized crowd lined up to pay their bill and maybe buy a few commemorative T-shirts. Like a swarm of bees, the mass of activity was interchangeable and in constant movement through the dining room hive, with everybody's voices melting into one surround sound buzz. As the lunch rush took shape and tensions rose, I even saw one of my new coworkers ready to sting.

A thick-necked waitress was at the completed order window, impatiently tapping on the ledge and coaxing Cal to hurry up with a grilled cheese sandwich, when her focus shifted to a new body that was slinking behind Cal.

"*There* you freaking are, you little turd!"

Immediately, it became clear that the turd she was yelling at must be Arthur, the other busboy. He walked with his shoulders held up near his ears, as if he was either constantly shrugging or having a hard time staying warm in the ninety-degree heat. I hadn't met him before, but he looked like he was my age, maybe an inch taller, with hair that had a reddish tint to it. Looking like he wanted to be anywhere else than at the restaurant, he slightly raised an eyebrow but answered only in a blank stare as both Cal and the shouting waitress gave him dagger eyes.

"Well? Grab an apron! I've got five fu—" she stopped herself, looking back to the busy dining room. "Five *freaking* tables that need to be cleared, and another little brat just spilled his Coke. Go do something!"

"Ok Merryll", he responded blankly.

Gloria came back around (surprisingly, I'd hardly crossed paths with Jimmy at all by that point) to give the other busboy an irritated but patient greeting. She gave the waitress a reminder about staying calm, which was then forgotten about ten seconds later as she muttered something about the dumpster to Arthur, rushed to grab her next order, and then almost dropped the entire tray of food on the parquet floor. Exhaling, Gloria asked me if I "was having fun yet" before sending me out to the dining room with Arthur to observe him bussing tables.

Around midday, after the lunch rush had cleared out, Staples came over to check in with me.

I was starving by that point; being surrounded on all sides by dozens of people chomping into delicious-smelling meals only amplified the fact that I hadn't eaten anything since breakfast. From Cal in the kitchen, there was an endless stream of cheeseburgers, baskets of chicken tenders, French fries, and Jimmy's famous club sandwiches, all passing through my eyes and nose every few minutes at a tantalizing distance, always meant for someone else. From the soda fountain, Staples supplied customers with Coke, root beer, orangeade, lemonade, and milkshakes to wash it all down, plus two dozen flavors of ice cream to choose from for dessert.

All of it had made my mouth water and my empty stomach groan while I was "on the floor" and shadowing Arthur as a busboy. I even flagged down Jennie to check whether staff was allowed to take lunch breaks. Jennie said a quick yes before gliding off to deliver a tray to Table 36, but then came back with the full story. In order to take a break, I would need to clock out on the system first, meaning I wouldn't get paid for that time. On top of that, the staff discount was only 25 percent off! Jimmy might run a successful business, but it definitely wasn't due to his generosity. I made up my mind that I wasn't that hungry after all, which was a little easier to convince myself of now that the dining room had mostly cleared out.

The past two hours on the floor had been sort of a dull blur, following Arthur around and observing, but not actually doing much of anything. Instead of a Cal-esque life story, all I got from him was that he was homeschooled and a year younger than me, so that meant he would have just finished 8th grade—that is, if homeschooled kids even have grades like that. Technically, they're in the same class year after year, aren't they? Arthur hardly talked at all though, so I didn't have a chance to find out. He also didn't give me very much in terms of tips or advice on how to bus tables, but after a while I realized it wasn't too difficult to figure out.

"How's the first day going?" Staples asked. "You having fun yet?"

Why do people keep asking me this? I wondered.

"This is fun for you, is it?"

Staples met my question with a good laugh, and I was glad that he appreciated the sarcasm behind it.

"Just messing with you—it's something the waitresses are always saying. I think Gloria started it. If I ever have a mental breakdown, it will be from hearing that stupid question one time too many. You doing okay though?"

From watching the dining room, I'd seen that the main job of a busboy is to get tables cleaned up as quickly as possible when someone is done eating. Wheel out a cart, clear off any leftover dishes and silverware, spray the table with cleaning solution and wipe everything off, toss any napkins and gunk into a garbage bag, take the dishes back to the dishwashers: that's about it, over and over again for as long as there are customers. The key thing is just to move fast. The new customers want you to clear up fast because they're hungry and want to sit down; the waitresses want you to be fast because they want to make money.

"Yeah. Seems a little bit stressful, but it's good I guess." Hearing this, Staples laughed again. This time it was out of mockery, though, not because he thought I said something clever.

"Stressful? Come on, Jelly Bean, there's nothing remotely stressful about this job. Don't let Merryll and them try to convince you otherwise either. What's the worst that can happen— some rich guy being pissed off because he didn't get his meal fast enough? If that's the worst part of your day, you've got no business pretending to be stressed in the slightest. We're not exactly crawling down into the mines here."

I felt slightly ashamed with how quickly he dismissed the "stressful" idea. I was going to have to play it a little cooler if

I was going to get any respect from this Staples person. And even though he sort of sounded like a university professor (a real professor, not someone teaching "Cal 101"), I instinctively decided that Staples was someone that I wanted to get respect from around here.

A little kid throwing a tantrum at one of the few occupied tables cut us off. His mom looked embarrassed as she self-consciously tried to calm him down. She wore a wide-brimmed sun hat that matched an expensive-looking dress with a zigzag pattern on it. Her blonde four-year-old knocked the hat sideways and then threw a spoon on the floor while the mom begged and pumped her hands in a rapid downward "simmer down" motion about twenty times, which had zero effect. Calculating the situation, Staples turned to start walking back to his post at the fountain.

"I guarantee that the Peninsula mom caves. She'll buy the kid an ice cream cone to make this situation go away." He motioned for me to follow, smirking. "Come on, you can tell me all about this mountain of stress you've been under."

Apprehensively, I went with Staples over to his counter, wondering if anybody was going to tell me I needed to stay by the waitress station. I was technically supposed to still be shadowing Arthur, but as he'd been on a bathroom break for at least the past fifteen minutes, there wasn't much to shadow. Plus, the little kid was now doing that thing where he's crying but gasping for air at the same time. The opportunity to get away from that for a little bit was the final push I needed. Staples casually flipped a scoop around in his hand and expertly straightened out the "Buttered Almond" sign on the flavors list, which had gone a little crooked.

"How long have you worked here, anyway?" I asked, checking out the long freezer packed with tubs of all types of ice cream.

"This year makes . . . six summers? No, scratch that—it's actually seven. I started here right after finishing middle school, as soon as I was old enough to get a work permit. Started off as a dishwasher, then was a busboy one summer; I've filled in as cashier from time to time, and now you see me at the fountain," he raised his arms out like he was a sarcastic version of Jesus, "and all of the *prestige* that comes with it."

"Have you ever been a waiter?"

"Nope, wouldn't want to. Too much talking to customers."

"What about a cook?"

He shuddered. "Too much talking to Cal."

For the first time in several hours, I saw Jimmy again through the opening to the back area, emerging from the top of the basement steps. He had two heavy tubs of ice cream stacked in his arms, probably five gallons each. Without acknowledging either of us, he decisively carried them to over to near where we were standing, then set them down with a strained grimace. That was when I caught my first real glimpse of his strange choice in footwear. On anyone else, those ugly black Velcro shoes that he wore would have looked infantile, but they somehow made Jimmy seem even more intimidating.

Looking back up to the jam-packed freezer, I realized that there was no way the new containers would ever fit. Just as I was going to volunteer to carry them back downstairs for him, Jimmy opened the freezer up anyway. Theatrically, as though he knew he was being watched, Jimmy reached into the back row and pulled out two tubs that were already there. With an embellished flick of the hand, he reached down and slid out the bottom of the freezer, revealing an extra hidden compartment. For a quick instant, I switched brains with that of a first grader, and all I could think was, *Whooaa . . . secret ice cream!*

Jimmy filled up the hidden section and slammed the lid to the freezer back shut, snapping me back to my teenage self. He then stood and stared at me for a few moments, apparently making some inner evaluation of me. Squinting at me, he leaned in within inches of my face, raising his pointer finger up to his gray, fleece-like moustache.

"Shhh!!" He vigorously hissed with a firm "don't-tell-any-body" glare that sat in place for a few seconds, even after he had turned around and marched back down to the basement.

Feeling as frozen as those two tubs of ice cream, I looked to Staples for help. He started cracking up laughing, which only added to my confusion. I guess he'd gotten used to this sort of thing.

"What was that all about?"

"Hey, Jimmy guards his company secrets very closely." He smirked again. "Whether he needs to or not."

Over the next few minutes, I was still a little bit rattled by my weird interaction with the boss, and maybe also still a little bit amazed by the secret ice cream hideout. Whatever the case, I made my first true mistake of the day when Staples asked for a little help arranging dishes on the dessert counter. My hand wasn't quite steady enough as I trying to recreate the mini-pyramid pattern that the rest of the sundae glasses were stacked in, knocking one of them to the ground and practically shattering it to dust.

With a rush of discomfort, I saw someone's head emerge

from the basement stairwell again, but this time it had a dark reddish tint rather than a shiny bald dome. Arthur was back from his extended bathroom break, just in time to grab a broom and dustpan and start sweeping up evidence of my blunder. Jimmy and Gloria were both out of the scene, but Cal heard the commotion and quickly appeared from the kitchen. Going for what I think was meant to be a concerned tone, Cal pulled me aside and reminded me the importance of being careful with the equipment.

"You know, it's okay since you're just a rookie." He was tall enough to literally talk down to me. "But after the third one, they start charging you to get it replaced."

"Is that true?" I looked to Staples again.

"Don't know—I don't break stuff," Staples replied. He was completely uninterested, folding his arms and shifting his attention back to the Peninsula mom and her kid, who seemed to be starting to calm down. "Either way, if Jimmy didn't see it, it doesn't count."

Cal looked a little put off hearing the power of his warning being called into question. He gave me one final reminder to just be careful with the dishes, and then sensing that his usefulness was finished, walked back to the kitchen rather carrotly.

Whether Jimmy caught me breaking the glass or not, I had to admit that I was relieved to stay away from him for most of the day—and I said that to Staples. I even asked hopefully if it was always like this, and if Jimmy took more of a hands-off approach to running things than I expected. Staples shook his head and explained he was only away since it was an ice cream day for him.

"Don't get used to it. Jimmy mixes all the ice creams by

hand down in the basement before the start of the summer." I couldn't deny it; that was actually pretty cool. "Once a month, he spends a day restocking anything that's starting to get low. He won't accept any help with it, so that slows down the process too."

"So then, what's the best ice cream here, anyway?"

"That's inconclusive, but I can tell you what the worst one is. That would have to be Superman."

"Superman? How come?"

"I really don't know. For some reason or another, he struggles with it and always has. We only go through one tub per summer, which Jimmy doesn't mind, because he hates making the stuff. He can't ever seem to get the proportions right, or get the proper marble effect from the red, yellow, and blue flavors. There are plenty of much more complicated recipes, and he gets those right. I don't know—just something about Superman."

My mind jumped back to the ugly plain black Velcro shoes that Jimmy, without a trace of embarrassment, was wearing around the restaurant.

"By the way, does Jimmy like, not know how to tie his shoes or something?"

"Jimmy's shoes would tie themselves if they knew who was wearing them."

That didn't answer my question, but interestingly enough, I was satisfied with the response.

"Hold on a second," Staples said, diverting his attention away from me. "I have to get this."

The mom had straightened up her floppy hat and tried to look dignified as she took her son's hand and walked him up to the counter. Staples was right; she had caved. Right on cue, she asked for two sugar cones of Superman. Staples gave her a skeptical look.

"Are you sure about that?"

3:30 rolled around after another hour or so, without a whole lot else happening besides Arthur getting sent out to the dumpster and Jennie coming over to tell me about a rumor that a couple of 8th-grade kids were planning on sneaking out to the haunted house at Five Mile Creek.

"You're not part of that, are you?" she asked cautiously. "I thought we agreed that whatever's in there, we'd leave it in peace?"

"No, that's not me. I'm done with that."

"Just checking." She seemed relieved that I was following through on our small agreement from the winter. "You working again tomorrow?"

It occurred to me that I didn't know. Laughing at me—but somehow in a way that didn't embarrassed me—Jennie took me back to the screen door of the employee entrance, where several sheets of paper were posted on the wall with a schedule for the week. My name had been added on at the very bottom of the chart, in a different color of ink than the rest of them.

"See, you're on dinner shift tomorrow, same as me. No early mornings—can't beat that. You going out tonight?"

I told her no, and that I was playing ball.

"With who?"

"By myself."

Jennie wasn't too impressed with my weekend plans, but she showed me how to clock out on the DigiServ screen, and that was it for my first day.

I hopped on my bike and pedaled as hard as I could to get up the steep hill leading out of downtown and back towards home. I smelled like French fries and bleach, but overall it hadn't been too bad.

I didn't care if it was somebody else's idea of a good time or not; in my mind, the only proper way to spend a Friday night early in the summer was doing ballhandling drills and shooting threes in the driveway. There was always something entrancing about working on my game and daydreaming while watching the blues, yellows, and reds of the Northern Michigan sunset slowly melt into each other (the same colors Jimmy could never get right in his Superman ice cream) before eventually fading off into a starry black.

CHAPTER SEVEN

Dumpster Duty

After a few days of work, I was getting a better feel for things around the restaurant. The bussing tables part didn't end up being that hard at all. It was fast-paced but pretty monotonous at the same time, and after clearing up those first few dozen tables, I could do it on autopilot without too much extra thought.

If I worked a lunch shift, the first few hours would go slow, the beehive would start swarming from 11:30 until about 2:00, and then it emptied out again for the remainder of the time. Dinner shift followed a pretty similar pattern, starting off completely barren, and then gradually building until reaching a fever pitch around 6:30. Even after the dinner rush died down, a steady stream of customers remained right until closing, mostly coming in for ice cream and other desserts.

The only big difference for bussers on the night shift was that before going home, we had to mop the bathrooms and dining room as part of the cleanup routine. The bathrooms could be done anytime within the final hour, but the main floor had to wait until the final set of customers had fully paid and taken off. I mentioned that they take mopping the floor pretty seriously around here . . . I found out just how much so near the end of my first night shift.

"Staples . . . take the kid down and get him started on the mopping tutorial," Jimmy barked. Jimmy and Gloria both made demands rather than asking questions when they wanted something done; the difference was that Gloria disguised hers with a welcoming question mark at the end while Jimmy didn't bother.

So they had a whole tutorial just to mop the floor. You know, you just splash some soap and water down there and *mop* it, right? But I guess there's more to it—so much more that I was forced to sit through a cringe-inducing ten-minute training video before I could even get started. Staples led me down into the basement, past all the aprons and into what looked to me like a makeshift storage room, library, and computer server all rolled into one. The floor of the tiny room was littered with boxes of "Jimmy's" T-shirts and dozens of old issues of *Restaurateur Magazine* arranged in small stacks. One wall was bordered with uneven bookshelves. Numerous computer modems, routers, plugs, and cables occupied another, while space was carved out on the final wall to allow for a small desk and a single three-legged stool. On the desk sat a twelve-inch Hitachi TV screen connected to an old VCR. Staples focused his attention on the middle row of one of the smaller bookshelves.

"Okay, which one of these is it?" he murmured to himself while running a finger along a series of plastic cases with thin printed labels stuck to the side. Some of the titles included *Putting Your Best Spatula Forward*, *Adventures in*

Dishwashing, and *Bleach, Lysol, and Tilex: the BLT of Kitchen Hygiene*. Overwhelmed by the variety of such random crap being kept in such a small space, my eyes continued wandering, causing me to briefly forget what I was doing down there to begin with.

My eyes twirled like a game of spin the bottle, eventually coming to rest on an object that was crammed into the top row of the taller shelf. It was just a grimy cardboard box, but the writing on it simultaneously caused me to laugh and get a small chill down my spine. On the side facing me was a warning scribbled by a thick black marker in all caps: *"TOUCH THIS BOX AND LOSE YOUR FINGERS!"*

"Look at that." I nudged Staples on the elbow, breaking his concentration as I pointed out the box to him. This warning was obviously only a bluff—just a clever way of saying not to look at Jimmy's private stuff. Still, an image passed through my mind of Jimmy having spring-loaded the cardboard with a bunch of razor blades that snap out and slice the instant a human hand makes contact. "You ever touch that thing?"

"Does it look like I have?" Staples blankly held up both of his hands, displaying that all ten fingers were fully attached. "Now quit stalling, you have some enlightening to undergo . . . Here, this is the one."

He pulled one of the videos from the shelf. Simple and to the point, this one was called *Mopping Tutorial*. Staples blew off the old cassette before sliding it into the VCR. As the video player started rolling to life, he gave me a small salute and began to leave the room.

"I apologize, Jelly Bean, but you're on your own for this one." Staples kept a poker face, but I had a feeling his was trying not to laugh at me. "Just remember, we've all been through this. Grit your teeth, and it will all be over soon enough. Make sure you're watching closely, though," he added. "Don't want to risk needing to watch it a second time."

Staples closed the door behind him, leaving me alone on the wooden stool, staring at the small TV as a grainy image of retro Jimmy appeared. The video was obviously made decades ago, as the boss had a full head of thick black hair, with a black moustache to match. His apron still looked new, and his tight '80s work shirt showed off a bulging pair of biceps. Despite his differences in appearance, he was wearing the same model of black Velcro shoes as the current version of himself.

In this low-budget production, Jimmy was the one filming, narrating, and also giving the demonstrations. He stood in the center of an empty dining room, which was set up virtually identical to the present day.

"Over the past eighty-eight years, this establishment has built a foundation of quality and safety for our loyal customers. All of this trust can vanish—like THAT," he snapped his fingers to add to the effect, *"if you go and do something stupid to get us a lawsuit. Proper floor-mopping procedures begin right here, at the ground floor."*

Jimmy stepped just off-screen for a moment and returned with a bright yellow "Wet Floor" sign. He held the sign up and slowly moved it across his body so that everyone from the imaginary crowd watching the seminar could get a good look at it. He talked with passion about the importance of putting out the "Wet Floor" sign first thing, before doing anything else.

"Let's say Joe Hungryman slips and breaks his hip, because YOU forgot to put out this sign . . ."

Jimmy pointed into the camera like he was Uncle Sam and he wanted me to join the army. He snapped his fingers again and then shook his head in dismay, unable to even consider the consequences of such an event.

With his public service announcement out of the way, Jimmy began to mop the floor, exaggerating the movements like a flight attendant giving safety instructions before a plane is about to take off. I would have thought the entire thing was hilarious, if not for the fact that in a few minutes, I would be expected to follow all of the precise instructions it gave.

"A clean floor can make all the difference. After all, if a floor's not clean, it's just a floor. Now the real key here is to get a nice smooth back-and-forth action going. Don't let the mop decide what it's going to do—you need to be in full control. Here we go," he encouraged himself, finding the type of rhythm he wanted. *"That's the real stuff."*

It continued like this for at least another five minutes, with Jimmy mopping, commentating, giving guidelines for hand position, and even offering little nuggets of wisdom about the job as he went. The only thing that kept me from turning it off was remembering what Staples had said, about paying close attention so I wouldn't have to watch it a second time. The most important (and most ridiculous) point that the tutorial kept coming back to was the twisting motion used to change directions with the mop, supposedly to make it go more efficiently along the edges of the walls.

"Palm-handle-pivot. Let's slow that down. Palm . . . handle . . . pivot." During the editing stage of this part, Jimmy must have been experimenting with the camera's special features. Everything went into slow motion as Jimmy repeated himself.

"Paaaallllllmmmm . . . haaannd-dulll . . . piihhh-votttt."

To close off the video, he wrung out the mop and set it off to the side, looking back at the floor. Wiping off his face with a rag, satisfied with his work, he gave a small fist pump and then a thumbs up back to the camera. Kneeling down, he ran his finger along the floor and then licked it to demonstrate how clean it was.

"Now that's a hell of a goddamn clean floor!"

"So, what did you think?" Staples asked when I made it back upstairs.

"That seems like a pretty idiotic way to mop a floor." I was having a difficult time containing my annoyance, just wanting to get on with the stupid task so I could go home.

"Careful—you don't want Jimmy to hear you saying that." Staples was grinning as he gave his warning. "Don't want to get Dumpster Duty."

We went over to the men's bathroom, where Staples had the mop and a full bucket waiting for us. I pulled the head of the mop out of the soap-and-bleach-filled water, which started dripping like a guy with grey dreadlocks who had just gotten out of the shower.

"You're the third person that's said something about that Dumpster Duty thing. What is it, anyway, just something made up to scare new people?"

Staples arranged his face in a slightly condescending but friendly expression, reminding me a little bit of a guy from my lunch table at school, Teen Wolf. Wolf was sort of a know-it-all, and I'd worked out that he was probably about 15 percent full of crap at any given time. I will admit that he's also a pretty knowledgeable guy, and the other 85 percent of what he has to say is usually pretty interesting stuff. Based on my interactions with Staples, his crap-fullness percentages seemed even lower than that. I decided I needed to hear his take on this so-called Dumpster Duty, which was always being mentioned in ominous tones.

"On your way in this morning, you might have noticed a big wooden fence in the shape of a rectangle. It almost looks like a toolshed, but with no roof," Staples told me.

I nodded my head while pivoting the broom handle in the palm of my hand, trying for the smooth back-and-forth mopping action that apparently was vital to the bathroom floor getting clean. I knew about the fenced area that he was talking about; I'd parked my bike near it. There was an empty bench next to it also.

"Inside that fence is where the restaurant's dumpster is kept. Probably wasn't part of your opening tour. It's the dishwashers' job to empty out the trash, so most of the time, they're the only ones who ever go back there. *Most of the time.* Any time somebody really screws up, that's where Jimmy sends them. It's one final task to check off before they're allowed to go home."

Staples was completely clean-shaven, and Teen Wolf had a full chinstrap beard, but the way his eyes flickered, the two of them could have been twins. It's the type of grin that someone only gets when they know something that you don't.

"So, what's it like?" I always got a little bit annoyed when somebody took too long to just get to the point.

"Oh, it's glorious," said Staples, beaming with false enthusiasm. "You're going to just loovve it. First off, picture the worst smell that you've ever—"

"Hold on, how am I supposed to *picture* a smell??"

"Well played, Jelly Bean. Okay then, if you can't picture it, then . . . how 'bout . . . conceptualize. Conceptualize the most wonderful, awful smell that you possibly can. Then multiply that by ten."

"But, if I already had the worst possible smell in my head, I wouldn't need to multiply it, would I? It would already be at maximum awfulness."

"Hmm. Good shit, Beans. Okay then, the most wonderful, awful smell you can think of. Multiplied by zero."

"If it was multiplied by zero, it would be nothing. That wouldn't smell bad at all."

Staples started laughing and shaking his head.

"You can go drink a bleach milkshake for all I care. All I'm trying to say is that the dumpster smells bad! Thick, hot, garbage smells bad! Can I go on now?"

"Yeah, go on. I think I have the smell nice and conceptualized now."

"So, over time, the dumpster gets pretty crusty and grimy, right? It needs a good cleaning occasionally. But cleaning the dumpster isn't part of anybody's official job description. By the way, if I see you try to switch your grip back again, you're doing this bathroom again."

I gave him a side-eye, but there wasn't anything I could do about it. He'd caught me, so I had to go back to the palm-handle-pivot move that was probably going to leave a blister.

"So where was I . . . Oh yeah, so cleaning out the dumpster isn't part of the job descriptions—Jimmy uses it as punishment instead. Whoever incurs Jimmy's wrath for one reason or another, well, they have to thoroughly clean it all out before going home that day."

"Is it really that bad?"

Staples raised an eyebrow at me.

"You really want to find out? First off, you have to take out all of the full trash bags that are already in there. Get them out of the way, you know? After that, you have to maneuver your way inside, climb right on in."

Okay, that part didn't sound all that great. Still though, between pulling an Oscar the Grouch or being Sara's frog-frying chef, I figured I'd still take the dumpster diving. That was before he told me about what happens once you get inside.

"For the next thirty minutes or so, there's no such thing as fresh air. You're living on fumes that have literally been chewed up and spit back out, over and over again."

"What do you have to do to clean it?"

"You basically have to scrape off every single piece of nasty gunk that has leaked out and gotten stuck on the sides since the last time someone had to clean it. A chisel usually does the trick. I've heard that dried-up chocolate syrup mixed with hamburger grease wins the prize for 'Hardest Thing to Scrape Off' in the dumpster."

I silently wondered whether Staples knew all this from personal experience, or if he was just making it up to mess with me, or if maybe there was also a "Dumpster Duty" training video on one of the shelves down in the basement. If my mom didn't need the extra money, I gladly would give a big part of my paycheck just to watch Jimmy climbing around in a festering dumpster and pretending to be cheerful about it.

"Sometimes a bag will also have opened while it's in there, so there's an extra pile of congealing trash lying on the bottom. You need to gather it back up and put it in a new bag. The worst, though, is when you're pulling the full bags out of there at the start. Sometimes one catches on a sharp corner and splits apart. That can leave you with a nice blanket of coleslaw, ranch dressing, and blackened banana peels dripping down your clothes and onto your legs."

"You're exaggerating."

"Careful not to do it around sunset, either—that's when the rats come out for dinner. You don't want one of those things to mistake your ear for a half-finished chicken tender and start nibbling away."

I flinched and splashed extra water onto the floor when I heard the part about the rats. On top of the gross-out factor, I felt my sense of justice violated as Staples continued to describe this demeaning punishment.

"And what if you just don't do it? I'm not subjecting myself to that crap! What if someone just refuses to go in there? You know, just go home after work and skip out on all that. You said it yourself—it's not even part of the job description."

"Well, you get fired. And then you still have to clean it."

"You *still* have to clean it?!"

That couldn't be right. How could you try to enforce a rule for someone that you've already fired from the job? I opened my mouth to protest, but Staples cut me off with one severe facial expression. It was a solemn look, clearly and wordlessly stating that the conversation was over. Apparently, there were no arguments or loopholes as far as Dumpster Duty was concerned.

When the bathroom was finally mopped up to Jimmy's specifications, I dumped out the bucket of cleaner and rolled it back to its slot near the dishwasher.

When I got home that night, I spent about triple the normal time scrubbing all of the filth from the day from my wrists, trying to cleanse myself of the mere thought of Dumpster Duty. My sleep was even interrupted by dreams of trying to play a basketball game but being forced to run at a slug's pace due to the court being knee-deep in garbage.

CHAPTER EIGHT

Open Gym

Now that my job dilemma was solved and I was reasonably settled in, getting back on the basketball court was a possibility—as long as I used my time wisely. I found out that one of the assistant coaches opened up the gym three nights a week, and anyone could drop in and play pickup games. That meant I was able to make it on days that I was only working the lunch shift at Jimmy's. As it turned out, my return to the court wasn't nearly as smooth as I expected it to be.

It would be pointless to argue otherwise, the gap between Blaise and me was growing wider and wider by the day. If I'd grown two inches since winter, Blaise had shot up about three or four. He was six foot one now, not that muscular, but lean and athletic. While I'd been grounded and on lockdown at home the previous season, Blaise had not only made the varsity team as a freshman, but he'd also led the Eagles in assists and steals. He was named All-Conference at the end of year banquet, and his reputation around the area was building.

The year before, the two of us—along with our friends Darko and Garrett—went pretty much everywhere together.

That meant playing ball, hanging out in Blaise's basement, and stopping by Jimmy's to see Garrett and get lunch or orange-ades. Unfortunately, it also meant a lot of sneaking around to where had no business being in the first place. Looking back, it was only a matter of time before something went wrong. Of course, eventually I got caught at a blue house on the Peninsula—the one time that the others weren't with me— and I took the fall for everything.

Darko, who was never much of a ballplayer anyway, went his own way after that and found a new group of friends. Garrett dated Jennie for a while, and after they broke up, I'd heard he had gotten into partying more than anything else and was sort of headed downhill. My best friend Blaise, on the other hand, transformed into a local hero, just a few months after I'd been found out and recast as a local villain.

If you'd seen Blaise hanging out downtown or at the beach, you wouldn't immediately think, *I bet that guy is a basketball star*. Up close, you might notice his feet were a little too big for his frame. The sandy-brown hair that he was always brushing off his forehead looked more likely to belong to a preppy Peninsula kid than a ballplayer. His facial expression these days was detached, as if whatever was going on inside his head required a lot more attention than the ease with which he moved through the outside world.

I hadn't realized just how good Blaise was getting until witnessing it up close at these open gym sessions. A year ago, I would have tried to convince myself that while I might not be *quite* as good as Blaise, it was at least close. Now it was like I didn't even belong on the same court as my old friend; not even I could deny it.

He was clicking with the upperclassmen on the court more than ever, threading passes that even the uncoordinated post players could catch in stride, sliding past bigger guys for rebounds, commanding the fast break. One second, he'd toss a perfect alley-oop for Derrick Blackbird, the Eagles' leading scorer a season ago, to throw down; the next moment, he'd anticipate a lazy pass and swoop into the passing lane for a steal. Just like always, he'd usually let other people take the shots. Blaise would only do the actual scoring when his team really needed it—and sometimes just when he got bored. He could dunk now too.

Whatever made me think that I'd immediately step back in and be successful was quickly wiped away. My timing and feel for the game were all off, and I was so out of shape that I got winded after only a few runs up and down the floor. It's one thing to do shooting and dribbling drills alone, but without testing my skills and adjusting in a game at full speed, they were almost meaningless. Even my biggest strength, shooting threes, was suddenly failing me.

After a demoralizing shooting performance for the second night in a row, I decided I needed to do something about it. I'd missed so many open looks at threes that day, the guy guarding me just started backing away and daring me to chuck up another one. It's the ultimate insult to someone who takes pride in being a good shooter. Since I had the dinner shift again the next day and didn't need to worry about an early wakeup, I stayed after the rest of the guys had gone home so I could get some extra practice.

The air in the gym feels extra heavy during the summer. The side entrance propped open by a chair was the only fresh air, and the flimsy metal fan in one corner did nothing to cool things off. This heavy air made my legs deaden and get weak faster too; maybe I was just out of shape, though. Derrick Blackbird didn't seem to have any issues with concrete legs when he was rising up for a two-hand dunk.

I had an entire half of the court to myself, shooting threes and running sprints. Blaise was staying as well, using the other side. He was doing layup drills while wearing a weight vest. That thing must have been suffocating in the heat, and probably weighed an extra three pounds of sweat as well. He had a full gallon jug of water next to the court, and it was about three quarters of the way empty. After about a half hour on our separate sides, Blaise invited me over, and I joined in his workout until my legs were wobbling too much to properly set up for a shot anymore.

We completed most of the workout without much side conversation, but we got to talking as we were packing our stuff up to leave. I told him about my mom's work situation, and how I ended up with a job bussing tables. Blaise told me about his summer plans as well. There wasn't any big mystery as to why he was getting so much better. He pretty much lived in the gym. When he wasn't running at open gyms or playing tournaments on his travel team, he was usually still working out by himself, either on the court or in the weight room.

"How did you get out of getting a summer job, anyway? Your mom isn't any richer than mine. Don't you have to save for college?" Blaise's mom ran a dry-cleaning service, and I knew Blaise had helped her out with tasks around the cleaners from time to time in the past.

"If I get a basketball scholarship, it's worth way more than

I could ever get at a summer job. So I convinced my mom that I should just focus on basketball for the time being. I've talked to a bunch of coaches at tournaments. They say I have a good chance, if I keep developing. Places like Northern, Grand Valley. Maybe even Central Michigan."

"What if you get hurt or something, and can't play anymore?"

Blaise tugged at his gym shorts nervously.

"If I couldn't play anymore, I don't know how I'd pay for tuition. Your brother might be able to pull that off, but I'm no Rodney when it comes to academics. Besides, if I couldn't play anymore, I'd probably be too depressed to go to college anyway."

I wanted to tell him just how stupid that sounded, but I knew what he meant. I'd just went nine months without playing any form of basketball, and it wasn't a scenario I wanted to put myself in ever again. It probably seems immature and shortsighted to say, but for us, it was more than just a game.

"Still, that's a pretty big risk all the same, isn't it?"

Blaise had little marks under his eyes. Seeing him up close, he looked exhausted. He gave me a tired look that was somewhere in between confidence and fear.

"The way I figure, doing something else all summer instead of working on my game is an even bigger risk."

CHAPTER NINE

Coworkers

By the time I had my first few days of work in the pocket, I was starting to sort out which of my coworkers I clicked with and which ones I didn't. Depending on how the schedule looked on any given day, the people I was matched up with could have a big impact on how tolerable the shift turned out to be.

Despite being the most outwardly friendly of my new coworkers, I started to groan every time I glanced at the sheet and saw that I'd be working with Cal. Maybe it was the black jeans that he often wore (cooks had a different dress code, since they're behind the scenes) with the black Nickelback T-shirt peeking behind his apron. Or the black size-fourteen basketball shoes that he had, even though he didn't play basketball. Or maybe it how quick he was to offer unwanted advice on all topics and try to establish himself as a mentor to me.

Of the three cooks, Cal was easily the youngest and least experienced, but he was somehow the only one who found pockets of free time to talk at whoever was passing by at all hours of the day. Passing by the grill was like listening to a talk radio show that only had one topic: all Cal, all the time.

He seemed to hope that everyone listening would receive each of his stories and comments with jealous admiration. Gloria would politely laugh at his corny one-liners, and Arthur thought they were actually funny, which only encouraged him to keep going. Even at his best, Cal had a shaky version of reality in terms of how he saw himself. He wanted to believe that he was a suave ladies' man—someone who is worthy of admiration and envy— and he wanted us to believe it too.

Maybe for Arthur he was something else, but I mostly saw as a wannabe and a mediocre cook. Standing six foot four at an absolute minimum, the only thing about Cal that I was jealous of was his height. I can only imagine what I'd be able to do on a basketball court with those extra inches.

When he wasn't hyping his upcoming twenty-first birthday party (he kept inviting me to come, despite knowing full well that I was nowhere near being old enough to be let in at a bar), Cal would turn the subject over to his skills with the opposite sex. According to him, half the order tickets chirping through the printer weren't food orders at all—rather, they were requests for his phone number from any female customer who came in.

This irritated me more when he pointed out Lacy, the incredibly gorgeous frizzy-haired girl who worked at the cashier's booth, and suggested that she was always checking him out. Part of that annoyance was probably because he was like five years older than us and sounded like a creep. Another part was because admittedly, a secret hope of mine was that *I* would be the one that she was checking out.

Not only was this Lacy girl stunning to look at, but she was unusual too. What I mean by that is that she was the rare Peninsula girl who also worked a summer job. Living out in the exclusive resort on the water, but also working in town among the locals: that wasn't common among the kids of the wealthy seasonal residents. I'd always thought of Bellview as having two separate worlds that mix at times, but very rarely mesh. Lacy was one of the few people I'd met who seemed to carefully balance between those two different worlds.

The first time I actually saw her up close, I was hypnotized by the greenish tint in her brown eyes. It made me want to spend more time in either one of her worlds; it didn't matter which. I felt like a punk though, because any time she started to make eye contact after that, all I could do is look down at my shoes.

The only reason I'd been over at her booth that time was because a customer had asked for a takeout menu to take home. After stumbling over my words with the menus, I ended up asking some ridiculous question about the tray of dinner mints at her desk, just to try and keep the conversation going for a few seconds longer. I spent many of my free moments during my first week glancing over to the cash register, hoping to be noticed by Lacy. Instead, it was Merryll who noticed me, and not for the better.

Merryll was the thick-necked waitress who had yelled at Arthur during my first day. She was in her mid-twenties and had worked there even longer than Staples. As long as the restaurant wasn't busy, she was tolerable. Whenever the dining room started to get that beehive effect though, it was only a matter of time before there would be an outburst from Merryll. If I was anywhere near her when she snapped, I learned fast that, just like Arthur, I would be on the receiving end of it. It was only another two days before I suffered the same fate as Arthur, and it didn't even take showing up two hours late to get it.

If things weren't going her way (which seemed to be fairly often), Merryll would look at me like I was something stuck on the bottom of her shoe; this would have been okay enough, except that most of the time she talked to me in the same degrading way. Somehow, she considered it *my* fault that Cal had burned an order of French toast, or that Table 23 had left without giving her a tip, or that *she* had forgotten to put no tomatoes on an unforgiving customer's club sandwich.

Her thing would be to wait until we were both at the waitress station or back in the kitchen before unleashing her anger on me, almost always for things I didn't even have control over. It wouldn't surprise me if I were to see flames come out of the small gap between her front teeth when she really got going. After that, she would give some sort of direct order like she was my boss, and then she'd huff her way back over to her tables.

One time towards the end of that first week, I even retreated to Staples after catching the brunt of another Merryll attack. This one had something to do with napkins; there were either too many of them, or not enough of them, or maybe there was the correct amount, but they were the wrong size, I honestly can't remember. Long story short, Merryll went off on me, and then told me to go and get more (or different?) napkins, and I couldn't stand her for much longer, so I went to talk to Staples about it.

More and more, he was becoming my go-to guy whenever there was a problem, or if I needed help with something during work. He had plenty of quirks, like his slow and deliberate "professor" way of speaking, or the thin vertical line on the lower backside of his head, where it looked like hair was never able to grow—a scar, maybe. He also always wore a pair of khaki pants that were a size too big and probably not that comfortable to be wearing in eighty-seven-degree heat, but I doubt that he cared too much about what others thought of his clothing choices.

There wasn't too much that happened around the restaurant that surprised Staples, and he didn't seem surprised in the slightest regarding what I was telling him about my run-in with Merryll. He methodically balanced a scoop of vanilla ice cream over the edge of a glass to provide the finishing touch to a root beer float as he nonchalantly gave his perspective.

"Look, Beans, don't worry about Merryll. She's like that around everybody—don't take it personal."

"Yeah. She's uh . . ." I was still the new guy around there, so I guessed it was a good idea to be as careful with my words as possible.

"She's a total bitch." Staples chuckled as he took note of my surprise. He wasn't the new guy, so I guess that meant he was free to speak the truth. I cautiously waited for Jennie to take the finished root beer float away before agreeing with him.

"Yeah, that."

The two of us watched Merryll up at the food counter, drumming the heavy rings on her fingers impatiently against the counter, causing a clicking noise that maybe she thought had the power to make food cook faster. Jimmy passed across the window, scratching at his mustache and looking indifferent to Merryll's show of urgency. She sighed dramatically and then drifted back to check in with the waiting customer, attempting a friendly smile that came off looking more like a painful grimace.

"She's always been like this, too," Staples noted, wiping a hand off on the elbow-length sleeve of his work shirt. "It was the same thing my first summer here, when I was a busboy. Merryll loves going on her little power trips, and she can't keep her composure during the slightest bit of pressure. Not a good combination if it's a busy day and she wants to pretend she's in charge of you. I got cussed out by her pretty much the whole month of July when I first started."

"That sounds horrible," I said with raised eyebrows and a hollow tone. The thought of entire month of this was a little demoralizing.

"Yeah, it was horrible. That's not to say I didn't get my little piece of revenge though."

Staples turned to face me, his angular face looking coldly mischievous. "One time, I unscrewed the tops of the salt shakers for every table in her section. Then I put the caps back lightly on top but without screwing them in. Five of her six tables dumped piles of salt all over their food during a span of about a half hour. Jimmy's rage that day . . . poor guy nearly put himself into a coma."

Staples glanced into the distance, savoring this triumph from the past.

"Wouldn't either Merryll or Jimmy suspect that you did it?"

"As far as Jimmy is concerned, it doesn't matter. It's the

waitresses' job to check sugars and shakers before seating any new table. It's written plain as day in the employee manual. No one ever does it because it feels like a waste of time, which the majority of the time it probably is. Ol' Jimmy hates it when people try to cut corners, though. Merryll cut a corner and got burned for it. Jimmy wasn't interested in hearing her try to blame us."

I laughed along with him, a small part of me trying to think of a similar way to get even with Merryll, but a large part of me thinking that I should just avoid her as much as possible moving forward. I changed the subject, thinking that Staples might be able to provide some insight on a completely different topic.

"So, by the way . . . you have any idea whether Lacy, you know, has a boyfriend or not?"

"I literally could not care less whether a fifteen-year-old Peninsula girl has a boyfriend or not. You'll have to ask her yourself." He didn't groan out loud, but I could tell he was close to it. Sometimes I forgot just how much older Staples was than me.

"Okay, okay—I was just asking. Forget I mentioned it." Then, trying my best to sound casual, I asked, "What about Jennie?"

Staples let out a joyless laugh. "Jennie. . . where to even begin?"

From back at the bussing station, I could see Jennie in perfect focus. I watched her glide across the floor like a comet, rushing underneath the old tin roof, through a tiny parquet solar system—a.k.a., the main dining room. She was laughing at something a customer had said, picking up a ten-dollar tip from one table while leaving the bill for another.

Jennie and I had actually started talking to each other pretty often since I started working. In a lot of ways, the social walls that exist during school were broken down at the restaurant. Everyone needs to interact with everyone in order for things to get done, so I found myself talking to Jennie much more in a typical week than we ever did during the school year. Plus, we did have the common bond of our trip to Five Mile Creek.

Her dark blonde hair, bleached lighter by the early summer sun, was tied into a bun with extra pens politely tucked into it. A little strand of hair was always slipping out, falling onto her forehead. When her hands were full, she puffed air up from the side of her mouth to push the disobedient strand back into place.

Jennie was really in her element at the restaurant. She could almost always memorize people's orders without writing them down, sometimes snapping her fingers three times to search her mind for that one final item that she knew would come to her in just another second. Her customers always seemed to be smiling and enjoying themselves more than those who had a different waiter or waitress (especially the unlucky ones who got paired up with Merryll). Furthermore, Jennie was the one and only employee who could sarcastically ask, "Having fun yet?" without it annoying the crap out of me.

One moment, she'd be up at the order window, lightheartedly talking trash to the cooks. She was always telling them to hurry up in a way that might have sounded mean if it was anyone else saying it. Then she'd be back at the waitress station, shrugging off the half-impressed/half-jealous looks that Merryll would always give her when it was time to count tips. Jennie's body language said, *Hey, do a better job then—don't blame me if your tips are low.*

How could this Jennie strike such a vivid contrast to the Jennie that I knew from school? School Jennie was always bored, always stoned, always too cool and standoffish. Work Jennie was patient with customers, friendly with even the lowliest of dishwashers, and even had a good rapport with Jimmy. She may have been a burnout during the school months, but around the restaurant her shine was brighter than just about anyone. It's no wonder that people were always asking specifically to sit in Jennie's section. Even without a nametag, she was well known.

By just about any standard of looks, Lacy over at the cashier booth should have easily been the most attractive girl that worked at Jimmy's. Something about Jennie kept bringing my attention back to her though, even as I reminded myself that she wasn't remotely my type.

FULL TIME-OUT

CUSTOMER RANKINGS

The Top 5 types of customer that ate at *Jimmy's Family Restaurant*:

1. **The Margaritavilles**

   This is what I called the middle-age dudes who would come in around dinnertime, all sunburned after spending the afternoon golfing or out on the boat or whatever. After placing their orders (and complaining that we didn't have any TVs or tequila), a pair of them would head over to the jukebox, and "Margaritaville" was, without fail, their track of choice. There's something about that stupid song, because it's on at least four times a day at Jimmy's. I wonder if it's the official "Hey, everyone, look at how much vacation I'm on!" anthem for rich summer guys in their forties.

2. **The Real Housewives of South Point**

   With floppy brimmed hats, shiny bracelets, and heavy makeup, I decided that these groups of Peninsula ladies were probably the ex-wives and future ex-wives of the Margaritavilles. When they weren't arguing over whose plastic surgeon was the best, they were leaving behind small piles of half-used blue artificial sweetener packets. Always the blue ones. They must rip the packets open, dump out the easiest grains, and move on to the next as soon as pouring from that packet starts to get more difficult. This meant dealing with an annoying trail of hundreds of sticky sugar crystals when cleaning those tables.

3. **The Old Guard**

The only locals to make this list, the Old Guard is made up of the senior citizens who would come in around three or four, when the place was mostly empty. They usually ordered coffee and bland sandwiches, sat in the same booths day after day, always wanted Jimmy to come out and chat with them, tipped a little and complained a lot, but at least they kept their tables exceptionally clean.

4. **The Families**

The waitresses loved this category because the combo of large groups and friendly people meant maximum tip money. However, the families with kids under the age of five are the worst tables to clear from a busboy's viewpoint. A large family with young kids meant crusts of bread jammed into the seats, milk in plastic kiddie cups with protective tops (which would spill all over the place anyway), booster chairs blocking aisles, placemats with partly finished mazes filled in by broken-in-half crayons. Even though I was working for a family restaurant, as a busboy, I have to say that I really wasn't keen about the Families.

5. The Peninsula Princesses

Always travelling in packs, forever talking loudly and laughing conspicuously, causing my imagination to run wild, these were the tables that commanded my attention. Never the same group twice, the teenage royalty of the Peninsula brought in their own flowery-scented galaxy of bright shirts, sunglasses, and flip-flops whenever they entered, placing themselves at the center of that galaxy. Despite Jennie's unhidden scorn for the attitude of superiority from girls like this, I couldn't help but to secretly hang on their every word when I cleaned a nearby booth, experiencing the secondhand excitement of their presence.

CHAPTER TEN

The Boss

Jimmy didn't move anything like what I would consider an "old guy." Any of the customers who were part of the Old Guard all seemed to walk a very specific way; with their feet slowly shuffling along the ground, hands hooked together behind their backs, and heads passively leaning out over their shoulders, it was like they were moved from place to place by a gentle and invisible current, rather than any true desire to get anywhere. Not the boss, though.

If you took away Jimmy's balding head, covered only by a U-shaped patch of gray hair around the perimeter, he could have passed for a guy in his thirties or early forties. Okay, I'm exaggerating. You'd also have to take away his gray Truffula tree moustache, grouchy demeanor, and insistence on referring to the DigiServ computer as "the machine." That's not the point. All of this is just a bad way of saying that Jimmy didn't *move* like an old guy.

He paced through the kitchen with a certain cadence and a clear purpose. He must have made dozens of trips up and down the basement stairs in a given day to take care of one thing or another, but rarely showed signs of tiredness or aching joints during the day.

As long as it wasn't an ice cream day for him, Jimmy was everywhere, from before the doors of the restaurant opened until long after they closed each night. Chipping in with the same machine-like intensity to whatever task was needed at any time, he set the standard for focus that everyone else on the staff was expected to follow. One time I saw Jimmy cook sixteen omelets, slice up a whole package of raw whitefish, fix a broken part on the dishwasher, calm down a dissatisfied customer (Merryll's table), re-sharpen each of the kitchen knives, and figure out why the orange soda was coming out of the fountain brown, all in a span of half an hour. His "lunch break" on some days consisted of telling Cal to toss a quick cheeseburger on the grill for him, then taking forty-five seconds to devour it before wiping away a string of cheddar from his mouth and moving on to whatever was next.

With that said, my early days at the restaurant involved a constant series of minor arguments with Jimmy. Surprisingly, it wasn't hard talking to him. The employees ranged in age, from dishwashers and busboys in their teens all the way to cooks who were pushing their forties or later. Jimmy talked to all of us the same—like we were adults, expected to do our jobs, and with little room or reason for any outside nonsense. In this way, talking to him turned out to be somewhat easy. The difficult part was getting him to listen.

A few times, to break up the boredom of wiping off hundreds of tables, I'd come up with a good idea or two. Small things—and I mean *really* small things—that I thought could help the restaurant. Like buying jam in shorter but wider jars, so that it would be easier to work the knife around and get out every last glob without getting the handle all sticky. Or keeping a stock of barbecue sauce on-hand, because a lot of people (including me) preferred barbecue instead of the homemade "J-Sauce."

I don't know what the full recipe for Jimmy's special J-Sauce was, and I'm also not going to say which gross substance Cal tried to convince me was used as the secret ingredient. All I'm saying is that regular barbecue sauce is better, and even if it's not, customers should still have the option, shouldn't they? Like, how is that even an argument? Jimmy was never interested in hearing any of it. All he said was that when I have my own restaurant, I can dip my chicken in whatever the hell I want. Until that day comes, though, he says he'll just stick with J-Sauce.

My best idea was that the restaurant should start doing deliveries for takeout orders. I noticed that whenever customers came in for to-go orders, the line at the cashier would get all backed up, and then the restaurant would become extra clogged while they waited for their food. It annoyed me that takeout orders seemed to take priority over the ones that actually came in to sit down, and only because those people were pushier about it.

Even the southernmost (and furthest) edge of the Peninsula was less than two miles away, so just a few extra workers on bikes would have been able to handle the range for quick deliveries. They could get some extra tips, the restaurant would be less jammed, and we'd probably even get more business as a result. Maybe I just caught him at a bad time, placing a tub of Neapolitan into the secret ice cream compartment, but it didn't end well. Jimmy immediately shot my idea down, and somehow got upset that it was even brought up to begin with.

"I've got enough to worry about with what happens inside these walls," he snapped. "Why would I want to add on another set of headaches outside them?"

Feeling myself getting frustrated by his disdain, I couldn't understand why he was being so unreasonably dismissive about this.

"Because," I said, speaking as seriously and businesslike as I could, "I think it would be a great new addition for the restaurant. I think it would help out in multiple ways."

"Of course you think that. You're fifteen years old, you're full of piss and vinegar, and you think every thought that crosses your mind is worthy of the Nobel Prize for Thinking."

"Yeah, but I really think we need to—"

Jimmy slid the hidden compartment shut and gave me what Staples calls the Stare of Unfathomable Disgust. The name for that look pretty much describes itself, so I'll leave it at that.

"You're so quick to assume that you know better than people who have done this for the last fifty years. You show up for a week or two, and you seem to think that I need to check every little decision for your approval first. If you'd just shut up and worry about getting the hang of your job, you could actually end up being a big help around here, so can you just do that?"

Having finished with me, Jimmy started violently scraping chunks of frost off the rim of the ice cream freezer.

"Yes, sir. I mean, Jimmy."

The ice shavings fluttered off in the air like snowflakes as they were set free. With the boss concentrating on this, I figured it was probably time to duck away and head back to the waitress station. All three waitresses were watching me with interest, obviously having watched the whole exchange.

Jennie used her left hand to try and shield the huge grin from her face. When Jimmy's wrath was directed at someone else, it was easy to find the humor in it. Since Jennie never seemed to get caught in the crossfire herself, she had plenty of chances to laugh at the rest of us.

"He got me with the 'piss and vinegar' line," Jennie said. She glanced over, playfully pushing me by the shoulder, trying to break me out of my sour mood. "You gotta admit—that's a good one."

Staples stopped by a little while later, just to tell me that the Nobel Prize for Thinking isn't an actual award. Cal came over too, and I thought it would be so he could gloat, but it was actually to tell me in all seriousness that he thought the delivery thing sounded like a great idea. For a second, I considered that maybe I had been wrong the whole time . . . If Cal thought it was a great idea, maybe there *was* something wrong with it.

But then I even got some validation from Staples, which gave me confidence and a renewed sense of frustration. After replaying the specifics of my idea to those who were listening, I ended up venting a little too loudly about Jimmy's refusal to hear me out.

"It's not a horrible thought, deliveries," Staples said, eyeing me keenly. "Yeah, that has potential."

"I know, that's what I'm saying! Just because Jimmy's a

stubborn old bat who can't handle any type of change . . ."

There was the moustache, the black Velcro shoes, and the Stare of Unfathomable Disgust again, bustling past at just the perfect time to hear me insult him.

"You hear that, Gloria?" he called back to the kitchen loftily. "I guess we're old bats now!" I wanted to correct Jimmy and tell him that only *he* was, but accurately figured that wouldn't help the situation any. Mortified, my face turned a deep maroon, and I kept my head down and started wiping down the coffee machine with a wet towel for no reason. Jimmy didn't bother sticking around to see everyone's reactions, which was probably a good thing.

Cal stood there with his mouth open and his hands on his head, like he was witnessing a natural disaster, both thrilling and horrifying. Jennie couldn't even look at me without surrendering to a wild fit of giggles for the remainder of my shift. Staples just folded his arms and shook his head.

It was great that Jennie and the rest of them were kept entertained, but all in all, I was pretty relieved when 3:30 finally rolled around that afternoon. I went home and napped for a few hours, and then biked over to the gym for a workout that was exhausting enough for me to forget about what had happened. After six days straight, I finally had a much-appreciated day off from work.

CHAPTER ELEVEN

Speaking of . . .

I went into Jimmy's on my day off to check the next week's schedule, and while I was in there, I decided to put that 25 percent discount to use for an orangeade.

Speaking of orange, Lacy was working at the cashier's booth. She wore an orange headband to keep all the black waterfalls of frizzy hair out of her face. I didn't even get nervous saying hi and doing a little small talk. I joked about being there on my day off ("had to make sure Jimmy doesn't get too overwhelmed without me"), which made her laugh. While we were talking, we were also joined by Jennie, who picked that time to come up and exchange a bunch of one-dollar bills for tens and twenties. Maybe it was in my imagination, but Lacy seemed a little tense around Jennie.

Speaking of Jennie—and maybe this was also just in my head—but I was starting to sense that there could be something between her and me. She was cool as usual, letting me know some of the funny things from that morning that I'd missed, like Arthur getting Dumpster Duty again when he came in an hour late. She had me cracking up with a perfect impression of his vacant expression, and his stiff and high-shouldered walk. It was still hard for me to get over the fact that Jennie had such a different energy around the restaurant, like she was more in her element than she'd ever be at school. She was a lot more relaxed and inviting and seemed to have herself really pulled together, although she apparently still got high quite a bit. She wasn't shy about mentioning smoking weed during everyday conversation. She calls it "blazing." As in, "JB, after work sometime, you should come blaze with us."

Speaking of Blaise, he invited me to the school gymnasium to work out with him a few times at the end of the week. I beat him in most of our shooting drills: spot-up threes, curls to the free throw line, step backs, floaters. Towards the end, we practiced finishing at the basket, with driving layups— well, driving layups for me, and driving dunks for Blaise. That guy was developing some serious hops.

Speaking of hops, I had a bad dream the other night, about Sara's house and all those frogs hidden in the porch closet. I woke up in a panic, confused and thinking that they were all jumping around in my bed. I started thrashing around in the dark, unsuccessfully trying to knock the non-existent frogs off of my sheets.

Speaking of sheets, when I'd gone into the restaurant on my day off, Gloria had put the new schedule up, so I went back towards the kitchen to take a look. I found my name on it (this time it was in the same color ink as everyone else), and without thinking, I checked for Jennie's name as well. We were scheduled for the same shift four days in a row on the following week.

Speaking of weak, my legs went a little shaky when I

finished my drink and got up to leave. Maybe it was due to all the sets of wind sprints that Blaise and me had run the night before, or maybe it was because of the way Jennie had nodded and grinned at me as she grabbed my empty orangeade glass.

CHAPTER TWELVE

Juicy Fruit

Staples wouldn't tell me directly whether Jennie had a boyfriend or not, but I got my answer quickly enough after returning from my day off. During the lunch rush, we constantly crossed paths while hustling through the swarmed dining room, Jennie delivering club sandwiches, burgers, and chicken tenders, and me taking back the emptied dishes once they were finished. During our brief interactions that were always quickly interrupted, she mentioned a party coming up that she was excited about.

It wasn't until we were hanging out near the soda fountain during a dead period later in the afternoon that I found out whose party it was. It was one that Jennie's boyfriend was hosting. Apparently, he had a truck and his own house, and they were going to invite people over and make a bonfire in the backyard.

Hearing her talk about this guy out of nowhere caught me off guard for a lot of reasons. Mainly because I was starting to feel a growing chemistry between Jennie and me, and I'd wondered if she had felt it also. When I'd been daydreaming during the slow parts of my day off, it was an image of Jennie—not Lacy at the cashier's booth, or the dozens of Peninsula girls who revolved in and out of the main entrance—that kept replaying itself in my mind. It also caught me off guard to find out that her boyfriend was a lot older than us.

Like our boss, his name was also pronounced "Jimmy," except he spelled it J-I-M-I, like Jimi Hendrix. He'd graduated (or maybe he didn't ever graduate) from high school around the same time as my brother. I didn't know much about him, but the impression I'd gotten overall from Rodney was that he was sort of a lowlife, and I made the mistake of saying that to Jennie. We had gotten along really well ever since I'd started working at Jimmy's, but she seemed hurt.

"In case you're forgetting, I'm sort of a lowlife too. You even said it yourself, remember?"

"I never said that." I scowled at the jukebox, my face turning red. Out of anger that she had a boyfriend with a truck and his own place to throw parties at. Out of feeling stupid for thinking that Jennie might have a crush on me, when apparently my competition was guys who were twenty-one and had trucks, and parties, and places of their own. Out of remembering that yeah, I did pretty much say that Jennie was a lowlife back in the winter. Staples generally got along with Jennie too, but a dark shadow also crossed his face when he heard her boyfriend mentioned.

"You're seriously still with that guy?" He unfolded his arms and held out his hands in disbelief. I felt a sudden rush of gratitude for Staples upon hearing him rant against Jimi's character. "The guy is a scumbag—pardon my French."

"Oh yeah? And what exactly is so bad about him, Staples?"

The challenging tone that Jennie used made it seem like she already thought she knew the answer. Staples narrowed his eyes, digging in.

"You can start at the fact that he's still dating high school girls, and then go from there! He's not funny, he's not nice, he's not cool. Ask anyone from my year, that guy sucks."

"Yeah, well," Jennie raised her eyebrows and answered defensively, "a lot of people don't know what he's really like."

"And I feel sorry for the people who do." Staples wasn't backing down. He scratched at the back of his head and snarled.

"Well luckily for you, that's something you don't need to worry about. You can mind your own business about my personal life, and I'll make sure not to invite you to the party. Sound good?"

Cal had been watching and trying to listen in from the background, making up fake work to do in order to bring himself closer to the heated discussion developing. After hearing the word "party," he couldn't hold back for any longer.

"Are you guys talking about my twenty-first birthday party again?" Cal seemed to have us confused with himself; literally no one other than Cal had ever talked about his birthday party. "You're all gonna be there, right?"

"We're not talking about your birthday, and I hope I have other plans for whatever night that is." Staples was in a sour enough mood that he didn't bother humoring Cal. "And if not, I will make some."

"Oh," said Cal, confused but not really that bothered by Staples's rudeness. "What are we talking about then?"

I think that Staples and I would have been perfectly fine

leaving Cal hanging, but after a long pause, eventually Jennie went ahead and filled in the blanks for him.

"It's nothing. Staples over here just has a personal vendetta against my boyfriend, that's all." She said it casually, as if this was a topic they'd discussed numerous times before, and neither side was planning on changing their opinions any time soon.

"Nobody needs a personal vendetta to hate your boyfriend, the guy is a complete asshat."

Nobody paid attention to Cal giggling to himself after hearing the term "asshat."

"Okay, so if you have such a strong opinion on my love life, who should I be dating then? I'll wait, Staples . . ." Jennie sarcastically leaned her elbow on the counter, her chin resting in the palm of her hand. "I'm soooo interested in hearing what you have to say about this, I really am."

"Shut up. I don't care, just anyone besides *Jimi Dandersley!*" He said the name like it was a bad takeout meal that he couldn't wait to vomit back up. "Maybe someone actually *in high school* would be a start—could be Jelly Bean, for I care."

He just had to say that last part. I shifted around uncomfortably, trying not to let my body language give anything away. I don't think it mattered though, because Jennie had already tramped back across the dining room and over to the waitress station, in as bad of a mood as I'd seen her since joining the staff. She must have been really fed up if she preferred Merryll's company instead of ours. Even Staples, who normally stayed cool and aloof, was still clearly agitated, rattling a tray of empty water glasses as he retrieved them from the dishwasher and set them extra hard on the counter. I wondered, did Staples have feelings for Jennie or something, or was her boyfriend just *that* bad of a guy?

"What is it that you were saying about Jennie's boyfriend earlier?"

It was nearing the tail end of my shift, a few more groups of customers had cycled through, calming down the tension from earlier. Staples was back to his normal self, leaning back against the counter, folding his arms across his chest. He smiled a little bit in a self-satisfied manner, like he'd been specifically waiting for me to ask that very question.

"Got a little crush, do you, Beanie?"

"No."

I lied. Maybe it was a lie, I wasn't sure. It could have been a little crush, could have been a big crush, maybe I was falling for her, or maybe it was just hormones acting up. This sort of feeling was still pretty new to me. Even just a year ago, I didn't really think about girls like that. Obviously, I knew they were out there, and I saw my friends starting to pair up with them from time to time, at school dances and dates and even parties on the Peninsula in Blaise's case, but it wasn't something that seemed accessible for me. Girls didn't seem to be very interested in me, which usually wasn't a big deal because I wasn't all that interested in them either. It was only when my friends were being pulled away from me on their account that it started to matter to me.

Now, it was like everywhere I looked, some female or another was catching my eye. There was Lacy and her tiny shorts and long tan legs over at the cashier's booth. Then there were the endless hordes of alluring but intimidating Peninsula girls, loudly talking and laughing as they ordered lemonades and club sandwiches during a break from the private beach. And of course, there was Jennie.

"Sure you don't. Listen, Bean, you don't want to get yourself mixed up with a girl like Jennie. It's not worth it. Her boyfriend? The guy is a total jerk. There's not much else to say about it. That's who the Jennies of the world go after. Don't ask me why, but that's who she goes for, and that's always who she'll go for. You don't strike me as a total jerk. Therefore, you don't want to waste your time worrying about Jennie."

"I don't think that's true about her." At least, I really *hoped* it wasn't true about her. "Thanks on the 'not a total jerk' part, by the way."

I put on some hand sanitizer—not because my hands were dirty, but just because I wanted to have something to do.

"All I'm saying is that dating a girl like Jennie would be a lot like chewing Juicy Fruit gum."

Staples could see the confusion etched into my face. Where exactly was he going with this?

"Sure, it would probably be pretty good for about twenty seconds, but then it loses its flavor and becomes stale and unbearable almost immediately. Would that pretty good twenty seconds really be worth it, knowing it will leave a bad taste in your mouth for the rest of the day?"

"Juicy Fruit isn't all that bad, is it?"

"Yeah, it is. And you're setting yourself up for a lifetime of Juicy Fruit if you let your emotions get taken in by girls like Jennie."

With the restaurant cleared out of customers and the jukebox in between songs, the whole space had become quieter than I realized. Jennie looked up from sweeping the floor near her section of tables. She was back on speaking terms with me, having broken the ice by asking what I was planning on getting Cal for his twenty-first birthday present a few minutes earlier.

"I heard my name," said Jennie, grinning over at the two of us. "Careful with the gossip, ladies."

CHAPTER THIRTEEN

The Restaurant Guy

J_{B!"}

"JB!"

It was about 9:30 in the morning, on the final day of June. Like a restless summer tourist, the heat wave that had gripped Northern Michigan for the past two weeks must have seen enough of Bellview and returned back down to the grind in the southern parts of the state. The lasting impact of the heat wave meant that the impossibly blue water on Lake Bellview was finally comfortable enough to swim in, and the sunlit seventy-five-degree temperatures were warm enough to enjoy, but not suffocating. It stayed light out until well after 9:30 each evening, and Jimmy's Family Restaurant stayed open for an extra half hour to accommodate the extra customer traffic, as the 4th of July and peak of summer approached.

Jimmy was calling me from back in the kitchen. My gut reaction closely mirrored whenever I heard my mom call my name and summon me downstairs at home. I tensed up, assuming that I either did something wrong or was about to be put to work.

Tightening my apron strings and cleaning some runny

drops of Table 27's spilled orange juice from the front of it, I walked past Cal and through the doorway to the kitchen. He nodded at me in a sort of way that made me think he planned on having a nice long pep talk with me afterwards. I tried to ignore him as I braced for Jimmy's Stare of Unfathomable Disgust. Despite being clean-shaven, Staples did a great impression of the way Jimmy scrunched up his moustache and leaned his forehead outward when giving that look.

There were plenty of different ways to receive that stare, and I was certain I was about to discover a new one. To my surprise, once I got back to the kitchen, I found that Jimmy was actually whistling as he directed traffic and sang out orders into the intercom. The intercom had been the previous system for calling meal tickets back to the kitchen, eventually getting replaced by the DigiServ computers. Once in a while, Cal would get a hold of the microphone and try to get cheap laughs by making Chewbacca noises or growling and making threats into the speaker like The Rock or other WWE villains. Besides that, Jimmy was the only one who still used this old-fashioned mode, taking a certain pride in his persistent old-school mentality.

"Ordering: one sal-edd . . . one chicken. . .sal-EDD. Light on the dressing." The boss took his finger off the intercom button and faced me. Someone wanted chicken salad for breakfast, which sounded gross to me, but Jimmy didn't mind one bit. "JB, I have a new dishwasher starting up today. I'm pretty sure he's in the same grade as you. You're starting to know your way around here a little bit . . . I need you to take an hour or so later in the morning to show him the place. We shouldn't be too busy yet, so the waitstaff can bus their own."

"Bus their own?" It took me just a tick too long to understand what he was meant by that.

"Their own *tables*. The job that *you normally do*?" There was Jimmy's stare of disgust, right on schedule.

"Oh, right. Sorry—I just misheard you. Yeah, that makes sense. So what should I show to this new guy?"

"He's going to be a dishwasher, but I want him to see a little bit of how the rest of the place runs. He'll shadow you for about an hour. Show him how to clock in on the machine, take him back to the freezer, the walk-in, dry storage, the bathrooms, that type of stuff. Just help him get settled."

It reminded me of my first day on the job, which really hadn't been very long ago. I felt a small surge of pride upon hearing Jimmy say that I was starting to know my way around.

"Yeah, I can do that. What's his name?"

"Trent Spencer. You know him, right?"

"No, that name doesn't sound familiar. Is it a summer guy?" There were very few summer residents who needed/wanted/decided to get jobs when they came to stay on the Peninsula. Then again, Lacy was also an exception, so it wasn't unheard of at Jimmy's.

"He's local. I'm pretty sure he said he goes to high school here. Anyway, he'll be here in about forty-five minutes. Make sure you help him get situated."

"Sure, I can do that. And you're sure the waitresses will be okay with bussing their own?" I still had Merryll's breathless scolding from a few days before fresh in my mind, when I had gone to the bathroom for three minutes and (according to her) ruined her tips at a bunch of tables. Jimmy brushed my concern off without much thought.

"They can manage."

Turning the corner into the back room, I could overhear Gloria talking with the new guy. They were back by the screen door of the employee entrance. With his back turned, I couldn't get a good look at him; I could only see the tangle of messy blonde hair huddled like a bird's nest on his head.

"And this board over here is where we hang up the schedule for the next week. I update it every Sunday, and all staff needs to make sure to check so all your shifts are covered. Oh, and if you have a Sunday off, feel free to just call and someone can tell you your times for the next day. You don't need to come all the way down here if you're not working. Any questions so far?"

"Is it okay if I use my own rubber gloves? I brought these from home."

Hearing that question, I instantly realized that I *did* already know my new coworker.

"*SPAZ?*"

I don't really know what made me so happy to see Spaz, but I didn't bother suppressing my wide grin watching him pulling on a large pair of yellow rubber gloves as Gloria reintroduced us. He wasn't a friend, but at least it was one more familiar face around the restaurant. Plus, as I found out that winter at Five Mile Creek, the guy's entertainment value was off the charts.

To his credit, Spaz was one of those rare people who's not constantly worried about his image. He likes what he likes, and he doesn't care in the slightest whether other people think it's cool or not. Going to high school, it seems like everyone does more acting than the theater club to appear a certain way and follow all the right trends. Yet somehow, kids who act in the school play (and actually admit that what they're doing is acting) are considered weird. In Spaz's case, it was refreshing to know that there's at least one guy who is his own person and fully unique.

Spaz could annoy me, make me laugh, surprise me, and confuse me, but in the short time I'd spent with him, I can say for certain that I've never been bored. An image flashed across my mind of Jimmy strangling him Homer Simpson-style at some point during the summer, which made me grin even more.

"Hey, Spaz. Nice gloves."

"Well then, seeing as you two already know each other, I suppose I'll leave you to it," Gloria said. "Mister JB, take good care of him, and I'll be back in an hour to show you the nitty-gritty of the dishwashing machine."

Once Gloria had left, I took Spaz on a tour of the restaurant, showing him the dry storage room in the basement, the *"TOUCH THIS BOX AND LOSE YOUR FINGERS!"* room where I had watched the mopping tutorial, the employee bathroom, and the brass hooks with all the aprons. Coming back upstairs, we continued to the walk-in fridge, kitchen, soda fountain, and dining room areas. While making the rounds, I introduced him to some of the other employees, including Staples and Cal. Merryll was bussing her own tables and looking thoroughly displeased about it. We skipped her, making a detour over to the cashier's booth instead, where Lacy was just arriving to take over at the register. My nervousness around Lacy had started to fade somewhat, and I enjoyed that I could be around her without constantly shifting around in place or acting strange. As she tied back her frizzy black hair, Lacy politely asked Spaz how he'd ended up working at Jimmy's.

"I started out as a dishwasher at another restaurant, Rivera. You know, my dad is the night bartender there." It's anyone's guess how Lacy was supposed to know that, but she nodded along anyway. "I got sick of him always telling me what to do, though. He's already doing that at home anyway. I figured someone else could have a turn bossing me around. Hey, are these mints free for anyone?"

Lacy laughed, helping tilt the tray so that two dinner mints dropped into Spaz's gloved hand. He popped them into his mouth, without saying thanks but clearly with gratitude nonetheless, and then went on explaining his previous jobs.

"After that, I worked for like three days at a nursing home. That was even worse. It was basically sweeping up old ladies' hair off the floor all day. Needed a change . . . I guess I'm a restaurant guy at heart."

Lacy and I looked up and shrugged at each other upon hearing that final part. I couldn't tell whether it was impressive or depressing that at fifteen years old, Spaz had already decided that he was "a restaurant guy" when it came to determining a career path. Taking no notice of our reaction, he adjusted his gloves and retied the apron strings that had gotten loose and now trailed to the ancient parquet floor.

"These are some nice aprons. They picked out a good font for the 'Jimmy's' logo. It's elegant." Maybe Spaz was really a restaurant guy after all.

I felt a small but noticeable change after Spaz began working at the restaurant. Since someone had joined after me,

I officially wasn't the "new guy" anymore as far as the others were concerned. Being the second newest instead of the absolute newest person there was a tiny distinction, but it made me feel just a little bit more confident and more useful as a result. Realizing that I was able to provide answers some of the time for that one person who came to me with questions, Jimmy was right: I was starting to know my way around.

The downside of Spaz's arrival was that the two of us became unavoidably linked in many people's eyes, just because we started around the same time and are the same age. Merryll assumed that we were good friends, even though we were barely more than classmates, and one of the cooks even accidentally called me Spaz once. I'll give Cal some credit here; at least he understood that Spaz and me were fully separate people, never bringing me over to help interpret the latest odd behavior or strange comment from the new dishwasher.

In fact, it was Staples who didn't seem to have much patience for Spaz's quirks, and it was him who probably connected the two of us most. When questioning me, Staples had taken to referring to Spaz as "your boy"—as in, "Jelly Bean, what's the deal with your boy? Does he need some kind of medication or something?"

From the start, Spaz was one of the most enthusiastic workers out of anyone; I mean, who else brings their own dishwashing gloves from home? I'll be the first to say that the guy is weird—and maybe a little too much at times—but for some reason it bothered me to hear Staples and the rest of them say it. When we were kids, Blaise had this pet dog that he would complain about. It was old and mangy and wasn't good for much, but when I said something about it being worthless, we ended up getting into a fight. It was okay for him to talk about his own dog, but me doing it was crossing the line. Maybe it was that sort of thing with Spaz.

The truth was that he wasn't my boy, my dog, or even my friend. I had no desire to be Spaz's keeper, but at the same time, I still felt protective over him and was quick to defend him when I felt people were going a little overboard. At the end of the day, maybe we *were* more connected than I wanted to recognize.

CHAPTER FOURTEEN

Jennie's Boyfriend

"Wurr's Jennie's table? I'm sittin' thair."

A wiry-looking guy with freckles and a buzz cut was hassling Lacy in the busy restaurant. It was 4th of July weekend, and even though the holiday wasn't until the following Monday, the town was even more crowded. Vacationers looking forward to the beaches, barbecues, families, fireworks, parade, and parties had filled up the dining room. All of them, plus one unpleasant-looking local, who was demanding a specific seat during the most hectic part of the afternoon.

Lacy's job wasn't to be a hostess, but trying to be accommodating, she motioned for Jennie. Jennie's section was completely full, but expertly switching between responsibilities, she was managing just fine. When she lifted her head and saw Lacy uncomfortably beckoning her, she snapped out of her zone for a moment to go see the visitor.

Seeing Jennie's face light up, there was no mistaking who was there to see her. She grinned and hugged him, leaving Lacy to continue handling payments from the long checkout line. Jennie was blushing and excited, and since there was a dirty table nearby, I kept an eye on the two of them while cleaning it off. Clearly, this was Jimi Dandersley.

I'd never spoken to him, but in that instant, I agreed with Staples and despised everything about Jennie's boyfriend: his freckly and sunburnt face, the heavy Fox Racing jacket that he was wearing with a plain white T-shirt underneath, the flecks of red in his brown hair that was buzzed down in range of his scalp, right down to the idiotic spelling of his name. Jennie explained that her section was completely full, but she had a small table of two that was bound to finish up soon.

"If you're okay hanging here and waiting for a few minutes, I can get you on that one as soon as possible," she offered, still smiling.

"I guess, if I don't have no choice," he scoffed. The idea of waiting didn't appeal much to him. "Thought I was VIP."

After ten minutes or so of impatient waiting, Jimi found himself seated at a thin table against the wooden dividing panel that separated the two halves of the dining room. As soon as he entered the picture, Jennie had become noticeably less focused with the other tables in her section. She forgot that a customer wanted wheat toast for their club sandwich, mixed up the bill for two tables next to each other, and came close to spilling a milkshake from her tray, bumping her leg while taking a corner too close.

Watching Jimi making comments, winking, or reaching out at Jennie each time she went past him, I felt a deep stab of jealousy that quickly turned into a storm of rage. I found unnecessary reasons to become even more annoyed at him: the way he held a fist up near his mouth every time he laughed, his stonewashed blue jeans, the fact that he wanted chicken nuggets when it clearly says "tenders" on the menu. While bussing table after table on autopilot, I started plotting ways to get revenge. When I thought about it more, I realized that it wouldn't be revenge at all though, since Jimi had never done anything to me. Even so, I wanted to do something.

Once Cal had placed the finished chicken tender combo meal in the window, Jennie delivered it over to his table with an extra flourish. Jimi set the little plastic cup of J-sauce off to the side and cracked his knuckles, prepared to dig in. Unsatisfied, he wanted his order of French fries sent back to the kitchen, saying they were overdone and too crunchy. Of course, he ate seven or eight of them first, dipping some into his milkshake. Jennie rolled her eyes and gently teased him as he complained.

"You didn't mind the crunchy Cheetos that we spilled on your couch." She touched his hand, apparently referencing a flirty inside joke that they shared. Jimi bit two more fries in half before frowning and handing the dish to Jennie.

"Cheetos are Cheetos, and they're fine. The fries here suck. Hold on, babe, lemme a grab a piss first. Thair' any bathrooms in here?"

Jennie pointed over to the door for the men's room. As he stood up to leave, Jimi reminded her twice that he needed a new order of fries, and that he wanted extra salt on them. The idiot didn't realize that there was a saltshaker right there on the table for him to do it himself. Hold on . . . *extra salt on his fries*! I remembered hearing Staples's story about his famous prank on Merryll. This would be a perfect opportunity for a return to glory. Staples wouldn't be working until the dinner shift, but I imagined the look of pride that would cover his face as I told him about this one—if I was able to pull it off.

Jennie looked slightly frazzled, but dutifully called back to Cal, asking for another batch of fries that weren't so well-done. Far from being irritated by her request, Cal smiled. That annoying, knowing smile that he always did.

"Oh, I know how it is. Don't worry about it. I know if my woman was eating in here, I'd have to get the fries done perfectly too."

"Your woman, eh? And who is that again?" Jennie walked back to the dining room without bothering to listen to Cal as he loaded up a wire basket for the deep fryer, stammering out a non-response.

Jennie had confused the order for another of her tables, so while she was busy sorting that out, Cal shouted over to me to deliver the new fries to Jimi. For the first and only time, I was perfectly happy to follow his directions. This was my golden opportunity. I seized the moment, putting the fries on his table and subtly unscrewing the cap from the saltshaker. Just as Staples said, I laid it gently back on top so it would look like it was still attached. If all went well, Jennie's lowlife boyfriend would soon have a fresh pile of extra salt covering his new order of not-well-done fries.

Jimi returned from the bathroom, surprised to see someone at his spot, and I thought he had caught me at first. I quickly rearranged the menus and ketchup bottle at his table, trying to look like I was just giving his area a special VIP treatment. The acting job was as good as it needed to be, because he didn't suspect anything.

"Here's your fries, hope these are better."

"Hey, thanks a lot, big guy."

I would have preferred for this dude to cuss me out and punch me in the face than talk to me like I was his eight-year-old cousin. *Big guy.* He might as well have ruffled my hair and offered to buy me an ice cream cone if I finished all my lunch.

For the next twenty-five minutes, I kept guiltily looking over at Jimi's table, fidgeting as I watched him eat his chicken tenders, wanting to capture the exact moment of his salty splashdown.

He stared with interest as a group of Peninsula Princesses walked in, begged Jennie to find him some barbecue sauce, and used two straws to drink his milkshake, but every time he started reaching for the saltshaker, something would distract him. My heart started pounding against my chest when he had the shaker raised up at one point—until Cal came out and interrupted him.

"Hey, man! Like those chicken tenders?" Cal seemed eager to show off to anyone watching that he knew somebody. "Yeah, when I heard they were yours, I made them . . . you know, extra good," he weakly finished.

They must have gone to high school together. The salt was put back down on the table, as Jimi returned Cal's attempt at a cool handshake without enthusiasm. A few seconds later, once he realized that him and Jimi had zero to talk about besides chicken tenders, the Human Carrot creeped back to his post at the grill (or maybe it was because the boss was standing in the doorway with his hands on his hips, asking, "What the hell is *he* doing out there??"). Whatever the case, the opportunity had passed. For some reason or another, he never got around to pouring the salt on his fries.

"I ain't eatin' these," he finally concluded as Jennie came by to collect his dishes at the end. "They're too soggy."

Jimi got up from his small table, asked Jennie what time she was getting off work, and used a handful of wrinkled one-dollar bills to pay for his meal. As soon as he left the building, it was like the spell on Jennie was broken. The blushing and the careless mistakes were over, and she was back to her usual collected and unbreakable self, which I assume her customers appreciated.

My great plan having failed, I regretfully screwed the cap back on the saltshaker as I cleared up his table. Then again, it was probably for the best. I hated the look of him, but at the same time, Jimi looked like someone I'd hate to pick a fight with. From the small scrape on the bridge of his nose to the cold glint in his stare, daring you to look at him wrong, I imagined that anybody who wanted trouble could get it in an instant from Jimi Dandersley.

CHAPTER FIFTEEN

Ghosts of the Past

Since it was a holiday weekend, the heavy flow of people coming through the restaurant never really calmed down that afternoon. Pedestrians passing by the giant windows at the front must have looked in and been drawn in by the wave of energy pulsating from the dining room. Everyone's spirits were especially high, and the sounds from the jukebox were fully drowned out by the echoing chatter from dozens of side conversations. Cal was really on top of his game as well, churning out egg sandwiches for the Old Guard, burgers for the Margaritavilles, and tuna melts for the Real Housewives, enjoying the challenge of keeping all these different people fed and satisfied.

The beehive effect lasted right up until the tail end of my shift. I found myself running low on energy and started glancing toward the back of the restaurant every few minutes towards the end, hoping to catch a glimpse of Arthur arriving to take over for me. With an early evening workout planned at the gym with Blaise, my hope was to have time to eat and rest up before heading over there.

Jennie's final table of the day was another one top (as in, only one person): a friendly middle-aged woman who wandered in by herself and quickly took a specific interest in Jennie. She carefully laid a few shopping bags in the seat across from her, filled with souvenirs from an afternoon spent on the downtown gift shop circuit. While most customers just want their meals as fast as possible and then to be left alone, this woman was striking up conversation with Jennie each time she went by, beaming as Jennie patiently answered her questions. I grilled her about it when she came back to type the order into DigiServ.

"What's that all about? Do you know her?" "No . . . at least not that I know of, but she says I look familiar." She shrugged. "Might get a decent tip out of it anyway."

Jennie loaded a tray with a refill of lemon water and went back to see the lady who may or may not have recognized her from somewhere. She usually got a decent tip no matter what, and just as my interest in the topic was starting to fade anyway, Gloria walked out from the kitchen to speak with me. She faced me with an expression that was equal parts annoyed and apologetic.

"Mister JB, just the man I need to see." She pulled a pencil from behind her ear and crossed something off from her clipboard. "You're probably not going to want to hear this, but our friend Arthur just called out sick. I know this is last minute, but I'd really appreciate it if you stayed and did a split shift tonight."

A split shift is basically a double. You work all through the lunch shift, take a short break, and then come right back in for the dinner rush as well. I hadn't had to do one yet, but

Staples and Cal had them commonly enough that I was familiar with the concept. It was extra money at least, but there went my basketball plans for that evening. Grudgingly, I told Gloria that I could stay, feeling like I didn't have much choice but to say yes.

When Jennie came back around, she brightly announced that the woman at the one top had lived in her hometown back in the day.

"Small world, right? She said it was only for a few years, but she had a daughter that was roughly my age too. Guess she must've seen me around when I was younger."

I told her about Arthur and the split shift.

"Ugh. That sucks."

Jennie could only generate so much sympathy for me, though. It had been a busy day for her too, even without a split shift, and it was clear she was getting that second wind of energy that comes from knowing that in a few more minutes, you're free. I knew the feeling, so I couldn't blame her for nearly skipping back to the friendly lady at her final table for one last check-in before logging off DigiServ and calling it a day.

The woman had already neatly stacked her silverware back on the football-shaped sandwich plate, and then even used her napkin to brush any stray crumbs from the table back into her hands. As Jennie was reaching into the pocket of her apron for the check, the customer's face lit up, as if a great idea had arrived out of nowhere and needed to be immediately written down or else forgotten.

"Hold on, hold on, hold on . . ." Her small hands flitted out over her plate, faintly shaking with excitement. "Is your name Heather Rawlings?" Jennie shuddered upon hearing the name, completely changing her mood.

I didn't know all that many of the details about Jennie's older sister, but still a lot more than most people in town. They were only a year or two apart in age, and Jennie had said they'd been extremely close to each other—shared a room, stayed up late talking every night; they were basically the opposite of me and Rodney, who hadn't been in touch since before Sara's froggy cottage. When Jennie was in 8th grade, her sister had gotten diagnosed with leukemia pretty much out of nowhere. She passed away six months later, and Jennie hadn't been quite the same ever since. Shortly after her sister died, the family packed up their lives and moved to Bellview.

"No . . . but Heather'uz my older sister." Her voice clouded over for the last part, blurring it somewhere in between "is" and "was." The woman heard "is" and fondly recalled how Heather would come over to their house to play with her daughter back in the day.

"Oh, Heather was a lot of fun! So much energy. And you do look a lot like her. I hope she's doing well."

Jennie chose not to set the record straight, instead forcing a short smile as she abruptly dropped off the bill and walked away. Hearing her murmur "me too" under her breath, I remembered a private confession that Jennie had made to me, that night at Five Mile Creek: *Every night since then, I've tried to somehow bring her spirit back to me. Like if I wish it and pray it enough, she'll speak to me, or appear in front of me.*

The friendly lady from Jennie's hometown looked confused, maybe wondering what she had said wrong. She grabbed the handles of her paper bags and went up to the cash register to pay, leaving a ten-dollar tip on the table for Jennie before heading back out into the festive downtown atmosphere.

Jennie wasn't as interested in rushing out anymore, trapped in her thoughts by the unexpected reminder of her sister and her previous life. Even though it was technically a job for the newly arriving waitresses, she stayed late and helped refill the sugars, ketchup bottles, and salt and pepper shakers that sat in little baskets at each table. Since I was going to be stuck there for the rest of the night anyway, I figured I might as well help, joining Jennie for this mindless but oddly relaxing task.

I went and grabbed the baskets from each of the empty tables while Jennie reached into the cupboard under the DigiServ computer for the box of sugar refills. She stayed silent at first, with a distant gaze out the massive front window, sorting through the different colors of the sugar packets.

"It's been almost three years since I moved here, and that's the first person I've run into from my hometown," she said.

"Why didn't you tell her about your sister?"

"Because that would be pointless, wouldn't it?" She spoke in a detached and logical tone, but I was starting to know her well enough to see that this was only a mask, which she put back on whenever she needed to play it cool. "She doesn't live there anymore, and I don't plan on going back. I'll probably never see her again; she'll probably never think about it again. No point spoiling her lunch over it. Plus, I kinda liked the way she remembered Heather."

I took a closer look at the tattoo on Jennie's left wrist as she reached for the tiny sugar packets and neatly arranged them in the baskets: whites, pinks, and blues. From my viewing angle, I thought it said "ANARCHY" at first. After a longer examination though, I saw that the message etched into her arm was a word I'd never come across before—something in a different language:

ANÁΓKH

I wanted to ask Jennie what the word was and what it meant, but when she caught me staring and modestly pulled her arm away, I quickly switched to a different question.

"Where did you live before coming here, anyway?"

"Zilwaukee." She seemed to welcome the change of topic.

"Wait, you're from Wisconsin? I thought you said that you were from downstate."

"I *am* from downstate. Not Milwaukee, dude. *Zil*-waukee, with a Z. It's down by Saginaw."

"No offense, but that sounds like a fake place."

"It sort of *is* a fake place," Jennie laughed darkly.

She told me that when the town first got formed in like the 1600s, 1800s, something like that, the guys who founded it were pretty much swindlers. They needed workers to run this sawmill scheme of theirs, so they gave it a confusing name on purpose. They were trying to trick recently settled foreigners into moving there without seeing it first, thinking that it was the real Milwaukee.

"So they just changed a letter. Zilwaukee. Genius stuff, right?"

"That couldn't possibly have worked, did it?" The unbelievable childishness of that scam annoyed me more than it probably should have.

"I mean, it's a really small place, so it couldn't have worked all that well. On the other hand, *my* ancestors must have been dumb enough to fall for it. We stayed there for multiple generations, up until . . . up until, you know."

Thinking back to my phone call with Rodney at the start of the summer, I thought that if they lived in the present day, the Zilwaukee guys would fit right in on Craigslist. With some of the messed-up stuff they show on the news, I wasn't so naive to think something like Zilwaukee couldn't exist, but the elementary school level of it is what bothered me. I'd assumed that grown-up lies would at least be a bit more complicated than just changing one letter of a word. Maybe that's not the case, unless there are some people out there who just don't ever grow up.

"That's crazy, though. Starting a whole town with a cheap lie like that, just to trick newcomers who don't know any better."

"Hey, welcome to America, right? 'Land of the thief, home of the slave.'"

"I guess . . . Even so, this knock-off Milwaukee place doesn't sound like somewhere that I would ever want to live, no offense."

"None taken—it's not somewhere I would want to live either. Zilwaukee sucks."

I had to bite my lip to prevent myself from laughing at that last part, just because I wasn't sure Jennie would get what was so funny about what she'd said. It made me immediately think of the Milwaukee Bucks, the NBA team. I imagined a T-shirt with a modified Bucks logo and that phrase on it. The cartoon deer guy, smiling and holding up a basketball. He's still wearing a green sweatshirt, but instead of a B, it has a Z on it. "Zilwaukee Sucks." I made a mental note to tell that idea to Blaise the next time I saw him. He'd get a kick out of it for sure.

"If the scammers with the letter Z tell you all you need to know about how the town formed," Jennie continued, "there's this huge concrete bridge that sums up my experience there."

Jennie told me about the Zilwaukee Bridge, an extremely expensive project that they finished building the same year she was born. It was a section of I-75 that crossed over the Saginaw River, replacing a drawbridge that would cause traffic backups for thirty miles or more when it was raised to let ships through. Started at the end of the '70s, while her parents were still in high school, it was meant to solve all sorts of traffic jam problems, especially for people driving up north during the summers and on holiday weekends.

"Instead, the thing was a total piece of crap. The summer that my parents got engaged, these massive sections of the bridge started to crack and break apart. It was supposed to open the next year, but they had to completely shut down construction for the next two years, trying to figure out how to save it. The final report showed that there were as many as five different things wrong with it, eventually causing it to break."

As if on cue, I heard a shattering noise from out in the dining room, making me flinch. Someone at a crowded table had lost a vanilla milkshake, leaving a wet trail of liquid in the aisle. I grabbed the "Wet Floor" sign and a mop and headed over to their area for a little palm-handle-pivot action. As the embarrassed offender stammered an apology for the spill, I ruefully thought that it should really be Arthur apologizing to me. This should've been his cleanup job, and I should be getting ready to hoop with Blaise.

"So did they ever get it fixed?" I asked Jennie when I'd

finished mopping, surprised that she hadn't left yet. "What happened with that bridge?"

"The original contractors got fired, and the new ones ended up doing all kinds of renovations on that stupid thing. My dad said that at one point, they were using an epoxy substance that made it look like they were trying to glue the broken parts back together. The building of that bridge had turned into a local joke."

I pictured construction workers with tool belts and hard hats, using small tubes of Elmer's school glue to reconnect the broken pieces of thousands of tons of concrete. It was completely ridiculous, but then again, no more ridiculous than X-ing out the letter M on a Milwaukee sign and starting a different town.

"By the time it was finished, it was five years later, over the budget by fifty million dollars, people didn't trust that it was safe yet, and me and Heather were both alive. Our old house on Sherman Road was less than a mile west of the new Zilwaukee Bridge, and my dad said he'd rather swim across the river than drive on it."

"So after all these years, has your dad ever driven over it?"

"Put it this way: whenever he travels downstate, he makes sure to take a detour around Zilwaukee. Ever since I got my license, I've done the same thing, for different reasons."

"What did you mean when you said that bridge sums up your experience there?"

"When you're a kid, you grow up always sort of trusting that you're building towards something. But then, when it seems like things are finally starting to come together, there could still be as many as five different problems without you realizing it until it's too late. Eventually it all cracks, and it can take years to make sense of it and start to repair."

She was probably being vague on purpose, but I kind of felt like I understood what she meant.

"Are you starting to repair yet?"

"Yeah . . . I mean, the last few months it's been starting to feel that way, at least. Anyway, I'm gonna head out now." She finished arranging one last basket of sugars. "That's enough volunteer work for one day. Good luck on the split shift, 'Mister' JB."

CHAPTER SIXTEEN

Jungle Juice

My worst day of work happened as a result of Jennie asking me to sneak some items out of the walk-in fridge for her: a few lemons, a few oranges, and a Tupperware of fresh cherries sent over from Traverse City. It was the 4th of July, the same night as the party at Jimi Dandersley's house; she said they were making "Jungle Juice." I didn't know what that was, but I pieced together that it was something alcoholic that had lemons, oranges, and cherries in the recipe. Jennie said it would look suspicious for her to be in the walk-in, but since I was back there all the time restocking anyway, I could pull it off without getting any funny looks. I immediately knew how bad of a move it would be to steal stuff from Jimmy's storage cooler. I agreed to do it anyway, without a second thought.

Jennie was causing my mind to behave in interesting ways. The way she squeezed my arm when asking for this favor made all the hairs on it stand straight up. When she was standing close, it made me want to puff the little extra strand of hair on her forehead back into place.

I knew that she was probably just playing me, flirting

and using me to get this favor; but seeing the gleam in her hazel eyes made me want to get played. She made me want to abandon all of my judgement skills if it meant helping her. So, checking over my shoulder at least four different times, I stepped into the thirty-eight-degree temperature of the walk-in and started filling my cargo pockets with fruits that didn't belong to me.

On the surface, there wasn't anything unusual about me being back there; Jennie was right. Filled with all sorts of miscellaneous food items, depending on where you stood, the walk-in fridge could either smell like lettuce, a mix of cold bread and noodles, or fresh lemons, which was easily the best of the three; that refreshing scent was a small reward anytime I needed to carry up a heavy box of citrus fruits from the truck outside when there was a fruit delivery. Not even the cool trace of lemons in the air could calm my nerves in this case though, knowing that someone could burst in at any time and catch me stealing from Jimmy's own shelves.

Instead of her usual drawstring bag that she kept in the cupboard under the DigiServ computer, Jennie had brought a full backpack to work. She told me that it was down in the basement, so all I had to do was transfer the goods down there and be all set. Trembling with anxiousness, I stuffed oranges into the left pocket of my cargo shorts, lemons into the right, putting the lids back on the cardboard boxes. Unless Jimmy came in at 4:00 a.m. just to count them individually, there's no way anyone would notice that the citrus boxes were slightly emptier than they should have been.

The industrial-sized container of cherries on the top shelf was a different story. Since it was far too big to take without it being missed, I would need to pour cherries out from the larger container into a smaller plastic one. With a lot more effort, I stood on my tiptoes and slowly nudged the heavy container in my direction, balancing it along the edge of the shelf until I could get a proper grip.

To my horror, the door to the fridge was suddenly jolted open, making my arm shake even more. The tub of cherries slipped off the shelf, crashing onto the cold cement floor, spilling out red syrup like the crime scene of a stabbing victim. Not all of them leaked out, but there were at least ninety cherries and a sickening red stain all over the floor, shelves, box of lemons—and, worst of all, Jimmy's apron. With cherry juice dripping from my fingers, I was literally caught red-handed.

Jimmy didn't have the full story. He didn't need to have the full story. It was so painfully obvious that I'd just gotten busted doing something I shouldn't have —no further details were necessary. I pathetically wiped my hands against my apron, expecting him to fire me on the spot, or at least start screaming loud enough to drown out the tones of Margaritaville on the jukebox.

Jimmy raised his foot to stop a rogue cherry that was trying to escape across the floor. I was ready for a similar state of bedlam as my incident at Sara's house at the start of summer. What happened next was somehow worse.

I felt the cold weight of silence as Jimmy decapitated me with his eyes. The vein on the side of his bald forehead reminded me of a fault line, about to split down the center and cause an earthquake. When he finally spoke, it was in such a vicious whisper that it nearly caused me to piss my pants.

"Clean this shit up." I nodded at his command with an

involuntary obedience. "And you'll be cleaning dumpsters. For the rest of the week."

My hands were still shaking as the red juice dripped from my fingers. I didn't even think about arguing. As far as Dumpster Duty goes, at least I had earned this one.

For the next two hours, customer traffic at the restaurant was going full throttle, so I didn't have much time to think about what had just happened. The 4th of July parade finished up, bringing in a new wave of Peninsula families waving little flags and wearing red, white, and blue, ordering disappointing cones of Superman ice cream and passing time until the fireworks later that night. I dropped my head and quietly got in the rhythm of bussing my tables, not daring to look up in case someone was watching. "Someone" meaning Jimmy. "Someone" meaning Jennie too. I was glad that it was so busy. I could blend into the surroundings better that way.

It's probably a good thing that I wasn't a waiter. If you're waiting tables, you can't let it show when you're miserable, otherwise the customers might complain about you, and you'll definitely get less tip money. As a busboy, though, nobody cared that I was furiously chewing on a pen as I scowled and rushed through clearing up the finished tables. It probably made my work more efficient, to be honest. Miserable, but efficient.

Refilling ketchup bottles, salt and pepper shakers, wiping up the remains of recently departed lunch diners. Handling the soppy mixture of milk, napkins, and crayons that every toddler seemed to leave behind. Spaz tried saying a few things to me on some of my trips back to drop off dishes, but I was too far gone in my own head to bother listening.

What the hell could I possibly have been thinking earlier? I didn't even want any of the freaking cherries! I'd never stolen anything in my entire life. Think about that for a second: I'd broken into seven houses and *still* never had stolen anything. All of that, just because Jennie had smiled and touched my arm and asked me to?

In the heat of the moment, maybe I didn't mind it being like that; now that I had more time to think about it, it bothered me a lot. Did I think by giving her oranges for her stupid drink that she might actually start liking me? I pictured Jennie and her twenty-one-year-old dirtbag boyfriend, clinking their Jungle Juice glasses together, toasting to my good health as they laughed and cuddled on his Cheetos-crumb couch. It made my stomach hurt to think about it. Why couldn't the cheapskate come down here himself and steal his own lemons?

After setting my latest tray of dishes down much harder than necessary (Spaz yelped when he heard the clattering of glass), I tossed my towel nowhere in particular and went downstairs for a bathroom break. Just in case some shame tears slipped out, I didn't want anybody to see. For a few moments as I was passing by the dry storage room, I thought about quitting. Forget Jennie and Jimmy, and the other stupid Jimmy who was really *Jimi*. Maybe Sara was still looking for frog catchers.

I just stood in the bathroom for five or ten minutes, my heart racing as I fought off tears of resentment and embarrassment. When I finally calmed down enough to head back upstairs, I realized that my cargo pockets were still full of fruits. I made sure to put them back in their boxes in the fridge before returning to the dining room. When I finally made eye contact with Jennie again, she looked concerned. I wanted to believe that it was because I'd gotten in trouble, but with a savage pessimism, I suspected that her main concern was that now she needed a backup plan for the Jungle Juice.

As the lunch rush briefly faded away around 2:30, Staples motioned for me to come over to his area and talk. He apparently was watching me over the course of the day and saw that something was wrong. Either that, or everyone was already gossiping about my incident in the cooler. Since I figured that second part was most likely true, I decided I might as well just tell him everything.

"Bad move on Jennie's part," Staples determined once I had finished with the play-by-play, "sending you in there to begin with. You're not what the kids call 'clutch,' my man."

The way he talked sometimes, I pictured Staples wearing tweed jackets and smoking a pipe all dignified-like when he wasn't working at Jimmy's. Despite how upset I was, I had to stifle a smirk when an image came to mind of him using his thumb and fingers to stroke a non-existent goatee. I mentioned Dumpster Duty and also confided that I was worried Jimmy might step out here and fire me at any second. I wouldn't blame him if he did.

"Say what you will about Jimmy, but he's not one to hold a grudge." Staples's slanting eyes surveyed the surroundings thoughtfully, as if the walls of the restaurant itself would agree with him and help to prove his point. "Do you have any idea how many immature teenage employees have probably tried stealing stuff from here over the years? He was probably more pissed that you made an idiot of yourself. And made a mess in that fridge."

I told Staples that Jimmy technically didn't have any proof about the stealing part, and that he hadn't even bothered to ask any questions. I also asked how often people got caught trying to sneak things out, but Staples brushed it off, saying that specific incident is actually pretty rare.

"It's not that he couldn't find out, he just chooses not to find out. If he went around and fired everyone who ever tried to sneak a brownie, or a milkshake, or a raw steak once or twice, he'd never be able to keep a full staff. And if someone happens to get away with it from time to time, it's not like it's going to make them rich; it sure as hell isn't going to put Jimmy out of business, either. Sure, it pisses him off, but he also sort of gets it."

"Gets what?"

"Gets that people are going to make mistakes. Mistakes that you definitely know better than to make. It's a long summer. People feel tired, annoyed, underappreciated, entitled: you name it."

In his cool and patient tone, Staples made the whole situation sound reasonable—normal, even. I felt awful though, especially considering that I needed this job and was putting it in jeopardy before my first paycheck even came through.

"That still isn't a good excuse for it," I told Staples flatly.

"Of course it isn't. So don't do it again! Jimmy's thing is, pay the price, learn from your mistake, and we all move forward. That's basically why Dumpster Duty was invented in the first place."

Dumpster Duty was pretty much how I expected it to be: no better, no worse. For half an hour after work, I began repaying my debt to Jimmy. I started to resent that I was out there alone, when really this was just as much Jennie's mess as it was mine. Still, I was too angry at myself to have much left over for Jennie, as I tried not to breathe too much and get the worst of it over. At least there weren't any garbage bags that split apart on me, and the dried chocolate syrup and hamburger grease mixtures were kept to a minimum. I probably smelled pretty bad when I climbed back out, but that hardly mattered to me by then. It didn't even cross my mind until I saw Jennie sitting on the metal bench next to the dumpster's fence, jingling her keys around in her hands as she waited for me.

"Is that your bicycle?" she asked.

"Yeah . . . I thought you had a party to get to," I added. I was not in the mood for this.

"It's not until later tonight." She pointed to the old ten-speed bike again, grinning. "Can I have a go?"

I couldn't tell whether she was making fun of me, or if this was her way of trying to clear the air from earlier. After I nodded my head yes, she playfully rode around the enclosed courtyard area, making mini-circles as she dangled her feet off the pedals. She had already changed out of her shoes and into a pair of thin flip-flops. The warm air was perfectly still, and through the buzz of people walking around downtown, I could faintly hear the splashing of the water out on the lake.

"Look, I'm sorry that you got sent out here and all that," Jennie offered, still cruising the tiny space in those slow circles, pushing her feet along the ground instead of pedaling. "You should come out to Jimi's party with us tonight. He said I could invite friends. I can give you a ride."

"I don't want to go to Jimi's party."

"Oh." Jennie sounded legitimately surprised that party invitations and Jungle Juice wouldn't automatically solve things between us. "How can I make it up to you then?"

Inside my head, the answer was simple enough. *Step one: you can break up with Jimi Dandersley. Step two: you can chip in with Dumpster Duty this week. Step three: you can tell me what ΑΝΆΓΚΗ means. Step four: you can try looking at me little bit differently for a change.* After sitting on the question for a little while though, my answer back to Jennie was even simpler.

"It's fine—don't worry about it. Just don't get me into trouble anymore."

"Oh." Now she sounded mildly disappointed. She hopped off my bike and leaned it against the bench, grabbing her backpack and struggling for additional things to say. "Well, Happy 4th. Sorry again about what happened at the fridge . . . at least it's payday tomorrow, right?"

After I'd biked up the winding hill and made it back home, my mom caught a whiff of the scent and forced me to get cleaned up immediately. I stayed in the shower for ages, frequently switching the water between hot and cold, using all the different soaps and body washes to rid myself of the lingering dumpster fumes. The scene in the walk-in fridge replayed itself at least fifty more times in my head: the fruits weighing down my pockets, the cherry juice splattering on the floor, my boss's icy rage. And four more days in the dumpster before I was back on even terms at the restaurant.

After I was finally suitable again, my mom ordered us pizza for dinner. I sprawled out on the couch right after eating, consumed by my thoughts and forgetting that I'd originally planned on working on dribbling and footwork drills in the driveway before bed. It was still partially light outside when I fell asleep. My alarm was set for 7:45 a.m., and I wanted nothing more than for the next morning to arrive so I could start moving forward again.

CHAPTER SEVENTEEN

Payday

The next afternoon, a dark gray sheet briefly closed around the town and the Peninsula, bringing with it a downpour of nonstop rain for about an hour. During this unexpected slow point for customers, Gloria walked around the floor from person to person, holding her clipboard and a large security envelope, calling out names and handing them smaller envelopes with our paychecks inside.

"Rawlings, Jennifer . . ."

Jennie celebrated sarcastically but cheerfully when her name was called. Since she got paid mostly through cash tips and had to declare them for taxes at the end of each shift, a low hourly wage turned out to be even lower on paychecks.

"Ayyo! Thirteen dollars and forty-three cents! Getting into the big time now!" Jennie rubbed her fingers on both hands together in a teasing money sign. She wasn't fooling anyone, though; the paycheck obviously didn't tell the whole story. It was pretty common knowledge that besides Jimmy and Gloria, Jennie might be the highest-paid member on the entire staff on a good week.

"To the artist currently known as 'Spaz' . . ."

Unfortunately for Spaz, his first paycheck *did* tell the whole story. The poor guy nearly went permanently cross-eyed looking at his final number.

"SEVEN BUCKS?!?"

Going by the tone of disbelief and injustice in his voice, inside Spaz's head, he was also adding, *Is that all?*, but with quite a few more swear words added. Jimmy, however, heard the commotion and put a stop to his crusade before it could even get started.

"You started on the last day of the pay period—some of it goes to tax, more for your work shirts, and your shift was only half the day."

Spaz didn't look completely satisfied with this explanation, but he carefully folded the envelope in half and slid it into his back pocket without another word of protest. He put it away in a guarded manner, as if Jimmy might come over and even take back that last seven bucks if he wasn't careful.

"Give it two more weeks, and you'll be good," encouraged Staples. He took one quick glance at his own check with only a mild amount of interest before it found a home in the side pocket of his baggy khakis. He'd been around long enough that the thrill of receiving a paycheck must have worn off for him.

"It's not like any of it is mine, anyway," Staples said. "I should just have Gloria endorse my checks to the University of Michigan and save everyone a little time." Gloria heard his comment and gave a quick chuckle to Staples as she moved back towards the kitchen to take care of the cooks.

"Waterson, Calgary. . ." she muttered.

With no college tuition to worry about, Cal grabbed for his paycheck with a much higher degree of excitement. He called Spaz over to tell him about all of his glamorous plans for that week's wages.

"Talk about a perfect birthday present—you know what I'm saying?" Yes, Cal's long-awaited twenty-first birthday had finally arrived. "Me and my roommates were thinking about pitching in to get a flat-screen TV. I don't know, though; I think I might fly solo with this one."

Spaz was straining his neck to try and catch a glimpse of how much money was on Cal's check, but Cal kept proudly flicking at the slip of paper with his pointer finger.

"What do you think, Spaz? Should I get an electric pasta maker for my place, or some subwoofers to put in the back of my car?"

"You make your own pasta?" Spaz sounded impressed.

"No, but I could start if I had a pasta maker." I knew that Cal enjoyed cooking even outside of work, but I think he was most excited to get "advice" on his upcoming purchases because he knew that Spaz couldn't buy any those things for himself. "I saw one online that has eight different shape attachments. All you have to do is add the flour, water, and eggs. A pound of fresh spaghetti in only fifteen minutes! And it's only three hundred bucks. How's that sound?"

"If you just buy a box of spaghetti, you have it in like fifteen *seconds*, don't you? It costs a dollar."

Spaz no longer sounded impressed. Cal had to stop and think about this one for a little bit. He'd probably expected Spaz to be so amazed by his riches that he wouldn't ask any further questions. Instead of trimming his sails though, consulting with Spaz energized him even more.

"You're right, Spaz, you're right, that's a good point. I'm gonna go with the subs after all. Get the Subaru bumping, you know . . . set the mood. I'll let you hear the bass sometime. If you ever want a ride to work, just let me know. You're cool paying for gas though, right?"

As Spaz started to tell Cal that he didn't want a ride to work, I looked at my first-ever paycheck with a mixture of pride and disappointment. I felt strangely like an adult, knowing that most of the money was going to help with my family's household bills. I knew that had been the point all along; it was the reason I'd gotten the job to begin with. Even so, it felt a lot less interesting than Cal paying for his unnecessary luxury items, Staples his college tuition, or Jennie spending it on . . . whatever it was that she spent money on. Seeing it right in front of me made me fully appreciate just how little of my money I would be getting to keep for myself. Maybe enough to get a few 25 percent off lunches from time to time, and hopefully a new pair of basketball shoes before the end of the summer.

By the time I had deciphered all of the other taxes (federal, state, social security, Michigan retirement fund, etc.), it was starting to make me envision a treadmill. The belt is cranked up to its highest speed, and you're running in place as fast as you can. The numbers on the monitor can tell you one thing, but in reality, you're never actually going anywhere.

CHAPTER EIGHTEEN

The Familiar Car

When I got back home late in the afternoon, after my final day cleaning the dumpsters, there was a car sitting in the driveway that I hadn't seen in almost a year. The 1994 Ford Taurus had a broken taillight, a few dents in the passenger side door, and left little drips of fluid on the ground anywhere it was parked for too long. If I were to look inside, I knew I'd also find the glove compartment held shut with bungee cords, a seatbelt in the back that didn't click anymore, a leprechaun Christmas ornament hanging from the mirror, and a collection of CDs that were mostly by British rock bands. Forgetting that I was supposed to immediately shower after stepping inside, I rushed into the living room instead of going upstairs, eager to see the only person I could think of who would dare get behind the wheel of that shaky old car.

Rodney hadn't even unpacked yet. A bulging duffel bag was laid down next to his feet as he lounged on the couch. He was digging into a giant bowl of Frosted Flakes (that I'd originally planned on having as a snack) and casually talking to our mom, who looked thrilled.

"So what time did you leave South Bend this morning, son?" Mom asked.

"Nah, nah, I wasn't coming from South Bend," responded Rodney, as if it were a dumb question. "I stayed at U of M with my buddy T for the last couple nights. I got moving at about 10:30 this morning, though."

"Oh, well, alright then," said Mom, a little confused but still obviously happy at this unexpected development, her oldest son dripping milk onto the living room carpet. "How was traffic?"

"Ehh." Rodney paused to load up another spoonful into his mouth before responding. "It got pretty backed up for a while around the Zilwaukee Bridge, but other than that, not too bad."

"Geez, boy, you're not smelling too good these days," said Rodney: his way of saying hello. "They cut off the hot water or something? Mom, I told you, you can't let—"

"I paid the water bill!" Mom spoke up, a little bit defensively. "And your little brother is a working man now, and he's working hard."

"Hmph. I thought to be a trash collector, you needed a driver's license and a high school diploma nowadays."

"Oh, stop picking on your brother!" Mom slapped him on the thigh. "He's not a trash collector, he's working downtown at Jimmy's Restaurant."

"Ah, Jimmy's?" Rodney perked up a little bit at that. "I should head down sometime for some chicken fingers then. I've always liked their J-Sauce. What kinda family discount action do they have going on?"

"Well, I get 25 percent off, so maybe like, ten or fifteen for you."

"Cheapskates."

Eventually, Rodney finally got around to telling us what he was doing back in town. Apparently, his difficulties finding a job down at college finally caught up with him, and when he couldn't make rent anymore, it didn't make any sense to try and stay. He was back for the rest of the summer.

"So then, what are you going to do for money?" I asked. "You have to help out now too, you know." I was curious of course, but there was some delight slipped into that question somewhere too. I was acting like Cal, but I didn't care. After all, my brother had made such a big deal about how he'd 'outgrown Bellview' back in the spring. It not only felt like a weight of responsibility had been lifted off of me, but I also felt a bit of guilty pleasure upon seeing him forced to come crawling back to us and home. "Got any leads yet? See, because I know this lady named Sara—"

Rodney cut me off. "Nah, nah, it's all hooked up. I made a quick stop downtown, Z said I can have my old gig back at the boathouse."

"Hey, no fair, I was *at* the boathouse, back in June!"

This was typical Rodney. No matter how little effort he put into something, he always seemed to have the best possible solution fall directly into his lap.

"They said they weren't hiring," I continued. "And why are all your friends' names only one initial now?"

"Why is yours only two?"

I had no answer for that one.

"Whatever, man, I gotta go take a shower. Enjoy my cereal."

As I turned to head back upstairs, I couldn't keep a small grin from escaping my lips. Rodney was back home.

Sauntering and snarling, condescending and critical, dragging his feet and draining my Frosted Flakes, but at least he was back home. That would help things.

CHAPTER NINETEEN

The Routine

Once the week of Dumpster Duty was finally over, I was determined not to screw up anymore at work. I didn't want to clean the dumpster again; I wanted to keep getting those paychecks, and I wanted to earn back Jimmy and Gloria's trust. As much as I could, I tried to follow the advice that Staples gave me, keeping my emotions away from Jennie before it got me in any more trouble. For the next three weeks, I was the model employee, dropping all the outside distractions, even going above and beyond my regular duties at work—and it was driving me crazy.

Arthur continued showing up late and calling out, at least once a week. He might literally be the most unreliable person I've ever met. Cal kept pretending that he wanted to kick Arthur's ass, but still never did anything about it. To show Gloria that she could count on me, I found myself staying for split shifts more and more, whenever they needed extra help. It wasn't always bussing tables, either. In addition to covering for Arthur, I also filled in as a dishwasher when Spaz's cousin was in town, and even once for Lacy as a cashier. Learning to work the cash register and the credit card machine was actually kind of fun, and it was a relief to break up the boredom that was starting to consume me, even just by a little bit.

For the remainder of July, it was the exact same routine almost every single day. It always began with me lying in bed for long past the alarm clock, finally getting up at the last possible moment so I wouldn't be late. At school, arriving late only means that you get a tardy slip and a desk sits empty for a few extra minutes. At the restaurant though, even one person being ten minutes late can throw off the whole day. It means that dishes are piling up unwashed, or tables aren't being cleaned, or food isn't being cooked, or a customer's order isn't being taken. If you're late for work, you actually screw a lot of people over: something I had carefully avoided ever since the incident in the fridge.

Every once in a while, Rodney would agree to give me a ride somewhere in the Taurus, but for the majority of the time, it was biking back and forth, up and down that daunting hill. When I arrived at Jimmy's, I could always count on the waitresses asking if I was having fun yet, Cal bragging about which girls he thought he could hook up with, getting my hopes up whenever it seemed like Jennie was flirting with me, and then reminding myself of what Staples had said. Even Spaz's weirdness had become strangely predictable. By the time I found out that he jogged over four miles to get work each day, the surprise barely even registered with me.

My job when it came to bussing tables was still the exact same as on day one; the only difference was that I did it a little faster now. Wheel the cart, clear off dishes, spray and wipe, toss extras into the garbage, take the dishes back. The same five groups of customers would still continuously rotate through the restaurant—different faces, different times, same types of people: the Margaritavilles, the Real Housewives of South Point, the Families, the Old Guard, and the Peninsula Princesses. All of it began to blend together like a tub of Jimmy's Superman ice cream, and it was just as unsatisfying.

When I got home at the end of a shift and finally made it back upstairs to my room, I'd automatically empty out my pockets on the nightstand next to the bed, and then change into my basketball clothes. Any free evening available, I made it a top priority to get on the court. Having already missed enough training time due to night shifts and covering for other people, the treadmill effect was happening to my basketball progress too.

Plus, it turns out that people take this stuff *seriously* in high school—most of all Blaise, but even the benchwarmers from the year before were putting in extra work, either hitting the weight room or doing ballhandling drills on the sideline while waiting for next in the pickup games. I used to think that training just meant shooting around in my driveway; now it seemed like that was far less than the bare minimum— at least if you were hoping to suit up for the Eagles.

One night, after getting lazy with the floor mopping and being forced to do it again, I shot two out of fourteen in a scrimmage at open gym. I know there are no stats kept at open gym, but it got so pathetic, I couldn't help but keep track of my own. I doubt there's anything more frustrating than shooting two for fourteen in a basketball game, even if it's just a scrimmage. To me, it said a lot more about my current condition than it would probably seem at first glance.

First off, I had a crappy game, and it wasn't due to any lack of opportunity. There were fourteen different chances where I got the ball and there was enough space available to take a shot: that much freedom, and I still couldn't find anything positive to do with it.

The other endlessly frustrating part was knowing that to get that many shots, I had to believe that somewhere deep down I *must* actually be a pretty good player. Otherwise there's no way my teammates would pass the ball to me fourteen times, even if I was wide open. Someone who is a truly awful player would never get more than six or seven shots before the rest of the team would freeze them out. I figured the other guys must have confidence that I would eventually come through, even as the evidence overwhelmingly pointed to the cruel fact that it wasn't my day. As for the two shots that I made? It was probably worse than if I'd just missed all of them.

I'm serious. To take that many open shots and somehow miss every one of them—there must be some universal conspiracy stacked up against you, right? It's something you can laugh about years later. *Zero* for fourteen is cruel fate. Two for fourteen, though? That's not fate. It was all in your hands, and you just blew it. A little false hope here and there, but the same outcome of defeat.

It made me realize just how narrow the line between success and failure really is. Out of those dozen misses, at least five or six of them were really close calls. One barely off the back iron, another one gets halfway through the basket before rattling back out, or a shot off the glass takes too steep of an angle and ends up just off target. All it takes is a few tiny details to go wrong, and it changes everything. Now almost halfway through the summer, it felt like I was going two for fourteen in a lot more ways than just basketball. Was constant failure just going to become part of the everyday routine?

CHAPTER TWENTY

Rain Day

Hundreds of thousands of dull liquid pellets plinked off the restaurant's old tin roof: a constant sound overhead that had been going on for hours. The dining room, half-darkened by the relentless storm, sat completely empty. A couple people trickled in as time passed.

Before I'd started working there, I would have thought that the restaurant would get extra busy when it was the opposite of nice outside, and that was true in certain situations. If a sudden downpour happened early in an otherwise sunny day, it would fill up with people coming in from either the beach or the pier, waiting for it to pass and go about their day outdoors. However, if it was rainy all day and with little hope of it passing, people just avoided coming downtown altogether.

It didn't matter since there were hardly any customers, but Spaz arrived late for work for the first time. He was yawning and rubbing at his face, his hair even messier than normal. Staples, who usually didn't care to interact with Spaz if he could help it, was quick to call attention to his wild appearance.

"Geez, Spaz, rough night?" Staples had a pretty good intuition about this sort of thing, and he seemed to think that there must be a pretty good story attached to Spaz's tardiness.

"I'll say . . . There's a freaking cricket sitting in the wall of my room, right behind my bed. That thing kept me up the whole night."

I don't think that was quite the explanation that Staples was expecting. He shook his head after a quick chuckle, ready to drop the subject, but Spaz apparently wanted to vent. He pulled at his hair with a yellow rubber glove and became a lot more animated.

"Yeah, it's like two in the morning, and he's back there with the whole 'Eeet-eeet-eeet-eeet!!', playing his music or whatever."

An elderly couple looked up from their twin bowls of runny oatmeal to see what was going on. They probably thought the smoke alarm was going off.

"And just when I'd start to get used to it and almost doze off, he went and stopped completely, and that would throw me for a loop. So then I'd settle down again and almost fall asleep, and then sure enough . . ." Spaz yawned again and pointed to the ticket printer sitting on the counter, with its shrill buzzing sound every time a new order came through. "It's like, imagine if you had to hear that machine going off every few minutes, for eight hours straight."

Staples rolled his eyes, looking over at me just to make sure I'd caught what was just said.

"I *do* have to, Spaz. Almost every day."

Spaz scowled and backtracked, claiming the two noises weren't similar, and that his was a lot worse. Jennie stopped by to ask Staples to take the whipped cream out of the elderly couple's hot chocolate, noticing Spaz for the first time that day.

"What's wrong, dude? You having *Chainsaw Massacre* nightmares again?"

"No, it's even worse than that." Spaz sighed meaningfully. "Crickets."

Jennie started to laugh, and then covered her mouth a little bit when she saw that he was serious. Staples had scooped out the spoonfuls of whipped cream from the top of the two mugs, wiping off the drips of hot chocolate from the sides before setting them back on the ledge for Jennie. He grabbed Spaz by the shoulders to stop him from doing the shrieking noise again.

"You don't believe me, but that thing was driving me crazy!" Spaz urged. "I asked it politely at first. And then I started yelling at him, but that didn't do anything either. He's still back there, playing his little violin or whatever, rubbing his legs together. You know, so I start rubbing *my* legs together, trying to speak its language, you know?"

"I gotta be honest, guys, I'm not buying this cricket story," said Jennie with a mischievous grin, grabbing the tray of mugs to take back to her only set of customers. "Spaz is hungover."

"But I guess it's true what they say," Spaz finished, as if he were affirming some long-held universal truth. "Not everyone can speak cricket."

"Crickets rub their wings together, not their legs," Staples corrected, expressionless. "Maybe the issue was that you were speaking grasshopper."

With Staples refusing to show him any sympathy, Spaz threw up his arms and wandered back to the kitchen, looking for Cal. The elderly couple finished their meal and left, meaning that the restaurant was now completely empty. This left us stuck with one of those rare stretches where there literally wasn't any work to do. Jimmy decided to turn it into an ice cream day for himself, disappearing into the basement for the majority of the day. Despite the fact that most of the staff members were huddled in various parts of the restaurant and idly chatting for large parts of the afternoon, Gloria chose not to say anything. She must have known it was a lost cause, as the storm continued to roll through from the lake.

Right around time for the lunch rush (which never even came close to happening), Gloria sent Staples out to the post office to pick up the company mail. He came back drenched, dripping straight through his hooded jacket, but with an interesting item in his hand. To be honest, on any other day, we wouldn't have thought of it as an interesting item in the slightest. On this rain day though, with less and less happening during each passing minute, this item became the source of a lot of entertainment and debate.

It was *Restaurateur Magazine,* a catalog full of all types of restaurant supplies. I remembered seeing a stack of them from the time I watched the mopping tutorial during my first week. The catalog advertised industrial-sized refrigeration systems, five-headed milkshake mixers, custom-made menus, uniforms, oven mitts, kitchen utensils, bulk orders of dinner mints, and everything in between. There was even a glossy full-page promotion for something called the "Nakayama Genesis," which according to the testimonials was the greatest kitchen knife in existence.

As the ad proclaimed, the Nakayama Genesis was *"The type of knife that you <u>could</u> bring to a gun fight!"* It came with a sharpening steel, a choice of three customized handles, and its own sheath that attached to a belt. As one satisfied customer raved:

> *I used to think that choosing between kitchen cutleries was tedious and like splitting hairs . . . until I got the Genesis. This knife is so sharp, it probably <u>could</u> split hairs, except I've been too busy slicing the #1 rated sushi in Manhattan to find out!*

I felt childish for thinking it, but it really hadn't occurred to me that all of the hundreds—maybe even thousands—of different tools and machines needed to run a restaurant had to come from somewhere. Without having thought of it, my previous mental image was that Jimmy's had just appeared one day, fully furnished and ready for action. Flipping through the pages of the *Restaurateur* catalog was like suddenly discovering an extra attic in your house—one you probably should have known about for years.

Without anything better to do, Staples and I started flipping through the catalog and imagining all the upgrades that we could make to the restaurant if only Jimmy would be willing to drop a few extra bucks. Staples found a temperature-controlled ice cream scoop, one that would stay warm at the head and carve through even the hardest frozen slabs without trouble. He massaged his right forearm while considering this possibility. It wasn't long before our coworkers came over to see what we were looking at.

"Holy crap, ten thousand dinner mints for only a hundred bucks." You could almost see the bootleg dinner mint resale business forming in Spaz's mind.

Cal was especially interested in the official-looking chef hats, while Jennie joked about finding a high-tech notepad that could translate Merryll's handwriting into something legible. The part of the catalog that interested me most was the kitchen shoe section, which filled a solid eight pages of the catalog.

It was like a bizarro world version of the Eastbay magazines that Blaise and me would flip through to pick out basketball sneakers each season. Instead of Nike, Adidas, and Reeboks filling up this section, I was looking at a full-page spread featuring dozens of different models of basically the exact same pair of plain black shoes. Pretty much all of them had rubber soles with something called "No-Slip traction technology." A few pairs had a very simple brand logo or a few shapes that I guess were supposed to be for style, but to my eyes, they were all nearly identical. The majority of them had regular laces, some others had laces and a strap, and then at the bottom corner of the third page was a familiar model of plain black No-Slips without laces, only Velcro.

I wondered if the really big names in the restaurant world, similar to NBA superstars, ever got their own signature kitchen shoe. An image came into my mind of Jimmy in that magazine, holding up a mop in perfect position and advertising his own equivalent of Air Jordans: *"At Jimmy's Family Restaurant, summer starts here, with a pair of No-Slip Jimmys. Take it from me . . . Do you really think the busiest feet in Northern Michigan would settle for anything less?"*

Everyone agreed that one welcome addition to the restaurant's equipment would be to get a silent printer for food
order tickets. No more incessant chirping from the machines
every thirty seconds during a busy day, driving Staples and the
cooks and anyone within earshot crazy. When the boss came
upstairs for a little bit to fill up the secret ice cream compartment, Staples even took a shot and asked if we could get them.
Jimmy of course said the fancy silent printers were way too
expensive, and that people would forget to check on orders
without the buzzing to remind them.

"Unless it's an emergency, I only buy new equipment at
the start of each season anyway," he said.

"Okay then," Jennie challenged. "Let's say you were really
going to splurge for something in here, anything you wanted.
What would you pick?"

"Oh, I dunno. I suppose it wouldn't hurt to get some
newer aprons with the Jimmy's logo on them."

The guy somehow *spoke* in cursive for just that one word.
I'm serious.

Jennie playfully groaned at the boss's lack of imagination,
while Jimmy smiled and shrugged. Taking advantage of the
boss's good mood, Cal worked up the nerve to ask if he could
order one of the chef hats to wear while he was cooking.
Jimmy gave a sharp "no"—quick enough that it was like the
answer was given and *then* the question was asked, instead of
the other way around.

"Why not? I think I really need one!"

"Because you're not a chef. And a hat isn't going to turn
you into one." Jimmy wrinkled his gray moustache scorn-
fully. I actually felt a little bad for Cal seeing him shot down

so ruthlessly by the boss in front of everyone. His demeanor reminded me of the boats in the harbor right before evening, when they drop their sails and quietly float back to the dock. However, after the rest of us lost interest in the *Restaurateur* catalog and cast it aside, I noticed Cal pick it up and start flipping through it again.

While the older cooks and waitresses had their own hangout back in the kitchen, and Cal and Spaz were challenging each other to try and eat six saltines in under a minute, I stayed with Staples over by the soda fountain. It occurred to me that I hadn't talked to him all that much recently. It felt good to relax and chat with him, sparking up any and every conversation to stay entertained during what was shaping up to be the slowest day of the summer.

I passed along that Merryll had left forty-five minutes earlier, grumbling that she'd only made twenty-three bucks in tips for the entire day. Even if I had the chance to skip out early, biking in this weather would be a death wish, so I stayed, and like Staples and everyone else, found enough pointless things to talk about to keep the afternoon moving. Somehow or another, the subject of Rodney being back home came up, and Staples surprisingly had a lot to say.

"I don't like your older brother very much, Beanie. I have no problem saying this. Even so, I've got nothing but respect for what he did in Mr. Morrison's world history class once when I was a junior."

"Morrison's class? What did he do?"

"Well, your brother is highly intelligent—you know that, right? I also have no problem saying this."

I had to roll my eyes at the "highly intelligent" part. I spent far too much of my own average brainpower trying to figure out whether Rodney was actually as smart as everyone said he was. The guy who got perfect scores on his college entrance exams is the same one who once tried to invent a new type of cereal by pouring a can of Dr. Pepper on top of Fruity Pebbles, and then heating them up in the oven.

As Staples told it, Rodney had been bored out of his mind in class one day. It must not have been your everyday type of boredom either, because that happened to just about everyone in Morrison's class. But something about that particular type of boredom had apparently pushed Rodney over the edge.

"Right as Mr. Morrison was going on about Marxism, and communism, and probably some other types of –isms, Rodney yelled right out loud, 'This class sucks!'"

I gasped. I know gasping is sort of old-fashioned nowadays, but I definitely gasped. It was partly because I was surprised at Rodney being so disrespectful right to a teacher's face, but also because it was so similar to an outburst that Spaz had in front of Morrison when we'd taken his freshman-level history class.

"Yooo, I never knew he did that. Hold on, we gotta get Spaz in here for this!"

Staples was a little bit annoyed that his story was getting interrupted, but he must have calculated that it was worth it in the long run, since he was now drawing in a bit of a crowd. Spaz came and joined us; Jennie stopped by too. Cal was very obviously listening to us from a distance, hoping to get invited in but trying to make it look like he wasn't. Staples started back from the beginning, and then made it back to the part where Rodney yelled out his opinion about the class.

"So what did Morrison do?"

"He snapped his neck around like it was spring-loaded, and Rodney dropped his head to the desk and pretended to be sleeping. Mr. Morrison immediately knew it was him though."

That didn't surprise me any. Rodney had been a bad liar growing up, and was still a bad liar now; I could picture his fake sleep routine being unconvincing.

"So then Mr. Morrison paused for a few moments, calculating what his response was going to be. I don't know—he must have run the numbers wrong or something, because he ended up saying the worst possible thing you can say to a guy like Rodney: 'I suppose you think *you* could do better?' It was meant to shut him up, but the exact opposite happened."

"Wait, what would the exact opposite of shutting up be?" Spaz wondered. "He started yelling at the top of his lungs?"

"No, it wasn't anything crazy. Rodney just shrugged. Then, I think he genuinely thought the question over in that moment and gave his honest response. He said, 'You know what? I actually think I could.'"

According to Staples's account of things, the two of them looked at each other, each sort of shifting around in their personal space. He said it looked like they were trying to decide whether or not they'd just made an agreement, and what exactly the agreement was that they may have just made.

"So Rodney makes the first real move. And he gets out of his desk kind of awkwardly, and right after that, Mr. Morrison sat down into his roller chair."

"Wait, Mr. Morrison used to be in a wheelchair?"

"Don't be a moron, Spaz. He's talking about those chairs with the little rollers—the ones all the teachers have."

Staples was more irritated at the latest interruption and appeared like he might be on the verge of cutting us off entirely. Jennie quickly apologized, and then backhanded Spaz on the ribs, causing him to apologize to our storyteller before glaring back at her. Staples resumed a stance that made him look like a teacher himself: frustrated but patient, waiting for his class to quiet down so the lesson could continue.

Picking up where he'd left off, he made it perfectly clear that Rodney had gone to the front of the classroom while Mr. Morrison sat down in his roller chair (which wasn't a wheelchair, just to clear up any remaining confusion).

My older brother really had once been given the opportunity to teach his high school history class. I know we didn't get along that well or talk as much as brothers probably should, but I couldn't believe that he'd never once mentioned it to me. I normally didn't mind keeping our distance, but this omission strangely disappointed me.

"The first thing Rodney did was pick up that giant-sized pencil that Mr. Morrison always kept next to his desk." Staples paused. "He still has that thing, right?"

Jennie was looking at him like, "How am I supposed to know?," but Spaz and I both nodded our heads, remembering the mega-pencil that Morrison always had as a classroom decoration. I was pretty sure I saw Cal slightly nodding his head in the background as well.

"So yeah, he has that pencil, and he's pointing it at everyone." Staples got a real serious look on his face and stabbed his arm out like a sword to demonstrate. "At first, I think he was just trying to be funny, but the second time, something about having that the pencil in his hands actually had a pretty imposing effect."

I couldn't really picture my brother having an imposing effect, but Staples had a knowing gleam in his eye.

"You'd be surprised. All he said was, 'Alright guys, listen up!', and the guys listened up. The girls did too. Rodney started his lesson. 'Look, here's the thing about Marxism...'"

Everyone started laughing, including Cal, who no longer bothered to pretend that he wasn't butting into the conversation. He was the first one (though it was on everyone's minds) to ask what happened next. Staples folded his pale arms across his chest and grinned.

"Well, he told us the thing about Marxism! I don't know where he learned it, but that day was legit the most I ever learned in that class by far. Jelly Bean's brother is telling us all about nineteenth-century Europe and all these economic theories like it's as simple to explain as reading off ice cream flavors." He tilted his head to the laminated list of flavors posted on the board to the left of him. "It was awesome."

Staples let his story sink in, and even I had to admit that Rodney pulled off a pretty impressive stunt—one that I would probably never have the guts or the brains to do myself. As a finishing touch, Spaz quietly spoke up.

"Morrison must have flipped out," he shuddered. I knew he was speaking from experience. From what I'd heard, Spaz's own history with Mr. Morrison involved him doing at least a month's worth of detentions. He pointed a gloved finger at me. "Your bro must have got demolished by him after that."

Staples considered this idea for a second, squinting his eyes to recall the aftermath of Rodney being the teacher for a day. He unfolded his arms, almost apologizing to Spaz for the lack of consequences.

"Morrison was embarrassed, but I think he actually sort of appreciated it. Think about it. It gave him an hour off from teaching, and the lesson was way better than it would have been otherwise. I bet he still uses some of the critical thinking questions that Rodney asked us when he teaches that unit too. Rodney was honestly a better lecturer than half of my college professors—I'm not joking."

Spaz barely had time for the relative unfairness to register before we were interrupted by an unimpressed voice from the kitchen. Without us noticing, Jimmy had made it back early from making the ice cream.

"Story time's over. From each according to his ability, to each according to his needs, find something to do and get the hell back to work!"

Most of us immediately scrambled to appear busy and stay out of the line of fire for potential Dumpster Duty. Staples didn't rush, though. Instead, he looked back towards Jimmy with a serene look in his eye, making me think he must have understood something that the rest of us didn't.

"Hey, JB, do you think Jimmy and Gloria ever, you know . . . here in the restaurant?"

I froze while I processed what Jennie was asking. Once I figured it out, I tried to pretend that I didn't. Jennie saw right through me.

Every time she mentioned something that she knew could make me uncomfortable, my instinct was to pretend that I didn't understand what she was referring to. Jennie had a huge grin on her face as she watched me squirm, getting an unwanted image in my mind of what she was suggesting.

"Why ya blushing, JB? I asked a simple question!"

It was 3:45. The rain was finally starting to slow down somewhat, but there were still hardly any customers. With only fifteen minutes remaining until the end of my shift, it was the perfect opportunity for Jennie to embarrass me before I left.

"Think about it. Gloria told me she's worked here since even before they got married. It's where they met. So that leaves at least like," she raised her eyes towards the ceiling, tapping at her fingers with a fork to do some sort of math, "thirty-five or forty summers together, at least. That's a lot of time spent in this restaurant nonstop."

"What's your point?"

"You really don't think that after closing up shop on a late night . . ." Jennie bit the side of her lip and looked for a reaction from me. She waved the fork around in circles, expecting me to put the final pieces together for her. "In here alone together . . . they might have gotten caught up in the mood? Maybe push a few boxes to the side in the storage room? Or step back to the walk-in fridge if they were feeling extra—"

"I don't want to think about that! That image . . . come on!"

"Oh please, JB, grow up a little bit. I'm just saying . . . maybe they'd even want to scrape the grease off the stove and—"

"CUT IT OUT!"

Staples heard my exaggerated yell and coolly strolled towards us to see what the fuss was about.

"What are we terrorizing Jelly Bean about this time?"

"Maybe you can help us settle a little debate." Jennie continued biting her lip with that mischievous look in her eye.

"Yes ma'am."

"Do you think Jimmy and Gloria have ever, you know . . . here in the restaurant?"

A quick blinking of his thin eyes was all the time that Staples needed to decide where he stood on the topic.

"Well, it's pretty obvious that they have, isn't it?"

"Obvious?? How is it obvious?"

"You've got forty-two summers cooped up in here, day after day. They run everything in here. It can be a hectic environment at times, all that tension just building up during the workday." Staples bumped his knuckles together to demonstrate the tension. "Yeah, they definitely have. Probably hundreds of times."

"Ha! Told ya!" Jennie taunted me with a quick victory dance.

I was defeated, and I knew it. As I'd unfortunately found out that first night of Dumpster Duty (and many times since), Staples usually knew what he was talking about.

My shift finished up, and I biked back home in the rain, greasy and drenched.

Probably as a result of that last conversation with Jennie, there were thoughts of . . . you know, rushing through my head that night when I turned the lights off for bed. Except it wasn't Jimmy and Gloria (thank God!) who I was thinking about as I tossed and turned. Even without Spaz's cricket friends hanging out in the walls, I had a difficult time falling asleep.

CHAPTER TWENTY-ONE

Wanna Chill?

By the start of August, any enthusiasm that I might have had right at the start of my time at Jimmy's had completely worn off. I was feeling lazy, annoyed, frustrated, sluggish: you name it.

I kept pace at the restaurant, keeping my tables clean, getting dishes back to Spaz as soon as a tray was full, and I'd even gone two weeks straight without having Jimmy get on my case about anything. Gloria had even been praising my work ethic, saying how reliable I'd been for them and how much they appreciated it. My satisfaction level, though— with this summer job, and with my summer in general—was at a low point.

I stopped bothering pretending to listen to Cal's corny jokes, or his tall tales about all the girls he supposedly had hooked up with. Any time he started to talk these days, I tuned out all content completely, but felt the rhythm of his monologues enough to give a partial reaction every once in a while: an occasional "for real?" or "no way!" when Cal looked over for approval, or a simple polite laugh if it seemed like he expected me to think whatever he said was funny.

As my patience for this performance faded though, my polite laughs had become little more than a head nod and a grunt. Those two things could pretty much sum up my entire spirit as I came into work on a Saturday morning early in August: a head nod and a grunt. I had a short enough shift planned, letting off at 3:30 that afternoon, but I still wanted nothing to do with it.

When my alarm went off at 9:00, it wasn't even that early. I'd gotten plenty of sleep, because it had been Friday night, and I had nothing to do and nowhere to be on pretty much any Friday night. Even so, I woke up that morning feeling half-dead. That's actually a little bit of an exaggeration. Not half-dead—probably in the range of 35 or 40 percent dead though, which is still not very encouraging. I wasn't feeling dead enough to blow off work and stay lying in bed all day, but not alive enough to put any effort into my morning routine.

I'd spent nearly a half hour staring at the digital clock and trying to avoid getting up. The reddish digits on the clock dug into my eyes, as if they were scolding me for my sudden weakness. Time is one of maybe like three or four things in existence that you'll always have until the very moment that you die, yet it somehow was starting to feel like there was never enough of it—or even worse, when there *was* enough of it, having the nagging feeling that my peers were all using theirs much better than I was using mine.

Time meant money for Jennie, quickly building up a supply of cash with each hour during the day, and then making sure to enjoy it at night. Spaz greeted it like a long-lost friend (that was never lost or a friend to begin with), skating his way through an eternal present. Blaise was making time itself work for him, as his hours in the gym were starting to multiply and would likely add up to a full basketball scholarship within a few years. Staples was biding his time, with the patient confidence that he'd go back to college and on to better and more exciting things soon enough.

Me though? At this point, it felt like I was being used, rather than using my time. Wasting it, dividing it, unsuccessfully trying to extend or condense it, depending on the scenario. It prolonged when I needed it to shorten, collapsed within itself like a black hole when I needed more of it. It's clear you've woken up on the wrong side of the bed when it feels like even time itself is conspiring against you. Yet I kept eyeing the intense red digits of that clock, and they kept glaring right back without blinking as the minutes ticked by.

I laid there with this stream of negativity in my head until the last possible moment, until I would be late for work if I stayed down a second longer. I didn't get any breakfast and didn't bother finding a clean pair of cargo shorts or a fresher work shirt to put on. Just the same stuff from the day before, as if anyone would notice.

If the season were developing a main theme, it would have to be this: the ever-widening gap between what I thought the summer would be, and what it was actually turning into. Being cooped up the previous winter had filled my head with all sorts of fantasies about how things would be once I was back. Now that I actually *was* back, it was a reality check, revealing the deep valley that separated my dreams from my existence.

It was like I'd woken up only to realize that half of the summer was gone, and I'd accomplished nothing from my top five list. In fact, I may have even fallen further behind in each category.

I stupidly thought that my re-entry into basketball should be smooth and triumphant. That I'd get my shot and my stamina back in no time and establish myself as an up-and-comer to make varsity as a sophomore. Instead, I clearly hadn't grown enough to match up with the upperclassmen, and all that time away had messed up my confidence on the floor. I never thought I'd feel out of place on a basketball court, but certain days at open gym, I almost felt like Darko out there: slow, uncoordinated, getting in everyone else's way, and probably better suited to choose a different extracurricular activity.

The plan was to completely stay out of trouble, but I ended up getting a week's worth of Dumpster Duty. I wanted to get a girlfriend, but I ended up catching feelings for someone I shouldn't have and who wasn't interested in me. Despite playing ball and working out with Blaise a lot more, he was becoming a mystery, speaking less and appearing more tired and troubled each week. Between filling in for others at work and feeling compelled to be at the gym or else lose even more ground, it often felt like my free time wasn't free at all. I couldn't shake the increasing concern that this was all my redemption summer was shaping up to be, and in only a month I'd be back in school with no way to reclaim the lost time.

"Ayy, JB, do you know where we keep extras of those Styrofoam-whatever thingies? Jimmy says the kitchen is going to run out of them pretty soon. He asked me to get some from downstairs."

"No, Spaz, I haven't seen any Styrofoam-whatever thingies." I was purposely being difficult, and I knew it. Spaz had caught me in a bad moment, and I wasn't in the mood to be civil. "Not in my entire life. Now if by chance it's *takeout boxes* that you're really looking for, I can help you; but as for Styrofoam-whatever thingies, I'm pretty sure we don't have any of those here."

"Yeah, it's that!" Spaz didn't seem to be put off by my sarcasm, which is just as well. Since I couldn't say that type of thing to Jimmy, Staples, or Jennie and get away with it, unfortunately for Spaz, he'd have to catch the brunt of my frustrations.

"Yeah I know where they are. You go downstairs and it's next to where the extra ice cream cones are kept."

"Gawt it." He gave me a thumbs-up but remained stuck where he was standing. "Uhh, and where are the extra ice cream cones?"

"In the dry storage room."

"Where's the dry storage room?"

"Damn it, Spaz, how can you not know this stuff?"

"Geez, who pushed your buttons? I haven't been here that long, and I'm a dishwasher. I don't usually need to worry about all that—I thought you could help."

"Dry storage is that dark room to the left of the staff bathroom."

Spaz rubbed his thumb and pointer finger together. He must have wanted to give another thumbs-up but couldn't do it. "What? Now don't tell me—"

He shook his head. "There's a *staff* bathroom? I've always just—"

I couldn't take this anymore. I cut him off.

"Never mind, Spaz! I'll just go down and get them for you." I smacked him on the shoulder with my towel and marched down to the basement, hurling insults under my breath at the poor guy.

There were probably some tables finishing up and getting ready to leave in the dining room. There were also probably more groups of people at the front door waiting to be seated. Spaz probably didn't really need his Styrofoam-whatever thingies at that exact moment anyway, but I felt like disappearing for a few minutes. Going downstairs to dry storage to dig up some of those boxes was a good excuse to escape for a little bit.

Dry storage was a weirdly comfortable part of the restaurant to visit, tucked away towards the very back of the basement. Large, neatly stacked cardboard boxes created a sort of 3D maze feel. They formed crisp aisles to step through in order to locate all of the non-perishables and non-food items that were kept out of sight until something went empty up above.

The air smelled musty and mildewy, but in a way that agreed with me. Like how old library books often vaguely smell like puke, but I can't help opening and taking a big whiff anyway. It was a universal basement-type of smell. It reminded me of the basement at Blaise's house. It also reminded me of the basement in the haunted house at Five Mile Creek.

Even pulling the small chain hanging from the ceiling to click on the dim light bulb in the room was somehow satisfying. The dusty bulb only lit up about three quarters of the room, with the stacks of boxes casting shadows along the remaining corner. It made me think of treasure hunters exploring a dark cave with those old-school lanterns, having themselves an adventure.

Despite my little tantrum at Spaz, I was secretly glad to have an excuse to come down here. I could still feel like I was doing my job and getting something accomplished, but without the distractions and annoyances and chaos of scurrying around upstairs.

Down in dry storage, I didn't have to worry about Jimmy's mustached scowl, and him finding another reason to send me to the dumpsters after work. There weren't any fake smiles or mechanical echoes of "having *fun* yet?" No glaring eyes or judgmental body language from the waitresses if I wasn't moving fast enough for their standards. There was no Spaz down there (since he didn't even know how to get there), and Spaz was hilarious if I was in a good mood, but infuriating if I wasn't. There also wasn't any Cal bragging about his exploits with the opposite sex, followed by the revealing silence that basically admitted that I didn't have any of my own to respond back with.

Most importantly, there was no Jennie to worry about. A few minutes without the burden of feeling like I was on a crowded stage, auditioning for her attention. No overanalyzing every interaction with, "Is she flirting?" . . . "Do I sound cool?" . . . "Do I sound like an idiot?" No seesawing between feeling admired and ignored, sometimes dozens of times in a single afternoon.

If I'm being honest, I probably wouldn't have been so bothered about the whole Jennie situation if I was at least getting noticed by other girls every once in a while. Staples pulled out the old "there's plenty of fish in the sea" line on me before. But if Jennie wanted to be with that barracuda Jimi Dandersley, then couldn't some other cute fish swim my way every once in a while?

None of the cardboard boxes were labeled very clearly, but I'd gotten familiar enough with the setup to have a good idea of where everything was by then. After only one false lead, which turned out to be a large box of plastic coffee cup lids, I found the one holding five hundred or so Styrofoam takeout containers. After lifting up a decent-sized stack of these, I decided that I wasn't ready to go back upstairs yet.

Sometimes I got sick of being the reliable one. The calm one. The one who people don't need to pull to the side every other day and ask, "Are you okay?" Why don't I ever get to have an outburst, or call off work if I'd rather be somewhere else? It was always, "Yeah, no problem. Sure, I can help. Of course, not an inconvenience at all." Why couldn't I be the one who gets to be pissed off from time to time? The one who is left alone, but also cared about at the same time? Maybe that's why I finally snapped last summer: too much trying to be perfect.

I thought about the time that Darko and I had hid down in the dry storage room for almost an hour, when Garrett still worked here. We crouched into some empty boxes and silently waited all that time until Garrett came downstairs just so we could scare him. Even in my dark mood, I couldn't help but crack a smile remembering that one.

I had a quick daydream about removing all the coffee lids from the biggest box and climbing inside for the rest of the afternoon. Someone else could be the reliable one for once, while I hid out in a cardboard fort. If anyone really needed any refills on the Styrofoam, they could come down here and get it themselves.

Obviously, the cardboard fort hideout wasn't going to work, but I wasn't ready to go back upstairs yet. To have a good excuse to stay in the basement, I convinced myself that the waitress station could use a refill on their sugar packets. All three kinds, in fact: the classic white ones, the pink ones with the music note on them, and the blue artificial sweeteners that groups of gold-digging Real Housewives from the Peninsula always seemed to choose. I guess if their tans, eyelashes, smiles, boobs, and marriages were fake, then their sugar might as well be too.

I got a cardboard cut along my right pointer finger as I opened the box holding the artificial sweeteners. It didn't sting quite like a regular paper cut, but it drew a sliver of blood. As I winced and examined my hand, I took special note of how my fingernails looked. They seemed extra-long and pointy. They looked cloudy and yellowish too, like a werewolf's claws. I reasoned that this must be from dipping my fingers into bleach all the time when I mopped up the floors. It felt like my nails had been growing twice as fast ever since I'd started this job. If only the rest of me would grow like that, I could really be in business for next basketball season. But no—my only superpower was growing bleach-induced werewolf claws. I ripped open a bag of napkins with those mutant fingernails, cleaning up the blood from my hand before running out of ways to stall and eventually heading back upstairs.

I managed to waddle one-by-one up each of the steps without dropping any of my loot from the dry storage cave:

Spaz's takeout boxes, plus all types of sugars, cups, and ice cream cones to top it all off. I half-expected some type of appreciation for helping to restock all of these items, but that was apparently far too much to expect (or even half-expect). Spaz didn't even notice me coming back up. He had his back turned as I emerged, and then he started walking away, holding his arms in front of him in a strange manner.

Still carefully balancing everything in my arms, I followed him out of the kitchen through to the dessert counter, where Staples and Cal were standing. I finally caught a better view of what was going on. Spaz was holding seven or eight knives of various sizes between his fingers, with the blades rising up from his knuckles like fingers. He proudly displayed the end result to the guys.

"Check it out, I'm Spazward Scissorhands!"

Cal busted out laughing, and even Staples couldn't keep himself from doing the same. Jimmy had walked past right as Spaz did his gag as well, stopping in his tracks.

"SPAZ!!"

Anyone else probably would have gotten Dumpster Duty. Jimmy just stood there in amazement though, his hairy forearms wringing out a yellowing towel. His moustache flickered. I swear, he was about to bust out laughing as well, but all he did was turn away shaking his head, pacing back to the kitchen.

It didn't exactly seem fair that Spaz was able to pull that off without any consequences, but I didn't have much time to consider it. My absence had been noticed.

"JB, where the hell were you just now?" It was Merryll, and she was furious with me. "I've got customers sitting at *dirty tables!!*"

The instinctive reply in my head was, *That's their problem*, but I looked at the ground and hustled back to the dining room without a word. Nobody thanked me for bringing up the stupid whatever thingies, either.

"Oh boy, Peninsula Princesses, ten o'clock," Jennie said later in the afternoon, as a group of five teenage girls walked through the front entrance. "Make sure somebody hoses down Cal."

The girls (three brunettes, a blonde, and a redhead, all with silky hair and cell phones) walked past Lacy with only the slightest nods of recognition. Each wearing a different-colored tank top, they sat down at one of Jennie's tables: the booth along the back window. Jennie puffed a piece of hair off her forehead, looking a little bit annoyed, which was the case whenever she had to wait on a group of Peninsula girls.

She rolled her eyes at pretty much everything they did. The way they took pictures of themselves, puckering their lips and holding up sideways peace signs, then instantly crowding around each other to see how the picture turned out. If it wasn't that, it was flipping their hair and shifting their eyes from side to side, trying to check whether other people were watching them without appearing too obvious.

"Um yeah, toadully." Jennie lifted her chin and flipped her hair in an exaggerated motion, imitating the girls while typing in their order. "It's like, soeww good!"

Jennie despised anything that she considered fake, and she felt like Peninsula girls were constantly overdoing it. Over-laughing all of the jokes, whether they were funny or clever or not. Showing over-interest in even the weakest topics of their own private world, and then making sure that everyone else was sucked into their orbit as well.

She claimed there was a hidden desperation to it, like they were trying to convince themselves that their own jokes were the funniest, that their conversations were naturally the most intriguing and important. Or when they were bored, sneering and sighing and dropping their heads, acting like even their boredom was somehow more glamorous than the regular kind. According to Jennie, their whole self-esteem was entirely dependent on believing that the ears of everyone in that dining room were fully concentrated on their every word. I would never tell Jennie this, but for what it's worth, I couldn't help listening in whenever I was flipping a nearby table.

While pushing my cart around, still in my dark mood from earlier, I found myself catching every other sentence or so coming from their area, Table 36. I didn't make any move to talk to them and avoided even making direct eye contact, but I found a strange satisfaction from my secondhand involvement in their lunch hangout. While talking and waiting for their food, each seemed to be testing the waters, taking turns guiding the discussion, jostling for social standing and figuring out which one was the true group leader. This made me think that they must live in different towns from each other during the school year.

"Yeah, she *would* say that. She absolutely would say that!"

I leaned in. I had no idea who "she" was and would probably never meet her, but for some reason I wanted to hear what she would absolutely say. I never got a chance to find that part out either, though.

"Ah, shit!" said Merryll, way too close to customers to be swearing like that. "Damn pens are all dead. June Bug, wait here for a second!"

I felt like a butler, standing at attention with a towel, waiting for a six-person family to announce their orders with Merryll (which she would probably forget immediately since she was all out of ink). She turned back to me after collecting all the menus from Table 33.

"Go grab me three new pens, would ya? They're under the computer, in the drawer. Next to where I keep my purse."

"I don't know where you keep your purse."

"The Bic ones too, not Pilot—those ones run too much. Bring them to me at the order window."

"Great. You want me to wag my tail too?"

She scrunched up her face, which was starting to sweat, before hurrying back to the order window. I could tell that she was backlogged on at least three tables. I don't think anybody needed to see a full Merryll meltdown, so I figured I might as well just get the pens for her.

Grudgingly following Merryll's command, I crouched down to the cupboard below the DigiServ system to find the replacement pens. I first had to sort through all of the wait-resses' purses and handbags that were blocking the shelves of the cupboard though.

Getting a little uncomfortable in my crouched position, I set Merryll's purse to the side, which was probably more expensive than what she should have been spending on an accessory. I figured this based on the fact that she's always grouching about having the lowest amount in tips, no matter which section of tables she was assigned or who else was working the floor that day. I also saw Jennie's small drawstring bag with some kind of notebook leaned up against it, a red bookmark poking out from the middle.

After pushing past of box of Band-Aids, a pair of empty red ketchup bottles, a few rolls of packaging tape, and the extra waitress notepads, I reached a fresh bag of Bic Round Stic pens on the bottom shelf of the cupboard. The glossy plastic bag reminded me of the packs of basketball cards I'd collected when I was younger. The bag even made the same half-pop/half-squeak noise when I pulled it open. I grabbed three new pens for Merryll and figured I might as well grab some for Jennie too.

As I started to put the pens back in the cupboard, I took a closer look at the front of the packaging. The logo was of a round-headed guy who was dressed in all yellow. He didn't really have a face, but he looked pleased with himself anyway, holding onto a pen that was almost the same height as him. I also noticed the slogan on the front of the bag: *"Writes first time, every time!"*

I had to read it three or four more times before it sunk in. I realized that this must be the absolute worst product slogan that I've ever seen. The pen *writes*? Even the *first* time that you try to use it? What they were basically saying is, "These pens actually work!," as if Bic should get extra credit for their pens doing the one and only simple thing that they're designed to do. I started to think about if other companies tried to get away with the same sort of mediocre standards that Bic was bragging about. Does anybody else notice this stuff?

Imagine if the companies in *Restaurateur* magazine took this same approach when it came to their advertising. *"The Nakayama Genesis: this knife is capable of cutting things."* What about Hollywood? I pictured a promotional poster to really hype fans up for the upcoming superhero blockbuster.

"*Magneto Man: The Induction—the plot mostly makes sense!*"
Or how about ol' Jimmy himself? "*Jimmy's Family Restaurant: now made with real food!*"

I tested out the new Bic Round Stics on one of the notepads before taking them back over to Merryll. The last thing I needed was her scolding me if I gave out faulty pens. Two of them wrote cleanly on the first try; I needed to scribble back and forth a bunch of times to get the other one going. The little round-headed guy on the logo probably thought he had it all figured out, though. Him and Cal would probably get along well, come to think of it.

Once Merryll was all set (she actually did say a relieved thank you), I carried the remaining three pens over to Jennie. After using two of them to tie back her hair, she grabbed the third to write with, even though she usually just memorized orders. She smiled gratefully and went to grab a drink order from Staples. Watching Jennie glide back out to check on the girls at the back window, I thought of one more slogan: "*Zilwaukee: we're not Mil-waukee, but now that we've got you here . . .*"

A little while later, Jennie stepped toward the waitress station with her classic mischievous grin, getting my attention as I scraped bits of whitefish and tartar sauce into the trash.

"What do you think about those girls over there, JB?"

The butter knife I was using slipped out of my hand. I had to reach into the garbage bin to pluck it back out. I wish I knew some sort of trick to prevent myself from blushing when I felt it coming in advance, but there was no way of stopping it.

"Which ones?"

"Sitting in my section. Table 36."

"Ohh. Which table is that again?"

"Stop pretending to be a moron. You know where Table 36 is, and you know exactly which girls I'm talking about."

"So?"

"So . . . just answer the question. Tell me what you think about them. Do you think they're *hot*, or *cute*, or whatever?"

"No. I mean, sure. At least, I can see why someone might find them to be, you know, fairly hot. You know, I guess they're . . . decently attractive."

Jennie kept grilling me. She bit her lip to cover up her smile and wrinkled her forehead, faking seriousness.

"Is this making you uncomfortable, JB?" Then she broke the serious face and started laughing out loud. To be honest, it was pretty annoying.

"Shut up," I snapped back. "It's just weird, that's all. You're not someone I'd expect to be talking to about which girls I think are hot. It's weird, isn't it?"

"Oh, grow up. Why's it weird? Would you rather I brought Cal over here instead?"

She flicked one of the sugar packets at me, then immediately turned to the DigiServ computer. The pink packet skimmed off my shoulder, but I was able to catch it before it fell to the ground.

"I'd rather that we just dropped the subject entirely," I continued. "What made you bring them up, anyway?"

"Because," Jennie said as she finished typing her next order onto the touch screen. I heard the printer in the kitchen buzzing to life with the newest food ticket. "I heard them talking about you."

"Huh??"

Jennie acted like she hadn't heard me, drowning out my follow-up questions by loudly singing the opening lines from "The Wreck of the Edmund Fitzgerald."

"The LEH-GEND lives on, from the Chippewa on down . . ."

She was simultaneously being infuriating and hilarious. Before I had time to decide which was more so, she turned away and walked back to her customers. Including Table 36. I tried to take a closer glance at the Peninsula girls without making it completely obvious that I was checking them out, but they must have been better at that sort of move than I was. Next thing I knew, I heard a calm and condescending voice from over by the grill.

"Whatcha' lookin' at there, Beanie?"

Cal looked enormously pleased with himself as his own eyes scanned the dining room and landed at the back booth. He flipped a hamburger patty up in the air with extra gusto, and actually got a good landing and a satisfying sizzle as the other side began to cook.

"That sort of clientele sort of makes me want to be a waiter, know what I mean?"

"Hi, Cal."

I didn't mind it when Staples called me "Jelly Bean" and "Beanie" and all that. He came up with it, after all, and he didn't seem to mean anything by it. It was just his bizarre sense of humor at work. Plus, I really liked Staples. Whenever Cal or Merryll did it though, there was something extra to it, like they were using the stupid nickname as a weapon over me. Anything to display that they were above me.

"They look like Peninsula girls, too . . . Peninsula girls are the best. They're also the worst—know what I mean? Maybe I should be a waiter instead of a chef."

"There you go."

I didn't know or care what he was trying to get at, but my easiest route in these situations was just to give Cal a quick affirmation and clear the runway.

"Maybe I'll go and get the blondish one's phone number before they leave." He said it with an unwarranted confidence that suggested there was no way anyone would consider saying no to that offer. "I'll only call her if I feel like it, but it'll be good to have as an option either way. Get something going at least." Cal slightly growled as he said the "get something going" piece.

For the next few minutes, Cal was back to his post, now putting the pieces together to load up Jennie's order for five identical club sandwiches.

With a surge of adrenaline, what Jennie had told me began to sink in. The Peninsula girls were talking about me. Was this just Jennie messing with me again? Or, if not, what were they saying?

After setting the club sandwiches up in the window, Cal was right back out in the doorway, grinning with his eyes glued to the back table, returning to his daydream about becoming a waiter.

"Then again, staying a chef is probably for the best. Waiting tables would only get me in trouble."

When I didn't give any type of response, he chuckled to himself and grinned at me even deeper, thinking I must not have heard him. "Yeah, I'd find myself in a lot of trouble if that were the case." He nodded his head knowingly until I couldn't take his stupidity anymore.

"Yeah, Cal? And how exactly would cute girls sitting in a restaurant in the middle of the day 'get you in trouble?'"

"Ahh." Jennie had caught the last part as she picked up the tray of sandwiches. "So, you admit you think they're cute! Want me to say something to them?"

"Sure, you can tell them all about me." It was Cal saying that, not me. Jennie laughed and balanced her tray and strolled back to the dining room, leaving me alone with Cal again. He again insisted on how much trouble he would get in if he were a waiter instead of a cook.

"Oh, I can be quite the flirtatious little bastard," he warned with pride, clearly trying to give himself a forehanded insult. I decided that I reached my Cal quota for the day.

"Yeah, well, I think I should go check on those pens for Merryll, and—I just gotta stop talking to you right now." Cal kept on cooking and grinning like the Cheshire Cat, unbothered as usual by getting the brush-off.

"JB, your friends have a message for you."

The next twenty minutes passed in a blur, with several tables to clear up, plus an ice cream spill near the soda fountain, plus an aggressive Margaritaville guy who loudly complained to me about the extra order of fries that was mistakenly added to his bill. When there was another free moment and Jennie came back around to find me again, I had already started to forget about what was happening at Table 36.

"A message? What friends?"

Jennie nodded to the back booth and pulled out a tiny slip of lined paper from the pouch of her apron. It was frayed along the edges, clearly ripped from a notebook. I unfolded the paper slip and saw a phone number, written underneath a quick note in loopy handwriting:

Wanna chill?

My first thought was to crumple up the slip of paper and say forget it. This seemed too much like another one of Jennie's tricks, and I wasn't going to take the bait this time. Even so, I had to pause. Just because something happens to be your first thought, that doesn't mean it's your *best* thought. My heart started beating extra fast, and I stared uncertainly at Jennie.

"Hold on a second, this is from . . . over there?"

"Well, it's definitely not from me." She smirked. "So, are you gonna call?"

I'd run into too many situations where I quickly said yes to something only to regret it, and just as many where I instinctively said no and regretted that too. I needed someone who would at least give me neutral advice, so I made a quick trip over to the soda fountain with Jennie trailing close behind.

I explained the situation to Staples. He said that unless I had the guts to go up and talk to the girls myself, I needed to leave the whole thing alone. Jennie was pretty quick to disagree with Staples. She said I should take the paper home, think about it for a bit, and decide later on whether I wanted to call or not. Looking at Jennie, then Staples, then back at the Peninsula girls, I stupidly wished that high school came with a quick one-page sheet of tough decisions that might come up, separating out the exact situations where I should say yes and all the ones where I should say no.

By the time I made it back to the waitress station, a pretty good idea had formed in my mind. Opening the cupboard under DigiServ, I retraced my steps from earlier and pulled out one of the notepads—the ones that waitresses used to put their orders on. I wrote my name and number to the house phone on a piece of the official Jimmy's stationary, leaving a message of my own:

Yes. Call me after 4.

It may not have been as brilliant as my meal delivery service idea, but this plan seemed to be the perfect middle ground. If this was legit, and the Peninsula girls actually wanted to hang out with me, they could get in touch when I got off from work. If it had been some sort of joke all along, I would be saved any additional embarrassment. Calling Jennie back over, I showed her what I wrote and asked if she could drop it off at the table when she delivered the bill. Jennie first looked surprised, and then as if she was trying to stall.

"Now . . . are you *sure* you're sure about that?"

"What do you mean? You started this . . . Time to back up your talk!"

"Yeah." Jennie bit her lip and took a longer look at me. "But I didn't think you'd actually do it."

"Well, I'm actually doing it." I stood firmly and handed her the paper. "They're almost finished eating, you can take it over now. I'll watch."

Reluctantly, Jennie walked back to Table 36, handing them my response along with the check for their club sandwiches. As she set it on the table, I made sure to find work to do, so I wouldn't have to endure the agony of watching their reaction. Even though it wasn't nearly full yet, I took the trash bag from my cart and started walking past the soda fountain to take it to the bigger garbage can in the kitchen.

"I saw that." The ever-omniscient Staples gently shook his head and smacked me across the chest with his dish towel. "You're digging your own grave, Beanie."

As I started to defend my decision, Spaz passed by with a tray of glasses and dessert dishes. He'd only caught the final part of the comment from Staples but decided to weigh in on it all the same.

"You say 'digging your own grave' like it's a *bad* thing. I don't get that phrase at all. I would want to dig my own grave."

For a moment, I forgot what Staples was even chastising me about; the blonde kid in his hair net, with those yellow rubber gloves that sort of matched his hair, had stopped us both in our tracks. As he always seemed to do, Spaz took the conversation in a much different direction than it was intended to go.

"Who else besides myself would I trust enough to prepare my final resting place? No one, that's who. I could get the plot dimensions measured out just how I want them, make sure the digging isn't rushed, and I'd be able to customize it better too. I'd probably only go like, maybe four feet deep instead of six. Make it easier to get out of there if I ever needed to."

As Spaz stopped speaking to consider his zombie apocalypse scenario, he looked up for long enough to take in the confused looks that both of us now had. Staples had mastered a voice tone when making a point that could somehow be both kind and cruel at the same time. He used this tone to respond.

"Spaz, there are many different follow-up questions that I

could ask right now, but I think it's best for everyone if you just go back and wash some more dishes."

"What . . . is that not what we're talking about?"

Spaz's face was a blank canvas, showing no hints either way to determine whether he was being serious or enjoying himself as he messed with us. He passed the dishes along to Staples, who casually began pulling sundae dishes three at a time from the tray, recreating their mini-pyramid formations on the countertop.

"I don't know, Beanie. You seem to have a lot of wild ideas that do nothing but ruin your self-esteem when all is said and done."

I liked Staples a lot, but that comment really irritated me. What did he know about it, anyway? Then again, the guy had proven time after time over the course of the summer that he generally knew what he was talking about. I think that's probably what bothered me the most: the possibility of Staples being right yet again. Maybe I was only setting myself up for another big disappointment.

Then again, as the Peninsula Princesses paid their bill with Lacy and started to make their way to the exit, one of the brown-haired girls briefly turned back. Unmistakably looking over at me, she smiled and waved, clearly holding the small slip of paper in her other hand. The redheaded girl snickered wildly and pulled her friend out of the restaurant by the arm. Staples folded his arms and reconsidered.

"On second thought, well done, Beanie."

CHAPTER TWENTY-TWO

The Peninsula

I rushed so fast to leave work that day that I forgot to take off my apron when I punched out. Jimmy would have to survive being one apron down until the next day, though, because I wasn't turning back. The straps of it came untied and flapped behind me as I biked back home at top speed to start getting ready for my big night.

Part of me was still a little bit skeptical about whether or not this whole thing was actually going to happen. Since I'd written my phone number down on that slip of paper, the ball was in their court. Even though I had the *"Wanna Chill?"* paper with a number on it, my game plan was just to sit next to the phone and wait for something to happen. This was one of those times that I wished I had a cell phone. In that case, at least I would be able to do something else in the meantime and still have a phone next to me. Since my brother and mom were both still at work, my only option was to sit anxiously near the home phone in the kitchen. I felt a little bit like a hostage. A very excited and hopeful hostage, if such a thing exists.

I'd been waiting for about twenty minutes when it finally rang. For a second, I felt like I'd been struck by lightning. Clearing my throat and wiping my sweaty hands against my shorts, I grabbed the phone and tried to answer it as calmly as possible.

"Hello?"

"Hey, man, what are you up to tonight?" It was Blaise.

It's not that I didn't want to hear from Blaise, but the guy picked the absolute worst time to call. On literally any other night this summer, I would have been available and grateful for Blaise to invite me anywhere. Now, though, the sooner I could get him off the phone, the better. He sounded a little bewildered.

"Not much. Well, I mean, actually I might already have plans, not quite sure. Do you . . . need something?"

"Ohh, well, I was just going to see if you wanted to hang out, that's all. No tournaments this weekend, so I'm in town. Figured I'd check in. You said you're busy though?"

For a second, I thought about telling him all about what happened at the restaurant—the girls and the note, and my nervous excitement as I waited for them to call. I strongly considered asking if he wanted to come along and join me on whatever the night had in store. Blaise was no stranger to having girls invite him places; he'd be able to handle himself and probably even take some of the pressure off me. This was my night, though—not his. Though we'd never fully talked about it since, the memory of him going without me to a party on the Peninsula a year ago was still fresh on my mind.

"Yeah, sorry, man, tonight doesn't work for me."

"Oh." Even through the phone, the disappointment in Blaise's voice was clear. "Don't worry about it. Workout still on Monday?"

"Yup, sounds good, see you Monday."

After another ten minutes of pacing around the kitchen and flinching every time I thought I heard a noise, the phone finally rang again. My right leg shaking on overdrive, I answered it again.

"Hello?"

From all the noise in the background, it sounded like there were numerous people on the other line. I must have been on speakerphone.

"Heyyy, are you JB? From the restaurant?"

"Yeah." Without knowing what else to add but feeling like it was still my turn to speak, I added, "That's me."

There was muffled speaking and what sounded like furniture moving around on the other end. I heard someone call out, "What does JB stand for?" and then a fit of giggling, with the main caller eventually hushing them up and returning to the speaker.

"Don't worry about them. So, got anything going on tonight, JB?"

"N-nope," I said, stammering a little bit. "I mean, not yet. But you know, if there's anything happening, I'm, you know, free."

"Well, me and my friends are having a few people over later on, at our place on South Point."

That was a small but defining difference between locals and summer people; we called it the "Peninsula," and they called it by its more official title, "South Point." I'm not saying one of those names is more correct than the other, but put it this way: summer people also called their mansions "cottages." Sure, *cottages.* Just a quaint little trip up to your *cottage,* with three floors, ten bedrooms, and a state-of-the-art security system. If they don't even know the right word to call their houses, why should we take their word for it on the name of the land? I'm not saying our way is right, but *our way is right.* It's the Peninsula, not South Point. Now wasn't the time to worry about it, though.

"That sounds cool."

"So you wanna come down and chill with us?"

I felt like Jimmy the time that Cal was asking if he could get a chef hat. Without a doubt, I answered yes before the question was even asked. Like one of the waitresses taking an order for an important customer, I carefully wrote down the address when she gave it to me and recited it back to make sure I heard it right: 15 South Beacon Street. 9:30 p.m.

"Alright, JB. I'll let the worker guys at security know you're coming. See ya later."

Pumping my chest and letting out a silent war cry, I hung up the phone before sprinting up to my room in an ecstatic one-person celebration. It was like the time Blaise hit a go-ahead shot and then stole the inbounds pass to beat our rivals from nearby Red Cliff back in middle school. When I calmed back down, I realized that there were still several hours to kill before it was game time.

Around 7:30, I started getting ready to leave, beginning with a shower. I worked extra hard to scrub all the ice cream residue that was caked onto my wrists and remove the smell of French fries and bleach from my body by any means necessary. Afterwards, I looked into the medicine cabinet and pulled out three different scents to put on: my Speed Stick deodorant, my brother's Old Spice, and some type of cologne in a dark glass container that was also my brother's.

There was no need to try and shave. I didn't have any facial hair yet—not even a little peach fuzz that could be scraped away. Even so, I slapped on some Brut aftershave onto my face and neck the way I'd seen guys do it on TV. It smelled kind of good too. Rodney would probably be pissed off if he knew I was using all his stuff, but since he hadn't come home from the boathouse yet, he had no way to object.

While doing all of this, I practiced making confident smiles and facial expressions in the mirror. I had to admit that despite my untamed excitement, I really had no idea what to expect from the night. "Chilling" was such a vague term when I thought about it, and I didn't even know what it consisted of. Was it like a date, or was it more like a party? Was the main girl from the phone call who I was being specifically set up with? Or maybe it was just a group hangout at somebody's house. For all I knew, maybe it was just sitting around watching TV and talking. That wasn't the most exciting thing in itself, but watching TV and talking with *Peninsula girls* made the idea sound exhilarating. I wondered why they had picked me out from the restaurant that afternoon, and what it all meant. It felt like it could be the turning point of my entire summer. Or maybe I was overthinking the whole thing and just needed to wait and find out.

I decided to put on my slightly fancy watch for the occasion. I say "slightly fancy" because I knew it wasn't a Rolex or anything like that, but it did have a leather strap, and a glass casing, and thin silver minute and hour hands. In my head, I liked to refer to it as a "timepiece" and not just any regular watch. It was a Christmas present from my aunt—one that I never really found many opportunities to wear, even though I liked how it looked.

I was smart enough to never wear it at work, imagining all the substances that would get crusted onto the glass if I had it on while bussing tables. Peering through the remains of lemon wedges and J-Sauce while checking how much time was left in my shift . . . no thanks. A night at the Peninsula seemed like the perfect chance to get slightly fancy though, so I put on the watch, along with a pair of khaki shorts (actually ironed) with a light-blue polo shirt. Instead of the Asics that I normally wore to work, I changed into the white Nike sneakers that had become my go-to for basketball ever since losing my old shoes that day at Sara's house.

As soon as I was satisfied enough with my appearance, I hustled across the living room, hoping to duck out of there without attracting any attention. Of course, my mom heard the screen door creak open and went into interrogation mode.

"Where are *you* headed?"

Even though I wasn't doing anything wrong, I was still hoping to avoid my mom and the need to give a full rundown of my schedule for the night. I turned back around and found her looking at me with a bewildered smile. I tried to just talk fast and get it over with as quickly as possible.

"I have plans tonight, Mom. Me and these girls, and uhh—I don't know who else. It's like a date/hangout thing."

"A 'date/hangout thing,' huh? And who are 'these girls?'"

It dawned on me that I didn't really know. It would have been impossible for me to properly explain the scenario to my mom in a way that made sense. When she was growing up, I'm sure that dating worked a lot differently than for people nowadays. For her, the guy probably showed up at the girl's doorstep with a flower and met her father and said, "I fancy your daughter" and stated his intentions and all that. Everybody was on the same page. *Things have become a lot more complicated since then*, I reasoned.

I opened my mouth to tell my mom that she just didn't get it, but I had to stop myself. Maybe my mom got it and maybe she didn't, but that was beside the point; I realized that I didn't get it either. Not being able to even tell her the girls' names was a bad look, and so was my failure to fully describe where I was headed and what I was planning to do. I sounded like Spaz trying to tell me about the takeout containers in dry storage.

"They live out on the Peninsula, Mom. They saw me while I was at work earlier and invited me down to hang out. It's not a big deal—I can go, right?"

She gave me a skeptical look after hearing that last part.

"So you put that much body spray on for things that aren't a big deal then?"

My face turned red. It was no use. I tried to explain things in a way that could add a little more context to the circumstances, but all I could get out were a few rounds of "the thing is . . ." and "see, it's like . . ." and pointing (kind of desperately) with both hands to the general direction of downtown. She had the type of posture that suggested she might put a stop to this nonsense all at once and tell me I was staying home.

"Look, son, I've really appreciated the way you've stepped up this summer. I know it must be frustrating having to work so much and not getting to keep all of the money. You've done a good job of staying out of trouble too, so I'm not going to stop you if this is really something that you want to do. Just be careful . . . and make intelligent decisions."

The two skateboard guys bustling around inside my head were having a hard time keeping a straight face at the "intelligent decisions" part, but I kept them quiet and nodded back at Mom as she finished. She added a part about not wanting to see me disappointed if the night didn't work out as I'd planned. I could tell from her genuine concern that this wasn't just one of her lectures; I couldn't let her see that, though. Without looking her in the eye, I shrugged and tried to play it off.

"Come on, Mom. I told you, it's not a big deal."

It *was* a big deal though, and I knew it. Leaving the house for the second time that day, I might have been unrecognizable from the person who had walked down those steps earlier in the same morning. Gone was the 40-percent dead feeling, and in its place, I was overflowing with anxiousness and life. Based on the electricity circulating through my body, I could have been going to the gym for the first game of a new basketball season.

I decided to walk down to the Peninsula. Somehow, that seemed more dignified than taking my bike. Plus, I still had extra time to kill before the meetup, and I was buzzing too much to stay in the house any longer. I calculated out that the walk downtown would take about twenty-five minutes, and then another fifteen to get over to the Peninsula from there. I dribbled an invisible basketball and did a few imaginary spin moves as I began to walk.

As I rounded the curve at the bottom of the hill to downtown, I walked past the green awning of the Number One Rebaires building. I hadn't noticed before, but there was a wooden sign featuring a cocky-looking cartoon tiger extending out from the building over the top of the awning. He winked as he signaled number one with his pointer finger. I still had no idea what was sold there or the type of business they did, but I couldn't help grinning as I looked at the tiger. Vaguely wondering just who these "Rebaires" were and which category they ranked at the top of, I kept on walking as my anticipation for the Peninsula built.

I got downtown and passed a group of high school guys and girls, summer kids laughing and flirting as they bit into ice cream cones near the waterfront. Ordinarily, I would have been annoyed and probably a little jealous too at their easygoing confidence, their effortless attractiveness and social dominance. Tonight, I grinned and gave a friendly head nod as I strolled past them. If they were members of some sort of unofficial but exclusive club of the social elite, then I was just a few minutes away from being fully initiated myself. Any other time, I probably would have seen them as being above me, but tonight we were equals.

Walking past the public beach, I felt a surge of superiority. It was nearly dark now, and another group about my age, all of them guys, were lounging and passing the time on the cracked stone structure surrounding the fancy public drinking fountain. I imagined that they hung out here pretty much every weekend, sort of entertained but secretly wishing for something more to do with their Saturday night. Once again, I got a thrill out of the feeling that this other glamorous world was about to be opened up to me: the exclusiveness of this other side to Bellview, with its security alarm systems, private beaches, and mansions posing as cottages, not to mention the parties and hangouts with the girls staying there. After another five minutes of walking, I reached the giant iron-wrought gates that marked the entrance to the South Point Peninsula.

CHAPTER TWENTY-THREE

Security

Since the Peninsula is a gated community, they have a security guard sitting in a booth at the front, twenty-four hours a day. Like a bouncer at a nightclub, the guard checks all visitors in to make sure they belong, preventing outsiders from stepping through the towering metal gateway entrance. Since the girl from my earlier phone call said that she would add my name to the visitor's list, I felt a little like a big-shot VIP as I walked up to the booth to announce my arrival. The security guard was sitting in front of four television monitors; three of them looked like surveillance cameras set up at various points on the Peninsula. On the other one, he was watching some sort of detective TV show—either *CSI* or *Law & Order*. He had on a nametag showing that his name was Marvin.

"Name?"

"Hi, I'm JB. I'm attending a gathering in the residence at 15 South Beacon tonight."

I don't know what made me say it like that, other than that the place seemed super fancy, with the front gates and security and everything. I was trying to make it look like I belonged, and they probably called date/hangouts "gatherings" around here and referred to their houses as "residences."

The guy behind the booth didn't strike me as a typical security guard type. He looked pretty young and didn't have a very tough or imposing demeanor to him, like I would have expected. He talked like he was still in high school.

"A 'gathering,' huh? Whatever, bro. Last name?"

I gave it.

"Cool. Just wait there by the entrance. I'll buzz you in."

I went and stood in front of the iron gateway, feeling like I was about to be granted an audience with royalty or something. Guess that explains where the term "Peninsula Princess" comes from. Thinking I was clever, I held my hands behind my back and softly whistled that royal-sounding Great Britain theme song while waiting for Marvin to buzz me in.

"Hold on, wait a second, dude . . . ha-ha-ha! Yo, this is nuts, you gotta see this."

I twisted my head to look back at him. I just wanted to get through the gate; I didn't care what was happening on *Law & Order*. What could be so funny that this security guard—who didn't act like a security guard—could possibly need me to come back and look at? He urgently motioned me back to the window of his station.

"It says here that you're banned for life, bro! Ha-ha-ha, that's awesome!"

I felt all of the color drain out of my face and settle down in my thighs, like twin anchors on one of the sailboats in the harbor.

"There's gotta be a mistake!" I said with more conviction than I really felt. I knew that there wasn't any mistake. A year ago, I got caught inside one of the houses on Perry Drive. In the end, the South Point Homeowners' Association had decided not to press any criminal charges. This must have been their way of getting even. Banned for life though? But I was *invited!* The security guard shook his head, basking in the glow of this unusual turn of events.

"I've been here for like five months, and this is the first time I've ever seen this, man. You're a total badass—what did you *do* to these guys?!"

I pleaded my case. I rambled on, telling him all about the restaurant, and the note, and the "*Wanna chill?*," and the phone call, and anything else I could think of that might make him push the button and just open up the gateway already. I asked for an exception. An amnesty. A grace period. Anything that might be able to get me out to 15 South Beacon.

"You're insane, kid. No wonder you got tossed from this place!"

"Couldn't you just, you know, *accidentally* let that gate swing open, and then maybe get caught up in your TV show for about the next thirty seconds? I swear, I'm not going to do anything bad, I just need to get through."

"Sorry, that's a no can do. I'm like, honored to be meeting you and everything, but the association would fire my ass in about two-point-two seconds if I let someone out there who wasn't supposed to be. Can't blame a guy for wanting to keep his job."

"Yeah, but that's the thing. I was actually invited! So you see, it's not a big deal. You can let me through."

Marvin stared at me, in the same way that Staples had when I was looking for loopholes to avoid Dumpster Duty on my first week of work. He wasn't budging on this, but my mind was on overdrive. I thought of one more way to solve the problem. I excitedly pointed out to the security guard that he must have a directory that keeps track of the names, addresses, and phone numbers of everyone that lived out there.

He could look up 15 South Beacon and find out their phone number, I could use his phone to call the girls, and they could come meet me at the front gate. If nothing else, I could at least explain the snag in the plans, and maybe we could still go someplace else to hang out. It sounded like a great idea to me, and I hurriedly asked the guard to look up the necessary information.

"That would be strictly pro-hibited."

I lost my temper.

"Ahh, screw that! I bet you don't know what 'prohibited' even means!"

"It means . . ." he snapped the fingers on his left hand and pointed at me in one quick motion, "you ain't calling."

He chuckled to himself, making me want to slug him in the face.

"Come on, you gotta understand—it was these five super, super hot girls! They were at the restaurant! I had it all set up! Come on!!"

From the other side of the glass, the security guard felt around for something unseen that was located in one of the desk drawers of the cramped booth. I wondered whether he was about to pull out a handgun on me, but instead it was a walkie-talkie.

"This is crazy. Come to think of it, I probably need BACKUP." He said it in a way that made me think he'd been waiting his entire life for the chance to call for backup. Holding the walkie-talkie up to his mouth and pressing the talk button with purpose he announced, "HQ, this is front desk, do you copy? Dewww, yewww, caa-pee?"

A muffled voice returned back through the speaker, sounding both bored and annoyed. "What do you want this time?"

"Hey, I got this kid over at the entrance gate trying to get to a gathering. Check this out, though—he is BANNED FOR LIFE on the Peninsula! You better get down here, Cap."

"I'm not coming down. Don't call me fricking 'Cap' either. Just tell him to go away or the police will be called."

"Roger that." The guard set down his walkie-talkie and dramatically cleared his throat. He wasn't smiling anymore, replacing it with a serious and grim appearance.

"Go away, or—"

"I KNOWW!!"

I turned and stormed off. I briefly threw my left arm up in the air over my shoulder as I walked, just because I was frustrated beyond belief and couldn't think of anything else to do. Back at the bottom of the driveway to the Peninsula entrance, angry and embarrassed, I made the puzzling decision to check my watch. Don't ask me why. Like what, maybe I'd just happened to choose a bad time to turn up? Maybe I was only banned for life because it was 9:43 on a Saturday night?

I wound up my leg and kicked a plastic grocery bag that was drifting across the sidewalk. It being 97 percent air, all that happened was that it moved about four inches before fluttering a little bit and then continuing to drift, giving me no angry satisfaction whatsoever. There was nothing left to do except turn around and start walking back the way I came.

I admitted to myself that the night was officially a lost cause. Even though my feet were aching, and it was pretty dark out, I trudged back, retracing the same route in reverse. I went past the public beach and grassy park on the other side of it, through the downtown area, and back to the base of the winding hill.

The big goofy tiger winked at me again as I slumped past the Number One Rebaires. I wanted to give a number one signal of my own to that idiot tiger, except using a different finger. I wanted to scream at him, to tell him that he sucks and that the Rebaires suck too, and that they're probably dead last in whatever the hell they even do and they're not fooling anyone, but no words would come out. That was my only lucky break of the evening, as there were still a few tourists walking around downtown. They likely would have been alarmed and called the cops if their nighttime stroll was ruined due to some unhinged teenager shouting obscenities at a wooden sign.

I continued back up to the top of the winding hill, and another fifteen miserable minutes through the buggy humidity until I was home again. Once upstairs, I passed by my brother's room, where he was collapsed on the futon and holding a videogame controller.

"Ayy, boy, 'ave a good time out there?"

I poked my head inside the doorframe to see what he wanted. He looked pretty mellowed out with beer; he must have been out partying with his college buddies after work. He was playing *Mario Golf* and paused to answer his own question.

"Naw. Naw man, of course you didn't. Yer's too young to do anything in this town, boy. That's why I gotta enjoy myself now. Yup, while I'm still young . . . but you're *too* young." Then he went straight back to playing.

I'm sure whatever he was talking about was making perfect sense inside his own head. He chuckled to himself, then sneezed and farted at the same time. Unbothered by this, he went on with his lecture—if that's what you want to call it.

"Don't worry though, boy, you'll get there. Oh yeah, you'll get there. I was just like you once. Yup, can't blame you. Good old high school Saturday nights, heh-heh. Just wait till college. Oh yeah, I got the job done!" I watched Rodney gaze fondly at the TV monitor as Luigi shanked a five-iron shot way to the right and out of bounds.

You've probably never "got the job done" in your entire life, you freaking idiot, I thought to myself, scowling and turning to leave the room.

"Ayy, just remember, man, it's really not that bad, once you git in there. I know wudyer thinkin', I know. Trust me though. Once yer innit, it's really not that bad."

I shook my head in disgust and didn't bother looking back.

"Sure thing. Have a good night, big guy."

Feeling more angry and sorry for myself than ever, I closed my door and collapsed into bed. When I finally worked up the nerve to change out of my clothes, I reflexively reached into my pockets to empty them out. Since I wasn't wearing my work shorts, this time around the pockets were already completely empty. No paycheck envelope, no stray napkins or forgotten pens, and of course, there was no "*Wanna Chill?*" paper, which had started this whole mess of an evening roughly ten hours earlier.

I flipped out my light and flipped on the window fan, which immediately started humming. The extra noise thankfully stopped Rodney from hearing the pathetic sobbing noises as I miserably plopped face-first back into bed and allowed my pillow to be drenched in salty, thoroughly defeated tears. So much for wanting to chill.

CHAPTER TWENTY-FOUR

Hangingness

I took a deep breath before stepping through the back entrance to Jimmy's on Monday. Not because the combo smell of fries and bleach was starting to nauseate me (which was also true), but because I was feeling like a gladiator about to be fed to the lions. Apart from two hours spent locked into a surprisingly productive basketball workout, most of my day off had been used to mentally prepare myself to face my coworkers once I returned.

Seeing Staples, Cal and the older cooks, Merryll, and Lacy (probably even Gloria) trying their hardest not to laugh in my face had gotten old pretty fast. Five or six times throughout the morning, in addition to my usual "clear, spray, and wipe" routine, I had the unwanted task of explaining my epic failure from the weekend.

I guess I could have lied and made up some wild story, with me as the charming hero, but what would the point of that be? Staples would've instantly seen right through me, Jennie would press for details until my story fell apart, and Cal would just tell an even wilder fairy tale, depicting himself as even more charming and heroic. Either way, I knew what had really happened, and that was bad enough. Plus, I'd accidentally had plenty of practice with this sort of thing last year, answering for myself any time a relative or friend of the family asked why I wasn't on the basketball team. Since everyone was suddenly so curious regarding my social life, I figured I might as well just tell the truth.

Certain parts I left out, like how I'd tried to call the number from the "*Wanna Chill?*" paper the next day, only to find out that the line was disconnected—it wasn't even a real number. I also didn't admit how many times that day I glanced over toward Table 36, just in case the girls came back in wondering what had happened and wanting to try again. I basically told them the rest though. About the call on speakerphone, the walk through downtown, and my conversation with Marvin the security guard. About my original trip to the Peninsula, and how I ended up getting banned for life.

"Wait a second—that was you?" Staples must have already been away for college when all that went down. He wasn't particularly bothered or impressed by it, however, only saying with mild interest, "I underestimated you, Beanie."

Jennie had kept away from us somewhat, not asking any direct questions, but quietly paying attention to the side conversations all the same. She wouldn't say it, but I got the impression that she was secretly glad that things hadn't worked for me on Saturday night. Whenever she came over to us to talk though, it was strictly business-related.

"Hey, Staples, just a heads-up, your next drink ticket is going to say Coke," directed Jennie. "But what the kid actually ordered is every single type of pop mixed together. There's not a name for it on DigiServ."

"It's going to get them sick," Staples protested.

"Nuh-uhh, I do it all the time!" said Cal, bringing his own XL plastic cup over to the soda fountain for a refill. He took the spray gun and filled the red cup with Coke, Diet Coke, Sprite, orange soda, Jimmy's Good Ol' Root Beer, iced tea, fruit punch, and Mountain Dew. "And it's called a 'Nuclear Fizz.'"

"Case in point," said Staples. He narrowed his eyes as he watched Cal take a satisfied gulp. "I'm not making this, Jennie. Go tell the kid to order something else. And to find a new role model."

The lunch rush went on until nearly three, but shortly after that was a steep drop-off in customers, leaving the staff with some extra time on our hands as the early shift crawled near its end. Teasing me about my misadventure on the Peninsula was probably the first time that Cal and Staples had ever teamed up on anything, so the soda fountain became a no-fly zone for the end of that afternoon as far as I was concerned.

"Ayy, JB," Spaz called out to me, carrying over a steaming plastic cylinder full of clean silverware to the waitress booth. "You doing anything after work today?"

Spaz was pretty much the only person who wasn't interested in getting the full rundown of my big night on the Peninsula. Naturally, by the end of the day, Spaz was pretty much the only person there that I didn't mind talking to. Wanting to avoid my coworkers, I'd made sure to keep to myself in the shadows of the waitress station

Before the end of my shift, I needed to wrap the fork-and-knife combos into individual napkins anyway, stacking about a hundred or so into a plastic tub to get through dinner. As I went to work on this, Spaz pulled off his elbow-high rubber gloves and set up next to me.

Apparently forgetting that he'd just asked me a question, Spaz grabbed out a napkin and turned his attention to rolling it around the silverware. He was the type of guy who always preferred to be moving around and doing something. Even though the vacant dining room meant time to relax for others, Spaz wasn't the sort of person who took much pleasure in relaxation. You could visibly see him start to twitch a little bit when he went even a few minutes without having something to do.

It reminded me of the time he said he was a "restaurant guy" when he first got hired. In an unexpected way, it made me a little envious to see Spaz enjoying his job so much. Jimmy and Gloria enjoyed having him too; the guy worked hard. Harder than just about anyone else there.

The more I got to know him, it wasn't all that difficult to see why dishwashing at a local restaurant meant that much to him. Around school, there wasn't really a specific person or group that he gravitated towards. This was probably how he ended up often sitting with me at the Lunch Table Democracy during freshman year, with a crew of misfits that was more like an Island of Lost Toys than anything. And even then, he drifted on and off the island depending on the week. I guess you could say he had a hard time fitting in. Then again, "fitting in" isn't really the goal for a guy like Spaz.

"At school, most people just think I'm goofy or weird. Half the things I say, and it's, 'Oh man, there goes crazy ol' Spaz again.' It's different around here. Yeah, people still give me crap sometimes here too, but they also need my help. I get to wash dishes and check out what Cal's making over on the grill, plus Jimmy and Gloria are always supportive." He stopped speaking long enough to stack a set of ten fresh silverware combos into the tub. "I always like bringing dishes out to the dining room too—there's usually something interesting going on. Mostly I just like the hangingness of it all. A lot of people to talk to, a lot happening."

I think "hangingness" was Spaz's word for the feeling of camaraderie that happens when everyone is working towards the same goal. I often noticed that feeling among basketball teammates during a close game, but I can't say I felt it while working at the restaurant. It never occurred to me that someone might consider washing dishes to be an exciting and interesting team effort. I'd always thought of my job as little more than showing up for my shift, counting down the minutes until it's over, trying not to screw anything up, and at least getting those paychecks to show for it. Or maybe Spaz was right, and I hadn't been paying enough attention to what it was really like.

During slow periods in his shift, it wasn't unusual for Spaz to be plucking bristles out of the brooms to keep them from getting ratty, running stacks of dishes through the conveyor belt to the washer two or three times in a row, or stacking all the half-pint cartons of milk in the mini-fridge.

"Thanks, man, it's cool though. You don't have to help."

I'd seen Merryll, Cal, and even Jimmy take advantage of this trait in him, asking Spaz to do some of their tasks for them when they simply didn't feel like it. It always made me vaguely angry watching it happen. Spaz didn't seem to mind, and he may have even been enjoying himself, but it made me a little uneasy for him to be working on something that was technically my responsibility. I appreciated getting that little bit of extra help from him; I just wanted to make sure it was entirely his call, and that he didn't feel forced into it.

"What were you saying about after work today?"

"Huh?"

"When you brought out the forks and all that . . . you made it sound like you had plans for after work."

Spaz rubbed his finger around the inside of his ear for moment, puzzled before searching through his memory bank and realizing that he in fact did have plans for after work.

"Right! Yeah, me and Marty are going to hang out. Do you know him?"

I had to laugh. Of course I knew Marty. Spaz *knew* that I knew Marty. All of us had been classmates since elementary school, when Marty first moved to town. I still felt a little ashamed at how badly we treated him in elementary school. Marty must be made of some stronger stuff though, because he never let it break him. By the start of middle school, he had blended in to the point where he gained something closer to acceptance.

Freshman year, when the roles were reversed and *I* was the one without any friends, I could always count on an open spot at Marty's lunch table. Over the years, I'd developed a weird type of respect for him. He was a welcoming face in the crowd, and definitely an underdog to root for, if never entirely a friend. We had all ridden out to Five Mile Creek together. I hadn't seen or talked to him since school let out in June.

"Yeah, I definitely know him."

"You should hang out with us too then," said Spaz, as if

that settled things. In his world, knowing somebody was apparently the only criteria needed in order to make plans with them.

"Can't tonight. There's an open gym up at school this evening, and I'm supposed to work out with Blaise after that."

"You can't miss one?"

"I've missed too many already this summer. I'm finally getting back in the groove a little bit, so I don't want to ruin the momentum."

Spaz's answer was the same—wait, that's not right. It was a *question*. With him, sometimes questions felt like answers, and the other way around. Spaz's *question* was the same.

"You can't miss one?" he repeated.

"I don't really have a choice—not if I want to make varsity next year, anyway."

I tried to convey to Spaz the difference between making the JV and varsity teams at school, and the status that comes with it. It was like night and day. Even in the summer months, the next Eagles' basketball season was never far from the minds of locals, the varsity team being the stars of the show. Especially the select few who make it as a freshman or sophomore.

"Does it really matter if you're not on the more prestigious team? As long as you're playing basketball, shouldn't that be all that matters?"

"No one cares about the JV team. It's completely different. You just don't get it."

"I don't think there's anything to get. There are two teams. Whichever level you're at, that's the one you can be on."

By this point, I was pretty annoyed with Spaz. I'm not sure whether it was because I wasn't getting my point across, or maybe just the fact that Spaz was disagreeing with me and I couldn't think of a good response to send back at him. So rather than just try to repeat myself again and hope for a completely different result, I did what any good debater would do. I flipped the subject back to him.

"Well, what about you?"

"What about me?"

To be honest, I didn't know "what about" Spaz, but at least my question bought me a little more time to think. I even purposely dropped a butter knife on the floor so that I'd need to take a couple extra seconds to pick it up. Seeing the fronts of his beat-up running shoes, a good response finally came to me and I rose back up from the floor.

"You've been running like five miles a day to get to work all summer, but you won't even join the track team!"

"So?"

"So, it's pointless. You do all this training, but you're not training *for* anything. You seriously don't think it would be cool to race against other people? You'd probably win most of the time!"

"Could happen, I guess. It still wouldn't be worth having to go to practice every day."

I'd completely given up on the silverware-rolling project and put my hand in my pockets. It was difficult to tell the direction that any particular conversation with the Spaz could go. I could feel this one slipping away from me.

"What are you talking about?? You go running just about every day anyway! You *like* it!"

"Well, yeah. I do it when it's time to come to work, or else just whenever I feel like it. If I was on a team, it would be like,

'Oh, it's three o'clock now, time to go run in circles for an hour just because a guy with a clipboard and a whistle says so.' That sounds like it sucks."

"Don't you want to, like, challenge yourself though? Every day, you can keep trying to beat your personal bests. Keep lowering your times, you know?"

"So then what—the faster I go, that means the more fun I must be having?"

Spaz shrugged dismissively. With the way he had his yellow rubber gloves tucked into the waistband of his pants, it was hard to take him seriously. However, I would be lying if I said he wasn't making some interesting points. Calling it like I see it, he definitely won the argument.

As I finished wrapping the remaining sets of forks and knives, there was a small part of me that sort of wanted to blow off basketball and go hang out with Marty and Spaz. By the end of my shift though, the feeling had passed. Before leaving, I reminded Gloria that I had a dentist appointment the next day and would be coming an hour late. Then, with an apology and some well-wishes, Spaz and I exited the back door and began heading separate ways. Spaz walked towards the docks, and I mentally prepared for the gym and the bike ride back up the hill, leaving the fumes of grease and cleaning solutions behind until the next afternoon. To my surprise, Blaise was waiting for me next to the dumpster, wearing a backpack and holding an outdoor basketball.

"Hey, Blaise, what's up? Thought we were meeting at the gym."

"I can't do gym tonight, man; I need to change things up. Let's go see if the Mirage is open."

CHAPTER TWENTY-FIVE

The Mirage

There's this tucked-away basketball court in a corner of the downtown area, nestled between the boathouse and a small cluster of condominiums. I'm positive that Blaise and I weren't the only two people who knew about this court, but it sure felt like it. Two years after we discovered it for the first time, we made at least a few dozen trips over to play on it. Sometimes squirrels would run across the surface of it, but we'd never seen another person on the court while we were there.

As far as outdoor courts go, this one was a ballplayer's dream. On a typical playground court, it can get pretty frustrating to play outside; gusts of wind and even light breezes frequently pushed longer shots off target and were impossible to predict. If that wasn't difficult enough, most outdoor hoops have such tight double rims that it's nearly impossible to get a friendly roll. There's very little room for error when aiming up a shot, and the harsh aluminum backboards at most of the school playgrounds weren't much help either. At this hidden court though, the conditions were nearly ideal.

The cement was painted a deep shade of blue, which perfectly matched the color of Lake Bellview on a sunny afternoon. It had a free throw line and three-point arc expertly stenciled in white paint, and the lane was filled in with a refreshing lime green. The whole scene gave off a real elite feel to it; like anyone who played on a court like that must really be able to ball. In my mind, it was as close to perfection as an outdoor basketball court could possibly be.

It was only a half-court, but the single basket had a clean fiberglass backboard and a forgiving breakaway rim. The pole of the basket support had thick padding wrapped around it, matching the lime green from the lane, in case someone got fouled during an acrobatic drive and crashed into it. The annoying breezes were never a problem there, because not only did the boathouse shield away the wind, but there were also thick pine trees in the surrounding yard area that offered additional sanctuary from the forces of nature.

There were a few layers of some sort of extra coating poured onto the cement, making it easier on the knees than asphalt or a typical slab of concrete. Plus, there were what looked like grains of sand mixed into the top layer of paint, providing nearly perfect traction (even without a pair of No-Slip Jimmys). Compared to the anthills that popped up on my driveway court, or the cracked and uneven ones at school, the traction was something to savor.

Blaise and I nicknamed it the "Mirage," because it seems to spring up out of nowhere. It's so out of place that when we first discovered it, it was almost like our eyes were playing tricks on us. As if it were only a mirage in the middle of a basketball desert, appearing through the haze, but ready to disappear as soon as we got close enough to touch it. As far as the atmosphere goes, the only place in town I could possibly think of that would be better to play would be to shut down traffic and set up hoops right in the middle of Main Street.

I'm not entirely positive that this hidden spot was meant to be a public court. On the one hand, it looks like it's placed in the backyard of either the marina or the condo association's property. At the same time though, there's a stone footpath to get back there, and there weren't any visible "Private Property" or "No Trespassing" signs around. If anybody ever came back there and told us to leave, of course I'd be disappointed, but I'd understand and go without complaining. Like I said though, no one had ever been out there at the same time as us. On a day where the stuffy indoor gymnasium had very little appeal, it's easy to see why the Mirage was the much more attractive option to play ball at.

CHAPTER TWENTY-SIX

Seagulls

The Mirage wasn't far from Jimmy's—probably only a walk of about ten minutes or so. I left my bike where it was and grabbed the basketball from Blaise, dribbling it along the pavement as we walked. One of the Real Housewives was talking on a cell phone without paying attention to where she was going on the sidewalk, so I made a quick juke and bounced the ball behind my back to avoid bumping into her. Blaise said I was showing off, which was probably true, but I didn't really care. I was excited about going to the Mirage, and it felt good to have my ballhandling skills slowly returning to me.

"My brother's probably working today," I mentioned, pointing at the boathouse as we started getting close to it. There was a flock of seagulls impatiently sitting on the grooved aluminum roof. Their ugly eyes were intently fixed on something concealed to us by the brown walls of the building. Blaise's eyes danced a little bit when I brought up Rodney.

"You wanna go in there and mess with him?"

I laughed at the suggestion, but quickly declined. "Aren't we retired from that sort of stuff?"

"Yeah, you're right," he said, slowing down his walk and gazing longingly at the front door. "Would've been great, though."

"So why no gym today?" I asked, changing the subject, just in case Blaise still had ideas about messing with Rodney while he was at his job. "What's going on?"

Blaise tugged at the side of his shorts, seeming like he was having a hard time turning whatever he was thinking into actual words. He had that exhausted look that was only noticeable when I was standing right next to him.

"Remember when we used to just play ball?"

"What are you talking about, isn't that what we still do?"

Blaise took a quick swipe at the rock as I bounced it, but I switched hands too fast for him. I picked up the dribble and faked like I was going to pass it straight at his face. He didn't flinch in the slightest.

"I've been *training* a lot. I've been *competing* a lot. I've been *working out* a lot. As far as actually playing, though? Nah, it's been forever since I've done that."

He talked about the intensity of his training, and the pressure of his weekend tournaments, where impressing the right person at the right time could make the different between going to college or not. Most of all, however, he seemed bothered and overwhelmed by the rising expectations of certain people around town.

"I was at the drugstore this morning, picking up some Advil and vitamins for my mom, and Mr. Floyd flagged me down. He told me all about how he used to play for the

Eagles, back in the '50s or something, when they won the state championship. He said that most of the local newspapers are already predicting us to finish first in the conference next year."

Personally, I would have been honored to be recognized in public for something positive for once. Besides, after working at Jimmy's all summer and seeing the area become overrun by vacationers and Peninsula dwellers, I would've welcomed talking hoops with a local.

"What's the big deal? That sounds cool. Would be nice for this town to be known for something other than the damn Peninsula. Must be cool to be getting that kind of respect from people."

Blaise lowered his eyes and slowly shook his head, smiling tolerantly as if something was being lost in translation.

"Yeah, it would be nice, if that's really what he meant by it. The way this guy said it, though . . . it sounded more like a threat than an encouragement. Like, 'So now you'd better actually go out and win the conference, and screw you if you can't.' We had a nice run over the second half of last year, with the winning streak and all, especially since it was so unexpected. Now, though, unless we do all that again plus a lot more, it's like in their minds we personally failed all of them."

On the outside, you would never know that Blaise felt any pressure. The way he played when he was on the court was always so confident and quietly intense. In his day-to-day life he had such a single-minded focus towards his own business that I was surprised to learn that other people's opinions affected him this much.

"I know it sounds kind of mean, but some of the people

around here, they're not all that different from those seagulls." He nodded back at the gritty group of white birds on the boathouse roof. "They see one tiny little piece of food off in the distance, and suddenly the whole flock shows up out of nowhere and wants a piece. And obviously that one little bread crust isn't going to feed all of them, so they demand more and more and more. Until obviously you have nothing left to give, and even if you did, they still would never be satisfied anyway."

Blaise seemed to get a cold chill at the thought, widening his eyes and blinking as if to jolt his mind back to the present.

"I'm telling you, JB, there are some weird 'fans' around here."

Noticing that his shoelace had come untied, Blaise stopped on the sidewalk, kneeling down to take care of it. He kept on talking.

"You know what some old guy said to me last winter? I was picking up breakfast at the IGA before open gym, the morning after the Silverledge game. You know, it was the one where we were up by 20 in the first half, but then fell apart towards the end."

"You still won, but they came all the way back to force overtime." Despite my best efforts to avoid paying attention, I had almost every detail about the previous basketball season memorized.

"Yup, that one. And this guy in the store comes up to me while I'm waiting in line—he recognized me. He's wearing a flannel jacket and an Eagles hat. I remember him having a gross boil on the side of his nose, and these full-rimmed glasses that made his eyes look huge. He walked at me with this really pissed-off look on his face. He's on that, 'How'd you blow such a huge lead? What the hell happened out there?' Not only was he acting like we'd lost, but he even seemed to think that it was his personal privilege to scold me about it! And this is early on a Saturday morning, while I'm already headed to the gym to work on my game."

Blaise rarely showed emotion, but this was something he was clearly getting worked up about, even remembering it months later. He pulled at his shoelace so hard I was surprised that it didn't snap in half. Not satisfied with how it felt, his undid the knot and tried it again.

"Keep in mind, this is after we *beat* Silverledge. So that should tell you what things can be like if we lose. I ran into that same guy again at the very end of the season, right after we got knocked out of the playoffs."

"You guys got destroyed in that one."

"Yeah, we got completely run off the floor—lost by twenty-five or whatever. After the game, I was walking out towards the bus, trying to get past this huge crowd of people in the hallway. I felt a hand pat me on the shoulder as I'm shuffling through there, so I turned around and this old-timer is standing there again. I thought he was about to be like, 'good game, good season, good luck next year,' that sort of thing. But no. He's staring at me all scandalized, like I was refusing to pay my taxes.

He says for everyone around to hear, 'So what *happened* out there??' I tried to shrug it off, you know, tell him we just couldn't get the offense going, all that. He scoffed at that and goes, 'Well, maybe next year will go a little better if you try to take your head out of your ass *before* the game."

"Hold on a second—he said what?" I stopped Blaise. "He did not..."

I was torn between whether I thought that was hilarious, or just disturbing. I could picture Jimmy saying that, except he didn't care one bit about basketball as far as I knew. Blaise raised up his hands, not knowing what else to say. He stood back up and we kept walking in the direction of the court.

"I can't make this stuff up, it's crazy. Keep in mind, I had one of my best games of the season, we just got beat by a better team. They're seagulls, man. Coming up through peewee ball and middle school, I remember people always asking how the team was doing. I used to think they were just happy to see us play, and that they just really like the sport. By the time you get up to varsity though, it's like they think we owe them something. When you really get down to it, what do they even get out of it? Like, what's the point? I dunno, man. If it weren't for all this other stuff, I might actually like basketball."

Blaise didn't realize it, but the way he was talking was reminding me of Spaz.

"What are you saying? You don't like basketball anymore?"

We weaved around the buildings of the condominium complex. We retraced the off-the-path route, pushing tree branches to the side and stepping through rows of woodchips that were laid out as part of the landscaping. Blaise answered my question.

"I *love* basketball. And it's going to give me opportunities that I'll never have otherwise, so I definitely appreciate it. But no, I don't like it. Not at the moment, anyway."

We passed through a narrow alley and came out on the stone path of the courtyard, right next to the Mirage. From well beyond the trees and the buildings, the lighthouse on the edge of the Peninsula was partially visible in the distance, just barely within my sight, but permanently out of reach. The glistening backboard and shiny orange ring of the basket came into focus. For the first time in more than a dozen trips down there, the court was already occupied.

CHAPTER TWENTY-SEVEN

Two-on-Two

The sight of someone else using what Blaise and I had started to think of as *our* court (even though it obviously wasn't ours) was unsettling. Pressing the slightly worn outdoor ball to my hip, I stopped in my tracks. The two people who were shooting around on the hoop were about our age. I didn't recognize either of them, figuring that they must be from out of town.

I looked at the two of them and immediately decided that I disliked them for a wide variety of reasons. There was the fact that they were rich Peninsula kids, that they were wearing indoor soccer shoes to play basketball, and they were on *our* court. Then, of course, came my wild speculations that their parents were probably the ones who'd banned me for life, and they were the ones who ended up getting to chill with the girls from the restaurant the other night, and that maybe they were the actual owners of the court.

Considering the trouble I'd gotten into in the past that involved trespassing, my initial feeling was that we should just call the whole thing off. These summer kids probably had security guards on speed dial and could get us dragged out of there in an instant if they really wanted to. It wasn't ideal, but we could always just go back up to the school gym like the original plan had called for. Of course, it was less scenic, more sweltering, and less exciting than playing at the Mirage, but at least we could get a workout in without any trouble. Before I was able to vocalize this thought to Blaise, though, he'd already strolled over to join the two strangers on the court, quickly striking up a conversation with them.

"You guys up here all summer?"

"Nah, just for a week. We have a cottage rented on South Point. I'm Weston, by the way."

"I'm Blaise. Where are you guys from?"

"Birmingham. Michigan, not Alabama. Our dads work together at Chrysler. We've been coming up here like what— six years, Reed?"

Weston motioned over to his friend, who was removing a wristwatch and a necklace, setting them on the lawn chair near the court, leaving them next to a hat and wallet that were already placed there. Reed was very tall with long limbs. He turned to face us, a little uneven looking, like one of his legs was a tiny bit longer than the other, causing a slightly off-balance effect to his stance. It was a little like seeing an alternate universe version of Cal—an opposite day, Peninsula-kid version—who does play basketball but doesn't wear basketball shoes.

"Yeah, bro, every summer, man, six or seven years at least." Reed nodded at Blaise and I, inhaling quickly from the side of his nose, maybe sniffing out that we were locals. "It's really cool coming up here—you know what I'm saying? This place is solid, you guys are lucky."

"Don't know about 'lucky,' but yeah it's alright," Blaise replied.

Making small talk came much easier for Blaise than it did for me. While he stood there calmly chatting with the Peninsula kids about how "solid" our hometown was (let's see them spend a winter here, and then ask them how solid they think it is), I just wanted to get the game started and crush these guys.

"Game is to fifteen?"

"Yup. All ones, or ones and twos?"

Blaise tugged at his baby-blue athletic shorts, which were long enough to just barely cover the top of his knees. On the left leg was the logo of the showcase tournament that he had played in at the very beginning of the summer. Him and Weston had been doing most of the talking up to this point, so it was natural that they were the ones negotiating the terms of our two-on-two game.

I was silently hoping that Weston would choose "ones and twos" so that my deadly three-point shot would be extra valuable. I imagined the look on Spaz's face if I had to sit down and try to talk to him about how pickup basketball works. The conversation would go something like this:

Why would threes only be worth two? That just makes it a little easier to keep track of without a scoreboard. *Wait—but if threes are only worth two, how is that extra valuable?* Because it's worth double the points of a regular shot when you play with that type of scoring. *So then twos are only worth one?* Now you're getting the hang of it. *Is there such thing as a one-point shot in a regular game?* Yeah, free throws. *Wait, how so much are free throws worth in this interesting format? Zero?*

I knew at that point of the conversation, I would break down and start laughing, and then admit that there aren't free throws in pickup, so they are technically worth zero.

Shoot—I would just foul every single time then. Never let the other guys score. That wouldn't work. *If there're not even free throws, what's the worst that could happen?* You'd probably end up getting in a fight. *Yeah, I don't really like fighting either.* Besides, that's not the point of the game anyway.

And then of course Spaz would hit me with the big question: *Yeah, so what is the point?* I wouldn't be able to come up with a good answer on the fly, but I'd know that deep down, there was some greater and more meaningful point to it all— there had to be.

This time I thought to myself, *Sure, keep telling yourself that.*

My daydream ended when Weston chose ones and twos, and I had to stop myself from doing a little fist pump of celebration. Blaise wasn't finishing ironing out the details of the game though.

"Want to do alternating possessions, or make it/take it?"

"Let's go with make it/take it."

"Fine."

Blaise slightly frowned as he agreed. I knew that he hated playing make it/take it because it didn't simulate an actual full-court game. In his mind, even pickup games should be as close to the real thing as possible. Plus, he genuinely enjoyed playing defense. In make it/take it, if a team scores, they automatically get the ball back for the next possession. In a sense, scoring was actually somewhat of a punishment for

Blaise in this format, since it deprived him of the opportunity to defend.

"Shoot for ball." Blaise rolled it to Reed, the tall lefty, whose shot from the top of the key rattled around on the rim before sneaking through the net.

"Nice shot. Your ball first."

"You sure you don't want a rebuttal?"

The Peninsula kid was probably being overly polite, giving Blaise a chance to match his shot. If he'd known better, he'd understand that Blaise actually *wanted* to play defense first. No rebuttal would be necessary.

"Nah, check it up."

Reed flipped the ball to Blaise to check the ball. Even in my daydream, I couldn't think of a simple way to describe to Spaz what "checking the ball" is; I could picture the bullcrap sensors in his retinas going mad as he stared me down and wondered why you have to pass the ball to the other team first, *before* inbounding it to your teammate. I would probably sigh and tell him that's just the way it was, but only in pickup basketball, and he again would remind me that he didn't like sports, and I'd probably give up from there.

Blaise used the bottom of his royal blue Adidas shirt to remove any extra moisture off the ball and rolled it back to Reed. I got low in a defensive stance, ready to chase Weston and keep my body between him and the basket. I wiped the bottom of my white Nikes off with my hands for added traction and dug in as the ball was put into play.

The Peninsula kids took an early 2–0 lead. The tall lefty hit a jump hook over Blaise on the first possession, giving them the ball again. Weston then caught me off-balance on a pass fake, easily driving by for a layup. Blaise came in at the last moment to try and block it, arriving at the backboard just late enough to watch it bank in off the center square. He glared at me for letting my man drive past me so easily.

Weston tried the exact same move again on the next possession, but I was ready for it. I stuffed him with my right hand as he rose to shoot it, knocking the ball out of bounds. After retrieving it from the grass behind the hoop, I started to check the ball back to Weston for the next inbounds pass, but he admitted that it had touched his hands last, giving us our first possession.

Blaise and I wasted no time from there. Blaise used a smooth spin move to get past the big guy, twirling in an all-blue blur towards the lane. Weston went over to stop the drive, leaving me wide open on the right-side wing for a three-pointer (well, a two-pointer by these rules). Blaise sent a pass my way, and I shot it with confidence. It sunk straight in, barely grazing the rim. Game tied, 2–2.

As if to make me prove that the first shot wasn't a fluke, the Peninsula kids tried the same defensive strategy on the next play. They stopped Blaise from getting to the rim, but I was left open again, this time on the left wing. Same result: Locals 4, South Pointers 2.

Weston stayed much closer to me from then on. I caught another pass from Blaise and pump faked. Weston jumped at the fake, reaching his highest to block a shot that was never coming. I sidestepped him, letting him fly right past me, and then launched another deep shot. I was catching fire, and Blaise knew it. He raised his fist as the ball left my hand, not even bothering to go for the rebound. We'd been playing with each other long enough to know when the other's shot was going in, or whether we needed to chase it. This one swished. Bellview Boys 6, Peninsula Princes 2. Their people may own all the mansions and sailboats in town, but we owned them for the rest of the afternoon.

The first game went by quickly from there. Weston had a few shifty moves from time to time, but he wasn't a very good shooter, so he missed of a lot of open looks. The tall kid had some skillful post moves, but he was too slow to fake out Blaise and kept getting his passes deflected. I hit another two-pointer and a layup. Blaise got to the basket without much trouble, banking in short jumpers and spinning reverse layups off the glass. The final score was 15–4.

We played a second game, and it was more of the same. Blaise looked a little bit passive on offense. We both knew that he could take Reed off the dribble any time if he really wanted, but Blaise didn't really seem that interested in driving. Still, he used his court awareness to make clever passes to me and continually tip rebounds away from the taller kid. I missed some shots in the second game, but still made enough to put the game out of reach.

With the score at 14–5, the Peninsula kids' frustration was finally showing through. After running a perfect pick and roll play, Weston turned a corner and looked to have a clear layup as Blaise and I tried to fight off the screen and make a defensive switch. Weston started raising up to shoot it, but saw Blaise soaring out of the corner of his eye.

Weston tried to change his mind at the last second and stalled in midair. Trying to decide whether to shoot or pass, he did neither, landing right back where he started. He loudly swore and slammed the ball against the ground as hard as he could, while we both called him out for travelling.

Reed was frustrated too, and let his teammate hear about it.

"Come on, man! Take care of the ball!"

"Well, what the hell was I supposed to do?" Weston shot back. He raised a pleading hand over in Blaise's direction. "You saw that—he came out of nowhere. The guy is like a frickin' . . . Smurf . . . on *springs!*"

Blaise, wearing his all-blue outfit, could only stare at the ground after hearing this; Weston's comment had to be right up there on his "Weirdest Compliments Ever Received" rankings, but the point was made. The guy was everywhere on defense. We had the ball back, and Blaise iced a step-back shot from midrange to finish up the game. Our opponents decided to call it a day after that.

Honestly, I was expecting them to be arrogant jerks, but I had to admit that Weston and Reed turned out to be pretty cool guys after all. Just as in any basketball game, there had been a few arguments over an out-of-bounds or foul call, and a few rough plays with a push or a stray elbow, but overall, they played a clean game and seemed really impressed with us afterwards.

"Nice hooping with you guys," Weston said. "JB, keep working on that amazing shot. And Blaise . . . when you're in the NBA, I want tickets bro."

"Tickets." Blaise quietly repeated that last part, more to himself than to any of us. He looked like he was about to enter a place of deep thought, before snapping out of it when he noticed that Weston and Reed were walking away. "Later, guys.

CHAPTER TWENTY-EIGHT

Five Guys

Before going home from basketball, I still needed to grab my bike from Jimmy's. Blaise agreed to walk with me, but when we were about halfway back to the restaurant, he randomly suggested that we take a detour.

"Any interest in going by the beach for a little while?"

"The beach?"

"Yeah. You know, cool off and take a swim?" He seemed a little bit anxious, maybe worried that I would turn him down again, like on Saturday. "If you're busy, it's cool though. Not a big deal."

I hadn't had anything to eat since that morning's breakfast, but I'd lasted long enough that another hour or so wouldn't make much of a difference. My mom had been starting to get more of her hours back at the plastics factory, so I knew I would be on my own for dinner anyway. Thinking that I'd probably demolish an entire box of Mini-Wheats as soon as I got home, I agreed to the beach.

"Nice—I haven't been over there all summer." Blaise looked comforted. "Let's do this."

Instead of making the final turn for the restaurant, we stayed along the waterfront area, walking past the edge of downtown. Five minutes later, we made it over to the public beach, across the street from a grassy park and the pavilion with the fancy drinking fountain. It was starting to get late in the afternoon, but it was still hot out, and the place was still crowded with people on all sides.

Finding a small patch in the sand to leave our shoes and shirts, we immediately dove into the water. Being late in the afternoon, the sun had moved off to the side and was lowering just a little bit, angling off the water and turning it a darker shade of blue. The lake had finally reached that perfect temperature where it was cool enough to be refreshing, yet warm enough that it didn't shock the system by jumping in.

A series of white-and-orange buoys bobbed from side to side in the water, forming sort of a border around the swimming area. We raced out to the furthest one, furiously splashing through the water and scaring a seagull that had been perched on top of it. Both of us claimed that our hand hit the buoy first. After some friendly trash talk back and forth, we couldn't reach an agreement on who the winner was.

Laughing and flipping into a backstroke, Blaise continued swimming away from the shoreline without saying another word. Putting more and more distance between himself and the crowded swim zone, he broke past the perimeter of buoys and out into the open water. The Peninsula loomed large to the right, but otherwise there was nothing but open water for hundreds of yards. With his head barely visible over the surface of the water, Blaise continued getting smaller and smaller as he advanced through the lake towards wherever he was trying to go. Even just staying at the buoy and watching, there was something sort of majestic about it. If not for the screeching whistle from a lifeguard that forced him to turn back around, who knows when he would have returned.

After his moment had been rudely interrupted, Blaise wasn't interested in swimming much longer. We came back to the shore and stood in the sand, waiting for the warmth of the sun to dry us off.

"I could have made it all the way to the lighthouse . . . if not for Baywatch over there."

Blaise brushed a patch of wet hair off his forehead and glared out at the lifeguard: a pretty blonde college girl wearing a red swimsuit. She sat authoritatively on the wooden swim raft, which was anchored in the middle of the busy swim area. From the top of her lifeguard chair, she continued to blow the whistle every few minutes, reprimanding younger kids for roughhousing or running too much on the slippery dock.

While Blaise lamented his majestic swim being cut short, I heard someone call out my name from behind us. Well, they didn't call out *my* name, but it was one that I'd gotten used to responding to. It was someone who I wouldn't have ever expected to run into at the beach.

"Jelly Bean?"

Staples was wearing a plain white T-shirt, wrinkled plaid swim trunks, and a fading gray bucket hat. The area just above his ankles and all the way down to his feet were fully pale; it looked like this was the first time all summer he'd taken off his shoes and socks. He had friends with him, two guys who looked a lot more enthusiastic than him about being there.

They dragged along a cooler and some folding chairs, weaving around families and sand buckets as they followed Staples over to where Blaise and I were standing.

I found it almost impossible not to grin seeing Staples out there, looking so visibly out of place. There really wasn't anything wrong about his set of "beach clothes"—just that they looked like someone else should have been wearing them. I remembered categorizing him has an indoor cat when I first met him, and now I had more evidence.

"Staples! I never pictured you as a beach guy."

"I'm not one." He slumped his shoulders and mock-glared at me. "I'm more of a 'restaurant guy,' you should know that."

I laughed at his reference to Spaz, while my coworker explained the inside joke to his friends. To my surprise, one of them nodded in understanding, setting down the cooler and raising his hands up like oven mitts.

"Wait—you mean Yellow Gloves?" he quickly asked with excitement. Staples must have told these guys some Spaz stories before. I nodded and grinned wider.

"Yup, the one and only!"

The guys laughed and set a verbal reminder to try and go into the restaurant while Spaz was working sometime during their trip. Blaise glanced at us, and then back the water with a puzzled look on his face, unsure whether he should join the conversation or not.

"Jelly Bean, this is Connor and Eli, they're my housemates down at college." Staples played the role of the welcoming host. "Connor and Eli, this is Jelly Bean. And . . ."

"Blaise. He's a friend of mine, we were playing basketball after work."

Blaise nodded and shook hands with the two of them. I wasn't sure whether him and Staples had ever met before either, even though they knew *of* each other. So they did an awkward handshake too, and I guess everybody was properly introduced.

"Okay, so you guys have seen the beach," Staples said dully, presenting the water as if it were a lame prize on a game show. "Does this mean we can go now?"

Eli groaned and lunged at Staples, pulling the brim of his bucket hat down over his face. He pulled out a drink from the cooler and unfolded one of the beach chairs.

"So," I asked, facing Connor and Eli. "How did you convince this guy to come out here in the first place?" Staples looked salty and readjusted his hat, answering the question before his college buddies had a chance to.

"These jerks told me that they'd feel—what was the exact phrasing . . ." There went Staples, sounding like a professor again. "Oh yeah, 'personally and unforgivably cheated' if their visit passed without me showing them the splendors of the famous Lake Bellview."

"That sounds about right," said Eli, digging the metal slats of his chair deeper into the sand. "And the more you complain, the longer we stay!"

"Apparently, I don't know how 'lucky' I am to have grown up here," Staples added. "I guess the best way to show gratitude is to waste hours of my life sitting around on a patch of bright dirt and exposing my skin to cancerous UV rays at every opportunity. The life of luxury, indeed."

"Seriously, though, all this stuff around you growing up," Eli pointed out. "What more could you want?"

"Easy." Blaise passively traced a series of shapes in the sand with his toe, not bothering to make eye contact with anyone. "To get out."

No matter what Staples or Blaise said, his friends were clearly enjoying their vacation up north. With his fast and friendly voice, Eli flooded us about all they'd been up to since arriving that weekend, appreciating the scenery and the "paradise" feel to downtown and the waterfront. They'd gone for a hike in the woods on Sunday, and Eli made Staples promise to wake up early and take them fishing out on the Eagle River before they had to leave the next day.

The three of them started talking about going back to college in a month, and everything they planned on doing once they got back to Ann Arbor. I was relishing the feeling of being able to hold up during the conversation so far, especially since it was a rare time where Blaise found himself lost in the shuffle for the most part. I wanted to stay involved, so I asked Connor the only college-related question that I could think of.

"What's your major?"

"Econ." He pronounced it "*eee-con.*"

I looked over at Blaise to see if he understood. All he did was raise his eyebrows a little and shrug back at me. Staples's friends seemed cool though, so I didn't mind if I sounded dumb. I figured I'd just say it.

"I don't know what that is."

"Economics," Connor answered patiently. "How business works, how money works, how humans figure out how to make the most of what we have—that sort of thing."

"Yeah, and Connor's been shoving all his new econ

knowledge down our throats all trip," teased Eli. "What was it that you said this area was, a 'typical visitor economy?'"

"That's right. And whatever, man, that type of stuff is interesting."

Eli had put his sunglasses on, but it was still obvious that he was rolling his eyes at his buddy as he lightly scoffed and then turned his attention to the action on the swim raft. The lifeguard was yelling at some middle school boys, pointing back towards the sand as they cannonballed off the giant raft into the water and started to frantically swim away from her.

Hanging out with Staples and his friends, I was really starting to enjoy the vibe that they gave off—how smart they were, but also how easygoing they were at the same time. They could sit there and go back and forth roasting each other, but they never took it too far. Instead of getting mad or offended, the other one would always send back quick responses that were just as sharp. I found myself gravitated towards wanting to keep up with them.

"So if you're not into econ then, what's your major, polly-sy?" I was proud of myself for knowing the nickname for political science; thank you to Rodney for that one. At the suggestion of it, though, Eli pulled back a little bit, like I'd offered him a plate of fries that were too soggy.

"Nah, man, the political system in this country is so messed up, what's there to even study?"

Staples and Connor both chuckled knowingly at this one, while Blaise and I shrugged at each other again. Eli explained that he was an English Literature major. Jumping back in, Connor joked that until he met Eli, he used to think the only purpose of bookshelves was to hold video games.

"Yeah, and now look at you . . . needing a whole video game shelf of your own, just to hold all your precious Adam Smith and Karl Marx books!"

"Still beats Harry Potter and Ernest Hemingway," Connor shot back in a superior tone.

Eli started telling him that Ernest Hemingway spent every summer in Northern Michigan when he was growing up, and Connor reminded his friend that he'd already said that two or three hundred times on the car ride up, and Eli insisted that it was still awesome anyway, and Connor reminded him that he still didn't give a shit, and Staples tapped me on the shoulder.

"You never asked me what my major is, Jelly Bean."

Hearing this, Connor and Eli instantly stopped bickering, now ganging up on Staples. Eli made another grab towards his bucket hat, but Staples casually moved his head out of reach, still pretending that he wasn't enjoying his time at the beach.

"Aww, what's wrong, Stape, feeling left out?"

"Come on now, this is Stape's favorite party line—let him have his moment."

Staples dug his feet further into the sand, clearly wanting to announce his major, but not unless he was asked first. Surprised that this had never come up during downtime at the restaurant, I went ahead and took the bait.

"Okay. Well, what is it?"

"My first year, the plan was to be an English major too, like this guy," he said, flickering his gaze over to Eli. "Then I had to write an eighteen-page term paper on Beowulf. You heard of him?"

I knew that name sounded familiar, but I couldn't place exactly from where. One of the guys in my head tossed a random dart somewhere into the back row of my knowledge section. Without taking the time to examine just where it landed, I answered.

"Beowulf . . . isn't he like a zombie? Where if you say his name three times, he shows up at your house and helps get rid of spirits?"

Staples surveyed me with his thin eyes, shifting into a wide smile, and his friends cracked up. "Ahh, you're worth the price of admission for lines like that alone, Jelly Bean. That's Beetlejuice you're thinking of. I'd probably still be an English major if I got to write about him."

A little bit embarrassed, I decided to sit back and listen for a little bit, making sure not to say anything else stupid.

"We got this Beowulf assignment towards the end of freshman year, and then the whole class goes into a long debate all about why Grendel is so angry in the story. Everyone's trying to outdo each other, coming up with all these crazy theories . . . You took that class too, didn't you, Eli?"

"Yeah, it was with that Scottish professor," Eli recalled brightly. "So you can't say theories, it's '*theedies*.'"

"Okay, *theedies*," Staples conceded, trying to stay on-topic. "I'm hearing everyone's *theedies* about Grendel, when I came to a realization: I'm sinking thousands of dollars further into student loan debt each month, and I'm sitting here listening as my classmates create fan fiction about a thousand-year-old monster. Didn't seem very practical on my end, so I switched."

"Switched to what?"

"Now I'm learning to become a drug dealer."

Staples kept a straight face under the shade of his hat, savoring my reaction while his friends continued to take in the surroundings, now looking with interest towards the Peninsula. They all laughed at how fast Blaise turned his head around to make sure he was hearing correctly.

"I mean, technically it's true. I'm a pharmacy major."

"Oh." That made a little bit more sense. "You gonna be like Mr. Floyd then?"

I was thinking of the little drugstore on the corner of Main Street, next to the sandwich shop. The owner was a withering gray-haired dude in his seventies who had been running the place seemingly forever. He wore half-moon glasses and was always twitching and muttering things to himself as he restocked cough syrup.

"I think Mr. Floyd has that place locked down for at least another fifty more years," Staples said thoughtfully. "Plus, I'm not planning on sticking around here after I graduate."

"So then, if not that, what else could someone do with a pharmacy degree?"

"The dream would be to create a new medicine that cures AIDS or something. The reality is that yeah, I'll probably be in the back of a CVS in ten years, filling prescriptions to help somebody's grandmother deal with arthritis. See, 'drug dealer' sounds a lot more interesting. Pharmacy isn't terribly exciting, but it pays well. If I need an adrenaline rush, I can always go skydiving."

Everyone—even Blaise—cracked up at that one. Parachuting out of a plane is probably the one activity Staples could do where he'd look even more out of place than lounging at the beach.

"What's that place with the big tower, and the blue houses?" Eli asked, his eyes still tracing along the right side of the horizon. He seemed bored by all the career talk. "We should go out *there!*"

Trying to explain the Peninsula to outsiders turned out to be more difficult than I expected. Not from a material wealth standpoint; with all the mansions, cars, and boats, that part was obvious. It was more the psychological hold that the part-time invaders had on the year-round locals, finding ourselves downgraded to being second class in our own town every summer.

"Did you know there's actually a road out there called 'Easy Street?'" Blaise finally said, after we'd all taken turns unsuccessfully trying to convey the aura of South Point. "For some of them, it's not even a metaphor. They *literally* live on Easy Street."

Rather than a place to live, Peninsula often felt more like a status—one that only a select few could attain. More than a home, people acted like it was an achievement, even more than a strip of land covered with fancy houses and surrounded by sparkling water on three sides. Most frustrating of all, Peninsula status also meant having the freedom to bolt out of town at the first sign of the season changing. Feasting on the best parts of the area and leaving the table scraps for the rest of us once they'd had enough.

Blaise and Staples gave his friends several reasons why an up-close tour of the lighthouse and mansions wasn't going to be a possibility. Blaise snarled at the unfairness of the iron-wrought gates and super strict guest policy that prevented outsiders from even stepping foot on the land unless specifically invited (and in my case, not even then).

"Locking everyone out like that, maybe they're really

doing us a favor," said Blaise. "Getting a small glimpse of that life every once in a while, it might make it even worse."

"What do you mean?" Eli asked.

"The one night I ever went out there, it was for this party at the end of last summer," Blaise explained. "Inside the house, they had like five TVs and a bunch of artwork on the walls. The living rooms and mantles were decorated with all sorts of other useless and overpriced items—things that no one in their right mind would ever buy. The girl throwing the party had gotten jet skis for her half-birthday, and all her friends were talking about trying them out the next day. Freaking jet skis, for *half* a birthday, and it was the most normal thing in the world to them. Being an average local, but every summer being surrounded on three sides by people who have more than you . . . It can seriously mess with you."

If you ask people who follow the Eagles, Blaise was anything but an "average local," but I got the point. That was the most I'd ever heard him talk about that fateful night—the same one where I got caught sneaking around in one of the same blue houses that Eli wanted to check out. With another six years of wisdom on us, and having never actually been on the Peninsula himself, Staples had a more indifferent approach to it all.

"Yeah, it is what it is. I suppose it used to bother me somewhat, but I've never considered it something to obsess over. I'm not planning on ever coming back anyway, as soon as I graduate from college. So what do I care what's going on at the Peninsula?"

Blaise and I were still working on that part, a few years away from that critical moment where we'd either leave or stay. For the time being, the Peninsula was still something I thought about, something that seemed significant, something that maybe I would rather do without.

"I get it, we're not exactly poor. I definitely get that. But still . . ." Blaise continued pushing little piles of sand around with his feet. "All the stuff that's right here in front of us, but that we can't be part of. It's like we can look but not touch. To be constantly reminded of all the cool shit that they all have access to that we don't . . . you can't help but want in on some of it."

"Either that, or you just want it to disappear," I added.

"You see how it all works though, right?" Connor eyed me quizzically.

I couldn't even begin trying to pretend that I saw how it works; after all, I was no econ major. Staples nodded his head in gentle agreement, while Blaise and I weren't keeping up. During his brief visit, Connor had apparently observed enough of the town to see how it functions. He coldly concluded that as much as we may resent the Peninsula and what it represented to us, the reality was that the rest of town was kept afloat financially because of it.

"Think about it. Let's just say there's no Peninsula anymore. The summer crowd just goes away, and you get 'your' town back; what would you really be left with? If they take off, they're taking everything with them . . ."

Blaise and I listened closely, having never considered this possibility before. Connor made a snatching motion with his hands, as if he were swiping imaginary items from the shelves of a grocery aisle.

"Their money, their yachts, their Peninsula houses, sure— but that's just the beginning of it. They're taking most of the local economy too. Say goodbye to the boutique stores, the waterfront area, the shops, those ski resorts in the winter, Jimmy's Family Restaurant. They'd probably even take that Spaz kid for good measure, anything they find entertaining. You guys may spend more time here, but if you follow the money, it's still their town."

"So what can we do about it?" Blaise asked. For him, there always needed to be something that could be done about it. He was far too competitive for the concept of hopelessness to sit well with him.

"I guess just drop to our knees and salute our Peninsula overlords!" Eli laughed as he raised a fist to the sky. "Fuck it, this place is still awesome, I'm going for a dip."

Eli took off in a sprint towards the water, splashing and kicking his knees above the surface until immersing himself and swimming off towards the wooden raft. Connor and even Staples were swept up by his enthusiasm and joined in.

This left Blaise and I still standing in the warm sand, watching Connor chatting up the girl in the lifeguard chair, while Eli did backflips off the dock and into the water. Staples, for his part, executed a feet-first pencil dive, generating a thin splash and a lot of laughter from his buddies.

I could tell that Blaise was still caught within his head about what Connor had said. For a guy whose every move was centered on trying to one day make it out of town, somewhere deep down, Blaise still felt a lot of pride for Bellview. Connor's suggestion that maybe it wasn't really our town after all must have stung.

"Hey, we crushed those Peninsula guys in basketball at least," I said. "We still have that over them."

Blaise grinned for a moment, before his eyebrows sank low again. He twisted at the leg of his shorts, squeezing out a few last drops of water that hadn't dried yet.

"Yeah, but they're not good at basketball because they don't *need* to be. Think about those guys, Weston and Reed. They don't need it to get money for college, they don't need it to have status or to get girls, and they already have all kinds of vacations and toys to keep them occupied in their spare time. If I had all that stuff, I probably wouldn't be able to ball either."

"Whatever. I'd rather play ball anyway. I like that people like Mr. Floyd make a big deal about it. Even with all the pressure." I built myself up to say something I'd never admitted out loud. "You have no idea how much I wish I was at your level."

Even upon hearing this, Blaise was still skeptical.

"But wouldn't it be nice if just playing two-on-two at the Mirage was what it was all about?" he said thoughtfully.

CHAPTER TWENTY-NINE

Dentist's Office

My shift the next day was shortened due to having a dentist appointment. With all that had gone on the summer before, my mom hadn't gotten around to scheduling cleanings, so it had been nearly a year and a half since I'd visited last. At the time when I'd normally be punching in on DigiServ, I was instead sitting in a plastic waiting chair at the dentist's office, running my tongue along the tops of my teeth and hoping for the best.

While riding in the passenger seat next to my mom on the way to Dr. Pharaoh's office, wordless except for a few brief observations here and there, it had occurred to me that I'd reached a weird in-between age. I was at some undefined period of development between being a little kid and something closer to an adult. I was old enough to hold down a summer job, but apparently young enough to get excused from it with a note signed by a parent.

Working with people who were almost all older than me every day made it easy to forget that I'd only turned fifteen about six months before. I felt too old to still be riding with my mom to a dentist's appointment—but then again, how else was I supposed to get there? Bike ten miles? Hitchhike?

I wondered if, when we got there, I'd be able to check myself in. You know, march up to the receptionist's desk and state my own name and my business there. Wouldn't that be more appropriate than Mom escorting me in and remarking that she hopes her little boy hasn't been eating too many sweets? It didn't seem right that someone with a steady paycheck and a lifetime ban from the Peninsula would need one's mother to announce their arrival to a dentist's appointment.

Once we arrived, I consciously made sure to walk through the doors ahead of Mom so that the receptionist would see me first. Staying as businesslike as possible, I cleared my throat and told her that I had an appointment for 3:45. My mom came in a few seconds later, rummaging through her purse as the receptionist quickly typed something into her computer.

"Okay, 3:45 . . . Does this mean that you're JB?" I nodded my head as she continued in a cheery voice, "And do you have an insurance card that I can put on file?"

"Uhh . . ."

Luckily, Mom was there on backup, already retrieving the plastic card from her purse and greeting the receptionist. There was that weird in-between age again: old to enough to independently announce my arrival, but not enough to have my own insurance card. If it turned out that I was taking good care of my teeth, I wondered whether they would still put my name on a cutout of an extra-large tooth and add me to the "No Cavity Club" on the outside of the door. And would I be a little bit offended if they didn't?

While I sat down and waited for the cleaning to start, I

noticed a large jar full of hard candy sitting on the receptionist's desk. There was a challenge for patients to try and guess
the exact number of candies. I marveled at the hypocrisy of it,
instead estimating how many cavities and chipped teeth were
caused by the contents of that jar. Then again, maybe this was
Dr. Pharaoh's way of making sure that she stays in business.

Just as I was starting to feel a little bit guilty about missing
the start of work, the door to the No Cavity Club opened and
I heard my name. An assistant called out for me with a smile
and walked me back to an open dentist's chair. She clipped a
paper towel bib to the front of my shirt and pushed a button
to send the chair into a full recline.

At Dr. Pharaoh's office, each of the four chairs has a different *Where's Waldo?* poster taped to the ceiling directly
above. When I had to get four teeth pulled a few years back,
staying distracted by a scene of witches and vampires partying
at a castle was the only thing that got me through the sting
of the piercing needle that she used to numb my mouth. The
poster this time showed hundreds of guys in different-colored
hoods running around and competing in a brutal four-
way type of ball game, looking like a mix of rugby, Hungry
Hungry Hippos, and complete chaos. As I was trying to sort
out what the rules of this game could possibly be, Dr. Pharaoh
appeared from above, wearing a blue mask that covered up
her mouth and clicking on a little flashlight attached to the
side of her glasses.

Instead of letting me zone out and get to work trying to
find Waldo, Dr. Pharaoh made sure to keep a full conversation going, even while cleaning my teeth. Her voice sounded
nasally and half-invested, like a guy working under the hood

of his car, and the prying neighbor comes by uninvited and wants to chat about nothing for half an hour. Only thing is, I wasn't a prying neighbor, I didn't really want to chat, and I could barely respond to her questions even if I did.

"Been a while since you've been in," she said in a thin and partially interested monotone, poking around at my molars as she spoke. "Was wondering when I'd be . . . seeing you again."

"Yaughh."

It had been a long time since my last visit, but as the cleaning progressed, I was reminded of the many different unpleasant sensations that are unique to being at the dentist. As she was talking to me and polishing my back teeth with that spinning mechanical toothbrush thing, my tongue kept getting in the way, no matter which way I tried to position it. I tried not to gag as the buffer loaded the side of my tongue with that extra dusty toothpaste stuff.

"You must be in high school by now, no?" I blinked my eyes twice to indicate yes. She pulled out a metal toothpick and started prodding the tiny cracks in between my teeth. After that, it was time for the portable chisel, which she used to forcefully scrape off any plaque from my teeth. "Right, and . . . what, grade will you be in this fall?"

"Ehhnt."

I thought about asking for a cup of water, but that wasn't likely to make much difference. Dentist water always tasted like they mixed it with mouthwash—or maybe it was just since I had too much toothpaste covering my taste buds to tell the difference, but I felt like a rinse would only make it worse.

"Right . . . right. Sophomore year. That can be a tough one."

Dr. Pharaoh put the pointy metal tools back on the tray,

and I was able to briefly loosen up my jaws in relief. I thought about replying that if it was any tougher than freshman year, I might as well drop out of school now and join the military; I didn't think I could handle another year like the last one. She then unrolled a strand of floss and wrapped it around her gloved hands to get some tension to it.

"And have you been flossing enough? It's something you really should do more of."

"I have been. At least, *I* think it's enough." Since I could actually talk now, I figured I might as well try to speed things up a little bit. Compared to this, I would gladly be bussing tables. "Look, I have to be at my job, so maybe I can just handle that part when I get home tonight . . ."

"Mmmm . . . nn-nn."

In case it was unclear what she meant by that, Dr. Pharaoh started violently flossing my teeth, sharply digging into my gums and choosing that exact time to pick up on the conversation again.

"And are you . . . keeping out of trouble?"

Is this something she asks all of her patients, or does this lady have a file on me that goes beyond dental records? I wondered.

"Arrh-uh," I replied.

"Good . . . good. And do you . . . have your eye on anyone at school?"

Dr. Pharaoh then moved on to the part of the appointment where she dug her mini-icepick into my gums, causing my eyes to water and leaving me incapable of even attempting a response. I tried to concentrate on the poster again, but my vision was too blurry from my eyes watering. Trying to find the little guy in his red-and-white stripes was like looking out to the South Point lighthouse on a foggy morning, and the shine from her flashlight was blinding me even more instead of guiding the way. At this rate, I'd need to see an eye doctor next. Had Dr. Pharaoh never heard of sunglasses?

The final step of the cleaning was a minute of swishing around some weird-tasting fluoride stuff. It was like a warm version of what I imagined Cal's Nuclear Fizz drink to be. While I tried to use my teeth to scrape the aftertaste off my tongue, Dr. Pharaoh pushed the button for the chair, and I was lifted back upright.

"I know I'm starting to sound like a dead horse, but you really do need to floss more. Other than that and a little plaque, looks all good. Up and at 'em."

I didn't even wait to check on my No Cavity Club status, rising from the chair, tossing my bib into the garbage bag, and practically skipping out the door.

Back at the restaurant, the first person I saw after punching in on DigiServ was Cal. He was shaking his head at me as he squirted oil onto the grill. His solemn frown gave off the feel of a disappointed parent, but the satisfied glee in his eyes made it clear that he thought I was about to get in trouble.

"You think it was daylight savings or something?"

"Why would I think it was—Cal, I was at the *dentist!* I told Gloria about it three days ago."

His disappointed frown was real now. He must have been hoping I was about to get a tongue-lashing from Jimmy, or Dumpster Duty or something.

"Oh. Well, I'll admit you needed an appointment there. Your teeth were starting to look like Cap'n Crunch." I clenched my jaw and felt my face turning red. It was irritating enough hearing all of Cal's corny jokes and comebacks, but it was even less tolerable when he actually had a good one.

"Shut up, Cal. Like you know anything about Cap'n Crunch." I don't know what I meant by that last part, but Jennie was approaching, and now I was getting self-conscious.

"Ayyo, where have ya been?" Jennie seemed both giddy and relieved upon seeing me.

"Uh, I was at the dentist. What's up?"

"Nothing's up. I just saw that you were scheduled, thought you might be skipping out."

"Well . . . here I am. You miss me or something?"

"Yeah, actually, I kinda did." Jennie reached behind her head to adjust the pens she kept in the bun of her tied-back hair, looking genuinely surprised by her answer. She grabbed a set of whitefish dinners from the counter and looked a little bit flushed as she walked away. I'll admit it, my teeth actually did feel a lot better after my dentist appointment, but that wasn't the reason I was smiling as I went to start clearing up my tables for the night.

CHAPTER THIRTY

Supper Wanted

Just that one small show of affection from Jennie might not seem like a very big deal. Even so, the echo of her confession, that she'd actually *missed* me while I was away, kept bouncing around in my head. The pleasant, warm feeling in my stomach was a nearly unbreakable shield from what was turning into an evening of chaos and aggravation for everyone else. For no apparent reason, the restaurant gods created an impossible set of customers for that particular night, with a pairing of impatience and clumsiness that seamlessly added to each other like a burger and fries combo meal.

Over at the soda fountain, a long line got held up even further as an idiot ten-year-old somehow knocked the whole top scoop of his frozen yogurt cone onto the floor on the very first lick. Then the kid got a replacement, took a second lick, and the exact same thing happened again. Turning a shade of pale that shouldn't have been possible for someone who was at the beach the day before, Staples looked like he wanted to crawl into the secret ice cream compartment and hide for the rest of the night.

Merryll was at her wits' end with a table that asked at the last second to have their final bill split eight separate ways, then didn't even leave her a tip. Gloria had to give her a long pep talk before the steam finally stopped coming out of her ears and she was ready to get working again. Even Jennie was having a rough go of it herself, as every other table seemed to either have a spill or some petty complaint that needed immediate attention. All of this outside noise made its way to the boss himself, when Lacy approached Jimmy apologetically, saying that someone on the phone wanted to speak with him.

"There's this guy who wants to make a reservation for 7:30," Lacy explained, holding the cordless phone and twisting her frizzy hair around with her free hand. Jimmy's eyes flared impatiently as he waited for the rest of it. "And I told him that, like, we don't do reservations, so then he said how about 8:30 . . . and I told him that we don't do, like, *any* reservations. He wouldn't give it up though, and then he told me I need to find a manager."

"If he wants a reservation that bad, tell him to go to Rivera," the boss sneered, refusing to take the phone. "I'm sure they have plenty of empty seats."

Maybe she had a fiery and sarcastic streak that hadn't yet shown itself, but I doubt that Lacy actually ended up saying that. Jimmy didn't stay around long enough to find out either. The vein down the center of his forehead bulged as Cal called him back to the grill to help with another remake of somebody's order, sent back due to some microscopic imperfection or another. It was that kind of night.

Jimmy couldn't snap at his own paying customers, so he was snapping at Cal instead, which led to Cal snapping at

Spaz, and Spaz snapping a rubber band that hit Cal in the ear, causing him to swear loudly and start the whole cycle again. Everybody was taking their turn being pissed off at somebody or something else. On top of that, there seemed to be a contest going on to see how many times "Margaritaville" could be played on the jukebox, and this night's customers were going for the high score.

None of this craziness going on in the beehive could dampen my own spirits though, not even when a crying toddler spilled an entire kiddy cup of lemonade all over the giant back window, and I was sent over to get the situation cleaned up. There's no way it could have made that particular splash, unless the kid purposely spiked it against the window. A smug-looking Real Housewife, who apparently was the kid's zookeeper, insisted that the loose-fitting plastic cap was to blame for the spill.

"And this restaurant is supposed to be all about the fff-am-ilies," she huffed before demanding a free refill.

While mopping the floor, and then using a squeegee and spray bottle of Windex to clean up the window, I kept observing the rising tensions of everyone else around me. Still basking in the glow of my interaction with Jennie though, I was miraculously immune through the first half of the night. I finished cleaning off the window and was double-checking that it didn't leave any streaks when a blur of fuchsia passed through the corner of my vision and instantly changed my entire demeanor.

I frantically turned and started wheeling the mop bucket to the back of the restaurant, pushing it along with my knees as I tried to balance the handle of the mop with the Windex and squeegee in my hands. The entrance door swung open behind me, sending a vicious chill through my body, as a voice that sounded like a push broom sweeping a rough patch of concrete buzzed out from the cashier's booth.

"Hallo honey . . . what's for supper tonight?"

I ducked into the kitchen just in time as Lacy directed the new customer towards an open one-top table across the restaurant and near the waitress station. Once I put the cleaning equipment away, dreading the thought of going back in the dining room, I approached Spaz with a proposal.

"Spaz, I think we should trade jobs," I suggested, trying to keep the desperation from showing. "Not forever—just for the next forty-five minutes or so. You bus tables, and I can wash dishes."

Spaz looked like he was about to agree—like the switch-up could be a fun little business deal that benefited both of us. Then he hesitated.

"What makes you so interested in being a dishwasher all of a sudden?" Spaz asked suspiciously. I didn't feel like explaining myself. I just needed him to grant me sanctuary for the time being and not ask too many questions. "Are you sure this is such a good idea?"

"Yeah, it'll be fine. I know what to do back here. Slide the tray of dishes through here, see? Rinse them all off, push that green button . . . and put them all back when it's done." I even grabbed the metal water hose that was dangling next to the washing machine and quickly sprayed it to further prove that I had it under control. Spaz continued to stall, neither denying nor agreeing to my request, until Jimmy inevitably came over to put a stop to it. Wrinkling his forehead, the boss's imperious eyes darted between the two of us and eventually settled on Spaz.

"What is *he* doing back here??"

Waving Spaz off, I fielded the question myself. Staring directly down at Jimmy's No-Slips (so he couldn't try my mom's "laser eye surgery" move), I started to explain.

"There's this lady who just walked in, and I sort of know her from the start of summer. Her name is Sara . . ."

While explaining the Peninsula to Staples's friends had been more difficult than I had expected, I can say that explaining Sara to Jimmy was much more straightforward. With Spaz listening intently, I gave the full rundown about the "Help Wanted" ad and biking out to the cottage with the pond outside of town, the paper bag in the closet and "keeping the numbers up," the smoky stove with the black frying pan, puking in the front yard and furiously biking away. I even admitted that while lying in bed at night, I'd jolt awake in a cold chill every once in a while, after hearing that prickly voice say, *"Come on out, frrr-oggy!"* in the back of my dreams. If there were ever a time for Jimmy to give into the voice of reason and sympathy, certainly this had to be it.

"So you see, I have to stay back here, and that's really all there is to it. You can give me Dumpster Duty if you have to, but I'm not going out there again until she's gone!"

Standing with his hands on his hips as I pleaded my case, Jimmy's face twisted into the Stare of Unfathomable Disgust. Not disgusted about the frogs in the closet, and the bubbling ones on the stove, but disgusted with me.

"You're gonna bus the fricking tables, you're gonna stop acting like a dumbass, AND you'll do Dumpster Duty tonight."

"Yes, Jimmy."

The people out in the dining room, staff members and probably customers included, probably couldn't understand why I was acting so strange. After Jimmy had been zero help at all, I wasn't about to tell my story again, so that made for an awkward hour or so. While still sort of trying to do my job, I found myself literally ducking behind counters, speed walking past that one table, and holding menus up to my face to avoid being seen by Sara.

The only area I was safe in was by the waitress station, where I at least had a dividing wall to block me from the creepy middle-aged lady in the fuchsia pants just a few feet away on the other side. The unlucky one who had to wait on her was Jennie. I thought that maybe I should give Jennie some type of warning leading into it, but when I had stopped quivering and started getting my voice back a little bit, Jennie was already set to take her order. From behind the divider, I listened closely.

"Hallo, honey, do you have any frogs?"

"I'm sorry, ma'am, could you repeat that?"

"Shoulda listened the furss time! Do you have any frogs?"

"Umm . . . you mean like frog legs?"

"Legs, arms, shoulders, the whole nine. Doesn' matter to me!"

Hearing this, Jennie somehow managed to both stay patient and (I think) keep her face from contorting in disgust, which shows just how good of a waitress she was.

"I'm sorry, we don't do that sort of thing here. Would you like to check out the menu for some other options?" I expected Sara to get up and walk out. To my surprise, she didn't seem to be all that put off.

"Can I have scrimp scrampi?"

"I don't know what that is."

"Ahh, screw it. How 'bout chicken tenners then, you 'do that sorta thing' here?"

"Yes, and our chicken tender meal comes with fries."

"That. That and a milkshake. Chocolate. And it better be extra runny, otherwise I'm sending it back."

Jennie caught my eye once she came back around the divider to type the order into DigiServ. She cupped a hand around her lips, silently mouthing "that-lady-is-crazy!" to me, and started to giggle uncontrollably. I think her annoyance from earlier must have been flipped, now replaced by an acceptance of our collective fate for the evening: like it or not, these are our customers. Merryll wasn't seeing the humor in things just yet, glowering impatiently as she waited for Jennie to finish typing in the special instructions for the drink order. Once the order ticket buzzed through on the other side, we heard the dry voice of Staples, raised to a higher volume than normal, calling out from the soda fountain area.

"Jennie, could you step into my office, please?"

I decided to follow Jennie over to see Staples, partly to get further away from Sara for a few minutes, but also curious to see what his issue was.

"Can you explain this milkshake order to me?"

Jennie took a quick look at the small slip of paper and handed it right back to Staples, leaning on one foot and looking at him as if issuing a challenge.

"Looks pretty clear to me. What's there to explain?"

"Jennie, how am I supposed to do 'extra runny?' The machine sends them all out at the same consistency, and you know that."

"Do hand-dipped then—that's not hard at all."

She had a point. Hand-dipped shakes from Jimmy's were a classic. Even though Staples would prefer to have his temperature-controlled ice cream scoop, making it this way wouldn't be out of the ordinary at all.

"Great, and then what? Wait an hour for the ice cream to melt? Why don't we just pour her a glass of chocolate milk?"

"I dunno, dude! Just figure something out, she's nuts!"

With that, Jennie glided off, leaving Staples to ponder his extra-runny milkshake. She had other things to worry about.

"Having fun yet?" I asked Staples, as he took a small sliver of chocolate ice cream out of the tub and gently set it in a milkshake tin.

"Don't you have Dumpster Duty to take care of, Jelly Bean?"

I kept watching as Staples squirted chocolate syrup into the tin and then loaded it with extra milk to try and get the proper effect. Since there was too much liquid in the tin, it splashed everywhere when he clicked it onto the electric mixer. He wiped drips of milk off his sunburnt nose, looking like he was about to grow fangs and attack somebody. I did a wide loop around Staples, and then a wider loop around the back edge of the restaurant—avoiding Sara's table, but getting the other empty tables cleared up—before Jimmy popped his head out and caught me slacking.

Back in the dining room, a table of four that had recently finished only left Jennie a fifty-cent tip. Shaking her head defeatedly, and jingling the change through her hand, Jennie walked up to the jukebox and used the two coins to play "Margaritaville" for the seventh time that night. When I got back to sort through a stack of dishes at the waitress station, Jennie's troubles still weren't over with.

"Hey, skinny, are my chicken tenners ready yet?"

After that fifty-cent tip, Jennie no longer saw the humor of Sara, or any other aspect of this senseless set of customers. She sighed heavily as she went back to Sara's table, staying as polite as possible, but the tone of her voice significantly dropped.

"I sent the order in several minutes ago, so it should be up soon," she told Sara.

"I am thirsty."

"Uhh, hold on just a second." Jennie started drifting away from Sara's table even as she was still talking. "I'll see how it's coming along back there."

I also wanted to see how Staples was coming along back there, so once again, I shielded my face with a menu and followed Jennie back to the soda fountain. Staples was now taking large scoops of chocolate ice cream and squeezing them through the lemonade juicer. The shake glass was sitting under the filter. It was half full and the level continued to rise, collecting all the drips as Staples twisted the metal handle down and juiced the ice cream. The process looked a little gross, but the end result was indeed an extra-runny milkshake.

"Okay, here goes," he declared once it was finished, sending the glass out on the counter with supreme skepticism. "Welcome to the end of my career."

Sara's chicken tenders were ready at the same time, so Jennie carried the full tray over to the table, setting everything out with a quick thud and then scurrying back over to the soda fountain as quickly as possible. The three of us watched from the counter with building anticipation as Sara reached for the runny milkshake first.

Taking out the straw, Sara downed the entire glass in one giant gulp, letting out a satisfied belch that I swear rattled the silverware on the three nearest tables. Oblivious to the Peninsula families that were now staring at her as she wiped off her mouth, she nodded and raised the empty glass like she was making a toast, looking for approval from no one in particular.

"*Ahhh . . . they don't makem' like this anymore, wooo-eee!!*"

Sara also must have liked the rest of her supper, because she ended up leaving a twenty-dollar bill as a tip.

Later, Jennie came out and helped me with Dumpster Duty. Since it was so dark when we finished, she gave me a ride back home too. Not a bad night after all.

CHAPTER THIRTY-ONE

The Top of the Mitten

Most people agree that the main part of Michigan is shaped like a giant mitten. There are all kinds of myths and legends about Paul Bunyan that supposedly explain how the state got its distinct shape—but I won't get into all of that. If you took off all the borderlines on a United States map, it's one of the few places that you'd still be able to recognize instantly.

If the mitten analogy works for you, then it becomes pretty simple to describe where most of the landmarks in the state are. It has a huge thumb region sticking off to the east, with Detroit all the way down at the base of it. Lake Michigan runs along the entire pinky-side of the hand.

The Mackinac Bridge rises straight out of the middle finger area, boldly flipping the bird to the massive Great Lakes that had once tried to separate Michigan from its other half, the Upper Peninsula (U.P.). Another world waits above in the U.P., which is almost half the size of the mainland, but nearly forgotten in the minds of outsiders. Even when Michiganders refer to Northern Michigan, we're usually only talking about the top part of the mitten.

Bellview is right around where the fingernail of the ring finger would go, which is fitting in its own way. As I was getting a little bit older, I started to decipher the town as a series of uneasy marriages between seemingly opposite things. Winter misery vs. summer bliss. Working locals vs. summer vacationers. People who go vs. people who stay. Somehow, all these contradictory ideas got together in Bellview right at the same time, right at the same place, and it worked. Might as well put a ring on it.

From the beginning of June to the end of August, the sun never ceases to generously rise, first over the bay, then through the downtown area, and eventually through the Tunnel of Trees beyond the western edge of the town. The Eagle River fills up with kayaks and paddleboards, traffic downtown quintuples, the beaches fill with swarms of eager vacationers, and the mansions on the South Point Peninsula are finally put to good use after sitting empty for three-quarters of the year. Everything speeds up for those three months, like it's a shortened year in itself, being played out in fast forward. Everyone is in a hurry to absorb and consume the perfect weather. It's a delirious rush to squeeze everything they can from the elements before the gray curtain drops down again to signal the season's final act.

Hidden like a little troll doll under the massive green bridge, our town name is barely visible on even the most detailed of maps. A summer daytrip along US 31 could take a family from Traverse City, through Petoskey, and then all the way up to Mackinaw City and back again without so much as a single road sign to point them in the direction of Bellview.

FULL TIME-OUT

CELEBRITIES

During my first two months, these are the Top 5 biggest names who came in to eat at the restaurant:

1. **Mr. Bridgeman,** the principal of the high school. He'd gotten takeout one evening back at the end of July. It was kind of disarming seeing him wearing cargo shorts and sandals, since he'd worn a sport coat, tie, and loafers for all of the other 180 times I'd seen him before. He arrived at the absolute busiest time of the night, but he didn't seem to mind waiting a little longer for his food to be ready. Bridgeman appeared quietly amused as he watched everyone shuffle by in a hurry: a mass of chaos that for once he wasn't in charge of controlling. He nodded his head in appreciation as I hustled some napkins and ketchup packets out to him. He seemed to be fully enjoying his summer vacation—even had a little bit of a tan.

2. **Officer Chiggins,** the cop who had arrested me a year ago. All he ordered was a cup of black coffee when I saw him talking to Jimmy one day. He tipped his police hat

toward me on his way out the door. He had a slightly suspicious look on his face, but seemed to prefer running into me there, rather than hiding in the bushes outside the blue Peninsula mansions after midnight.

3. **Some politician,** maybe from the state Senate or something. He looked too young to be a real politician, but Staples always pointed him out when he came in. He was always with a different group of two or three other men and women with briefcases. Maybe they were his advisors, or secretaries, or colleagues—I don't know who Senators eat their meals with. I can't think of the guy's name at the moment either, but Staples would definitely know. I see his re-election campaign signs posted in people's front lawns every once in a while; I'd recognize it if I saw it. One time, Jimmy gave the guy a long and disapproving stare when he caught him taking a whole handful of dinner mints. It was while one of the advisers was paying his bill. Jimmy never broke eye contact until the young Senator's face got all red and he put some back.

4. **Jimi Dandersley,** Jennie's boyfriend. It still made me angry to think that he was the type of guy Jennie preferred. Swaggering through the doors like it was "*Jimi's* Family Restaurant," complaining about his fries, and worst of all, flirting with Jennie. Luckily, he only came in the one time. If that guy became a regular, I don't know how I would manage.

5. **Sara:** what else can even be said?

I should add that I know none of those people are actually famous. Calling them "celebrities," even by the loosest definition of the term, is completely wrong. The summer crowd referring to their mansions as "cottages" is more accurate than me saying that Officer Chiggins, Mr. Bridgeman, the Senator whose name I forget, slimebag Jimi Dandersley, and Sara the Frog Lady are celebrities.

With that said, those are the types of notable customers who would cause a little bit of a stir when they walked into Jimmy's. Where we're from, the chances are better that you'll get hit by a deer while out on a bike ride than to ever run into somebody famous. Which is probably why no one really knew how to react when someone who was about to become one of the biggest movie stars on the planet sat down at Table 17 one afternoon.

CHAPTER THIRTY-TWO

The Celebrity

Even though my summer wasn't exactly filled with a lot of TV-watching, I'd still managed to see all of the commercials for the release of the first live-action Magneto Man movie, "*. . . coming August 19th:* The Induction." I highly doubted that I would go and see it once it hit theaters, though. Superhero movies weren't really my thing. However, I had to admit that the customer at Table 17 looked just like the guy from the previews, except his hair wasn't styled, and he wasn't wearing Magneto Man's signature burgundy-and-light-blue suit.

"You seeing this, Spaz?" Cal asked, nudging him. "You seeing this? That's gotta be him! The actor playing Magneto Man!"

"Prove it. Go get his autograph then."

"Can't wait to cook up this order! I bet he gets . . . probably a . . . I don't know."

People in our part of the country probably had a much higher level of enthusiasm for the new movie than anywhere else. Magneto Man was like a third-rate superhero at best, but it was well known that the creator of the old comics had grown up in Michigan. The rumor was that for the superhero suit in the movie, there was going to be a block M stitched onto the shoulder, taken from the University of Michigan logo.

Hollywood must have decided to skip out on yet another Superman or Batman remake for its big summer blockbuster, and maybe that's why *The Induction* wasn't being released until the middle of August. Either way, Magneto Man was about to finally have his moment on the big screen.

"That's definitely him," Cal assured us, listening from the grill. "I can't remember his real name—I think it's like 'Thom' or something."

"Magneto Man's real name is Glenn Murray," said Spaz.

"No, that's his alter ego. I'm talking about the *actor*. You going to the midnight premiere next week?"

"No. Magneto Man is weak."

You need to be a pretty big fan of comic books to really know much about Magneto Man. That was all about to change, though. The humble food delivery guy who gained mysterious magnetic powers would soon become the number-one movie in the country, and the star of the film (either that or a perfect lookalike) was sitting in a booth at the restaurant. Instead of getting somebody like Vincent Chase or Matt Damon for the lead role, they went and got someone who was previously unknown, though it wouldn't stay that way as soon as the movie came out.

The guy on Table 17 looked as if he knew that all of his movements were being closely watched. Everything he did looked like it was carefully calculated, from sitting with his hands on his thighs near the front of his chair, to every head nod and remark he gave to his companion, and even the way he carefully squirted a lemon wedge into his glass of water. It was like the inside of his head was currently programmed to "act normal" mode, while people in the restaurant stared at him with expectation, as if he was a rare flower that was about to bloom at any second.

Even though Spaz claimed to despise the Magneto Man comics, he seemed to have an encyclopedic knowledge about them. I turned my attention towards the heated discussion he was having with Cal.

"The origin story doesn't even make sense, Cal. Even if the magnetic poles in Breadville *did* randomly switch in just that one specific location, how would that make him able to suddenly fly?"

"If that's the only part that you find unrealistic, there's not much I can do for you, Spaz. It's a comic—why can't you just enjoy it and leave it at that?"

One by one, Spaz counted off his reasons on the yellow fingers of his rubber gloves.

"Umm, the one-dimensional characters, the recycled plotlines, the attempts to be much deeper than what it really is . . ."

Jennie went out to the table and calmly took the order of the guy Cal was convinced was Magneto Man. The rest of my coworkers in the dining room remained transfixed, watching his every move.

Cal cooked up Magneto Man's whitefish dinner confidently and set it out on the window with an extra flourish, holding his follow-through like he was playing Frisbee at the beach. As Jennie delivered it, I could feel the area around me become suddenly extra crowded. Word had gotten back to the kitchen that there was (maybe) a celebrity in the building, and the dishwashers and cooks now came out to see for themselves.

Jimmy recognized the commotion, coming out and squinting hard in the direction of Table 17. "Who's that supposed to be?"

Snorting in a rare fit of girlish laughter, Merryll was the only one who knew the actor's real name. Blatantly goggling at him, she said it out loud, but I forgot what it was just as quickly. It wasn't "Thom, or something," though. It didn't make much of an impact for Jimmy either, because he kept up his perplexed squint without showing any sign of acknowledgement.

"You possibly know him as Magneto Man," said Cal importantly.

"I don't know anything about any Torpedo Man," Jimmy responded with a dismissive scrunch of his moustache. "Don't you all have work to do, or did we shut down early tonight without telling me? Let the poor man eat."

"Yeah, let the poor man eat . . . mm-hmm! Bet you wouldn't mind a piece of that, would ya, Lace?" Merryll called over to the cashier's station. "Not till you're grown up, though!"

Cal was now somehow personally offended by all the attention that the movie star customer was getting—even though most of the attention had been coming from him just a few minutes ago.

"You only think he's attractive because he's famous."

"Yaaookay, Cal," Merryll said. "We don't even know for sure if that's the guy, but I'd take him down to dry storage right now either way!"

"Come on, he's not the only good-looking guy in here."

"You can't be referring to yourself."

"All I'm saying is . . ." Cal tilted his head a little bit to the side, giving what was clearly a try at a charming, smoldering gaze. "If you went around and asked all the girls in here who the best-looking guy in the restaurant is . . . sure, he might win overall, but it would be a much closer vote than you think."

It's a good thing that we weren't standing at the salad bar, otherwise Cal would have been pelted with a round of tomatoes from all the women on staff. Merryll clutched her gut, shaking with derisive laughter. Jennie and Lacy exchanged a look of obvious disagreement that I can't even try to describe, as Cal tried to figure out what he'd said.

"I can't always tell if you guys are laughing *with* me or laughing *at* me."

"It's neither," Staples muttered, supremely uninterested in all of this. "We're laughing *through* you."

Cal had no hope of a comeback, but with the hint of a scowl, he returned to his previous delusional statement.

"Well, at the very least, I'm the best-looking guy *working* here—I think that's clear enough."

"Yeah." Merryll rolled her eyes. "And this dump is a regular Abercrombie catalog."

"You even sure that's true, Cal?" Jennie now had a small smile that was equal parts mischievous and thoughtful. "Who's to say . . . JB isn't the best-looking one here?"

After Jimmy demanded that no one disturb the guy at Table 17 or ask for his autograph, things mostly went back to normal until Jennie delivered his check. Before heading to the cash register, he slowly walked over to the grill, as Jimmy was helping Cal put the finishing touches on an unexpected takeout order for a dozen hamburgers. Now wrapping them and placing them into paper bags, the boss found himself interrupted by the guy who we were convinced was a movie star.

"Excuse me, you wouldn't happen to be the owner of the restaurant, would you?"

"That would be me. Unless there was a problem with your meal. In that case, the owner is him." Jimmy pointed at Cal, who had been loading fries into takeout containers and staring from a distance, but clearly wasn't prepared to be referenced. He stupidly straightened himself up and waved hello, while the movie star cracked up laughing at Jimmy's comment.

"No, sir, no problem with my meal at all! In all seriousness, I think that was probably the best whitefish dinner I've had in my entire life. Thank you."

Jimmy held his hands on his hips, shrugging his shoulders without any change to his unimpressed facial expression. "Well then, you haven't been alive very long!"

Magneto Man started laughing again, as I tried to make sense of what I was witnessing. Did Jimmy not realize that he was talking to someone who would be world-famous within the next week? Did Magneto Man not realize that he was talking to my old grouchy boss who wore plain black Velcro No-Slip shoes in public? This who situation was making even less sense than the "Palm-Handle-Pivot" video I'd had to watch during my first week on the job.

Jimmy finally broke character and grinned. "No—I'm glad you liked your meal then, thanks for coming in. Make sure to give Jennie a nice tip, she does a good job."

"Definitely, man. This place is great." He introduced himself and extended his hand,

"Jimmy." The boss gave him an aggressive handshake. Magneto Man's eye's widened. He turned and pointed emphatically to the front entrance.

"So then it's really . . . you know, on the sign!"

"My grandfather. He started the place and ran it for about forty years, my father for thirty, and I learned it from him and have been running it for about thirty-five now."

"Pretty amazing. This place is a true classic."

I took a closer look at my surroundings: the chipped paint on the walls, the old jukebox, the tin roof, the massive front window, the retro ice cream fountain, the wooden planks that the fish dinners were served on, even the whiny ticket printers that drove us all crazy. Hearing this sort of praise from Magneto Man himself was causing me to rethink my stance on the restaurant a little bit; after all, I guess it did have quite a bit of history. Maybe in some way, I was actually fortunate to be a small part of this continuous chain of tradition.

"Would you mind signing a menu for me? As a souvenir? This is my first time in the area—don't know the next time I'll be able to travel up here again. Things are about to get pretty busy again on my end."

Jimmy casually signed a menu for him. I pictured it being the exact same cursive font that was on the storefront. He pulled out a glass jar from a cupboard near the stove.

"In that case, better have an extra J-Sauce for the road."

Smiling and clutching the jar of J-Sauce like he'd just won an Oscar, Magneto Man paid his bill and walked out of the restaurant, as the girls stared at him one last time. Meanwhile, the celebrity of the moment grabbed a spatula and went back to the glamour of scraping blackened remains of hamburger from off the top of the stove.

CHAPTER THIRTY-THREE

Split Shift

The biggest news of the next week was that Cal had purchased a new kitchen knife for himself. I know, I know, it's a far cry from Magneto Man coming into the restaurant, but to hear Cal tell it, you would have thought that the Zilwaukee Bridge had fallen down again.

"Look, Beanie, the Nakayama Genesis." he gently held it out at me, the way a king might present a special sword to a heroic knight. "Seventy-two pieces of steel, grinded and melted into an indestructible core."

"Hey, there you go," I said with vague approval. As long as I just went with it, but without asking questions or appearing overly interested, maybe Cal would leave me alone. Coming in at 9:30 for a split shift, I knew that I had a long day ahead of me. Long enough to hear the origin story along with every single detail of Cal's wondrous knife. Over and over again.

"I found it in that catalog we were looking at a few weeks ago. Knew right away that I had to have it. Gloria let me use the store's membership code, so I got a great deal on it—nearly half off the standard price. Not that I couldn't have paid full price if I needed to," he was quick to add.

As everyone knew, Cal's career goal was to be the head chef at a major restaurant someday. Despite the title not existing, he had even let slip to me and Staples earlier in the summer that he considered himself pretty much the Head Chef at *Jimmy's* already.

"Umm, I'm pretty sure Jimmy is the Head Everything around here," Staples had said, flicking the idea away like a housefly had briefly landed on his arm. "Nice try, though."

Cal wanted to give me a demonstration on all the different capabilities of his new knife, so he started pulling out a bunch of bell peppers and a head of lettuce from the mini-fridge, even though the place was semi-empty and most of the customers only had coffee and toast. Thinking on my feet, I came up with the easiest excuse I could find to avoid being an audience member for this spontaneous "Cutting with Cal" cooking special.

"That sounds great, but I really need to get started with silverware wrapping. It's going to be a pretty busy day for me, split shift and all."

"Split shift? You're brave," Cal said sarcastically. "For me, only having a split shift would be a blessing."

The next person Cal approached to tell about the knife was Jimmy, who was taking advantage of the calm morning to sort through a stack of mail that had gone unread for over a week. Cal showed the Genesis to him, smiling so brightly that it wouldn't surprise me if he saw his own reflection on the boss's glistening bald head.

"Most Japanese sushi chefs use them. *All* of the top ones."

"We don't have sushi here." Jimmy tossed the newest issue of *Restaurateur* to the side.

"Heh-heh, touché. I'm sure I'll put it to good use around here though, don't worry."

"We have a lot of knives sitting in the drawers of the kitchen, and they work just fine . . . *sharp* ones." He continued sorting through the mail, not looking worried.

Nobody noticed, but I began deeply blushing when Jimmy mentioned the knives in the kitchen. It's difficult to get anything past Jimmy, but here was one mystery of the restaurant that I was hoping would forever go unsolved. There were an extra seven or eight knives back there that had appeared out of nowhere one year earlier: unexpected souvenirs from the first house that I'd snuck into with my old friends.

As Cal went on making sure that everybody was fully aware that he had a new knife, I relived our midnight bike ride out beyond the north edge of town. It was on the 4th of July, about an hour after the fireworks ended. While we were bored and making prank phone calls the week before, a guy on the other line had threatened to slit Blaise's throat. Rather than being scared by it, Blaise rallied us all together to go out to the guy's house in the dead of night. We ended up sneaking around inside while the owner was asleep. Without saying anything to us, Garrett slipped a set of large kitchen knives into his backpack before leaving.

Blaise said it was payback, but in reality, it was more like a mix of a practical joke and finding an excuse to go off on an adventure. Once our excitement had worn off the next day, Garrett had a backpack full of kitchen knives to get rid of. It was his day off from running the cash register, but we sat at

Jimmy's and drank orangeades at Table 36, trying to figure out what to do with them. Jennie was our waitress that day, but this was back before we talked to each other. While Jimmy was out chatting with a customer, Garrett had slipped back to the kitchen, pretending to check the next week's schedule. He dumped the knives in the drawer with the rest of the cooks' silverware, and I hadn't thought about them since.

We got away with it, which was probably the worst thing that could have happened. The first time sneaking in with no consequences made us think there wasn't anything wrong with it, encouraging us to take on even more midnight adventures. Only a year had passed in real time, but it now seemed much farther back: the beginning of my downfall.

The early period of the shift was slow, meaning Merryll was extra surly since her tip money was adding up at a snail's pace. It was a no-win situation with Merryll. She was ornery when the restaurant was busy because she had a hard time keeping up, but maybe even more so when it wasn't. Stressing out about upcoming rent and car payments, she wasn't in the mood to hear about the Nakayama Genesis. Not the seventy-two pieces of steel or the finely polished chestnut handle, which Cal raved about as he set a rare order for French toast out on the window ledge.

"Are we seriously still talking about your knife, Cal?" Merryll sneered. "Why don't you jam it into my heart and put me out of my misery, please."

Maybe there was some magic to Cal's knife after all, though. As Merryll sniffed at the wisps of steam coming up from the plate, she no longer looked like someone in misery. Briefly closing her eyes to soak it in, Merryll licked her lips and looked back up, the malice in her expression temporarily replaced by adulation.

"Geez, Cal, this looks like some *good* fricking French toast!"

Cal twirled the straps of his apron in his hand after hearing Merryll's unexpected compliment. He stood there awkwardly, grinning and clearly proud, but not entirely sure how to address it. In Cal's mind, everything he ever made was amazing, whether that was the case or not. He wasn't used to hearing other people say so though, and he seemed uncertain on how to handle it. Staples came by the grill, a little bit sheepishly, after he'd seen Merryll pass through to add a glass of freshly squeezed orange juice to her brunch tray.

"Got any more of that French toast, Cal?" Staples asked.

"Nope. How come—you want to laugh *through* me again?" Cal had been uncharacteristically cold towards Staples ever since the day Magneto Man came in.

"Not this time," he said drily. "Was hoping you made extra. I've never been a fan of your work, but that looked *perfect*. What did you do to it?"

I thought that Cal was going to pompously display his knife again, and maybe talk about how it allowed him to get a thin, precise cut of bread that would have been unimaginable without the Genesis. Instead, though, he looked confused, and even a little overwhelmed as Merryll delivered the tray to an enthusiastic mom sitting with her young daughter at a side table.

"I just made it like I always do." He looked at each of us, as if to ask for help. "At least I think I did. I can't remember— people don't order French toast very often. I just . . . made it."

"Do you think you could do it again?"

"I honestly don't know." It was the first genuinely humble thing that I'd ever heard Cal say.

Standing back by the grill, the three of us looked on as the woman with the French toast took gentle, rapturous bites of her meal. She cleaned every last drop of syrup from her fork on each bite, closing her eyes to chew, quietly smiling with every piece. She cut off a piece to share with her four-year-old daughter. The little girl squealed with joy and giggled after tasting the small wedge of bread. The mom gave her a mildly annoyed side-eye at the noise, probably hoping to get back to the intimate moment with her meal. The two slices of bacon on the plate were forgotten as she sprinkled another round of powdered sugar onto Cal's unbelievably good order of French toast.

Watching his customer eat made Cal even more uncomfortable with his fragile triumph. Going through what was clearly a peak moment in his time as a cook, he looked indecisive of how to commemorate it, how he could possibly duplicate it, or what his next move should be. After shifting his feet restlessly, he made a small move to go out to their table, but Staples wisely held him back. Once the woman had finished the final bite of the French toast, the crisp golden top layer blending with the steaming, cloud-like interior of cinnamon and vanilla, she gave a nostalgic dab to the corners of her mouth with a napkin. I unceremoniously cleared the dishes off the table, and that was that. Cal was oddly quiet for the remainder of the afternoon.

With less than an hour to spare between my two shifts, I didn't have enough time to go home or even try to do anything interesting downtown. Instead, I grabbed a three-quarter-price club sandwich and orangeade from the restaurant and went across the street.

Jimmy's was located only a few blocks away from the harbor of Lake Bellview. One quick turn after leaving the back exit and you could already see the impossibly blue water splashing against the docks, as well as the spectacular sails rising out of the bay like the fins from a team of gigantic great white sharks.

If I had walked far enough out onto the docks, I would have been able to clearly see out onto the Peninsula. Looking out towards the horizon, the Peninsula's giant cottages crept from right to left along the shoreline, like a sentence being written backwards. The scene was punctuated by an ellipsis of three blue houses, right at the middle of the thin strip of land. From where I was, though, all I could see was the candy-cane-looking lighthouse that sat on the southern tip like an upside-down exclamation point. On the public side of the downtown waterfront, there was a small park with picnic tables, a gazebo, and two tennis courts running alongside the pier.

I sat down at a table and took partial interest in a couple that was probably in their twenties, playing tennis together. For some reason, they looked to me like newlyweds who came up to Northern Michigan for their honeymoon. She was wearing a short tennis skirt that made it hard for me not to stare at her smooth bronze legs while she chased after the ball.

The guy on the other side of the net looked like he was starting to get agitated with his girlfriend—or maybe his new wife, or other half, or whatever. He was trying to stay calm and encouraging, but the way he kept slightly dropping his head or gritting his teeth every time she missed (which was basically *every* time) gave him away.

The only time I'd played tennis before was on a video game. From what I could see, though, the guy had a lot of experience; as for his girl, not so much. When she wasn't missing the ball completely, she was sending it flying past the baseline and into the fence. She gripped her racket like it was a snow shovel, and she looked like she'd learned her swing technique from watching Staples scoop ice cream. She had already launched one ball all the way into the water, and her wild inaccuracy meant that another one would surely be taking a bath soon; it was just a matter of time.

Slipping into a daydream about what it might be like to teach someone like Lacy how to play basketball, I felt a tap on my shoulder, and quickly spun my neck around, seeing a familiar face grinning at me.

"Planning your next *Ocean's Eleven* escapade?"

At first I didn't know what Jennie meant, as she shuffled a set of keys in her hand and flicked her gaze off towards the horizon. The lighthouse with the red-and-white candy cane paint job loomed in the distance. That must be what she was talking about.

"Nice one. Couldn't go back there even if I wanted to. How long have you been standing there?"

"Long enough." Jennie coolly flipped the questioning back at me. She put the keys in a denim drawstring bag and sat it on her shoulder, and she held a notebook with a red bookmark poking out; it was the same one I'd seen once before, in the cupboard under DigiServ. "Shouldn't you be at work?" she asked. "I know you're on the schedule tonight."

I nodded towards my half-eaten club sandwich. The remaining fries had scattered across the white Styrofoam takeout box, looking like broken twigs on a patch of fresh snow.

"I'm on split shift. I was there all through lunch too. Between Merryll and Cal, I had to get out of there for a little while at least—get some of my sanity back." Jennie smiled and nodded in sympathy as I mentioned our coworkers, when a flash of alarm shot through me. "Wait, what time is it?"

As I sat by the pier, I hadn't been paying much attention to how much time had passed. For that brief uneasy moment, I worried that I might have overstayed my lunch break. Jennie glanced at her left wrist. A silver analog watch with a thin turquoise band was partially covering up her tattoo.

"3:25."

"Good," I exhaled. "I have another twenty minutes out here then. Where are you coming from, anyway?"

"I'm on night shift dude, you forget? I parked over in that lot." Jennie's keys jingled again as she gestured to the courts. "At first, I was watching these lovebirds attempt to play tennis, and then I noticed that you were over here too. Besides, it doesn't always hurt to get away from my boyfriend for a little while, ya know?"

I didn't know what Jennie meant, but I nodded along anyway as she finished this thought with an eye roll and a dry laugh. It didn't take much imagination for me to assume that anyone would need some time away from Jimi Dandersley every now and then. That wasn't enough, though. If it were up to me, she would need *all* of her time away from him.

"What's that word tattooed on your wrist?" I asked,

changing the subject. "I've been meaning to ask about it all summer."

At first Jennie looked like she was pretending not to hear me, but eventually unbuckled the strap of the watch and held out her wrist.

ANÁΓKH

"I don't even know how to pronounce it," she said, "but I saw it in a book once. It means 'fate.' It's Greek."

"I'll have to take your word for it."

Jennie slid the denim bag from her shoulder and set the watch inside of it before yanking on the string to close it again. She kept holding the small notebook in her right hand, tapping it against her hip and looking pensive.

"Remember that night at the haunted house?" she asked. "The Five Mile Creek one?"

Adding "the Five Mile Creek one" to the end of her question was pointless; as if Jennie needed to make sure that I wouldn't confuse it with one of the many other haunted houses that the two of us had visited together. On the basement steps, Jennie had been trying to communicate with the spirits of the haunted house, and I kept interrupting. It was the first conversation that her and I ever had, back when I dismissed her as a burnout, and she dismissed me period.

"Yeah, I remember. What does that have to do with your tattoo?"

"You said something that night, that sort of . . . resonated."

"Really?" The thought of me saying anything that resonated with somebody else was surprising. "What did I say?"

"I asked why you went out to the house, when you'd already gotten in a lot of trouble. You said that somewhere deep down, you knew that you should be there, even though you couldn't logically explain why. So then I told you maybe it was fate. Like every decision we make has already been determined by a higher power, and we're just reading the lines and acting out the grand script. We talked about fate, and for some reason, that conversation stuck with me."

"You got that tattoo because of *me*?"

Hearing that felt like some kind of strange honor, but Jennie gave a casual shrug.

"Indirectly, yeah. Because of what we talked about, anyway. I was tired of hurting so much and feeling sorry for myself too. It's a reminder that the past is always going to hurt, but that doesn't mean I can't try to take fate back into my own hands a little at the same time." She glanced at her wrist again, forgetting that the watch wasn't on it anymore. "I should get in early and take care of sugars and shakers. It's 'all hands on deck' lately, with how busy it's been."

I knew that the waitstaff was responsible for making sure that the various little packets of sugar—as well as the salt and pepper shakers—were consistently refilled and kept tidy in their sections of tables; like Staples told me (and as Merryll had found out firsthand), this small task was easy to ignore, but the results weren't pretty if we stopped paying attention to it.

"Ehh, this afternoon was really slow. I wouldn't rush it," I said.

"That guy's backhand is terrible, by the way," Jennie said, returning her attention to the courts. "He's supposed to be teaching the girl—so who's teaching him?"

"I didn't know you were a tennis connoisseur."

"A connoisseur, huh? Someone's been spending too much time around Staples." Jennie motioned for me to make space at the picnic table and sat down next to me. "He's gotta stop leaning back every time he hits it, otherwise it'll keep floating off so weak. And he's not following through at all."

"Didn't you say you had to do sugars and shakers?"

Jennie shook off the suggestion. "What's the worst that can happen? Merryll actually has to help someone for a change?"

Jennie stretched her legs, settling in. She reached into her bag and rummaged around in it for a second or two, pulling out a small rectangular box. It was her pack of Marlboro Reds, which she set on the table before going digging in the bag again. This second round of searching took quite a bit more effort on Jennie's part, but eventually a small plastic Bic lighter emerged from one of the hidden pockets. I wondered if Bic's marketing team used the same slogan for lighters as they did with those pens from the restaurant: *Lights the first time, every time!*

Preparing for Jennie to light her cigarette, I felt like I should be doing something at the same time—but if not smoking a cig, then what? I went back to nibbling at the club sandwich, looking away but still paying attention to Jennie from the corner of my eye. Jennie reached for her reds, then paused for a second, brushed a strand of hair from her face, and decided to put both objects back in the bag without doing anything. About a minute later, she pulled out the lighter for a second time, and then put it back again. I perceived an internal battle going on in Jennie's mind—one that she was winning for the moment. She looked back out at the newlyweds on the court.

"Mom got us these old rackets at a garage sale once. There

was a playground near our house, like only a five-minute walk or something, and they had tennis courts. The rackets were from like the 1980s, but Heather went through a huge tennis phase for a while. She was always making me go down and practice rallying with her."

"Hey, I guess it paid off. You know a lot more about it than I do—I thought that guy was pretty good."

"Nah, that's all Heather. One summer she kept making me watch all the big tournaments on TV with her. And got mad at Dad because he couldn't mow the yard extra short to make a grass court like Wimbledon. She said that we could be the Zilwaukee version of the Williams sisters. I was like, 'Okay, but you'll have to be both Venus *and* Serena.'" She grinned widely, obviously enjoying the memory.

"There aren't many people in this town who know about your sister," I stated, remembering the day that the woman from Zilwaukee had come to the restaurant. "What made you tell me?"

"I don't know." She saw that I wasn't satisfied with the answer, but firmly doubled down on it. "Seriously—I don't. It just felt like I could, so I went with it."

"Does Jimi know about her?" I sort of suspected that she was ducking the question.

"My boyfriend, or our boss?"

"Your boyfriend."

"We've only been together for a few months . . . It hasn't come up yet."

I gave her a facial expression that I'd learned from Spaz. I call it the "bullcrap sensor," when you know beyond a doubt that the person you're talking too isn't giving you the full story. Jennie shifted a little bit on the table and looked out at the lighthouse again.

"Look, Jimi's past is out there in the open. Plenty of people know that his dad committed suicide when he was like six. And everybody knows what happened right when he started high school, and they made up their minds that he's a bad guy. He's got enough to worry about without me getting all tragic. Anyway, I'd better get inside."

"Alright, see you in a few minutes. By the way, when you go in there, Cal is going to try to tell you about his new kitchen knife. If you act like you give a crap, I bet he'll send your orders out first for the whole evening."

"Ha-ha, thanks for the tip. I'll remember that."

I watched her leave. If Jennie didn't like me on some level at least, then why was she watching me from a distance and going out of her way to come hang out for a little while before work? I couldn't deny that at this point, there was definitely some sort of connection between her and me. But on the other hand, she could have been making out with Jimi Dandersley on his couch just an hour ago, for all I knew. So how's that for a connection?

After that uninvited thought, I decided that I wasn't hungry anymore. I wound up my arm and chucked the last bits of my sandwich off the edge of the pier and into the bay. A team of ducks looked very happy as they huddled around their free snack. I grabbed my backpack and brushed the loose crumbs from my shirt, leaving the waterfront as a few stray seagulls flew in to where I'd been sitting.

CHAPTER THIRTY-FOUR

Wildest Moments

What happened when he started high school?" After leaving the restaurant that night, I biked over in Jennie's direction, catching up to her at the edge of the parking lot. She was starting to unlock the door of her station wagon and looked confused. "Your boyfriend. You said that everyone knew."

Jennie had only meant it as a small detail in our conversation, but that question kept popping into my mind during the second half of the split shift. She hadn't noticed, but I was paying close attention to her right when the dinner crowd started arriving, when she winked at me before going over to see—with way too much enthusiasm—how Cal and his new knife were doing. She'd asked Cal whether it was true that part of his soul was infused in the center of the handle.

Watching the way Jennie's hazel eyes lit up as she both roasted Cal and egged him on at the same time, my mind was troubled with the echo of her throwaway comment on the picnic table. Jennie's boyfriend did something at the start of high school that completely ruined his reputation around town. Sound familiar?

"What, you never heard about that?" Jennie was forgetting that most of the people she hung out with were closer to my brother's age than mine. There was a bit of a generation gap in terms of relevant gossip.

"Jimi was kicked out of school for a while." She said it so nonchalantly that it was like she was telling me he'd slept in and come in ten minutes late one day. "He missed his entire freshman year."

"Seriously?" My mouth dropped. I never expected to have something in common with Jimi Dandersley, but maybe he was the one person in Northern Michigan who'd had a worse freshman year of high school than me.

"It was way before I moved to town—I would have still been in what, like 5th grade?" Then, seeing the look on my face, she said, "Okay, I know that sounds weird, shut up. He's a little bit older, whatever."

"And he got kicked out of school?" Figuring that Rodney absolutely must have known about this, it was yet another subtle reminder of just how little him and me talked.

"Yup. Jimi was suspended for his entire freshman year. He took extension courses at Fresh Start Alternative, but he was still way behind when he returned the next year. And he's always been kind of insecure about school, so that made him struggle even more when he got back."

"What did he do?" I asked quietly.

"It was sometime during the first week of school. He attacked another student, completely lost control of himself. Slammed the kid up against a brick wall in between classes. He probably didn't mean for it to cause quite as much damage as it did, but it cracked the back of the guy's head open."

"That's . . . pretty bad."

"Look, I didn't say he should have done it. Everyone makes mistakes, right? What makes you so interested in my boyfriend all of a sudden, anyway?"

I got on the defensive real fast after she asked that. If she hadn't already figured out how much I liked her, I was right on the verge of blowing my cover. So I did my best to deflect the situation.

"No reason. I guess I just thought that, you know, you and Blaise might have had a thing, that's all."

"You think me and *Blaise* would ever get together?"

Before Jimi Dandersley came along, there was a time when I'd thought that. Backtracking, but trying to think fast, I then mentioned that I knew the two of them had hung out a lot towards the end of the winter. And that I knew Jennie had started going to a lot of Eagles games near the end of the season, and that she didn't care anything about basketball. Also, the fact that Jennie was the one who took him out to Five Mile Creek.

"I took you out there too. Y'saying *we* had a thing?" she countered.

I heard a round of laughter from the background: a group of Margaritavilles enjoying a few cocktails out on their boat. Gentle waves splashed against the docks, and I thought of something ridiculous that Spaz had said once, about there being freshwater jellyfish out in the lake. Dusk was turning into nightfall, and the full moon was becoming a lot more prominent in the late-summer sky. Jennie leaned against her car.

"Sure, Blaise is kinda hot. That doesn't mean he's the type

I would go for. We were hanging out a lot, but it wasn't like that at all," Jennie continued. "You weren't talking to him, and he was feeling a ton of pressure, whether people realized it or not. I think what he needed most at the time was a friend who doesn't care in the slightest whether he was good at basketball or not."

"But you never thought you'd be a good fit . . . you know, together?"

Jennie vigorously shook her head no.

"He's such a perfectionist, it's freaky. He can't zip up his jacket without redoing it three or four times, because there's always something about it that feels slightly off to him."

I nodded and grinned. I knew exactly what she was talking about. He did the same thing with his shoelaces, his basketball shorts, the dollar bills in his wallet, you name it, always checking repeatedly to make sure everything was perfectly in place.

"Besides, Blaise is going places. Whether I like it or not, I'm here to stay. That's probably the biggest thing."

Going places. From the time we became aware enough to understand that a larger picture existed, our lives, decisions, and dreams were framed by this idea of going somewhere. In order to matter, eventually you had to go, even if it was just to say you did it.

Whether it was to try and get rich or become famous, to get a better job, a better education, a wider perspective, or a fresh start, the reason hardly mattered. If you decided that you were going to be somebody (or in some cases, if it was decided for you), the general thought in our town was that you needed to go somewhere else in order to be it.

"Is Jimi Dandersley going places?"

Jennie reached into her drawstring bag and pulled out the Bic lighter. Once again, I watched her internal battle play out in front of me, except this time Jennie was on the losing end of it. She looked exposed as she slid a cigarette into the corner of her mouth and lit it.

"Nope. So maybe that means we belong with each other. Can be stuck here together."

As the small cloud of smoke sailed off towards the water, Jennie shrugged off that somber thought. She seemed to be gathering her next question from the now-emerging awning of stars.

"Are you better than your wildest moments, JB?"

"What do you mean?" That was a question that I'd never been asked before, but it felt heavy.

"Are you better than yourself when you're at your worst? I want to believe that I am, and I want to believe that Jimi is too. You don't want your whole life to be affected by one time you went a little crazy, or even a few times. Nobody wants that."

I never thought I would have sympathy for Jennie's boyfriend, but I had to agree. I admitted that my entire summer had been built around trying to make up for a few wrong things that I'd done in the past, and how it was sometimes an agonizing and impossible task. Sharing that obstacle with Jimi made it a little bit more difficult for me to hate him.

"I feel bad for the kid who got his head busted," Jennie said, stamping out her cigarette on the ground. "But Jimi still got the worst of it in the end by far. He got booted from school for a year, and people think he's an idiot because it took him longer to graduate. He barely got out of high school with a degree, he's had this negative reputation following him around for . . . who knows how long—forever? And the other guy? Sure, he needed to get the back of his head stapled up, but he was completely fine." She opened up the car door and climbed inside. "And he even got a cool nickname out of it."

"Hold on a second . . ."

The ignition of Jennie's station wagon blared to life. She drove away as I looked in astonishment back at the outside of the restaurant.

CHAPTER THIRTY-FIVE

The Dream

Whenever I get a good night's sleep—a *good* night's sleep, which I'd say is about a third of the time—my dreams involve playing basketball in some way or another. That night after my split shift, and with all the new information I'd received, I fell into a deep dreamworld almost the instant my head landed on the cool pillow. It was one I'll remember for a long time—not only for how vivid and hyperreal the dream felt, but for what it made me realize, as well.

I dreamed about a basketball game taking place on Main Street of downtown, played in the middle of winter. The weather was light snow flurries and the trademark listless gray skies of February, but the mood of downtown in the dream was anything but dreary. Bellview was facing Red Cliff in the regional championship game.

Instead of uniforms, each team was bundled up in coats and gloves, with only their wool hats to tell them apart. Cliff's players were wearing their classic brick red, while we had navy blue knit hats with the outline of an eagle stitched on them. Main Street was shut down to all traffic to make room for the game, with the same baskets from the Mirage court set up in the middle of the road and facing each other. As you lined up for free throws on the west end of the court, the massive spires of the Catholic church loomed straight ahead in the foul shooter's line of sight.

Since my gloves prevented me from getting a proper grip on the ball, instead of shooting threes, I dribbled my way into the lane and shot only floaters: high-arching one-handers with no spin that either swished or softly sat up on the rim before falling in, as long as they were shot with the right touch. In the dream game against our biggest rivals, I couldn't miss, hitting all six of my shots in the first half. We went into halftime leading by eight.

Instead of a locker room, we spent the break in the dining room at Jimmy's Family Restaurant. The lights were turned off and the building felt cold and clammy, unused and forgotten in the dead of winter. The wooden chairs were stacked upside down on top of the empty tables, and the boss appeared from the back kitchen to pull them down for the team to sit on during our unusual halftime meeting. I noticed that Blaise was wearing gray No-Slips to play ball. Jimmy scowled as Blaise stamped his feet on the floor to knock off all the snow that had attached to the soles.

As I opened up the door to return to the game, dream Jimmy called back to me. He was holding the Nakayama Genesis knife, passionately stabbing it into a tub of red ice cream. Looking eerie and ghost-like, he kept repeating, "Finish them off. This is for your town. This is for *your town*, remember that."

The otherworldly game of snow hoops continued outside,

and our team picked up where we left off. By the middle of the third quarter, we led by at least a dozen (there was no scoreboard set up out there), and shoppers and pedestrians were coming out of the storefronts and gradually gathering around the curb of the street. There were way more people in the area than you'll ever see during the winter; it was like the 4th of July parade was taking place five months early.

I got the ball along the left wing and watched as the defender backed away from me. Disregarding my gloves, and the cold and damp leather from the ball, I decided to launch a deep three, knowing with full confidence that it would find a way through the hoop. It wasn't a swish, but after rattling around both the rim and the backboard, the ball convinced the hoop to let it through.

The snow was thickening, and the smell of hot chocolate swirled through the scene like an oil painting. Holding my arms out like an airplane, I ran and slid across the icy asphalt court as the Red Cliff team called for a time-out. Like what always happens in dreams, right when you feel like you're getting to the most important part, things slowed down and faded out, until the almost supernatural downtown scene disappeared and I was back in bed, awake and staring into the darkness.

While trying to get back to sleep, I was reminded of what Staples's friend Connor had said down at the public beach, about the Peninsula royalty taking everything with them if they ever decided to leave town. It occurred to me that there was at least one thing that they couldn't take: Eagles basketball. It may be our one and only outlet for excitement, drama, expression, and pride during the otherwise dreary Northern

Michigan winters, but Eagles basketball belonged to us and only us. I wasn't exactly sure what that meant in the grand scheme of things, but I knew it meant something.

The first beam of sunlight pierced through the curtains in my bedroom at 7:23 a.m. the next morning, pulling me out of my deep sleep. The events of the remainder of that day made me question whether I'd actually woken up at all.

CHAPTER THIRTY-SIX

Sunshine and Shadow

Jennie showed up at the restaurant the next day wearing a stylish pair of green-tinted Oakley sunglasses. The temperature outside was over eighty degrees already, and the sunlight was blinding by this point, but that didn't explain why she kept them on indoors.

"Magneto Man comes in one time, and now you've gone all Hollywood on us?"

At first, I thought Jennie might not have heard my try at a joke, but the exaggerated way she then turned away made it clear that she'd heard me and didn't find it funny. Fully ignoring me, she set her bag and notebook in the storage cupboard and found the large salt and pepper containers to start refilling the shakers. Anyone else in the area helping prepare for the day was wise enough to give Jennie her space from there on. No one approached her again until five minutes before the doors opened, when Gloria came out with a friendly dress code reminder.

"Miss Jennifer, those are some spiffy-looking shades, but unfortunately they do need to come off before we open up for customers."

Jennie nodded and briefly flashed an obviously fake smile as she turned on the coffee pots, continuing with her pre-shift routine. She waited until the last possible moment before taking the sunglasses off, revealing a massive bruise around her left eye.

When I reflexively asked about it, she snapped, and it was the last time she spoke to me during that day's shift.

"How 'bout you don't worry about it JB? Y'think you can do that for once?"

Retreating to the background for the remainder of the morning, I quietly went about bussing tables and trying to make sense of the change that had occurred since I'd seen her last. Both before and after work the previous day, we had breezed through our spare time talking by the waterfront. Jennie had shared stories from her past, I'd found out that her *ANÁΓKH* tattoo was inspired by me, and she had even unleashed a mind-blowing piece of history between her boyfriend and Staples.

Only twelve hours had passed, but it was like the magnetic poles of our shared world had suddenly reversed, while the vivid Main Street basketball scene from my dream distracted me. When we'd parted ways that night after work, some overwhelming force must have visited while I slept. It had left Jennie not only bruised, but also dispirited, and me shut out of her world completely.

Gone was the extra glimmer of life that had been apparent in Jennie's expression all summer. In its place was a dark shadow surrounding her hazel eyes, the ones that caused me to fidget with anxiousness every time they lingered on me for too long. Even with heavy makeup on, the deep bruise was impossible not to notice—definitely for our coworkers, and most likely from the customers too. In the absence of an official explanation from Jennie, the rest of the waitresses, along with Cal and Spaz, whispered amongst themselves and created their own conclusions of what had gone down the night before. In my own head, I tried to do the same as I bussed that day's tables mostly on autopilot.

The promising start to the morning slowly and imperceptibly faded away. Degree by degree, the temperature dropped. Cloud by cloud, the horizon flipped from shiny light blue to white splotches, then to a blanket of silver, and finally to an imposing shield of gray by mid-afternoon.

FULL TIME-OUT

THE TWO JIMS

Jimmy: About sixty years old. Restaurant owner. The "Busiest Man in Northern Michigan" during the summer. Keeps a yellowing towel over his shoulder and wears an apron that matches his black No-Slip kitchen shoes.

Jimi: About twenty-one-years old. Part-time construction worker. Probably the least busy man in Northern Michigan for most parts of the year. Has yellowing teeth and wears a black jacket that says Fox Racing no matter what the temperature is.

Jimmy: Arrived at his restaurant through the back entrance at 7:23 that morning, according to the DigiServ records.

Jimi: Arrived at Jimmy's restaurant through the front entrance at 3:28 that afternoon.*

*Neither of them looked like they'd gotten enough sleep the night before.

Jimmy: Must have wondered why Jennie showed up at work with a black eye.

Jimi: Knew exactly why Jennie showed up at work with a black eye.

Jimmy: Watched with interest through the kitchen window as an unshaven customer in a Fox Racing jacket started to argue with his best waitress.
Jimi: Walked with a limp through the dining room of the restaurant and demanded to talk to Jennie.

Jimi: I've gathered that he's the type of guy who selfishly stirs up problems at almost every opportunity.
Jimmy: I've learned that he's the type of guy who doesn't take shit from anyone.

Jimi: Didn't take kindly to his girlfriend giving him the cold shoulder. Started swearing and making a fuss, even though the dining room was full of a late-arriving group of families with young kids.
Jimmy: Probably didn't like the fact that this guy was hijacking the calm atmosphere of the late Sunday brunch crowd.

Jimi: Shoved Spaz out of the way as he tried to follow Jennie into the kitchen, yelling that she'd better turn around and face him.
Jimmy: Shoved Jimi up against the wall near the back entrance, pressing both hands around his throat, whispering that he'd better not come within a hundred feet of his establishment ever again. The schedule for the next week had been knocked off the wall. The paper casually floated to the ground.

Me: Silently watched all of this go down with a mixture of excitement and fear.

Jennie: Looked unsure of herself, alone and shaken, folding her arms across her chest. She was frozen in place, with an empty stare from across the kitchen, and every bit of her demeanor seemed to be asking, "What should I do next?"

Spaz: "Yo, Jimmy's a lot stronger than I would've imagined."

Cal: "You see the veins popping out of those hairy forearms??"

Staples: "I'm telling you, it's those mopping hands! (Acts out mopping the floor, like a game of charades.) Don't underestimate the technique!"

Jimmy: Scraped the smiles off my coworkers' faces with one death stare. Their glee may as well have been unwanted grease on the stovetop, and it was removed just as fast.

Spaz/Staples/Cal: Went back to work.

Jimmy: Walked over to Jennie and calmly whispered something in her ear.

Jennie: Walked out the back exit of the restaurant and didn't return for the rest of her shift.

CHAPTER THIRTY-SEVEN

Like a Comic Book

I'd thought the guy from Magneto Man coming into Jimmy's the week before was a surreal experience, but it had nothing on the events unfolding as Jennie's boyfriend had pushed in to dominate the dining room. The whole thing was so choppy and disjointed, my memory kept flashing from one specific image to the next in the series of mayhem. My imagination had to fill in the blanks to put together what had happened in the space between. Like panels in a comic book, it was like one scene moved to the next in small, broken-up sections.

Jennie holding a pot of coffee, looking towards the front door with an exaggerated raise of an eyebrow . . . The aggressive villain with a red buzz cut storming in to take over the scene . . . POW! A tray of dishes soaring through the air as he shoves an innocent bystander to the side . . . Jimmy swooping in quicker than a man his age had any right to move, his apron swishing behind him . . . The boss with gritted teeth, shoving the villain up against the wall, veins bulging out of his hairy forearms as the villain sweats heavily and turns blue . . . one panel of the comic empty, except for a screen door snapping shut . . . Jennie becoming even more noticeable by her absence.

The scene back at the restaurant was mixed once things had calmed down. Numerous customers had ended their meals early, hurrying up to the cash register just to pay and get out of there, while others continued eating and tried to return to normal. Either way, a tangible uneasiness hung in the air for the last hour of the shift. The tension in the room was thick enough to cut with Cal's knife. Thin, precise, slices of tension. Japanese-sushi-restaurant-quality tension.

Arthur arrived on time for once to take over for me, and I handed over my apron with an intense sense of relief after one of the most uncomfortable days of the whole summer.

Before I could walk out the screen door and head back home, Gloria called over to me with one final task. She was holding a drawstring bag, a notebook, and an apron filled with small bundles of cash.

"Would you mind returning Jennifer's things to her on your way out? She hasn't left yet."

CHAPTER THIRTY-EIGHT

Benched

Jennie was sitting on that out-of-place bench tucked away behind the restaurant, close enough to the dumpster to catch the fumes if the wind happened to blow in the wrong direction. She was leaning out with her arms folded across her stomach, as if she was trying her hardest not to be sick. She had the green sunglasses on again, even though the sky had progressively turned gray since earlier that morning. It looked like she was either covering up her bruised face or concealing tears; Jennie doesn't cry, though, so it must have been the first thing.

I was fully prepared to quickly finish off the errand that Gloria had assigned and leave Jennie by herself. Her position, sitting alone and all the way to the side of the bench, made it look for all the world as if she wanted to hide. However, my next thought was that if this was true, there were plenty of better places she could have slipped off to, unseen and unbothered.

I took a closer look at Jennie and changed my mind. By sliding over to the right-hand side of the bench, Jennie was just slightly signaling an invitation for someone else to sit down as well. Maybe what she secretly wanted was someone to hide *with*.

"Gloria asked me to bring out your tip money—you left it in your apron. It's all here." I handed over the roll of cash, which was already folded and sorted into ones, fives, and tens, as well as her notebook and denim bag. "She gave me your other stuff too."

"Thanks."

I reasoned that if Jennie really didn't want anyone to join her, she would have made it obvious. I used to do the same thing on the school bus if I wanted to keep a seat to myself. It's easy; all you have to do is sit in the very center and take up enough space on both sides so it doesn't look like there's any room on either. Jennie could have stretched her feet out wide and set her hands down at the sides, but she did neither. She didn't even use her book bag to cover up the open area on the bench when I handed it to her, instead setting it on the ground, directly at her feet.

A gust of the cool cross-breeze swirled through our area of the pavement, creating a curious smell in the air. It was a combo of the fresh lake scent from the docks a block away and the wet coffee grounds, vegetable stems, and orange peels from the partially contained dumpster shed just behind us. Strangely, the resulting mix wasn't all that unpleasant. Without any further plan in mind, I went ahead and sat down on the bench next to Jennie.

FULL TIME-OUT

THE RIGHT THING TO SAY

I'm not very good at picking out the right thing to say, even in regular situations. How was I supposed to approach this one? Seriously, what do you say to someone whose boyfriend gave them a black eye, raged into their workplace like a jackass, only to have our boss nearly strangle him up against the wall, with all her coworkers and half the restaurant watching? I've never seen a Hallmark sympathy card for that particular scenario. It never occurred to me to consider what I might say when facing such a situation.

It felt it was my responsibility to say something, though. Here's what I came up with:

A. **"Listen, Jennie, I may not have a truck, or my own place, or any facial hair, but I guarantee I would never leave your face looking like that."**

B. **"Does this mean you and Jimi are broken up now?"** The answer had better be yes, but this wasn't the time to be asking.

C. **"It's not your fault."** I don't know exactly what I would mean by that, but I saw it in a movie once. Robin Williams was a therapist. He keeps saying "It's not your fault" over and over again until they're both crying in each other's arms.

D. **"Did you see how the veins on Jimmy's forearms were popping out earlier?"** I could already envision Jimmy's ten seconds of fury becoming the stuff of legend around the restaurant.

E. **"Are you alright?"** Even I knew better than to ask that question. Exactly what part of this entire screwed-up day was Jennie supposed to be alright with? If she *was* alright, I'd think there was something wrong with her.

I wasn't convinced that any of these conversation starters were the right thing to say, so I decided to wing it.

"Wanna walk around a little bit?"

"Okay."

CHAPTER THIRTY-NINE

Curiosity is Heavier than Guilt

Jennie walked next to me timidly, like the sidewalk was a frozen pond that could crack with each step. It was as if she was feeling her way through an entirely different world than the one she knew the previous day. In my mind, I pictured an astronaut cautiously testing out the terrain and gravity on a new planet. In Jennie's case, it was an even meaner planet, less forgiving and more confusing than the one that ripped her sister away from her just three years before.

We didn't say anything to each other, though there were a few times where I thought I noticed Jennie whispering to herself (no idea what she said). Being a pretty fast walker, I found it awkward to slow up and still try to time my steps with hers. We ended up wandering about five blocks or so, over to the grassy park across from the public beach.

Reaching the middle of the park, Jennie raised her arms up and to the side in a long and exhausted stretch. Without warning, she plopped down on the dry grass (if the misty clouds turned into rain, it would be the first time in over two weeks). She extended her legs straight in front of her and blankly watched ahead. Again, it looked like the only thing keeping Jennie from bursting into tears was the simple fact that Jennie *doesn't* burst into tears. For a second time, I sat down next to her.

Jennie caught my eyes lingering for too long on her notebook, which rested on the grass in between us. She took off her sunglasses and gave me a disapproving look.

"What do you write in there anyway?" I asked.

"Oh please . . . I bet you already went through the entire thing."

A little offended that Jennie assumed that I'd already opened it up and looked, it took me numerous rounds to convince her that I hadn't. I didn't pretend that I wasn't interested, but it seemed important for her to know that she could trust me. Eventually, with exasperation in her voice, she told me to just go ahead and read it if I wanted.

"Nah, that's not what I meant. I was just asking what you use it for, like in general. I wasn't trying to be nosy."

"Go ahead. You're doing your whole polite thing, but I know you want to read it. I actually sort of want you to."

"What do you mean you *want* me to?

"Some of the stuff in there . . . well, you are referenced—put it that way. If you opened it to the bookmarked page, you'll know what I mean. Might as well at this point—I doubt it would make things any worse."

Jennie handed over the notebook, pulling aside the red ribbon and opening it to the most recent page that was filled. I took a deep breath, my curiosity outweighing my guilt. The date written on the top margin of the sheet was August 12th. I began to read.

CHAPTER FORTY

The Diary

I'm trying to navigate through my mind right now, but a drive through my brain at the moment is nothing scenic or majestic like going through the Tunnel of Trees. A road trip through my current thoughts probably wouldn't end up anywhere worthwhile, like the Grand Canyon or whatever.

I should not have just used the Grand Canyon as my number one example for a destination that's worthwhile. The Grand Canyon sucks. We drove out there during Spring Break in 5th grade. It took like three full days just to look at a big hole in the ground and then turn back around. Heather barfed all over the back seat of the station wagon. She never wanted to eat at Arby's after that happened.

So screw the Grand Canyon, seriously. But a road trip through my head wouldn't end up anywhere dope like Coachella or Bonnaroo either. Instead, I'd probably end up lost in a giant corn field somewhere in the middle of Ohio, surrounded by nothing but fucking silos.

Forget any sort of GPS or navigation device, there's not even an old wrinkled road map in the glove box of my mind. There's no veteran tour guide making corny jokes and telling anecdotes as he calmly leads me from one place to another. Instead it's like I'm being led by a couple of crazy monkeys with daggers, waiting for something to attack. Any time a positive thought, or a special moment, or hope or excitement creeps in, it immediately gets stabbed out of there by the monkeys.

I can't concentrate long enough to figure out where I'm trying to go, I'll admit it. So I shouldn't really be surprised if I always end up somewhere else. I don't know.

I don't know why I put up with Jimi's constant bullshit. I just know that it feels better when I'm with him than it does without him.

I don't know when I'll finally come to grips with losing Heather. All I know is that I feel worse in every moment without her than any point when she was with me.

I don't know why I keep flirting with JB when we're on the same shift at the restaurant. I just know that I keep saying in my head that I don't like him like that, but I need to work way too hard to convince myself of it.

I don't know why I got so jealous when those girls from the Peninsula were in there checking him out. I just know I wanted to spit in their orangeade. And I'm not sorry for changing the last digit on the phone number either.

I don't know why I used the fifty-cent tip from Table 32 to play Margaritaville on the jukebox the other day. I legitimately hate that song.

I don't know what it is about JB, but whenever I talk to him, I feel like. . .open.

I don't know why I'm writing any of this, but my boyfriend would probably freak out if he was interested enough to read it. Oh well, time to go pretend again. . .

CHAPTER FORTY-ONE

Slam

I'd seen enough. Not wanting to say the wrong thing or draw attention to how vulnerable she looked, I kept quiet and purposely looked away from her. I pretended to be deeply interested in the group of guys trying skateboard tricks over by the pavilion with the fancy drinking fountain. My pretend interest must have fooled the mini skateboarder guys inside my head, because they stopped skating laps around my cortex and zeroed in on their real-life counterparts by the drinking fountain as well.

There were six of them, mostly guys I've seen around, some a little older, some a little younger than me. I recognized them from the night of my failed excursion on the Peninsula. They looked like they were having a great afternoon, laughing, swearing, and videotaping each other's trick attempts. None of them could even land a simple kickflip, but that didn't dampen their enthusiasm. I kept watching them closely to avoid witnessing Jennie go through an obvious inner battle.

One of the older skaters almost landed a pop-shuvit (I only recognized it because of that Tony Hawk videogame), which was greeted with a round of high fives from his buddies. I heard Jennie's voice to my right.

"That was…so crazy. At the restaurant earlier. Unexpected."

I figured Captain Obvious would show up at any second. No crap—it was crazy and unexpected. Was she just making small talk?

I watched another kid lose control of his board and have it narrowly miss running over a little toddler who was playing in the grass near the sidewalk.

"I feel so . . . messed up, right now." I nodded at Jennie's statement. Not in like an "I agree, you're totally screwed" sort of way. Just because I had nothing to say, but still wanted to show support, I guess.

The next skater up had a bad wipeout. I winced a little bit watching his knees and hands slam against the concrete. His friends groaned in excitement and then crowded around the camera to watch the instant replay. Then they groaned in excitement again as the unlucky dude tried to shake off his injuries.

Jennie leaned across my line of sight and began kissing me.

CHAPTER FORTY-TWO

How's That for a Connection?

Explain this to me again . . . you made out with Jennie . . . and your boss nearly strangled a guy. And these things are connected to each other in some way?"

In between an exhausting circuit of shooting drills and conditioning, I'd been recapping my day at work to Blaise. I was just as confused as him regarding what to make of the day's events, so it took both of us to try and piece it all together. I'd spent half the summer daydreaming about a moment with Jennie like the one on the grass. After having more time to think it over, though, I wasn't sure whether my encounter with Jennie was something I should be celebrating or be freaked out by.

The jolt of excitement I'd felt when I was kissing Jennie was now balanced out by the reality of the situation. It must have started raining at some point while I was riding my bike, but my mind was so flooded with other thoughts that I didn't even notice my clothes were wet until I got inside the gym. There was the diary page, Jennie's back-and-forth emotions, Jimi Dandersley's reaction when he found out about all this, and yes, all those things connected back to me. Jennie and I had abruptly gone our separate ways from the park without saying much, and I had no idea what the earlier events would mean for us when we went back to work the next day.

"So was that like, the first time you've ever kissed anyone?"

"No . . . first *real* kiss though."

"Real? What do you mean?"

"Brien's birthday party, start of 7th grade. It was right before he moved. Remember, he invited all those girls from class?"

"Riigght. The spin the bottle game."

"Yup, that one. I got paired up with—" I couldn't even get to her name without Blaise exploding with laughter.

"RIIGGHT! I almost forgot about that!!"

"Yeah, I *tried* to forget!"

"Ha-ha-ha, that was a true CIL moment."

I'm not going to say what "CIL" stands for, but you'll have to take my word for it—that moment definitely was one. We both laughed again at the embarrassing memory.

"Alright, time's up," said Blaise. "Sixteen lines in under a minute, let's go!"

CHAPTER FORTY-THREE

Jennie's Suggestion

Over the next week and a half, Jennie and I were like the characters in an old Western movie, like with Clint Eastwood and all that. Keeping our distance, yet always aware of the other, neither wanting to fire first and give anything away, always with an unspoken tension. All that was missing was the single guitar galloping along ominously, with the sounds of crows and spooky whistling in the background as we circled each other carefully and suspiciously. On top of that, I sometimes caught myself defensively glancing over my shoulder as I grabbed my bike at the end of the day, half expecting Jennie's (ex?) boyfriend to jump out from behind the dumpster and start pummeling me.

As I expected, even as the days passed, the boss's actions during the sudden ambush remained fresh on the minds of most people on staff. The tale of his No-Slip grip on Jimi Dandersley's neck grew closer to mythic status with each new retelling. Though Staples never cared to get much into it either, the question of whether or not Jimi would turn up again was a topic of heavy discussion whenever Jennie was out of listening range. The boss's simple expression of defiance when Gloria suggested the risk of a lawsuit showed that if the villain ever returned, he wouldn't think twice about doing a repeat performance.

"Oh, if he ever comes in here again, Jimmy will have to wait in line to strangle him, because believe me, I'm going to kick his ass first . . .Yeah." Cal added that last "yeah" because he must have sensed the disbelief of everyone else who was listening.

Merryll and I didn't see eye-to-eye on most topics, but this was one we could both agree on; she actually snorted when Cal mentioned his ass-kicking agenda.

"You couldn't beat up Jimi Dandersley's little sister." Merryll didn't bother to stay in the area long enough to witness Cal's puffed up chest deflate like an old basketball after she said it.

I think in his mind, Cal beats up a lot of people. In this latest fantasy, he seemed to picture himself being a hardened street brawler, in addition to a smooth ladies' man. In reality, my guess was that Cal would probably have a difficult time beating up an ice cream cone; raspberry sherbet maybe, but Moose Tracks and above he would struggle with. Jimi wasn't that big, but the guy was wiry and crazy aggressive. Even with Cal's knife, I'd still probably put my money on Jimi for that fight.

With his face turning red and nobody coming to his defense, Cal started cutting up an onion, dicing it way harder than was necessary. No one had ordered anything requiring onions either; he was doing it just to prove a point. I'm pretty sure he proved it too.

The only problem was that nobody really knew what point he was trying to make. Judging from Cal's defiant-but-a-little-bit-confused posturing, he wasn't entirely sure which point he had proven, either. That left the rest of us at a bit of a standstill, Cal nodding "so there!," but also searching with his eyes for a little more clarity from the crowd. It reminded me of the story about my brother and Mr. Morrison, where the teacher and student stare each other down, but weren't sure whether they had made an agreement. By the way, the poor guy had picked the wrong vegetable to cut up. The sharp fumes from the onion rose up and caused his eyes to water, now making it look like he was crying because of what Merryll had said. Even by his usual standards, Cal looked completely ridiculous.

During work hours, I would still talk to Jennie, but neither one of us was willing to bring up the topic of our kiss on the grass across from the public beach or get any closure from it. Our interactions took on an odd dimension of formality. I found myself saying "good morning" instead of "what's up" when I saw her at the start of our shifts. I even called her "Jennifer" one time—no idea where that came from.

Just like with the building tension in those cowboy movies, something had to happen eventually, and as I maintained my ground, it was Jennie who made the first move. She walked over to me at the end of a late dinner shift. I had just finished mopping the bathrooms and was starting to wheel the bucket of dirty water to dump out in the kitchen. I heard the clicking of a handful of Bic pens as she approached, all tucked into her apron like pistols in a holster.

"Let's go see *Magneto Man* tomorrow night."

I looked around me and saw that the dining room was

empty besides the two of us. Surprised by her sudden direct-ness, I stayed neutral in my response, wanting to make sure I was hearing correctly.

"Hmm. I wouldn't have expected you to be into super-hero movies."

"I'm not. I think we should hang out though. We're both on day shift tomorrow. Let's go check out that movie after-wards. I'll pick you up in the evening."

Jennie's famous composure had returned once again. She wasn't asking me out on a date. She was *telling* me that we were going on a date together. She shifted her weight from one foot to the other, holding eye contact as she waited for me to confirm. The bruise under her eye was finally disappearing. At this point, it could have just as easily been a smudge of dirt at the top of her cheekbone if you weren't looking closely and didn't know the story behind it.

Most people didn't know the story behind it—not the full story, at least. It was clear by now that dirtbag Jimi had punched her, in one of those wild moments of his, but what wasn't as clear to outsiders was the page of Jennie's diary that he snuck a peek at: the final spark leading to his explosion. Specifically, a page that was talking about *me*.

"And this means," my left leg shook a little as I ner-vously brought up the question that had been on my mind, "you and . . .?"

"Over." Jennie said this with finality to her tone.

I imagined how each of my coworkers might respond if the secret of my upcoming date with Jennie slipped out.

I could picture Spaz back in the kitchen, with his rubber

gloves on his hips as I announced that I was taking Jennie to the movies. He would probably give me that suspicious look that he always does. Like I'm trying to sneak something past him, but he's determined to not let it happen. It's like the intense bullcrap sensors installed somewhere in his retinas were always going off at all the wrong times.

Spaz would probably say something like, "You can't drive, remember? So really, Jennie is the one taking *you* to the movies."

After that, he would probably ask to come along with us too, but to see a different movie. *That actually wouldn't be so bad*, I considered. Spaz could serve as a cushion for any awkward silences or dry spells in conversation on the ride there. The whole romantic aspect would probably go straight over his head; he'd be too busy critiquing all of the ways that *Magneto Man* movie would be a massive disappointment compared to the original comics, and that the original comics sucked to begin with. Jennie would probably ignore it, but I would take the bait and ask Spaz what he had against *Magneto Man* anyway.

Enough about Spaz, though; the reactions from everyone else would be plenty entertaining as well. Staples would of course give his words of warning, but potentially also some useful advice. I could picture him gently shaking his head, and then hitting me across the shoulder with a dishtowel. "Juicy fruit, Beanie. Juicy fruit," he'd probably say, very solemnly. At some point, I might have to ask him for the details about his run-in with Jimi Dandersley that Jennie mentioned, seeing as how I could potentially be facing a similar fate once Jimi found out.

Upon hearing the news, I was certain that Jimmy the boss would scrunch his face up into that disbelieving squint of his.

That vein on his forehead was likely to overflow with the amount of brainpower he would need to try and figure out what his best waitress could possibly see in me.

"You gonna see the *Neato Man* movie? Isn't he the one who ordered whitefish?".

I guarantee that by the time I even started to correct him on the name, he would already be back to taking inventory on a delivery of lemons and oranges, or heading back downstairs to premake ground beef patties with Cal.

If I didn't need a new pair of basketball shoes, I would gladly give a portion of my paycheck to avoid the wide grin of shock and intrigue plastered on Cal's face once he heard about Jennie and me. Within the course of a few minutes, he would likely flip from a stance of complete disbelief into a breezy claim that he'd known all along.

"I had a feeling something was going on with you two," he would pretend, beaming as he carefully wiped off his Genesis and placed it back in its sheath. "I just had a feeling." A carrot's intuition, I suppose.

What about Merryll? As far as I could tell, Merryll didn't like either of us, so that didn't really matter. As long as we didn't enjoy the date and had just as miserable of a time as her, I'm sure she would be quite happy for us. Then there was Lacy.

It was now hard to believe, but at the beginning of summer, she was the one that I would have hoped to go on a movie date with. Not that I had anything against Lacy as time passed; she was cool and everything too, and I even thought I caught her looking at me from time to time. As I got more and more fixated on Jennie, though, the frizzy-haired Peninsula girl who didn't act like a Peninsula girl slowly faded from my mind. Now she was barely even on my radar, and it didn't really even matter whether or not I was on hers.

CHAPTER FORTY-FOUR

At the Movies

Without my noticing it, the month of August was nearly creeping to an end. Like a giant roll of paper towels, I hadn't realized just how much of summer had been used up until I was down to only the final square and the cardboard tube. In just over a week, the Peninsula crowd would head back downstate for the next nine months, emptying the town back out just in time for the start of school and the changing scenery as the season slowly died.

As the temperatures dropped and an extra bite was added to the wind, my mom hopefully would be fully back to her old work schedule. Rodney would be going back to Notre Dame, and Jimmy's Family Restaurant would close its doors until June of next year. Jennie would be starting her senior year at Bellview High School, I'd be a sophomore, and depending on how this trip to the movies went, maybe we would be together.

It had been hot during the day, but temperatures in the evening were already cooling down to the mid-sixties. I wore a zip-up hoodie and khaki shorts. Even though it was getting chilly, I wanted to resist switching back to pants for as long as possible. I didn't go to the same extreme as Blaise, who wore shorts all through the winter no matter what, but I still wanted to hold on to the last crumbs of summer while I could.

Jennie's station wagon pulled into my driveway, sending a wave of relief through me as I stood in the driveway. She was about twenty minutes later than we'd planned, and before seeing the car I was starting to think that she had bailed. She had on a pair of ripped jeans and a purple windbreaker: a similar color to the jacket she'd worn when we went out to Five Mile Creek in the winter. Unlike Five Mile Creek, however, she wasn't wearing a beanie this time. Since she wasn't waiting tables, Jennie was able to keep her hair down, and her flow of dark-blonde hair dropped diagonally in front of her left eye, like a fancy silk curtain in someone's living room. She pushed it away from her eye as I got into the car.

"Sorry I was a little late. We might end up missing the previews."

That was fine with me, as long as it was fine with Jennie. After all, I was out of my element, and it felt like she was the one calling the shots. Riding alone with Jennie on the way to the movies felt a lot different than the other times I'd spent with her. In the past, it never seemed like there was much at stake during our interactions. Either I wasn't interested in her, or she wasn't interested in me, or we were both interested in each other but pretended otherwise. Now that we were riding in the station wagon alone together, on a genuine date to go see *Magneto Man*, it was like all our built-up comfort around each other had been reset back to zero.

All through that summer, conversation had always been easy, with a lot of interesting things to talk about and always a lot of joking around between us. Now it felt oddly official. I suddenly worried about how Jennie would feel being seen in public with me.

It occurred to me that this sort of unusual pairing was probably only possible during the summer. When school is in session, any number of unwritten social rules always would have prevented it. The simple truth was that at our school, people like Jennie just didn't go out with people like me, and vice versa. That's probably what originally convinced me that she was nowhere near my type.

The scene at Jimmy's Family Restaurant allowed for those unlikely connections between people to exist. I wasn't sure whether this summer and working at Jimmy's was an entrance to the real world or an escape from it, but here we were. The world we currently occupied was one where people like Jennie and me were going to try to give this thing a go and see where it leads.

Pulling into the movie theater parking lot, Jennie decided to get any awkwardness about who should pay for tickets out of the way up front.

"What do you think, Romeo? You wanna cover tickets, or we just get our own?"

"Uhh, I guess I'll get them." I opened up my wallet just to make sure. All I had was a pair of tens, but luckily that would just be enough. "Yeah, it's on me." I didn't add that she was on her own for snacks.

"Maybe they'll let us in for free. Seeing as I'm friends with the star of the movie."

Jennie kept a straight face as she steered the station wagon into one of the few empty spots in the parking lot of the cinema. I smiled and played along.

"Oh, so you put a few fish sticks on a plate for a guy, and suddenly that makes you friends with him?"

"Correction: Cal filled up the plate, I just delivered it. And you know Jimmy doesn't have fish sticks—it was a fillet."

I laughed. "You're proving my point."

"Okay, so maybe 'friend' isn't the accurate word for it. I'd say it's more like, *best* friend."

Walking in the glass double doors of the multiplex, I paid for the two tickets and we parted ways to use the restrooms before going inside the theater. While I was getting ready to wash my hands, a dorky teen wearing a Marvel Comics T-shirt turned the faucet on too hard and splashed it all over himself, getting water on the front my shorts in the process. I spent some extra time standing in front of the blow dryer just so Jennie didn't get the wrong impression. I figured that when I came back out, she'd be waiting for me already. As it turned out, she was nowhere to be seen, and the corridor was nearly emptied out, since it was well past the start time of the movie.

Thinking she was still in the bathroom, I passed the time wandering up the patterned carpet that every movie theater seems to have in the hallway, past the posters for new releases and observing each of them. I stood in front of the one for *Magneto Man* and saw the tagline: *"Trouble was his polar opposite."* I was nearing the end of the corridor, facing the lobby and the snack bar. I heard a voice from just beyond the turn that sounded like Jennie's.

"Hey, Kim," she said, then going silent for a beat. "Can't . . . uhh, because I'm busy, that's why . . . busy doing other stuff—what do you care?"

I moved up one spot closer to where the voice was coming

from, stopping in front of the sign for *Aladdin 4:* "*Sometimes, the Genie gets a few wishes of his own.*" Around the corner but now in clear hearing range, Jennie sounded irritated with her friend, who apparently kept pressing for details on what she was up to.

"Okay, fine. Since you're sooo interested, I am about to see a 'film.' A 'moving picture.' I am at 'the thee-ayy-ter.'"

Jennie laughed about something her friend must have said on the other end. Despite not being involved in the conversation in any way, I felt like I knew exactly what was coming next.

"That new superhero one. *Magneto Man* or whatever."

I found myself annoyed that she added the unnecessary "or whatever" part, acting like she didn't fully know or care which movie she was about to see. As if she was trying to distance herself from the evening.

"No, not with Jimi. Are you forgetting?" Another pause. "Yeah, I *know* he wanted to see it—whatever though, he'll have to figure that out for himself."

Losing my concentration in the *Aladdin 4* poster, I felt my eyebrows stiffening and dropping closer to my eyes as I became more and more irritated. The phone call clearly wasn't meant for my ears, but it's hard to unhear something, especially since it concerned me. After finding out that Jennie's movie date wasn't Jimi Dandersley, it wasn't too difficult to put together what the next question of her friend would naturally be.

"I'm there with . . . JB." I felt myself sweating and holding my breath, listening closely even though I knew I shouldn't be. "You do know who he is, he goes to our school . . . No, two grades behind . . . Yup, that's him . . . Hey, he kept asking and bugging me about it, so whatever. It's one date."

Wow. That's all I could think. I strolled out into the lobby, trying to look casual and hoping not to give away that I'd heard anything from the phone call. Jennie gave a quick double take: the type that people only do when the person who they were just talking about catches them. She flashed a smile at me and quickly ended the conversation.

"Oh hey, there you are! Look, Kim, gotta go . . . Yeah, maybe I'll come out after. Bye."

Since we apparently weren't late enough yet, Jennie decided that she wanted to get some candy from concessions before we went inside. Back in the lobby, I noticed someone who looked familiar; he was filling an XL plastic cup with Pibb Xtra. When his cup was filled to the brim, he let the fizz die down a little bit, and then sipped some off of the top. Then he put the cup back under the fountain to top it back off before finally adding the lid. He turned into full view, unmistakable in appearance due to his full chinstrap beard.

"Hey, Teen Wolf."

Neither of them realized this, but it was indirectly due to Teen Wolf that Jennie and me were there together in the first place; the whole chain of events had begun with Wolf, going all the way back to February, like some butterfly effect type of stuff. If he hadn't told the Ghost of Five Mile Creek background story back at the lunch table on a gray Monday in the dead of winter, we probably never would have planned to explore the haunted house. Jennie never would have found out about the trip or offered to drive. I never would have sat with her on the last of the basement stairs and talked while the others were outside.

Without Wolf's influence, I never would have learned about the tragedy in Jennie's past, or reached out for help when I couldn't find a summer job. I wouldn't have worked at Jimmy's or gotten to know Jennie better as the summer gradually crept away from us. The guy tells one little story that I didn't even fully believe, and then six months later, I'm at the movies with Jennie, he's standing right in front of us, and I can hardly think of anything to say to the guy.

"So," I asked, "what are you here to see? *Magneto Man*?"

Teen Wolf used his free hand to brush off the notion, as if the movie title had no business entering his airspace.

"Noo thanks. I don't care to see the dollar-store Batman fighting to save bootleg Gotham from the knockoff version of the Riddler."

To be honest, I don't know why I felt the need to defend the movie; if Jennie hadn't suggested it, I probably wouldn't have wanted to see it either. Even so, I didn't like the snobbishness of his tone.

"Oh, come on. I'd say Magneto Man is more like Spiderman than Batman. Breadville isn't *anything* like Gotham, and the Riddler . . . Alright, I guess Doctor If is a lot like him, I'd never thought of that before. Whatever, though."

I mentioned the lead actor eating at the restaurant a few weeks before, but Teen Wolf acted unimpressed by this, which was typical. He always liked to be on the inside and one step ahead of all the latest buzz; in cases where he wasn't, he just played it off like it wasn't worth his time to begin with. Jennie came back with a pack of gum and a box of Sour Patch Kids, and we finally went inside.

The movie had already started by the time we stepped through the dimly lit aisles and settled in a pair of empty seats about ten rows back. I didn't have a full interest in the movie itself, so I wasn't particularly bothered that we'd missed a little bit. Glenn Murray hadn't even turned into Magneto Man yet. Even so, despite holding my tongue, I was feeling disrespected by Jennie's cold attitude towards the whole night so far.

On screen, the main character was still riding around on a motor scooter, navigating the congested streets of downtown Breadville, dodging cars, trolleys, and buses as he delivered sandwiches to the crowded offices of the Financial District. His little vehicle was always breaking down or getting mud splashed on it by trucks, and the businessmen and women in the offices always seemed to say or do something rude to him when he dropped off their food. The actor had been done up to look nerdier and a lot less movie-starrish than the day he was at Jimmy's. His hair was pushed down over his forehead in a sort of bowl cut, which was much different than how he had fixed his hair the first time I'd seen him. I figured he would almost certainly return to the gelled and styled look once he turned into a superhero—that's usually how these things worked.

As Glenn Murray ran into minor problem after minor problem as a humble commoner on-screen, I found myself thinking back to the bits of phone conversation that I'd heard from Jennie near the bathrooms.

I scoffed out loud as I replayed the "he kept bugging me about it" part of her talk with Kim. Jennie probably just thought I was mocking the series of ridiculous circumstances that led to Glenn Murray being in the basement of a magnetics company headquarters after midnight with a tray of hoagies. *There's no way that being on a date is supposed to be this unenjoyable, is it?* Jennie made me feel a lot of things inside that I'd never felt before, but not all of them were pleasant. I wouldn't even say that the majority of the things I felt at the moment were pleasant, or even tolerable. Jennie was the one who had shown me the diary, *she* had leaned in to make out with me, and *she* had been the one who asked me out—so why was she acting embarrassed to be seen near me, or like being here together was a burden to endure?

I caught myself daydreaming and returned my focus back to what was going on in the theater. Magneto Man was now transformed into his true self, much to the delight of the guy in the Marvel Comics T-shirt who had splashed water all over it in the bathroom. He turned to his friend and whispered something in a giddy excitement that I guessed was, "I remember that part from the book!" Upon discovering that he could fly, Magneto Man did a loop around Breadville before triumphantly landing on the rooftop of his high-rise apartment building, planning out how to put his new powers to use.

Trying to change my mood, I thought back to all the moments that had made me fall for Jennie to begin with. Talking at Five Mile Creek, how she'd put in a good word for me with Jimmy, all the inside jokes at the restaurant, "The Wreck of the Edmund Fitzgerald," the way she puffed the hair out of her face when her hands were full. Then there was her saying that she missed me when I was at the dentist, sitting together by the docks during my split shift, *ANÁΓKH,* and our moment on the grass by the fancy drinking fountain.

Now wearing a mask with his burgundy-and-blue suit and cape, the superhero attached himself to the metal tower of a suspension bridge, where a vicious car wreck had happened moments earlier. He was getting ready to swoop up any injured passengers and take them to the Breadville General Hospital, as the ambulances stalled for hours in the resulting traffic jam. I stopped paying attention to it as my positive memories slipped away from me again.

I remembered how Jennie hadn't seemed too bothered when I got a week of Dumpster Duty around the 4th of July, even though it had only happened due to her influence. Or how she wanted to sabotage my hangout with the Peninsula girls, changing the phone number so I couldn't call them back. Or bringing me to the movies but telling her friends that I had basically begged my way into it.

Back in July, all I wanted from her was to look at me differently. Now it felt like I was the one finally seeing the whole picture. The friendly, hilarious, exciting, seductive Jennie that I had a connection with was still there; the only problem was this other Jennie, who used me and acted too good for me unless she needed something. This second Jennie messed with my emotions, got me in trouble, and would constantly defend Jimi Dandersley, just as long as all the crap he pulled wasn't happening to her. If we kept dating, which of these two Jennies would I really be getting?

The movie was already finishing up by the time I got out of my head and really started focusing on it again. Magneto Man flew a lap around his city before perching himself back on the roof of the apartment. The sky around him was gray. The smoldering ruins of a collapsed skyscraper were still blazing: a result of what must have happened earlier in the big scene.

Magneto Man looked around the metropolis with a steely gleam—what was it, triumph?—in his pensive eyes. The sinister Dr. If was still out there somewhere, but Magneto Man was safe, and that meant Breadville was safe as well. The camera zoomed in on his face, and he murmured to himself, "Everyone wants to wear the cape. But not everyone is meant to soar."

A crew of enthusiasts a few rows over erupted in applause as Magneto Man blasted off one last time and the end credits began to roll. Once the lights came back on, I stood up a little too fast and got light-headed for a couple seconds, seeing stars and trying to keep my balance as I regained my bearings. Jennie yawned and gave a cat-like stretch to reset herself. She stuck her chewed piece of gum on the back of a seat and motioned us to the nearest aisle.

As we arrived back in town, Jennie parked the station wagon back in my driveway. Mom must have been asleep by then, but the light in Rodney's room was still on. Jennie and I didn't kiss this time. She looked at me like I was expected to lean in and go for it, but something stopped me. I said good night and veered off at the last moment, confused at why it didn't feel better to have something I'd wanted all summer finally in range.

CHAPTER FORTY-FIVE

Blaise's Alternate Universe

I stayed away from Jennie at work the first day after our movie date. Of course, our paths naturally crossed dozens of times as we made our intersecting routes through the dining room. We didn't speak like usual, though. There was none of the banter, or inside jokes, or little secret coded comments about the customers no one else was likely to pick up on. Without any direct plan in mind for my next move, I was stalling as far as Jennie was concerned.

If our coworkers had heard anything about the two of us, they were doing a pretty good job of hiding it. I didn't hear a single comment or receive a wink or sly smile from anyone—not even a disapproving turn of the head from Staples. Jennie approached me towards the end of our shift, wanting to hang out by the docks again when we were done with work. That in-between state—being somewhat friends, somewhat dating, somewhat nothing at all—must have been just as uncomfortable for her as it was for me. The workout I had planned with Blaise for that evening gave me an easy excuse to avoid facing her. I needed more time to stall.

"Ever wonder how things might have been different if we'd picked something other than hoops to get into?"

As we pulled out our basketball gear and started getting ready for the shootaround, Blaise was getting philosophical again. I wrinkled my lip and squinted at my friend—the way Jimmy probably would if one of us had accidentally put the salt and pepper shakers in the walk-in freezer.

"Something else?"

The thought of being into something else had honestly never occurred to me. What else would we possibly want to get into besides basketball? My memory of trying out a different type of hobby at this time a year ago was still vivid, and that hadn't exactly ended well. Blaise slid out of his Adidas flip-flops and pulled his sneakers and a thick pair of white socks with the NBA logo out of his bag.

"Yeah, like if we were like Darko, and had a mind for computers and technology and all that. I've always been a little bit jealous that he can figure that type of stuff out so easily."

Jealous of *Darko*? It was disorienting hearing him talk like that, which he'd been doing more and more as we moved through the fourth quarter of summer break. I waited for him to finish tying his shoes up, which was taking even longer than usual.

I'd told Blaise all about the movie date and how things had only gotten more complicated, rather than better or worse, since the whole turn of events with Jennie. He gave a tired laugh and said he felt the same thing ever since getting promoted to the varsity team last winter. Now he seemed to have this idea that maybe life would be a lot simpler and easier if only we'd chosen a slightly different path.

Blaise was back at his strange routine of tying and retying his shoelaces obsessively when getting ready for basketball, whether it was for tryouts, shootarounds, or the biggest game of the year. He said he couldn't stand it when one of his sneakers felt tighter than the other, even by just a small amount.

I had gotten used to watching him retie one shoe, and then groan that now the other one (which was fine originally) felt too loose in comparison. He'd tighten the other one up further and then walk around for a few steps, realizing that now *both* of them felt too tight. So he had to stop and unlace them and do the whole thing over—sometimes two or three more times before being satisfied that it was perfect. He did a similar thing adjusting his basketball shorts: just below the knee, but not far enough to touch any part of his shins. His mini-sermon about computers, and Darko, and getting into something besides basketball was slowing the process down even more than usual.

"Yeah, I've never really had the patience for programming and all that though. It's like a whole different language that I can't figure out. Computer language is even harder than Spanish class too . . ." He switched his train of thought unpredictably. "Basketball isn't the only sport either, you know. Even if people around here seem to think it is. I bet I'd be pretty good at soccer."

"I told Spaz he should join the track team. He won't listen to me though."

"That guy's crazy." Blaise shook his head and laughed to himself. "I saw him out running on the side of the highway last week."

Folding my work T-shirt into my own bag, I was all set

and ready to get started with our practice session. Blaise might have unlimited time to practice, but I needed to get back home soon enough to actually get a decent rest; having a bunch of night shift and then morning shift days back-to-back on the bussing schedule wasn't doing me any favors in terms of sleep. Blaise, however, stared thoughtfully into the distance.

"I wonder what it would have been like if we'd just formed a band instead . . . done the music thing, and not ball."

I shook my head at him in disbelief. "Oh yeah? What instrument do you play?"

"Shut up. I dunno, man, just thinking out loud."

He finally got his shoelaces the way he wanted them and stood up.

"Alright, let's do this thing. Midrange drill: five spots, ten makes at each spot. I'll rebound first."

He jogged a few steps to get his legs under him, and then ran over to grab a basketball, passing it to me and positioning himself under the nearest hoop. We did shooting and ball-handling drills for another ninety minutes. I didn't hear any more mentions from Blaise about taking up soccer or starting a band, but his mind seemed to be somewhere else for the majority of the session. We played one-on-one to finish things off: a series of five games. I beat him for the first time since elementary school.

As unexpected as my victory over Blaise was, it was nothing compared to the surprise I received as we were gathering up our stuff and getting ready to shut the lights off and lock up. And no, Jimi Dandersley didn't kick down the double doors, slash the basketball with a switchblade, and challenge me to a death match. Blaise's summer team had their final tournament downstate that weekend, and he told me that they needed an extra player.

"One of our shooting guards is injured, and another guy said he can't make it either. You think you could fill in? You'd have to be good for the whole weekend, though—it's in Mount Pleasant. I'm leaving Friday evening and coming back Sunday."

Beyond excited for this opportunity, but also trying to play it cool, I paused and pretended that I was considering whether it was worth my time.

"Yeah. Yeah, that sounds good." I pulled the hood of my sweatshirt up so Blaise wouldn't see how hard I was smiling. "I think I'll have to run it by Jimmy and Gloria first, though. Oh, and my mom too."

CHAPTER FORTY-SIX

Dry Cleaners

I made sure to get in three more tough practices with Blaise to get ready for the weekend tournament with his travel team. While it was just the normal weekend routine for Blaise by that point, I was buzzing with excitement and could barely stay focused at the restaurant in the days leading up to it.

At work on Tuesday afternoon, the single tub of swirled red, yellow, and blue ice cream finally reached the bottom. After a satisfying sound of metal scraping across cardboard, Staples handed the final Superman cone of the summer across the counter and announced the landmark moment to Jimmy. The boss grinned as Staples removed the Superman label from the flavor list behind the fountain.

"One of these years, I'll finally just stop making that stuff." Jimmy stamped the word "stuff" with a dry laugh. "More trouble than it's worth—always has been."

"We should do Magneto Man ice cream instead," I blurted out, before letting the skateboard guys get hold of the thought and talk me out of it. "Burgundy and blue."

With his signature folded-arms stance, Staples tilted his

head slightly and coolly said that he didn't hate the idea. Cal's face lit up and he boldly claimed that he would order Magneto Man banana splits every single day if it were an option. Even Jimmy, that ice cream fascist, basically admitted it was a good one. He didn't say he was going to try it, but he took a long and thoughtful pause in front of the list on the wall, maybe playing out possible combinations in his mind for the potential new flavor.

For the next order of business, I made sure to see Gloria instead of Jimmy to ask for the whole weekend off. Maybe it was my nerves playing tricks on my eyes, but it looked like she was about to shake her head, apologize, and say that since the schedule was already up, it wouldn't be possible. Making me feel a little bit guilty about leaving, Gloria exhaled and patiently said she wished I would've let them know sooner. With the guilt trip out of the way, she said that she could put Arthur on split shifts for both days, and they'd manage. Labor Day would be my last shift at the restaurant when I got back from the tournament, with the first day of school right after that. As long as I could get my mom to agree with it, I was set.

When I talked it over with her, Mom got that same concerned look as when I'd told her about the (ultimately doomed) date/hangout with the Peninsula girls a month ago. Rodney was in the living room watching the guys on ESPN give their season preview for Fighting Irish football. Glancing up from the TV, he couldn't hide his surprise when Mom reluctantly gave permission for me to go downstate with Blaise.

She gave me the laser eye surgery treatment and used those famous three words: "I'm trusting you." Rodney was itching to leave for South Bend on Monday morning, and the trunk of his car had been packed for over a week. As his last act of service while in town, Mom volunforced him for pickup duty at the bus station when I got back Sunday night.

Same as Rodney, Staples was starting college back up too, so that Friday was his last day of work. His shift finished up a half hour before mine, so I made sure to track him down before he left to say goodbye. Staples said to hurry up and turn sixteen so I could get my license and come visit him at U of M. As he wiped down the ice cream counter and turned to leave, the thin vertical line on the lower backside of his head became visible. I still wanted to hear the full story of what had happened between him and Jimi Dandersley all those years ago, but I decided it could wait for another day. If anything, it would give me an excuse to stay in touch with Staples.

As I untied my apron thirty minutes later, wanting to make moves and get out of there to meet up with Blaise, Cal made sure to stop me for a quick interrogation. He sarcastically asked if I had a hot date that I was scampering off to, chuckling to himself at the idea that a girl would agree to go anywhere with me. When I gave him the real answer, he acted just as skeptical.

"You sure you're tall enough to be playing basketball?" He raised his knife gingerly and leveled it out a few inches above my head, as if to say that the Nakayama Genesis determined the minimum height requirement for basketball. I was in a rush and in too good of a mood to raise an objection.

"Guess I'll find out! Later, Cal."

At 4:30 that afternoon, Blaise and I were packed and standing inside the Full Court Press dry cleaners, waiting a little impatiently for our ride to the Greyhound bus stop. Blaise's mom had been in charge of the dry cleaners for as long as I can remember. She ran it mostly by herself, besides a few part-time staffers helping out from time to time. Based on how familiar Blaise appeared to be with all the procedures at the place, he also had more responsibilities around there than he'd let on.

A quick burst of people had come into the dry cleaners right after I'd arrived, either to drop off piles of jackets and dresses or to pick up a finished order from inside. Ms. Hornby was shuttling back and forth from the cash register to the main floor, calling out further directions to Blaise as she went. I marveled at the amount of organization it must take to keep track of so many different identical-looking items, the clothing with the same thin plastic sheaths covering all of them, hanging from the movable clothes racks like a troop of ghost soldiers—ones that floated rather than marched.

One lady came in wondering about a particular stain on her shirt, and Blaise gave her an expert do-it-yourself tip to fix it, like it was the easiest thing in the world to figure out. She took down a few notes on the quick process and brightly thanked Blaise on the way out. Watching from across the room, his mom gently teased him for sending away someone who gladly would have been a paying customer.

"I'm not sure our budget is large enough to be revealing all our trade secrets, son."

"That's fine." Blaise shrugged, furiously wiping a small piece of lint from the front of his shirt. "They can figure it out on their own for once. You don't have time to waste on something small like that, anyway."

"Well, Blazer, if you're sooo worried about my time, here's

something else I don't have time for." His mom held up a stack of hangers, smiling at her son. "Would you mind running these suits across the street for me?"

The way she said that first part gave my senses a strange jolt. In that brief moment, it felt like I was seeing and hearing Jennie, twenty years into the future—like a weird, opposite déjà vu thing. Even while wearing flared jeans and a loose-fitting sweatshirt around at work, it was clear that Ms. Hornby was still thin and stayed plenty active. Her teal eyes gave away hints of youth, with her true age only shown by a few extra wrinkles in her face and dark blonde hair that had a few tiny strands of gray and was just a little bit withered.

"You do deliveries?" I asked her. I then remembered how unreasonably upset it had made Jimmy when I'd suggested he start doing deliveries earlier in the summer.

"Not usually. I'm running two days late with this order, so I promised to drop them off in person." She turned back to Blaise. "It's just the office next to the new yoga studio, Suite C. Thanks, sweetie."

Blaise quickly printed off the receipts and stuck labels on the plastic coverings for each of the suits, sending a small puff of dust up from the floor as he dropped his gym bag.

"Okay," he said, "but you know it's a quarter to five though, right?"

"*Yes*, I know it's a quarter to five," she said with a bit of an edge to her voice, checking her watch anyway. "Let me finish a few more things, and then I'll get you to your bus."

Antsy but still obedient, Blaise took the pile of suits and walked back outside. Shortly after he left, I heard the chorus of an old '80s heavy metal ballad blaring from the center pocket of Ms. Hornby's sweatshirt. Blushing slightly about the ringtone, she pulled out her cell phone.

"*Scorpions* . . . can't beat that, right?" Looking closer at the screen as the electric guitar chords rang out from the tiny speaker, she flipped the phone open and started to glide away in the direction of the back room. She let the song go on for a few seconds longer, before snapping out of what looked like a mini trance. "Sorry, but I need to take this call. JB, honey, can you handle things in here for a few minutes? Thanks."

I assumed that it must be an important business call (maybe a conference call, whatever that is) that Ms. Hornby didn't want me listening in on. Before leaving, she gave a severe look, trusting but not really trusting me. Blaise's mom was the type of person who didn't have enough free time to be as strict as she wanted to be. Of course, she knew all about *my* mistakes from last year and didn't view me as innocently as when we were younger, but I was able to laugh off her suspicious look now. Any judgments she wanted to make about me, she would also have to make about her own son, if only she knew. I didn't consider it my place to break the news to her—plus, that chapter of our lives was over as far as I was concerned.

I sat down in the rolling chair behind a computer, cash register, and credit card machine, hoping like hell that no one would come in and there wouldn't be any things that needed handling until either Blaise or his mom came back in. As I sat there, I felt my right foot shaking uncontrollably. I was excited, but also nervous for a lot of reasons: the tournament, the bus ride, leaving town on my own for the first time, supervising an independent business for a few minutes, uncomfortable thoughts about Jennie that kept diving into my mind at random splashes. My nerves put me on hyper-alert, and I began noticing a lot of things surrounding me that I probably would have otherwise ignored.

The room was a little grungy, yet meticulously organized at the same time. There were different-colored stains on the floor and dust settled in the corners, but all the pieces of clothing were arranged by customer, size, and type, and finished orders were spotless and crisp. The mixture of chemicals in the air gave off an overall smell that made me think of artificial grape.

On the wall next to the computer desk, there was a collage of newspaper clippings thumbtacked to the wall from the previous basketball season, along with the team schedule that the bank always gives out for free every year. Blaise's name was mentioned in the majority of the articles. Final scores from each game were filled in on the bank schedule with a black Sharpie marker. The stain-removing chemicals concentrated in the room must have an effect on the newsprint, because the articles were beginning to turn pale and fade, as if they were from an earlier decade or even further back, rather than one long winter ago.

Underneath the wall of game scores and newspaper articles, I saw a bookshelf displaying a handful of retro-looking basketball trophies. Maybe Blaise was running out of room at home to store his growing repertoire of awards and championships. Either that or his mom just wanted to show off to her dry-cleaning customers that there was a star in the family.

While scanning across the bookshelf the first time, I thought that the same early aging process from the newspapers was also affecting the trophies. The shine was nearly gone from each of the metallic basketball guys, frozen in various positions on their marble stands. One of them was badly chipped, and the tiny basketball being held on another one looked fragile, like it had broken off before and been delicately reattached. It wasn't until I squinted and took a closer look at the engravings on the base of each trophy that I realized why they looked like they came from nearly twenty years ago. It's because they *did*.

"Arcadia Conference Champions 1986" . . . *"Eagles Basketball-Varsity MVP 1986"* . . . *"Eagles Basketball-Varsity MVP 1987"* . . . *"All-State First Team 1987."* Okay, maybe Ms. Hornby wanted to show off to her customers that there were *two* stars in the family.

Blaise walked back in from his errand across the street, and I spun around in the roller chair, quickly turning my focus away from the trophies and newspaper articles.

"Where is everyone?" he asked anxiously, coming back to find the store emptied of both its customers and its owner. "And why are you sitting back there?"

"I got a big promotion. It's my store now."

"No wonder they all took off," Blaise replied without missing a beat, breaking into a faint smile. "Seriously, though, where's my mom at?"

By the time we were both legitimately worried about missing the bus, Blaise's mom re-emerged from the back room and rushed us off to the Greyhound stop. As we climbed out of the car and flagged down the driver, she shoved a handful of cash into Blaise's hand, kissed him goodbye, and said to call once we made it to the hotel. With the window on the driver's side rolled down, she held Blaise by the wrist for a few extra seconds, firmly repeating to him to keep his focus during the tournament, no matter what happened.

"Does she always tell you that?" I asked as we walked away.

Blaise gave me a puzzled shrug and climbed onto the bus without any other type of response.

CHAPTER FORTY-SEVEN

Bus Ride

Having never been out of town on my own before, even something as small as boarding the Greyhound with Blaise felt like some sort of profound coming-of-age moment for me. Our bus driver apparently didn't see it that way, hustling us on to stay with the route schedule and cutting short my savoring of the moment. He grunted a short hello as he took our tickets and impatiently pointed out two open seats a few rows back.

I kept my eye on the bus driver, breathing heavily and inefficiently as he pulled out of the parking lot of the bus station. His head was covered with graying hair that probably had been slicked back all the way earlier in the morning, but now it just looked stiff and porcupine-like. Overheating almost immediately, he removed his jacket about two miles into the ride, revealing a pair of thick, scabby arms and the outline of a naked woman inked onto his forearm. I turned to Blaise to see if he'd noticed, but he was leaning fully to the inner edge of the seat, his face uncomfortably pressed against the glass window but somehow already fast asleep.

For the first hour or so of the trip, I made several attempts to take a nap as well. Even if my nerves weren't already on overdrive, the consistent wheezing sounds coming from the front seat would have made that difficult enough. Combining that with my excitement of the trip and a difficult decision to make as soon as I got back, a nap was pretty much impossible. That, plus the air conditioning had stopped working before we were five miles out of town, leaving a heavy feeling to the air that smelled vaguely like sweat and chips. Reasoning that if the driver had a heart attack and someone needed to take control of the wheel, maybe it was best that I stay alert anyway.

I'd only driven once before in my entire life, but I figured as long as I kept it slow and cautious, I could handle all the essentials if needed. Gas pedal on the right, brake on the left, green is go, red is stop, keep it between the lines, do whatever the traffic signs say. The yield sign was the only one that I really didn't know what to do with.

After the movie date, Jennie and I kept unpredictably bobbing in closer and then apart, like a series of buoys in the boat harbor. She had taken me out for a driving lesson after work on Tuesday afternoon. She sat in the passenger seat of the station wagon with a huge smile on her face, guiding me through all the basics on the back roads past the North Point gas station, leading us out of town and into the woods. Holding the top of the steering wheel with sort of a double palm-handle-pivot grip, I kept weaving the car back and forth over the lines, nearly knocking over somebody's mailbox at one point.

With the window down, the breeze from outside kept blowing Jennie's hair around, and eventually she positioned her green sunglasses at the top of her forehead to hold it out of her eyes. From the passenger seat, she maintained a relaxed smile for the entire ride, giving me tips and gentle teasing for every mistake that I made. The scattered rays from the sun unpredictably beamed across her face at different angles as it poked through endless rows of pine trees. Riding shotgun in her own car as it curved through the winding roads, Jennie was undeniably beautiful in every way that afternoon.

We kissed again at the end of the drive, while switching places outside the car. It wasn't planned, and neither of us really made the first move. Jennie was getting ready to take the wheel back and turn us back into town. As our paths crossed around the front of the hood, we impulsively drifted together and didn't pull back apart for several minutes. Remembering this moment on the bus, I noticed that my right hand had bunched up the bottom part of my T-shirt. Running my fingers through the cotton, I wasn't able to recreate the feeling of the vertical ridges from the fabric of Jennie's tank top.

That whole day had been infinitely more enjoyable than our time at the movies, and I kept coming back to the thought of how much potential Jennie and me could have together. If only the rest of life could be like the back roads on that Tuesday afternoon: just the two us, on the outside of town, and in our own world. Unfortunately, that thought was always followed by the harsh reminder that the very next Tuesday, we'd be back in town, and back in high school. What would happen when it was just the two of us, plus everybody else?

"Next stop is at the Grayling McDonald's, exactly halfway to our destination. We'll be making a pit stop for about the next twenty-five minutes, so feel free to go inside if you need your sodium and cholesterol levels replenished."

Blaise stirred a little bit and then fully woke up as the announcement crackled through the intercom. A few of the people on the bus chuckled, while others didn't seem to get the joke. Maybe the bus driver didn't get it either, because once we arrived at the McDonald's pit stop, he went inside too. Judging from the breathing and the way his gut hung out over his belt buckle, his sodium and cholesterol levels were nearly maxed out already.

After slowing all the way down and coming to a stop in the fast food parking lot, I heard a screeching noise from behind me. I turned and took a closer look at our fellow bus riders for the first time. An overweight woman was trying to get her three young kids to quiet down and settle back into their seats, but they were too busy climbing around and grabbing at each other as they celebrated the McDonald's announcement.

In the row across from the mom and her squirrelly kids there was a tired-looking man sitting by himself next to the emergency exit. He was wearing a wrinkled suit with sweat stains under his arms. He'd set his BlackBerry on the window ledge, which caused an annoying buzzing every two minutes or so as he received another message. It was like being back at the restaurant with the ticket printer, but he still refused to put it on silent.

Towards the back, I saw three separate Jimi Dandersley types, each sitting silently at separate window seats. Each of these Greyhound Dandersleys had buzzed heads and different styles of facial stubble, and all of them were scowling into the distance and looking angry at the world. If this were a weeklong journey across the country instead of an evening trip downstate, I wondered whether they would've ended up becoming friends with each other. Or maybe enemies.

In the very front row was a gray-haired woman with a lost look in her eyes. She was holding a toaster under her right arm like a football and had gruffly thanked the bus driver at least eight different times so far. With a quiet laugh to myself, I thought that maybe she could be Sara's sister. Then I needed to block an unpleasant image out of my mind, imagining what she might be using the toaster for if that were the case.

Surveying the rest of the crowd, it seemed to me like everyone on there was out of place in one way or another—including me and Blaise. Even in his modesty, when Blaise talked about travelling around the state to all these different basketball events, it made it seem a lot more glamorous than this. Not that I thought we'd be taking a limo or anything, but here we were on a Friday night, sharing a stuffy bus with this drawer of mismatched socks, waiting in a parking lot while they all got McDonald's. By the time Blaise had fully woken up and made sense of his surroundings, the rest of the crew had filed past and stepped off, leaving us as the last ones still in our seats.

"Aren't you going in?" I stood up and stretched out a little bit in the aisle, ready to follow the rest of the bus crew across the parking lot and into the restaurant. Blaise stayed in his seat.

"Nah, I'm good here." He unzipped his backpack, which had a large container of trail mix and at least a dozen energy bars packed inside. "We're supposed to ball out tomorrow morning—we don't want that other crap in our systems while we're trying to play."

Blaise made a good point, but at the same time, I was starting to get hungry myself. The greasy French fry smell in the kitchen at Jimmy's had stopped being appetizing many weeks ago, but my thinking was that anyone else's fries would really hit the spot at that moment.

"Either way, I don't have much extra cash," Blaise added sheepishly. "Still got the hotel to pay for and everything. Go ahead if you want though."

Since my mom's work was picking back up and Rodney had been chipping in at home too, I was able to keep a decent amount of money from my latest paycheck—enough to cover me for this trip without worrying too much, and definitely enough to spare for fast food. I could either stay with Blaise and his trail mix and granola bars or follow the trio of Jimi Dandersleys inside for a Big Mac and fries. It was a tiny decision to make, but as Blaise looked up at me keenly, it felt like one that would say a lot, depending on which side I picked. Annoyed but grudgingly certain that I was making the right choice overall, I sat back down.

The remainder of the ride was uneventful, though the roles reversed a little bit from before stopping at Grayling. Most of the other riders quickly fell asleep once the bus started moving again, while Blaise stayed awake and alert for the rest of the way. He kept pulling a sheet of paper from his pocket and diligently looking it over, the directions for finding our hotel and the address for the tournament the next day. It was starting to get dark out when we finally arrived at the bus station in Mount Pleasant. With a quick grunt to show that we'd reached our destination, the driver scratched at the top of his porcupine hair and stepped off to unpack luggage from the storage compartments underneath. Blaise and me had both kept all our stuff with us onboard, so while most of the others arranged an informal line to wait for their bags, the two of us quietly walked off.

Blaise turned a few slow circles as we got to the nearest street corner, staring at his sheet and trying to get a sense of direction. Since he traveled alone so often, I thought he'd have a better idea of exactly what to do. Then again, he was in a different town every week, so each set of bus stations, street corners, gyms, and hotels would always be new.

"Okay, so it says the tournament location is just a couple blocks from here, but the hotel is one-point-five miles west." He looked up again, straining his eyes for something in the distance. "Which way is west?"

"Umm . . ." Navigating new places wasn't really my strong suit. "West is always on the left if you're looking at a map. We could try going left."

"Your left or *my* left?" We were standing facing each other. I was stumped.

Having me hold his duffel bag, Blaise jogged back towards where the Greyhound was parked. The driver was finishing unloading the luggage and appeared startled to be tapped on the shoulder. Sighing, he slowly raised his arm into a point and held it up towards me for a three count. Blaise jogged back, looking skeptical.

"It was neither of our lefts, he says we're supposed to cross the street and go up that way. That's what he *says,* anyway."

After at least twenty-five minutes of gradually getting farther away from town, more and more nervous that we'd been led the wrong way, we reached a dimly lit sign on the side of the sleepy road, welcoming us to The Pleasant Inn.

CHAPTER FORTY-EIGHT

The Pleasant Inn

Seeing the outside of our motel, I was secretly glad that we would only be there for the weekend, because the building looked like it might not be standing for too much longer than that. Even in the twilight, the chipped paint, overgrown lawn area, and missing shingles from the sloping roof were noticeable. The dark brown building had two floors of small rooms stacked directly on top of each other but slanting just a little bit. It was as if the whole thing had once tried to collapse, only to lose interest partway through and stay right there, frozen and warped. I shook my head grimly as I followed Blaise inside to the main lobby, amazed that my mom had given permission for me to be out here unsupervised late on a Friday night. Seriously, what had she been thinking to give *this* her blessing?

"Ayy mans, what kin I do you for?"

We made it to the front desk and were greeted by a man with a long-sleeve flannel shirt rolled to the elbows and long gray hair. His jaw was stretched low in a substantial underbite, and an endless grin was chiseled into his leathery face. The absent way he grinned and nodded made me think that he was telling himself a series of really funny jokes in his head—ones that he wasn't letting anyone else in on. For the second time that day, I had the disorienting feeling that I was seeing someone I knew, but a future version of them. It was like seeing Spaz in another lifetime, one where he grows up to be an innkeeper rather than a restaurant guy, holding on to every bit of his weirdness all the same.

"I have a reservation for two nights." Blaise was the pro at this check-in stuff, and I was glad to step back and let him handle this guy. "It's under the name 'Hornby.'"

The manager was already wearing rectangular glasses, but he had another thinner pair hanging on a chain around his neck. Rather than using a computer, he kept all of his reservations in a thick ledger that was bound in leather. His thin and spindly fingers set the second pair of glasses on top of the first and started casually paging through the book with mild interest, like it was the latest issue of *Restaurateur Magazine*.

"Horn-bee . . . yerp, there's the one alright," he said, stopping at one of the pages and tapping it twice with a pointer finger. "Now, are we here for business or pleasure?" Right as I said pleasure, Blaise told the manager it was business, confusing the man momentarily.

"We're here for a basketball tournament," Blaise clarified.

"Aye. Roundball." He slowly held his wrist out over the desk, continuing that goofy smirk as the narrow fingers of his right hand carefully bounced an imaginary ball. "I thought this was the year for the Pistons, I really did."

Blaise gave a polite laugh, attempting to stay friendly but clearly wanting nothing more than to just get his room assignment and get out of there. If this was a business trip for him, then talking basketball with the night manager of The Pleasant Inn was an unneeded and unwanted part of the transaction.

"Then again, last year *was* the year for them, so I guess we can't complain too much now, kin we?" Neither of us had complained about anything, but the guy was already getting on a roll. "You know, because for a while there, this is late '80s/early '90s, they were callin' em the Detroit 'Bad Boys.' And everyone liked Laym-beer and Dew-mars, and Thomas. Now that was a great team."

The night manager would have been disappointed to find out that I hadn't paid much attention to the Pistons or the NBA over the past year. Watching games was something Blaise and I had done a lot with Garrett and Brien in the old days, plus Darko once he moved to town in middle school. That stuff just never felt as interesting or relevant ever since I'd gotten in trouble though. Plus, as soon as I'd started going to high school, basketball started and ended with the Eagles in my world. The Pistons were a different league and might as well have been in a different universe, with no similarities except the team colors.

"And then a team like *this* comes along . . . you've got Chawn-cey and Wallace, and then that curly-headed guy . . . his name's Wallace too." The manager took off the second pair of glasses, looking proud of himself for remembering the second Wallace. "And unless you're a total scuff, you're thinking, 'Oh, it's this type of basketball all over again.' A little less rough, but all the same . . . people are reminded of the old days. Kin really go for that kinda stuff, you know? I know

I could, anyway. Would've been nice to have another set of back-to-backs, but those are the breaks of the game."

"You *do* have a room for us, right?" Blaise didn't bother to hide his annoyance this time.

Shaking his head wistfully, the manager looked back down at his ledger, finally getting back to the topic of our hotel stay.

"Aye, here we are then, Hornby. So it's thirty-five per night, plus a cleaning fee, and then the guhv-ner takes his share. Ninety dollars even—but that includes breakfast." He gestured to a small table in the corner of the waiting area; on top of it was a pair of oranges and a muffin that must have been sitting out there all day. Handing my share of the cash across the counter, I made a mental note that the next morning's meal would probably be another round of trail mix and granola bars. The manager stapled one piece of paper to another piece of paper, and then gave Blaise a small envelope. Blaise pulled out a pair of rusty metal keys and frowned.

"Room thurdy-one. Take a right once yer outside and turn the corner. It'll be there waiting for ya."

"Thanks."

"Oh, and if the phone in yer room is working, you can dial nine to call the front desk if ya need anything . . . or is it eight? Well, either way, dial either nine or eight, and one of those should git ya in touch with the front desk. If not . . . just come in here and find me."

"Thanks, I guess." I had a feeling that a phone call to the front desk would be about as helpful as calling Rodney at the start of the summer had been.

Blaise and me picked our bags up and exited the lobby,

leaving the manager at his desk, singing or humming to himself. "A-roo-tee, too-tee, too . . . a-ROO-tee, too-tee, TOO!"

"Alright 'mans,' you ready to do dis?" Blaise gave a stale but accurate impression of the manager once we were out of the lobby and away from hearing range. He sounded like Randy Newman singing "I Love LA."

I replied to this by pushing my jaw outward and dribbling around the imaginary basketball, causing Blaise to break out into the type of uncontrollable slaphappy giggles that are only possible when it's the end of a long day and you're too exhausted to do anything else. We turned a corner, leading past a series of doors numbered in the mid-twenties and rising as we walked.

"That dude could have pulled out either a bong or a shotgun from under his desk," said Blaise, now calmed down and slightly short of breath as we arrived at our door, "and neither one would have surprised me."

The old metal key barely worked, but after shaking the door handle vigorously for thirty seconds or so, we pushed through into the dark space of Room 31. Dropping his bag on the floor next to the closest bed, Blaise immediately turned the window fan on full blast, probably more to block out the noise of the car alarm going off in the distance than any hope of refreshing the air in the dry and stuffy room. It felt like the makeshift storage room in the basement of the restaurant, where I had watched the mopping tutorial, only this one smelled a little more mildewy.

"Is this usually what the rooms are like?" I asked. Any illusions of glamour that I had about Blaise's summer tournament travels had been nearly broken by this point. If this evening was any indicator, chasing the dream of basketball glory and college scholarships involved a much higher dose of dreary bus rides, late-night walks in the middle of nowhere, and rickety motels than I would have imagined.

"I don't normally stay at five-star hotels or any of that sort of stuff if that's what you mean, but this place is a new low," said Blaise, unsuccessfully clicking away at the remote control for the TV.

"Yeah . . . didn't realize how much of a grind this was."

"That's what I've been trying to tell you. You think these weekend excursions are vacation . . . If this was just for fun, I seriously would never play ball anywhere except the Mirage. Bellview gym on game nights isn't bad either." Giving up on the remote, Blaise reached over towards the phone that sat next to a blinking digital clock reading 3:47 (I think the real time was somewhere around 10:30). "Do you think I need to dial nine before calling my mom? Or is it eight?"

Against all odds, Blaise's call went through, and he spent the next twenty minutes or so talking with his mom, telling her about the bus ride, assuring her that he didn't forget anything, and promising not to go hungry. He smartly left out most of the finer details about The Pleasant Inn. Blaise asked his mom about the rest of the day at the dry cleaners, and while he lay down on his bed and listened to her recap, I started to set out my basketball gear for the next day.

Drawing my attention back to the tournament, it made it much easier to forget about the less-than-perfect hotel accommodations. By the time Blaise hung up the phone, my navy-blue shorts and socks, gray Eagles T-shirt from 8th grade, and white Nike shoes were all neatly placed at the foot of my bed. Visualizing the perfect release to my jump shots, I imagined myself as the breakout star of the competition, drilling clutch shots from all over the court. I could almost feel the leather of the ball smoothly rolling off my fingers for yet another three points when Blaise interrupted me.

"I'm setting the alarm for 6:30. We need to be at the school by eight for registration, and then hopefully there will be some extra time for a shootaround. Games start at nine."

"Where are the other guys, anyway?" I got up and went to the bathroom to brush my teeth, calling out from the sink while Blaise fiddled with the buttons on the alarm clock. "And why can't we stay at their hotel?"

"Everyone else is from around the area—they're not at a hotel. Some are coming from Saginaw, a few others from Midland, and there are these two brothers who live right in Mount Pleasant, I think. We're meeting them at the gym in the morning."

I continued pressing Blaise for more details about his teammates while he brushed his own teeth and then settled into his bed. Behind my visualization of instant success was the uneasy knowledge that I was the odd man out for this team—only there as a last-second replacement, and maybe I wasn't even good enough to be that. Meeting a half dozen strangers for the first time would be nerve-wracking enough, even without the pressure of showing that I belonged on the court with them.

"You need to remember that you're coming into this thing as a sub, so don't be surprised if you don't play very much in the first few games; you're new and still need to prove yourself.

Plus, there are some *really* good players here."

Clicking the light switch, Blaise sleepily gave me the rundown on his summer team in the final few minutes before he nodded off.

"There's this guy, Jermaine, he's easily the best one. The dude can do just about anything out there. Michigan State is already going after him. There's a pair of twin brothers too. One of them could play D1 in college for sure, but he's always getting in trouble so who knows. His brother's not anywhere near as good, but he's a lockdown defender at least, so he can hold his own. Then there's Victor. Not the best shooter, but he's a freak athlete. Can't even drive yet, but he can jump over a car. You think I'm exaggerating ... you'll see tomorrow though. Some of the dunks that guy can do—"

"Better than Derrick?"

In our area, Derrick Blackbird was the leading dunker— at least for the time being. I had a feeling that Blaise would surpass him by the end of the next season, but around Bellview, Derrick's double pumps and alley-oops caused a lot of amazement and envy. Apparently not anymore for Blaise, though.

"Completely different level, man," said Blaise, his words slurred together by an extended yawn. "You'll see."

"You think I'll do alright out there?" I wasn't sure if my shaky self-confidence would be able to handle the truth, but I asked anyway. "Be honest."

Blaise had drifted off to sleep, so I never got an answer.

CHAPTER FORTY-NINE

Registration

We grabbed bagels from the breakfast table at 7:30 the next morning and trekked back towards town on foot. The tournament site was at one of the local schools, with about a dozen registration tables set up in the cafeteria, to cover all the different teams and age groups who were filing through the double doors to get signed in.

Blaise found the rest of his teammates sitting at a round lunch table. He introduced me and announced that I was filling in at shooting guard. I immediately tried to store their names in my memory: Jermaine, Victor, two guys both named Mike, and Darius. Besides a few head nods, I got a cold reception from the rest of the table, all of whom looked pretty serious and skeptical.

I heard one of them snicker a few seconds after I awkwardly waved, making me wonder self-consciously whether it was being directed at me. I thought I heard someone mutter, "Doesn't look like much of a baller to me"—or was it just one of the guys in my own head inventing that line? Maybe I was sitting at the wrong table, and there was a Lunch Table

Democracy of misfits in Mount Pleasant that I belonged at instead, one for us regular guys who weren't being recruited by Michigan State, or who couldn't jump over cars, or play lockdown defense, and were starting to feel like this whole tournament might not have been such a good idea.

After waiting uncomfortably for fifteen minutes or so, Blaise made sure to find his coach and introduce me as well. The frazzled-looking coach was sitting alone, one table over, anxiously sending texts on his phone. Then he quickly sized me up and grabbed an extra jersey out of his bag, but otherwise didn't appear too interested in me or what I could offer to his team. Plus, he was preoccupied with another concern.

"Darius . . . DARIUS!!!" the coach said, raising his voice.

Blaise nudged the kid sitting on the other side of him. After going through a detailed handshake routine with nearly everyone at the table, he'd stuck in a cheap pair of earbud headphones and zoned out to his music while waiting. He was about the same height as Blaise, but thinner and lankier, with dark skin and thin twists in his hair. His shoelaces were untied, and he wore an XL white T-shirt under his jersey, matching the headband that lassoed his hair back from his forehead. He turned and pulled out one of his earbuds to check why the coach was already yelling at him when the game hadn't even started.

"Darius, where's your brother at now??"

As it turned out, I wasn't the only one on the team who the coach wasn't all that interested in. His harsh tone and obvious annoyance told me that this wasn't the first time the brother had gone walkabout, or the first time that he addressed Darius only when his more talented sibling couldn't be found.

Darius's casually raised eyebrows told me that he wasn't too concerned about either side of the issue, his brother's whereabouts, or the coach's growing frustration. Nevertheless, Darius walked over to see what the coach was getting at.

"I'aint seen'im this morning."

"You live in the same house as him, don't you??"

"He was with my cousins last night."

"So then where is he now?"

"Don't know, but I know where he *ain't,* and that's right here!" Darius got a sudden glimmer in his eyes, grinning and showing a set of teeth that Dr. Pharaoh would have been proud of. "Don't worry, Coach, I got you though. I can put up some triple-doubles today if you need it!"

He patted the coach on the shoulder while the rest of the guys broke their stone faces and started laughing. Their reaction implied that Darius was the last guy to expect a triple-double from. The coach bit into his knuckles, either to stop himself from laughing or to stop himself from punching Darius in the nose. Maybe both.

"Well, if he doesn't make it here in five minutes, he's out! I mean it, we need to register."

Darius gave a "not-my-problem" expression, shook out his hair, and returned to his chair next to Blaise. When the coach later motioned for us to stand up and get ready to sign in, Darius was the only one who went out of his way to come introduce himself to me. His brother never arrived, so five minutes later, we moved on to get in the registration line without him. That left only seven players, including me, leaving a definite possibility of getting more playing time than I'd expected at first.

"Alright, we're in the Aux Gym, court number three." Once he shuffled our team through the line and got us checked in, the coach took a look at the schedule for the day, glaring at the paper and scratching at his gut. "Get stretched out and then run layup lines. We start in fifteen minutes, so I don't want any screwing around, neither."

Judging from the seriousness of everyone else, that last part was meant mostly for Darius, who had his ear buds back in and probably didn't hear him anyway. With his long neck rising above the crowd, Jermaine found a sign pointing to the Auxiliary Gym, and the team started to move as a pack.

"You gotta be kidding me." Blaise stood frozen in place, suddenly looking like he wanted jump off the Zilwaukee Bridge.

"What's wrong, man? You forget something?"

Blaise was skeletal. It was as if someone had stolen his wallet, jacket, and sneakers all at once without laying a finger on him. His eyes were fully locked in on another team's coach, who was standing at a registration section three tables down and glancing at his own schedule, chomping a piece of gum and nodding his head in rhythm with each chew.

"I can't even . . ." Blaise started, his voice trailing off in the middle of the thought.

Finding the information he needed, the other coach airily gestured towards one of the exits as he tried to herd a team of younger kids through the crowd, 6th and 7th graders from the looks of it. They must have been playing in the Twelve-and-Under division. After a quick look at him, it became clear why seeing the other coach had stopped Blaise in his tracks. Blaise hadn't forgotten anything; the forgotten one was *him*. I'd never seen this man before, but there was no mistaking his identity.

Even though he was clearly in his early thirties, the guy looked youngish and in shape, like he could just as easily still be playing rather than coaching a team of peewees. A fresh blue Nike warm-up jacket covered this coach's thin but wiry frame, his right-hand tugging at the knee of his khaki shorts. His sandy hair had the exact color and shape as Blaise's.

"Hold on, that's . . .?"I began.

"Yup."

"You gonna talk to him?"

"Nope."

An unwritten rule of our friendship was that Blaise and I made sure to never talk about our dads. It's one of those things where if you hide from it for long enough, it's almost possible to forget that it hurts. That was my reasoning for it, anyway.

I kept close to Blaise as we left the cafeteria, turned down a long hallway, and found the auxiliary gym, which had four basketball courts but no bleachers, and a row of folding chairs where we set down our bags and warmed up for the first game.

CHAPTER FIFTY

Proving Yourself

On one of my turns through the layup line before the first game, I got a little stronger push than usual on my way up. As I started to release the ball, I felt the knuckles of my right-hand bump against the lower edge of the backboard, higher up than I'd ever been able to do before. When I landed from my jump, a surge of pride in my achievement washed through me. That feeling of triumph lasted for about two long seconds—long enough to get a better look at the new pond I was swimming in.

First Blaise threw down a smooth one-handed dunk, and then Victor raised the bar with a two-handed reverse that was way too easy for him. Jermaine nearly broke the rim with a powerful windmill that all the guys yelled about. I shot a jumper on my next turn, not quite as pumped about my slap-the-glass layup anymore. Even Darius got up just high enough to grab the rim as he released the ball, rattling in a semi-dunk of his own. He stumbled a little bit on the landing, flapping his arms around and cackling as he looked for high fives while jogging back to the line.

To start the opening game, I took a seat on one of the folding chairs along with Darius, feeling more like a passenger than a player as the team took the court. I wasn't even sure what the team's name was, but whatever we were called took full command from the moment the ball was put into play.

At 6–5 and with arms like tentacles, Jermaine was easily the best player on the floor. He had three dunks, a smooth spin move in the post, and two demoralizing blocked shots within the first few minutes. The scouting report on Victor had been accurate, as well: when one of the Mikes threw a bad lob pass that I was sure would sail way out of bounds, Victor rose up above the square of the backboard and cuffed the ball behind his head before slamming it home. Even surrounded by a team of stars though, Blaise was still probably the second or third best out there. The shock of being hardly a free throw away from the father he hadn't seen in over ten years didn't affect Blaise's play at all; if anything, he was more focused, more composed, and had an extra level of the quiet intensity that defined his style of play.

Every time Darius entered the game, him and Blaise ran a vicious two-man press, trapping and marauding the opposing team's ball handlers and making it difficult to even set up an offense. Darius wasn't very coordinated with the ball, but on defense he was like a more hyper version of Blaise, yelling and pumping everyone else up as the two of them collected steals like dirty dishes on a corner table at Jimmy's.

When I finally got on the court for the first time, the score was already 35–9. I felt like an impostor, playing with such a dominant group but knowing full well that I'd done nothing to contribute to it. The unshakeable feeling of wanting to prove myself made me tense up and affected how I played. It didn't help that the other guys on the team weren't very interested in getting the ball to me either, but I couldn't blame them. Especially after I'd missed a pair of open threes and let a bullet pass from Victor slip through my hands on a fast break.

Since we were playing multiple times that day, the games were shorter than a normal high school one would be. With only fifteen minutes in each half and the clock continuing to run even after fouls and out-of-bounds plays, there was barely enough time to even settle in before the opening game was already finished. I rotated in for either Darius or the shorter Mike a few more times in the second half.

The score was so far out of reach that I got a few more shots off as the others started coasting. Blaise was basically the only one passing it to me, maybe trying to convince the other guys that I wasn't as useless as I appeared out there, but the shots kept bricking. I missed all six of my attempts in the 74–36 win.

Out of the three games played on Saturday, we won all of them without too much difficulty. My confidence stayed low and I had that nagging impostor feeling for most of the day, though. I missed way more shots than I made, was generally out of sync with the rest of them, and despite Blaise's quiet encouragement, didn't look like much of a baller to anyone else who was watching. The schedule for the next day was one more regular game, followed by the knockout rounds until there was one champion.

Both Blaise and I were in bad moods as we sat with the TV on, probably watching us more than we were watching it, at The Pleasant Inn that night. After sharing a pizza for dinner,

Jeopardy turned into *The Simpsons,* which turned into *Family Guy,* and then *Law & Order* as it got later. I hardly paid attention to any of them, lamenting how poorly I had played and thinking that I was probably the only thing that could stop us from leaving with the trophy the next day. Blaise was consumed with something going on in his own head, going hours without adding much to the conversation beyond the typical "your shots will start falling, just relax," or "gotta have confidence, that's all." When he finally opened up though, it was to take a surprising break from our unwritten rule.

"I still can't believe my dad was there," he said abruptly, his voice sounding more gravelly than normal. "How messed up is that?"

"You still played great, though." The theme song to *Law & Order* came on as a new episode started up.

"Yeah, it's like I told Goober at the front desk: business trip." He took a long pause before continuing. Like it was a mantra that he'd repeated over and over until it sunk in, he said, "Gotta take care of business, no matter what happens."

If I randomly ran into my dad right before a tournament, I don't know how I'd be able to "take care of business." I asked Blaise if he'd been going extra hard during the games that day to prove something to his dad, just in case he was watching. Blaise didn't think much of that suggestion, openly scowling in disgust.

"If anything, he should be the one trying to prove something to me!"

"What could he prove?"

"That he's not a useless ... deadbeat ... coward ... piece of shit ..." Blaise couldn't even finish his rant. His chest began heaving uncontrollably as he punched the mattress and broke down crying into his pillow.

With his old wounds freshly open, Blaise laid there, face-down and sobbing. I could feel his supreme embarrassment to be crying in front of me. Not knowing what else I could do for him, I finally told Blaise about my own dad, and the real reason he had to leave Bellview.

I wasn't positive that he was even listening, but I told Blaise how my dad had started hearing voices when I was in elementary school. That they kept growing stronger and more persuasive day by day, seemingly coming to life until he was seeing things as well as hearing them. Eventually they took him over; he couldn't separate the voices from reality anymore, and it all fell apart from there. He'd been recovering downstate for nearly three years now, but like my mom kept reminding Rodney and me, "it's a long road back to normal." Feeling exposed, I left out the hidden fear that one day the skateboarder guys would turn on me and send me down that dark path as well.

Eventually Blaise stood up and walked over to the bathroom. He turned on the faucet and let it run for several minutes. When I went in to check on him, he was leaning on the counter in front of the sink, still crying but more rhythmic, settling down and regaining control. He stared into the water while he fought off the tears, his demeanor so much older than his fifteen years. Lifting his head again, he looked up at the mirror, inspecting himself up and down as he used a hand to wipe his wet eyes.

"He could ball too . . . that's the even shittier thing." Remembering the name Craig Hornby from all those old trophies back at the dry cleaners, I nodded. "Bet he could have taught me a lot."

Blaise splashed water on his face, jolting himself closer to his usual manner. He grabbed a towel from the rack and dried off as he walked back to the main part of the room, looking pensive but regaining the strength in his voice.

"I don't want these to be the happiest days of our lives, JB. If there's something better than this out there somewhere . . . at the very least, I owe it to myself to go looking for it. I owe it to my mom, anyway. She told me she always dreamed of going to college, and then moving and living in a big city after that, just to see what it felt like. She was never meant to be someone who stays in town and spends her whole life at a dry cleaner—it just happened."

"Do you know what made your dad . . . you know, move on?"

Blaise spoke without emotion, his chest rising as he breathed, but otherwise he was eerily still as he sat down at the edge of his bed and looked down absently at the clock.

"My dad's whole life revolved around being the big star for the Eagles, and he would have liked nothing more than to stay a high school hero forever. He never wanted to leave. I don't think he ever thought about what would happen once he graduated though, so that's what happened for him: nothing. No college, no real skills or interests other than basketball, no one was in awe of him anymore—all he had was my mom and then me. After a while, I guess that wasn't enough for him, so he takes off. He takes off, while my mom had all these goals and plans for life, and she's the one who got stuck in one place. How's that for fate?"

I didn't mean to change the subject, but my response drifted away from the topic of Blaise's dad.

"Jennie got a tattoo of the word 'fate' on her arm," I said, holding up my left wrist and pointing to it. "It's in a different language, but that's what it means, anyway."

"Yeah, that reminds me, what's the deal with you and Jennie?" Something closer to a smile crossed Blaise's expression. I guess he was ready for a change of topic as well. "Garrett said he saw you with her the other day. He didn't look too happy about it either."

Any other time, I probably would have gotten a cheap thrill knowing that Garrett was pissed off; a little bit of karma biting him back was long overdue, after all. Instead, it was an insignificant detail, one that wasn't even relevant to my complicated situation with Jennie, where everything I thought I wanted was clashing with everything it ended up being.

I told Blaise that Staples was wrong. Being with Jennie wasn't like chewing Juicy Fruit at all; it was way more unpredictable than that. It was more like listening to the edited version of a rap song on the radio. Every time a swear word comes up in the song, that little part gets cut off, and it's empty noise for a fraction of a second. Even though you still have 98 percent of the song, those tiny extra pieces that aren't there can ruin the whole vibe of it. Those little "off moments": the cherries and the fridge, changing the Peninsula girl's phone number, slighting me at the movies, Jimi Dandersley still potentially lingering in the background.

"So what, you think she's like, using you?"

"No. That's the thing I really don't get. Deep down, I think she actually really likes me, there's this connection that probably neither of us would deny. But on the way down, there's so much other stuff that jumps out and gets in the way. It's going to break me in the process unless something changes. We're not 'official' or anything, but I feel a big decision coming up, either by me or by her, before we get back to school."

"That's on Tuesday."

"Yeah, and I'm confused."

There were plenty of great parts about hanging with Jennie, but I also couldn't shake off the small missing pieces that didn't seem to add up. I couldn't decide whether the edited version of Jennie would be worth it in the long run. Blaise gave his take on it.

"You're hanging out with a cute senior girl. She's actually really cool and down to earth, she lets you drive her car, she makes out with you, and will probably do a lot more than that before too much longer . . . I don't see what there is to be confused about."

"Yeah, when you say it that way it sounds perfect, but you're only seeing it from a distance though. Day to day, it's a lot more complicated, which you wouldn't see unless you've gotten closer and have gone through it."

"Like a mirage?" Blaise asked. "I've been trying all summer to tell you that about basketball, man. That's the real Mirage for you."

"But you still play ball."

"But I still play ball. Go figure."

"A man often meets his destiny on the very road he took to avoid it," I blurted out, surprised at my memory of Jennie's quote on the bottom stair at the haunted house that winter. "That's what Jennie told me, anyway."

CHAPTER FIFTY-ONE

Clutch

We checked out of The Pleasant Inn the next morning, nearly arriving at the gym late because the manager delayed us for over ten minutes, practically telling his life story to the family in front of us as they tried to pay.

"So I worked for the city for about fifteen years, and before that I was at a crematorium. Ehh, that kinda thing makes ya sweat, does it?" The mom must have given him a look, hearing about the manager's previous career as a manager of dead bodies. "Well, I kin see where yer comin' from, but someone has to do it! And I tell you what, it's not a bad way to urn a living! Not bad at all."

If the family ahead of us mentioned basketball, we probably would have been stuck in there for the rest of the afternoon, but finally they were able to pay (the "guhv-ner" took his share), we grabbed some rather dry-looking bagels from the breakfast table, and then we hustled back to the gym just in time, to the coach's annoyed relief.

I finally got a little bit of a hot streak going in the last game before elimination started, hitting two three-pointers in a row and following up a steal with a layup at the other end. Blaise and Darius both over-celebrated, finally with something to cheer me for, while the others didn't acknowledge it at all; they were probably thinking that unless you're a total scuff, you *should* be able to make a wide-open shot that you've practiced millions of times before.

Once we moved into the knockout rounds, we weren't in the Auxiliary Gym anymore, moving onto the Main Court and seeing the bleachers start to slowly fill up with spectators as other teams were eliminated. With Blaise dictating the pace of the game from the point guard spot and Jermaine's dominance inside the paint, we won both games by about twenty points each and moved into the championship round. As the intensity started to build, the games got a little bit edgier, with harder fouls and a greater sense of urgency. Not wanting to take any chances, the coach started substituting a lot less also. I wasn't sure if I was upset or relieved that I only got to play for eight minutes in the quarterfinals and five minutes in the semis.

The first half of the championship game was pretty much a replica of how the other games had gone. On the very first possession, big Mike missed a shot from the free throw line, but Victor skied for a rebound and a reverse layup. Blaise stole the inbounds pass and found Jermaine on an alley-oop, and almost unbelievably, stole it back again on the very next possession. Once Darius came into the game, he picked up two quick fouls, but his suffocating defense was a nightmare for the other guy, who was wildly trying to protect his dribble against the hyperspeed swipes at the ball.

The championship trophy sat in plain view at the scorer's table, and as our team blitzed through the opening minutes, anyone watching the game would have little doubt about who was going to end up with it. A rare three by Blaise pushed the score to 26–10 as the other team called time-out, clearly sensing that things were slipping away.

I only played for a single minute in the first half. The only time I touched the ball, I passed it into the post, where Jermaine did a series of head fakes before spinning in for a layup to make the score 34–19 at half. I thought to myself that if nothing else, at least I'd made that one small contribution to the final game. While I took a few more practice shots towards the end of halftime, I saw Blaise's dad walk into the gym, followed by his own team. The place was pretty much full by then, so they stood in the corner to watch the second half. Blaise went in for a dunk as the whistle blew and the ref started the game back again, pretending to be unaware of the new group of spectators.

As the second half started and the other team grew more desperate, the defensive intensity on both sides picked up. For the first five minutes after halftime, nobody on either side was able to score a single basket except Victor, who made one of two free throws after a hard foul. Victor felt the opponent had taken his legs out on purpose and glared and swore under his breath as he set up for the foul shots. Darius came into the game so Victor could calm down, but he picked up another foul after getting his legs tangled up, arguing with the ref since he thought it should have been a charge instead. The opposite bench erupted loudly when one of them finally made a three-pointer. It was their first points of the half and we were still up by thirteen, but suddenly the lead didn't feel quite as comfortable.

Darius picked up his fourth foul after getting the ball stolen from him at half-court and trying to block the layup attempt at the other end. He returned to the bench and Victor came back in. Both of the Mikes looked like they were wearing down as the clock dipped under ten minutes, but the coach kept his eyes nervously glued to the court and apparently didn't consider putting in his other sub.

From my spot on the bench, my mind switched back and forth between the game and thoughts of my final day of work on Monday. Before I'd left for the weekend, I'd agreed to hang out with Jennie at the end of my last shift. Since subbing into the game didn't look like a very high probability, I started mentally preparing for what that might be like, and what I should say to Jennie. With the lead at ten but needing a basket to get momentum back, Blaise called for a time-out. I barely listened to what was talked about in the huddle.

Coming out of the time-out, Jermaine set a back screen for Victor, who sprinted at the basket as Blaise lobbed the ball up next to the rim. Darius and I both stood out of our chairs as Victor gathered his feet for takeoff and then rose up. The spectators let out a small roar, the peewee players ready to lose their minds after Victor's highlight reel dunk to cap off the weekend. Instead, the defender clipped him again right as he was going airborne. The ref's whistle blew as Victor landed hard near the baseline. For a split second, I thought he was injured, but he popped right back up, heated.

Victor confronted the guy who fouled him, yelling at him

over the dirty hit, but the other guy postured and bumped back at him with his chest. Before Jermaine could arrive as the peacemaker, Victor had thrown a punch, and both him and the other player were thrown out of the game. With an exaggerated shrug that made me laugh, Darius came back into the game; he was maybe the only person there who wasn't feeling the rising tension in the gym.

Both teams traded baskets over the next few possessions—a tip-in here and there, a jumper that came off ugly but ended up banking in off the backboard, but nothing came easy. With just under seven minutes left, for all their work in the second half, the other squad just couldn't chip more than a few points off our lead. Blaise was calmly running the offense, and even though every possession was becoming a grind, his presence must have been endlessly frustrating to the other team, resorting to anything to try and throw him off his rhythm.

Darius was all over the place defensively, deflecting passes, chasing rebounds, and hounding his man whenever they touched the ball. Then he went a little too hard trying to get a steal along the sideline. He missed the ball and accidentally hip-checked his man, immediately shrieking as he realized what he'd done. The whistle inevitably sounded; Darius had fouled out of the game. Feeling a little bit numb, I walked out onto the floor, trying to channel my energy from the time I'd beaten Blaise at one-on-one. Down to only five players, for better or worse, they were stuck with me for the remainder of the game.

Our opponents inbounded the ball. Knowing that I'd hardly played at all until then, they decided to come right at me. They passed it to the guy I was guarding, and everyone else cleared out of the way while I dug into my stance. He faked a pass and then started dribbling, swaying back and forth with a wave of crossovers, then darting past me right as I was getting comfortable. Just as he turned the corner and started driving in for an easy shot, I extended my hand and flicked towards the ball as a last-ditch effort to save the play. I timed it perfectly.

I knocked the ball loose and straight into Jermaine's hands, and then took off running as he led me with a pass towards the basket on the other end. All alone and with an open layup to pretty much ice the game, I scooped up the ball and adjusted my steps to rise for the layup. I saw Jermaine following at full speed out of the corner of my eye, so I decided at the last second to give Coach Hornby's peewee team their final highlight reel moment. Instead of taking the layup, I bounced it off the backboard so Jermaine could swoop in and slam home the rebound.

What I didn't see was that Jermaine had a defender on his hip who was just half a step faster. Instead of a SportsCenter Top Ten moment off the glass, both guys flailed at the ball at the same time and Jermaine knocked it out of bounds. I clapped my hands in frustration, but also determination. It wasn't a smart play, but this wasn't the time to beat myself up about it. It was a good defensive play on my part to start off the sequence, and with just over four minutes left, we still had a seven-point lead. We still had Jermaine and Blaise out there, and that should still be enough to hold on.

"You good man, You *good!!*" Darius was calling out, now standing up and rocking from side to side, a towel wrapped around his head. "Just lock up now, you got this!"

And I probably would have been good too, until I heard Jermaine howl something at me, watched Blaise turn away like he didn't know me, and the Mikes whisper something to each other. Now my mind was racing. All in all, it had been a memorable weekend, hanging out with Blaise and travelling on our own, getting to share the court with a group of such talented players. But maybe I was overmatched and not ready for all this. Not ready for select teams and weekend tournaments, college scouts and main courts, crappy motels with weird managers. Sometime shortly after that pass off the backboard, it was like I'd left the back door to my mind unlocked, and every feeling of self-doubt had snuck back in and made itself comfortable. I tried to push the uninvited negativity out. Digging into my defensive stance again, I vowed again that I wasn't going to be the reason that we lost.

But it *was* just like me to do something like that. One of the skateboarders in my head even went so far as to say that my whole life could be explained just by that one ill-advised pass off the backboard. A fast break that gets botched at the last moment, just because I overthink it and do something stupid. Setting off the burglar alarm at the blue house on the Peninsula, getting caught right on the final day of summer. Walking all the way down to the gates of South Point, only to be turned away by the security guard at the last second. Spending the entire next summer trying to get close to Jennie, only to get second thoughts right as she's finally available and into me.

A vision flashed through my mind of the smirk Staples had the day I spilled all those cherries in the walk-in fridge at Jimmy's. "You're not what the kids call 'clutch..'"

The guy I was guarding drove straight past me on the next possession. Jermaine's tentacle arms swooped in and blocked the shot, but the ball deflected back to the other team and they still scored. The lead was down to five.

To an outsider, all of these things would probably seem unrelated. What does a burglar alarm have to do with a carton of cherries? What connection was there between a security guard and Jennie? How would a restaurant or a locked gate or even Staples explain why I made a bad play in a basketball game? As we took the ball back down the floor, I was left open along the wing, but nobody looked my way. Without saying it out loud, their message was clear: they weren't giving me the ball again.

Now with confidence as well as desperation, our opponents tightened up the defense even further. Blaise tried an aggressive spin move into the lane, but a swarm of arms swiped at the ball as he tried to gather it back. Jermaine picked up the loose ball and forced his way back inside furiously. Double-teamed at every turn, he landed on a defender and was called for charging. He was still arguing the call as the opponents pushed it back up the court, filling the lane for an open layup. Now with under two minutes left, it wasn't just me; we were spiraling.

They fouled big Mike on purpose on the next possession. He wasn't a great shooter to begin with, and he was worn out from the long weekend of games. He'd hardly subbed out at all the whole time. On top of the heavy cement feeling that must have been growing in his legs, now came the pressure of a crucial free throw. He bricked it badly, there was a wild chase for the ball, and the other team came down with it.

"No threes, y'all! NO THREES!!" While the coach was now biting his knuckles in silent disbelief, Darius was pacing the sideline with a towel around his head, begging us to make just one more defensive stop.

Back at the other end, we pressed our coverage up around the three-point arc, patiently switching on all screens and rushing with a hand raised any time one of them caught the ball. This went on for six or seven passes, as we were determined not to give up a long game-tying shot. As the clock ticked away, Blaise tried to play the passing lanes, searching for a steal to finally clinch the game. His eyes wandered away from his man for a split second too long; the guy did a quick backdoor cut across the wide-open baseline, caught a bounce pass, and laid it in. With a little more than a minute left, the lead was down to one.

Feeling like a non-factor, I made a few cuts and drifted around the three-point line, bracing for the reality that this is really how we were going out: blowing a huge second half lead right at the very end of the championship game. Suddenly, nobody wanted the ball. Jermaine caught it in the post and passed it right back out to Blaise. Blaise had an open three but decided against it and dribbled it back near half-court to reset. He reversed the ball over to small Mike, who didn't want it either but was open and left with no choice but to catch it.

Instead of purposely fouling, the other team was going for steals, taking risks and not worrying if they got beat or not. Mike's defender sailed over to him a step too late as Mike took a powerful first dribble towards the lane. The defender tried the same desperate swipe at the ball as I had earlier. I watched with dread as he timed it up perfectly too.

The ball was knocked free, setting off a mad dash for possession. Blaise was the first one there, sliding across the floor to corral the ball. It was wrestled away from him though, and sensing a turnover, their players started sprinting off to get a fast break going. With Blaise still on the ground, the guy who stole the ball fired a pass up ahead. Jermaine launched himself across the court and deflected it. After that chaotic round of hot potato, with five different players touching the ball in a span of a few seconds, now the ball calmly bounced to me at the top of the key.

When you really break it down, there are about a dozen different things that go into a basketball shot, and one tiny hitch at any point can cause the whole chain to be broken. There are times when the exact instant the ball leaves my hand I already know that it's going to be a miss, just because of how it felt on the release. When that happens, it's best to alert your teammates immediately that there will definitely be a rebound to chase after. I always yelled "OFF!" and would make sure to shout it when something didn't quite feel right on the way up. Every once in a while, the shot would go in anyway, but that was rare.

Derrick Blackbird would yell "UGLY!" when he knew his shot was about to be a bad miss. Blaise was even more specific, calling out the directions of the basket that he thought the ball would hit. He'd call out left or right, or "SHORT!" or "FRONT!" if he expected the ball to carom off the edge of the rim. Other guys weren't as precise, but they would yell out other words that started with S and F when they felt a bad release happening.

Unexpectedly finding the ball in my hands just outside the three-point line, I wasn't thinking about any of that though.

I could have held on to it and let the seconds run down until I got fouled. Or I could carefully pass it back to Blaise and let him handle things. We still had one time-out left too, so calling for time to set up a new plan of action was also an option. Instead, I let a shot fly and left it up to fate. I didn't say a word as the ball rainbowed its way to the rim.

In the movies, whenever somebody takes the big shot right at the end, everything always goes into slow motion, and there's a close-up of the ball as it floats through the air at a snail's pace, and of course it always swishes right as the clock hits zero. None of this happened for my shot.

With a satisfying "thNNk!" sound, the ball just grazed the back of the rim, tumbling through the net like I was shooting into a giant vacuum instead of a basketball hoop. I watched the hands of my teammates do quick fist pumps as things went into fast forward and they all got back on defense. Before having time to register that I'd just made the biggest shot of the tournament, the other team had already rushed down and missed another shot. Blaise grabbed the long rebound and found me on the opposite wing.

Suddenly, I wasn't out of my league in a select tournament, thrown into an epic endgame meltdown. I was right back at the Mirage, catching a confident pass from Blaise, roasting those kids from the Peninsula. I launched it again; this time it was a clean swish. The lead was back to seven, twenty seconds remained, and all of us could relax, with the game now out of reach. I made two more free throws in the closing seconds to push the final score to 60–51.

When the final buzzer sounded, Blaise jumped on my back, while the rest of the guys approached almost cautiously, just as surprised as I was about the sudden burst of clutch right at the end.

"This is why we brought you here! *This* is why we brought you here!" Darius kept repeating, smacking my hand until it started to turn red. If everything that had happened over the last year was just one long and complicated way of getting me to that moment, it was still all worth it.

At the final awards ceremony, the tournament directors announced the winning teams from every division and handed out the giant championship trophy to each team. Mr. Hornby's juniors were the champs of the under twelves tournament. Blaise looked at his shoes as they stepped up to bask in the applause. A few minutes later, the All-Tournament team was announced over the loudspeaker. Blaise was recognized as one of the top players, and they gave him a clear individual trophy, which he didn't appear too enthusiastic about. It wasn't a surprise at all, but Jermaine was named the tournament MVP. Even though I didn't get any trophies or awards to take home, knowing that I'd come back to hit some of the biggest shots of the weekend was more than enough for me.

As we were getting ready to leave and walk back to the bus station, Darius came up to us to say bye.

"What school you play for?" he asked.

"Bellview High, same as Blaise. The Eagles."

I don't know why I added that last part, other than that I'd always wanted to play for the Eagles. What I didn't tell Darius was that I hadn't been on any team for over a year, or that my spot on the varsity in the winter was still very much up in the air. Those seemed like details that could be sorted out on another day. Darius grinned after hearing my answer. With a deep laugh, he put his arm around Blaise's neck and fake strangled him.

"Bell-view High! Damn, y'all are gonna be a *problem* this year!"

The Greyhound arrived late to pick us up, so there wasn't any McDonald's stop on the ride home. While I had a hard time sorting out east from west back in Mount Pleasant, getting a grasp of direction on the bus couldn't have been much easier. Once we took the exit to get on US 127, it was a completely straight shot for dozens of miles at a time as we headed back, farmland turning into forests as the sun started to go down over the state.

At first, me and Blaise tried to make the ride go a little quicker by playing that old A-to-Z car ride game, where you have to find a word starting with each letter on road signs, going in order through the alphabet. We were probably several years too old for that game to be very exciting, but after an emotional weekend, a childish way to make the time pass wasn't the worst thing that could happen.

Around Houghton Lake, I saw signs leading to North Bay, then Old Highway 27 and Prudenville to take the lead, but from there the game pretty much tailed off. Signs for Q, X, and Z were always tricky. I knew that Zilwaukee was in the opposite direction, so even finishing the game may have been beside the point.

The bus pulled off the highway and slowed down into a back road before ending up at an empty parking lot somewhere around Roscommon. The driver came on the microphone and announced a quick five-minute break. Why this parking lot was built in the first place was a bit of a mystery. Forget any downtown area with restaurants, shops, or other attractions to visit from there—this sad patch of concrete didn't even have a building in front of it. The driver and many of the other passengers didn't seem to mind though, pulling boxes of Marlboro Reds out of their pockets as they stepped off. This time, it was apparently nicotine levels rather than sodium and cholesterol that needed recharging.

"You boys coming out?"

Blaise and I sat still, both a little bit annoyed, not because our A-to-Z game had been interrupted, but because this stop was one more delay to the end of the trip. The driver, cracking his neck and letting out an anguished sigh, asked again.

"You sure you don't want to stretch out a bit?"

"No thanks . . . really, I'm good," Blaise answered. After playing nearly every minute of seven games in two days, I knew that Blaise's limbs were probably begging for a good stretch, but he stubbornly stayed in his seat on principle.

"Yer good," the driver grunted with a half-laugh. "Give it another twenty years, and then we'll see."

After the short break, which featured a lot more smoking than stretching as far as I could tell, there was another hour and a half of driving before arriving back in Bellview. Blaise and I didn't bother continuing with the game, and it probably would have been too dark by then even if we wanted to. The driver's "give it another twenty years" comment stuck with me as I stared into the purple fabric of the seats one row up, my imagination extending towards the future and considering what he meant. It occurred to me that just as much as events from the past can change the future, the future can affect the past just as much—or at least how we feel about it.

Twenty years from now, would Blaise's distant and concerned expressions from this summer finally untangle into a full smile again? Would his talent and vision leave him satisfied with what his life amounted to? Or despite his dreams for more, would he remember high school and basketball as the best days of his life?

That Friday afternoon spent at the dry cleaners seemed farther back in time than it really was; I remembered looking at the shelf of old trophies while Mrs. Hornby talked on the phone in the back room, strangely looking like a future version of Jennie. Twenty years from now, would Jennie realize that whether she went places or stayed, whether her heart was broken again or her body bruised, a road trip through her soul would show that she's untouchable?

I thought about the others too. Did Cal really have any hope of becoming a head chef somewhere, or even having his own restaurant like Jimmy? I bit my lip as I imagined him pompously tightening a pair of his own black Velcro No-Slips. Whether he was curing AIDS or writing prescriptions in the back of a CVS somewhere in Middle America, would Staples still be called "Staples" by most of his world in twenty years? Would Spaz still be a "restaurant guy," basking in the fast pace and the "hangingness" of a common mission and busy atmosphere? Or would he end up at the front desk of a sleepy motel in the middle of nowhere, bored and lonely and telling everybody he sees about the "guhv-ner" taking his share? Would Jimi Dandersley still be defined by his wildest moments, with the only memorable ones being those that had painted him at his very worst? Would the same be true of me?

It struck me that as much time as we spend in life trying to become something that we're not, maybe an equal amount of wasted time is spent trying to avoid becoming what we're afraid we *are*.

Or maybe I could string together more days like this one, where I'm able to step up at the crucial times. Where I can keep my head while everyone else is losing theirs, making difficult decisions with a peaceful mind. Where I can be remembered not for my trespasses, but for my triumphs—not for my defeats, but for my redemption.

We rolled back into town after eleven. Thankfully, Rodney was already waiting for us at the bus stop. He didn't look all that happy to see us, but at least he was there.

"What, I suppose you volunteered me to drive Blaise home too?"

Blaise looked a little bit embarrassed, but my brother motioned for him to get in the back seat. He sheepishly tossed his duffel bag across the seat and climbed in. Rodney made a wisecrack about Blaise's All-Tournament trophy and started to drive. It reminded me of the old days, and I had to pause a few times to convince myself that it wasn't.

CHAPTER FIFTY-TWO

The Last Day of Work

Labor Day was the final day of the season at Jimmy's, meaning one last lunch shift for me before starting school again. Despite the triumph at the basketball tournament, my spirits weren't very high as I floated from table to table that afternoon. The emptiness of the dining room barely registered: Staples back at college, Lacy back home downstate with the rest of the summer crowd, and the only customers being occasional groups of locals. Without anything else to distract it, my mind was preoccupied by a difficult conversation, one that I was debating whether or not to have as soon as I left the restaurant.

While I cleaned up my final table, a three-top group of the Old Guard was sitting one spot over, senior citizens there for an early dinner. They had been in the restaurant for a half hour or so, ordering coffees and camping out at one of Merryll's tables. They all had on similar snapback mesh hats, perched high on their heads with words stitched across the front in all capital letters—things like "VETERAN," "USMC," and "EAGLES," all accompanied by various buttons attached to the sides of the hats. Merryll had been out there to check on them at least four times, but each time they were either too involved in their own banter or unmoved by anything on the menu, searching it up and down through thick aviator-style glasses, but not deciding on anything to order.

Merryll had been acting strange all day, and when I say strange, I mean *nice*. She kept getting all emotional anytime someone on the staff came in or out of the building for the last time, making people promise that they'd come back and work there the next year. It was like she forgot that we were all the same people that she'd been constantly bitching about for the last three months and somehow got the idea that we'd all been together at summer camp instead. When Spaz came by to help out with sugars and shakers, I swear I even saw a few tears slip out from her round face, much to his confusion.

Back at the table with the Old Guard, the one with the mesh "EAGLES" hat ordered a whitefish dinner. The "VETERAN" hat guy asked Merryll if it would be possible to order French toast even though it's dinnertime. Hearing that, "USMC" guy laughed and importantly announced that he was just about to ask that very question. Merryll agreed that the cook would be able to make a French toast order for them. She stood fake-patiently at the table as they marveled at the accommodation and tried to convince their friend to change his order into what they're having.

"C'mon, Hank, have a go!" said Veteran, as his friend started to get agitated. In addition to his Eagles hat, Hank had on a plaid shirt and a slick pair of gray Velcro shoes— ones that actually would've sort of looked cool if anyone else was wearing them.

"No, no . . . I don't want that. I've come here for decades to get th'hwhite-fish, and I intend on getting th'hwhite-fish once more. If I wanted French-toast, I would have stayed in Normandy!"

"And yeh shouldah stayed there, yeh old bastard!"

The two others cackled as Hank kept his arms crossed and grimaced.

"H'okay, Missy, we're all set!" said USMC, all of them turning their attention back to Merryll. "That's two special custom orders for some French toast—"

"—and one of th' planked 'hwhite-fish!" added Hank, with sour satisfaction. Merryll announced the French toast order to Cal and watched his face light up from the kitchen.

Cal had become oddly modest in the weeks following his perfect order of French toast. Not entirely modest—this is Cal we're talking about; but he was strangely detached from his bravado. Until then, it had been rare for Cal to see himself validated by others. He talked himself up a lot, but maybe that didn't necessarily mean that he believed all he was saying. The perfect French toast moment seemed to have put him at the crossroads. Maybe this meant he really *did* have a future as a head chef somewhere: the puffy white hat, a kitchen full of all the latest culinary equipment, drawers full of Japanese sushi knives, some No-Slip shoes of his own.

"Humbled by his success," was the assessment from Staples. He said it as a joke, with a little bit of mockery in the suggestion that cooking one good breakfast could be an iconic moment of success for someone. But Cal had different goals than Staples, a different way of attaining them, and probably a different definition of what success really looks like.

The Veteran limped up to the jukebox. After reaching into his pocket and coming up empty at least six times, he produced enough quarters to play a song on the machine. An old Frank Sinatra song called "That's Life" blared out of the jukebox, as the Old Guard did something that I guess certain dictionaries might define as dancing when they heard it come on. They even sang once the words started up. I wished that Staples was still around to observe this; if he weren't already back at college, he'd definitely have some sort of comment. I pictured what he might say—scratch that, I didn't picture it, I *conceptualized* it.

"Jimmy's: where else could guys in their seventies and eighties walk in during 2005 and use a machine from the fifties to play a song from the thirties? Maybe it's true that this place is timeless after all."

Thinking that at least it wasn't "Margaritaville," I listened to Frankie croon away about his philosophy on life.

> *"I've been a puppet, a pauper, a pirate, a poet
> . . . a pawn and a kiiingg . . .*
>
> *I've been up, and down, and over, and out,
> and I know one thiiinng . . ."*

I didn't get a chance to find out what that "one thing" was though, since Merryll had tracked me down.

"You're coming back next summer too, right? You'd better." Next summer seemed twenty years away to me.

"Ehh, I'll probably look for something that suits my skills a little better. Maybe go and work for the city instead."

I only said this to bug Merryll, but my gloomy overall mood made it even easier to keep a straight face. Merryll punched me on the arm and then hugged me.

"You're such a little shit, June Bug," she chuckled and wiped away another tear that had slipped out. "But I'll miss you anyway."

Gloria looked on from the background during my moment with Merryll, smiling and shaking her head gently, as if to wordlessly tell me, "She does this same thing every year." I found myself wondering what Merryll did during the winter, whether she had another job—like waiting tables at another restaurant—and whether she was lonely. I finished stacking that last set of plates on the dish tray and washed my hands.

On my way out, Gloria came to up to the front with a warm smile, thanking me for staying until the last day and saying I'd be more than welcome to come back the next summer. I also tried to say goodbye to Cal, who was so intensely focused on recreating the perfect French toast that he didn't even acknowledge me. No patronizing smile, no friendly but condescending advice, only full determination towards the task at hand. In that moment, I had to admit that I was fully rooting for him.

Pulling a clipboard from behind his apron, Jimmy also came over to see me off with one final surprise. Squinting his eyes and looking over his shoulder to make sure we weren't being watched, the boss flipped through the clipboard for a few pages.

"New ice cream flavor," he said severely, holding the clip-board up to my face. "Coming out next year."

Sketched onto the page was a swirling maroon and blue dome of color, sitting on top of a pizza slice-looking shape. It looked like something Spaz could have done left-handed with his rubber gloves on, but there was no mistaking the meaning behind it.

"Magneto Man," I said, unable to hide my satisfaction over Jimmy using one of my ideas. My grin widened as that victory sunk in, even when he hid the clipboard back out of sight and cracked two of my knuckles with an unexpected handshake.

The restaurant shutting down for the season didn't mean saying goodbye to everyone though. I crossed paths with Spaz, who was carrying out some dishes and was hardly sentimental.

"Ayy, JB . . . you're going to class tomorrow, right?"

"It's the first day of school, man, of course I am." I handed him my apron and didn't bother to add the obvious: "We sort of *have* to be there."

Frank Sinatra and the Old Guard kept singing in the background, and I clocked out on the DigiServ system one last time.

FINAL TIME-OUT

END OF SEASON RANKINGS

My Top 5 priorities for the summer:

1. **Stay out of trouble.** Unless you count a few rounds of Dumpster Duty, ✓.

2. **Set myself up to make varsity.** Bellview High's gonna be a problem this year. Nothing is guaranteed yet, but I'm closer, ✓.

3. **Enjoy my new freedom.** Sure, I spent I lot of time scrambling through the dining room at Jimmy's, but I was also allowed out of the house for a full weekend to play basketball downstate, so ✓.

4. **Reconcile with Blaise.** It's not like the old days and never will be, but that could be a good thing overall. We've definitely moved forward, ✓.

5. **Get a girlfriend?** It's complicated.

CHAPTER FIFTY-THREE

When School Starts . . .

Arthur arrived on time, and I handed over my apron and left the restaurant through the screen door exit. Jennie was waiting for me next to the dumpster. The late afternoon sun darted indecisively in and out of the clouds as Jennie and I slowly walked around downtown. Nearly all the tourists and summer residents had gone back downstate by this point, leaving the town with a gutted feeling to it. It was like wandering through a house with all its furniture removed, preparing for a winter-long renovation.

We didn't have any set path or destination as we walked—only a general sense of when we felt like making a turn or trying a new street or alley. Most of the other restaurants and shops were also closed early. We went down a winding alleyway behind the old Tin Soldier toy store, one with a garden, small fountain, and ivy coils wrapped around the light posts, which had just been switched on.

I was pretty certain that very few people in town knew about this little out-of-the-way path. I'd often walked through it with my mom as a kid: a quick shortcut as she finished errands to the bank and post office. It always gave me a faint feeling of magic that I couldn't quite place. The miniature wind chime hanging from the balcony above the book store gave a gentle clang in the breeze. For some reason, this noise made me picture fairies and pixies hidden within the plants and ivy. I would have felt stupid mentioning any of this to Jennie.

We passed wordlessly through the fairyland alley and came back out on Main Street. Jennie paused and scanned the area for options on where to head next. In the back of my mind, I knew that we had something important to discuss, and that it was likely to come up in conversation at any moment. Maybe that's why I tried to stay quiet.

"Left or right?"

I pointed to the right. That way would lead us back around to the docks and the water, and of course, the Peninsula houses filling out the rest of the landscape. The sun was still out, leaving an impossibly blue horizon that was upstaged only by the even bluer water rippling in the warm breeze.

Jennie's hand kept brushing up against mine as we walked stride for stride. Only a few weeks ago, I probably wouldn't have been able to resist grabbing it, squeezing it, hoping to attach myself to it. As we walked now though, I basically ignored it, set in my conclusion that it would only make things more complicated. This was easily the most romantic walk that I'd ever been on, but romance was the very thing I knew I needed to avoid. We took a turn out onto the wooden planks of the pier, and I felt a mixture of sadness and guilt as Jennie's hand once again started to brush against mine. I flinched before pulling it away.

"Damn, JB, what's with you tonight?"

Jennie had been about two inches taller than me when I first started at Jimmy's, but now I looked at her eye-to-eye.

"School starts tomorrow," I said vaguely.

"And . . .?"

While walking next to her, I once again compared the two different sides of her personality that Jennie shows the world. Looking more closely, my conclusion was that *both* of them were only masks; between the disaffected burnout seen at school or the sunny but mischievous personality shown at work, neither was completely real. Each is needed at separate times in order to keep going, but Jennie's true self is only revealed in the hard-to-catch moments when she forgets to put one of those masks on.

"I don't want to always be wondering if you've really just been pulling a Zilwaukee on me this whole time." My voice was shaking a little bit, but I was grudgingly certain that this is what needed to happen.

"Huh?"

"You know, lead me along and get me thinking this could be something real, when really it was just an extra Z put in there to fool me all along. I don't want to have to wonder if you actually like me or not, or if you're just playing me. Or if both of those things are true, but you can't figure out which one is more convincing."

With the way the sunlight hit her face as she turned towards the water, the color in Jennie's steely eyes looked more teal than hazel. A strand of hair had fallen across her face, but she didn't puff it away.

"Are you breaking up with me, JB?" I should have known better, but I was still surprised with how directly she said it.

I leaned back and thought about it for a second, eventually working up the nerve to say what I needed to.

"I don't know if we're even together, so I don't know if we can break up. But when school starts and we run into each other in the hall, are you going to use that half-embarrassed tone of voice like at the movie theater, explaining to your friends why you're being seen near me? Or if dirtbag Jimi shows up next week and apologizes and flirts and makes a bunch of promises, can you honestly say that you wouldn't fall back into that again?"

Jennie looked out towards the Peninsula lighthouse and couldn't even come up with a response; without going right out and saying it, there was our answer.

"Besides," I asked, "in another year, are you even going to care that any of this ever happened?"

I knew Jennie wasn't going to cry if this moment came, but she didn't get desperate, or ask for a further explanation, or start yelling, or try to change my mind either. Instead, she dropped her head just slightly.

"I barely knew you when we were at Five Mile Creek last winter . . . and to be honest, I didn't even want to know you. But somehow after we talked, I felt close to you."

"Same."

"So then when you showed up at the restaurant, I don't know if that was a sign or anything, but I was paying attention to you. You weren't who I expected you to be . . . I felt this connection."

"Same."

"When I realized you had feelings for me, I guess I sort of led you on, and it felt good knowing that you would be there if something went wrong with my boyfriend. It took me a while to make sense that I liked you back. I had a hard time getting over that part, because people—"

"What about them?" I asked. "So you like me, but only if no one else is watching?"

Again, Jennie was having a hard time giving a full answer. As she stammered, I thought back to sitting together on the bench outside Jimmy's, the crazy afternoon that ended up with us kissing for the first time. Jennie wanted someone to hide with that day, and I guess not much had changed in the weeks since. But I'd spent most of a year shut off from the outside, and I was done hiding.

"People just . . . wouldn't expect the two of us to be together, put it that way," Jennie said slowly. "Not only my friends, yours too . . . and you know it. But I didn't want anyone else to have you either—there was still that connection. And then when things started going wrong with Jimi, I felt it even more. Then when it *really* hit the fan . . . there you were."

The championship game in Mount Pleasant was also still fresh in my mind. I'd sat on the sidelines for almost the whole game, but when the team needed a sub, I was able to prove myself in the end. That was just a weekend tournament, though. I thought of myself sitting on that metal bench outside the restaurant, watching life go by and waiting for guys like Jimi Dandersley to foul out. I shook my head.

"I'm not interested in being a sub anymore."

Jennie's invisible mask had melted away, leaving her exposed as she looked to me significantly.

"You shouldn't be. But a year from now?" Jennie's voice broke by just a fraction. "I'm definitely still going to care that all this happened."

EPILOGUE

The First Day of School

Have you ever gotten that weird sensation where you can't really tell whether you're awake or dreaming? Imagine spending an entire year like that.

Situations and scenes that rapidly change and don't seem to have any logical connection to them. Conflicts that only become partially resolved, disappearing in the mind for long stretches before randomly returning when you least expect it. Coming face-to-face with your insecurities and fears, but not always grasping what there even is to be scared of in the first place. Getting what you thought you wanted, only to realize that sometimes even the real thing is still an illusion.

For the first day of sophomore year, I woke up extra early and biked to school. I put on my slightly fancy watch for the occasion, and when I arrived with an extra half hour before the start of biology class, I walked around to the back entrance of the brick building. Looking out over the bluff at everything—including the border of trees hugging the rows of streets and buildings, now shifting into various shades of orange and red—downtown Bellview had a drowsy look to it.

Jimmy's Family Restaurant was now officially closed for the season, but a few residual smells of French fries and grease had still managed to sneak up the boardwalk and into my senses. Beyond that was the lake and the harbor, the houses on the Peninsula, the docks, the public beach, and that famous drinking fountain. The Mirage basketball court was hidden away somewhere underneath the canopy of trees, but I was able to locate it without any trouble.

The two skateboarder guys in my head slowed down long enough to let me fully process everything that had happened in the past twelve months. All of the triumphs, all the mistakes, all the lessons learned, plus a lot more lessons that weren't learned yet, but probably could be with a little more time.

Even though I had accomplished nearly everything from my original Top 5 list, the summer still didn't exactly have a happy ending. Looking back, I guess it was pretty successful, but it felt like I still had a long way to go. But that's also okay, because as you get a little bit older, you realize that there really aren't any endings, happy or otherwise. Every day is another challenge, a next chapter, another chance to either be clutch or spill all the cherries, with a persistent series of struggles and villains, and maybe even frogs and runny milkshakes, but it's never over. After one last sweeping view of my town, I glanced at my left wrist and saw that it was time to go inside.

I went past Jennie in the hallway and gave her a small wave and a head nod but didn't slow down. I walked into the classroom as the bell rang and looked for an open seat, quietly confident and ready for another new start.

ABOUT THE AUTHOR

Payne Schanski is an American author who has worked as an educator, coach, and mentor for middle school and high school students over the past decade. Working closely with these students has meant revisiting the fears, insecurities, and mistakes that make adolescence the turbulent learning experience that it is. These observations, as well as the author's own experiences growing up in Northern Michigan—a quiet, wooded region shrouded with mystery and local lore—inspired him to write *The Ghost of Five Mile Creek*, his first publication.

After eight years living in Boston, Schanski recently moved back to Northern Michigan with Cathy AuGuste Schanski, his wife, first reader, collaborator, and unending source of inspiration. After thousands of hours of free time on the East Coast devoted to writing about Michigan, eventually moving back was (in Payne's words) "just a matter of time."

Redemption Summer is the final book of a three-part series, along with *The Ghost of Five Mile Creek* and the soon-to-be-released *Blue Houses on the Peninsula*. Together, the books follow JB's road towards identity formation and maturity, a path with as many sharp twists as the famous Tunnel of Trees.

The author hopes that young adults everywhere—but

especially those he had the joy of working with at Tenacity and the Curley K-8 school in Boston—will connect with, benefit from, and enjoy reading these books.

Printed in Canada